CONNEMARA

CONNEMARA

NICOLAS MATHIEU

Translated from the French by Sam Taylor

OTHER PRESS
New York

Originally published in French as *Connemara* in 2022 by Actes Sud, Arles, France
Copyright © Actes Sud, 2022
English translation copyright © Sam Taylor, 2024
Published by special arrangement with Actes Sud in conjunction with their duly
appointed agent 2 Seas Literary Agency

Production editor: Yvonne E. Cárdenas
Text designer: Patrice Sheridan
This book was set in Cochin and Trade Gothic
by Alpha Design & Composition of Pittsfield, NH

1 3 5 7 9 10 8 6 4 2

Library of Congress Cataloging-in-Publication Data
Names: Mathieu, Nicolas, 1978- author. | Taylor, Sam, 1970- translator.
Title: Connemara / Nicolas Mathieu ; translated from the French by Sam Taylor.
Other titles: Connemara. English
Description: New York : Other Press, 2024. | "Originally published in
French as Connemara in 2022 by Actes Sud, Arles, France"
Identifiers: LCCN 2023030077 (print) | LCCN 2023030078 (ebook) |
ISBN 9781635423563 (paperback) | ISBN 9781635423570 (ebook)
Subjects: LCGFT: Novels.
Classification: LCC PQ2713.A8767 C6613 2024 (print) |
LCC PQ2713.A8767 (ebook) | DDC 843/.92—dc23/eng/20230919
LC record available at https://lccn.loc.gov/2023030077
LC ebook record available at https://lccn.loc.gov/2023030078

For Elsa

1

THE ANGER CAME as soon as she woke. All it took to put her in a rage was to think about the day ahead: so many things to do, so little time.

And yet Hélène was an organized woman. She drew up lists, planned her weeks. In her mind, even in her body, she knew the exact amount of time it took to run a load of laundry, to give the youngest a bath, to cook noodles or get breakfast ready, to drive the girls to school or wash her hair. She'd had to get her hair cut twenty times to save on the two hours per week it took her to care for it. And she'd saved those hours, twenty times over. Was that the kind of sacrifice she had to make—the loss of her long hair, treasured since childhood?

Hélène was full of all these counted minutes, these little scraps of daily existence that made up the jigsaw puzzle of her life. Occasionally she would remember her adolescence, the lethargy that you're allowed at fifteen, the idle Sundays, and later the hungover mornings spent lazing around in a daze. That whole vanished period...at the time it had seemed to last forever, but as she looked back now it seemed so brief. Her mom used to bawl her out for the hours she wasted lying in bed when she could have been outside enjoying the sunshine.

Nowadays her alarm went off at six every weekday morning, and on weekends, like an automaton, she woke at six anyway.

At times she had the feeling that something had been stolen from her, that her life was no longer really her own. Now her sleep patterns were in thrall to some higher power, the rhythm of her days ruled by family and work. Everything she did, and the speed at which she did it, was for the greater good. Her mother could rest content: Hélène, a mother herself now, was useful at last. She'd been dragged into the adult mire, and she saw the sun all day long.

"Are you awake?" she whispered.

Philippe was lying on his front, a solid presence beside her, one arm folded under his pillow. He might have been dead. Hélène checked the time: 6:02. Ugh, not again...

"Hey," she said in a louder voice. "Go wake the girls. Hurry up or we'll be late again."

Philippe turned over with a sigh, lifting up the comforter and releasing the warm heavy familiar smell, the dense air accumulated from one night and two close bodies. Hélène was already on her feet, in the biting cold of the bedroom, hands searching the nightstand for her glasses.

"Philippe, come on..."

Her partner grumbled, then turned his back on her. Hélène was already mentally running through all the tasks she had to tick off.

She took a shower, her jaw still tensed, then checked the emails on her phone as she went to the kitchen. She'd do her makeup later, in the car. Every morning the kids would get her hot under the collar so there was no point putting on foundation until after she'd dropped them at school.

With her glasses perched at the end of her nose, she warmed up their milk and poured cereal into their bowls. On the radio it was those two journalists again whose names she could never remember. She still had time. The morning show on France Inter provided her with the same easy markers every day. For now, the house was still cocooned in that nocturnal calm, the kitchen like an island of light where Hélène could savor a rare moment of solitude. She drank her coffee, enjoying the respite like a soldier on leave. It was 6:20 and already she needed a cigarette.

She put on her thick cardigan and went out to the balcony. There, leaning on the railing, she smoked while gazing down at the city below, the first red and yellow lights of traffic, the scattered dazzle of streetlamps. On a nearby street a garbage truck was going through its routine drudgery, all sighs and beeps and blinking. A little farther to her left loomed a highrise, its dark outline studded with rectangles of light and flitting silhouettes. There was a church over that way. To her right, the geometric mass of a hospital. The city center, with its cobbled alleys and fancy stores, was a long way off. She watched as the city of Nancy stretched and came back to life. It wasn't too cold for a morning in October. The tobacco crackled and glowed and Hélène looked over her shoulder before checking her cell phone. A smile appeared on her face, highlighted by the gleam of the screen.

She'd received a new message.

Some simple words saying I can't wait, I'll see you soon. Her heart gave a brief jolt and she took another drag on her cigarette, then shivered. It was 6:25. Time to get dressed again, drop the girls at school again, lie again.

"IS YOUR BAG packed?"

"Yeah."

"Mouche, did you remember your swimming stuff?"

"No."

"You need to remember."

"I know."

"I reminded you yesterday, weren't you listening?"

"I was."

"So why didn't you do it?"

"I just didn't think."

"That's the point. You have to think."

"Nobody can be good at everything," Mouche replied, like a learned professor with her Nesquik mustache.

She had just turned six and she was changing before her mother's eyes. Clara too had been through that phase of accelerated growth, but Hélène had forgotten how it felt to see her children suddenly becoming *people*. So she was rediscovering, as if for the first time, that moment when a child shakes off the torpor of infancy, stops acting like some greedy little creature, and starts thinking, making jokes, coming out with stuff that changes the mood of a meal or leaves the grown-ups agape.

"Well, I should be off. Bye, everyone..."

Philippe had just appeared in the kitchen and he was going through the morning routine of tucking his shirt into his pants and running a hand under his belt, from his belly to his back.

"You're not eating breakfast?"

"I'll grab something at work."

He kissed his daughters, then gave Hélène a peck on the lips.

"You remember you're picking up the girls tonight?" she said.

"Tonight?"

Philippe's hair was thinner than it used to be, but he was still a handsome man: well-built and well-dressed, nicely scented, the gleam in his eye undimmed. He was still the boy who breezed through his exams without trying, the kid in the know. It was annoying.

"We've been talking about this for the past week."

"Yeah, but I might have to bring some work back."

"Call Claire then."

"Have you got her number?"

Hélène gave him the babysitter's phone number and advised him to contact her ASAP to make sure she was available.

"Okay, okay," Philippe said, typing the number into his phone. "Do you know if you'll be home late?"

"Shouldn't be too late," Hélène replied.

"It's a pain, though," said her partner as he scrolled through his emails.

"It's not like I'm out all the time. You got home at nine last night, remember? And the night before."

"I was working. What do you expect me to do?"

"Yeah, well, I'm volunteering."

Philippe looked up from the blue screen and gave her his usual thin-lipped, mocking smile.

Ever since they'd come back from Paris, Philippe seemed to think that nobody had the right to ask him for anything else. After all, he'd given up a brilliant job at AXA for her, not to mention his badminton buddies and, in general, the kind of prospects that simply did not exist in Nancy. And all that because she had not been able to handle Paris. Although it was debatable whether she was handling Nancy any better. That forced departure remained like an unpaid debt between them. Or at least that was how it seemed to Hélène.

"Well, see you tonight," Philippe said.

"See you."

Then Hélène rallied her daughters: "Okay, brush teeth, get dressed, let's go. I still have to put my lenses in. I'm not going to tell you twice."

"Mommy..." said Mouche.

But Hélène had already stalked out of the room on her long legs, hair tied back, checking her WhatsApp messages as she went upstairs. Manuel had sent her a new message, saying see you tonight, and she could feel it again: that delicious sting of fear in her chest that made her feel like a teenager.

THIRTY MINUTES LATER the girls were at school and Hélène wasn't far from the office. Automatically, she ran through her list of meetings for the day. At ten she was seeing the Vinci people. At two she had to call the woman from Porette, the cement works in Dieuze. They were planning layoffs, and Hélène had an idea for reorganizing cross-functional teams that could save five jobs. According to her calculations, she could save them almost five hundred thousand euros annually by modifying their organizational chart and optimizing the purchasing department and the vehicle fleet. Erwann, her boss, had told her this was a must-win situation: it was huge, symbolically, and she simply couldn't fail. And then at four she had the big presentation at the mayor's office. She had to check the slides one last time before she went there. Ask Lison to print files for each participant, on both sides to make sure she didn't get crucified by some pedantic tree hugger. And don't forget the personalized cover sheet. She knew the staff in places like that, the department heads, all those anxious, influential cliques that made up the ranks of municipal administration. They were always so thrilled if you printed their name on a folder or on the first page of an official document. After a certain point in their cluttered careers, lording it over their underlings, distinguishing themselves from their colleagues, became the most important part of their job.

And then tonight, her date.

From Nancy to Épinal, it was just under an hour's drive. She wouldn't even have time to go home and take a shower. Not that she was going to sleep with him on the first date anyway. Yet again, she told herself she should cancel, that this was a really bad idea. But Lison was already waiting for her in the parking lot, leaning against the wall and sucking greedily at her vape, her peculiar face hidden behind a cloud of apple and cinnamon smoke.

"So? Are you ready?"

"You must be kidding... I need you to print those files for the mayor's office. The meeting's at four."

"I did it yesterday."

"On both sides?"

"Of course. You think I'm a climate change denier or something?"

The two women hurried toward the elevators. Inside, as they ascended toward Elexia's offices, Hélène avoided her intern's gaze. For once, Lison did not look half-asleep. There was a gleam in her eyes, in fact, as though she were the one with a date that night. At the third floor, the door opened, and Hélène went through first.

"Follow me," she said, walking across the vast open-plan office for the consultants, with its archipelago of desks, the narrow red carpet showing people which way to go, and the numerous green plants thriving in the deluge of daylight that poured through the high windows. Red armchairs and gray couches sat waiting for employees to chill out on with their colleagues. At the back of the room, a small kitchen equipped with a microwave allowed people to warm up their lunch and gave rise to arguments over food items left in the fridge. The only enclosed spaces were on the mezzanine floor: a meeting room known as the Cube, and the boss's office. Hélène and Lison headed for the Cube, where they could talk without being overheard.

"This is a mistake," Hélène said.

"No it's not. It'll be fine."

"I'm acting like an idiot, checking my phone every five minutes. This is ridiculous. I have a job, I have kids. I can't get sucked into stuff like this. I'm going to cancel."

"No, wait!"

Lison sometimes forgot that Hélène was her boss and spoke to her as if she were a friend. Hélène didn't mind. She tended to rely completely on this strange, comical girl with her Converse sneakers, her secondhand designer coats, her horselike face. Even those long teeth and widely spaced eyes were not enough to make her ugly, however, and in all honesty she had changed Hélène's life. Before Lison turned up, she had long felt as if she were standing at the edge of an abyss.

On the surface she had everything she could want: the architect-designed house, the important job, a magazine-photo-shoot family, a good-looking partner, a walk-in closet, even her health. But her existence was undermined by a sort of negative *je ne sais quoi*, an impossible combination of satiety and lack. The crack that ran through her entire life.

The condition had first come to light four years before, when she and Philippe were still living in Paris. One day, at the office, Hélène had locked herself in the bathroom simply because she could no longer bear seeing the emails pile up in her inbox. After that, withdrawal had become a habit. She would go into hiding to avoid a meeting, a colleague, the necessity of answering the phone. And she would sit on the toilet for hours, improving her score on Candy Crush, incapable of reacting, lovingly imagining her own suicide. Little by little, the most ordinary things had become intolerable. She had once burst into tears while reading the office canteen menu, for example, because there were grated carrots and dauphine potatoes for lunch again. Even her cigarette breaks had taken a tragic turn. As for work itself, she simply hadn't seen the point anymore. Why bother with all those Excel spreadsheets, those endlessly interchangeable meetings? And, oh God, the jargon. She would practically retch every time she heard someone use the verbs "impact," "empower," or "prioritize." Toward the end, she couldn't even hear the note that her Mac-Book Pro made when she turned it on without sobbing.

She had started losing sleep, hair, weight. She had gotten eczema on the backs of her knees. Once, on her daily commute, catching sight of a man's pale scalp beneath his comb-over, she had fainted. She had felt alienated from everything. She had lost all desire to go anywhere. She had fallen into the void.

The doctor had told her she was probably burned out, and Philippe had reluctantly agreed to leave Paris. At least there were a few advantages to living in the provinces: a better quality of life and the ability to afford a spacious house with a large yard, not to mention the possibility of obtaining a place for her children at a local day-care center without having to sleep with someone at the mayor's office. Besides, Hélène's parents lived nearby, so they could always help out from time to time.

In Nancy, Hélène had immediately found a new job thanks to one of Philippe's friends. Erwann ran Elexia, a company that offered HR advice, audits, and recommendations, the same thing she had been doing before. And for a few weeks, the change of setting and the slower pace of life had been enough to keep her depression at a distance. But not for long. Soon, without falling back into the same bottomless abyss, she had started feeling frustrated again, out of place, often exhausted, sad for no reason, filled with rage.

Philippe did not know how to react to these black moods. They had tried discussing it once or twice, but Hélène had been left with the impression that he was just acting, trying to look earnest, nodding at regular intervals: exactly the same routine he went through when he was on Zoom with his colleagues. Deep down, Philippe's instinct was to *manage* her, just like he managed everything else.

Thankfully, there had been a light in this fog of fatigue: one day she had received a strange CV and a letter asking for an internship. Normally, that kind of request did not reach her, or she would instantly delete the email. But this one caught her attention because of its almost ludicrous simplicity: no photograph and none of the usual inane padding—social skills, wholesome hobbies, driver's license, etc. It was just a Word document with a name, Lison Lagasse, an address, a cell phone number, mention of a master's degree in economics, and an incongruous list of work experiences. Léon de Bruxelles, Deloitte, Darty, Barclays, even a fishery in Scotland. Rather than passing on her application to the HR department, as required by the recruitment process, Hélène had called the woman's cell phone out of curiosity. Because this girl reminded her of someone. Lison had picked up on the first ring, responding to Hélène's questions in her clear, reedy voice, interspersed with brief bursts of laughter: yeah, no way, totally. She sounded amused and straightforward, not like someone trying too hard or putting on an act. Hélène had arranged a meeting with her one evening after seven, when the office was more or less empty, as if she had something to hide. Lison turned up at the appointed time, looking like a party girl the morning after: tall and ultra-thin, skintight jeans and fringed loafers, bangs of course, and that long face, with her lips almost constantly pulled back to reveal those dazzling, horsey teeth.

"You have a strange CV. How do you go from Deloitte to Darty?"

"They're both on the same Metro line."

Hélène had smiled. So Lison was Parisian... The girls of Paris had intimidated Hélène for years with their special, advanced elegance, the way they felt at home everywhere, their inability to put on weight, and that imperious, unanswerable attitude, their every gesture saying: the best you could do, girl, is to try to be like me. It was strange seeing one there, in her office in Nancy, at nighttime. Looking at her was a bit like receiving a postcard from a place where she had once spent a complicated vacation.

"And what are you doing here?"

"Oh!" she said, waving her arm dismissively, "I got kicked out of college, and my mother found a guy down here."

"Are you acclimatizing?"

"Kind of."

Hélène hired Lison on the spot, handing her all the "reporting tools" that Erwann had made mandatory since embarking on his crusade against waste, his quest to "refine the process," which effectively meant the obligation to justify every little trip, to note even the tiniest tasks on gargantuan spreadsheets, to scroll through endless drop-down menus in search of the cryptic title that corresponded to what had once been an unquantifiable activity, and in this way to waste one hour every day explaining how you had spent the other eight.

Against all expectations, Lison was brilliant at her job. After a week she knew everyone in the building and all the office gossip. The secret of her success was simple: everything amused her. She floated through the open-plan office like a bubble, efficient and indifferent, irritating but mostly well-liked, incapable of stress, giving the impression that she could not care less, never disappointing anyone, a sort of Mary Poppins of the service sector. For Hélène, who spent her time struggling, desperate to be made a partner alongside Erwann, Lison's carefree attitude was utterly alien and enchanting.

One night, while they were having a pint in the pub next door, Hélène grew curious.

"Is there anyone you like at the office?"

"Never at work, that's taboo."

"But that's mostly where you meet people, isn't it?"

"I prefer not to mix business and pleasure. It's too stressful, especially in an open-plan office. Afterward, the guys circle around you all day like vultures. And those dickheads can never keep it to themselves. They always have to brag."

Hélène laughed at this.

"So how do you manage? Do you go out dancing?"

"God, no. Nightclubs around here? Ugh." She shuddered. "I just do what everyone else does: internet dating."

Hélène forced herself to smile. She was barely a generation older than Lison and yet she no longer understood anything about young people's romantic habits. Listening to the intern, she discovered that the possibilities of hookups, the length of relationships, the interest shown afterward, the time between affairs, the tolerance for multiple lovers and overlap, the rules, in short, of fucking and feelings, had undergone massive changes.

The primary difference was in the use of messaging services and social networks. When Hélène explained to her intern that she had never heard of the internet until she went to high school, Lison had looked at her with frank astonishment. Of course she knew that a civilization had existed before the web, but she tended to think of that period as belonging to the sepia decades, somewhere between the Nazi-Soviet Pact and the moon landing.

"Yep, it's true," sighed Hélène. "I got my baccalaureate results on 3615 EducNat, or something like that."

"Okay, boomer…"

Lison's generation had grown up inside the internet. At middle school, she had spent whole evenings flirting online with total strangers on the computer that her parents had given her to help with her schoolwork, talking endlessly about sex with kids her own age as well as with fifty-year-old perverts who typed one-handed, people in Singapore, or her neighbor, with whom she would never have exchanged a single word if they'd been sitting next to each other on the bus. Later, she'd had fun carrying on long, epistolary relationships with dozens of boys she knew only vaguely. All you had to do was contact a hot guy from your school on Facebook or Insta—hey, hi there—and the rest followed easily. Through the digital night, conversations flew back and forth at dizzying speeds, annihilating distances, making waiting unbearable, sleep superfluous, exclusivity unacceptable. She and her friends always had three or four discussion threads on the go simultaneously. The conversation, trivial at first, begun in a bantering tone, would soon take a more personal turn. They would express their dissatisfactions: the parents who pissed them off; Léa, who was a slut; the science teacher who was a narcissistic pervert. After eleven, when the rest of the family was asleep, these interactions between peers grew more clandestine. They started to really heat up. Fantasies were expressed in few words, all abbreviated, coded, indecipherable. They ended up sending each other photos of themselves in underwear, erections bulging, suggestive low-angle shots.

"Ideally you'd take a picture where they could see your ass but not your face. Just in case."

"You weren't scared the guy would show it to his friends?"

"Of course. That's the price you pay."

Those images, taken in her bed, chiaroscuro selfies, erotica under some degree of control, were exchanged like contraband money, unknown to the kids' parents, an illegal currency that brought into existence a libidinal market over which hovered constantly the threat of exposure. Because sometimes a dirty picture would find its way into the public domain and a half-naked minor would go viral.

"I had a friend in my sophomore year who had to change schools."

"That's terrible."

"Yeah. And that's not the worst of it."

Hélène feasted on these anecdotes, which, like potato chips, left her feeling vaguely sickened while continuing to want more of them. She also worried for her daughters, wondering how they would cope with these new forms of danger. But most of all, those stories turned her on. She envied all this desire aimed at others. She felt diminished by her lack of access to it. She remembered the permanent lust that had once been her normal waking state. She once told her psychiatrist: "I feel like I'm old already. All that is over for me."

"How does that make you feel?" the shrink had asked, as usual.

"Angry. Sad."

The bastard hadn't even bothered noting this down in his Moleskine.

The time had passed so quickly. From her high school exams to her forties, Hélène's life had taken a high-speed train, abandoning her one day on an unfamiliar platform, in an altered body, suitcases under her eyes, with less hair and more fat, kids hanging on her apron strings, a partner who said he loved her but who disappeared as soon as she asked him to run a load of laundry or look after the girls during a school strike. On this platform, men did not turn around very often to look at her anymore. And those looks that she used to hate, that were of course no measure of her value, she somehow found herself missing. Everything had changed in a flash.

One Friday evening, when she was at Le Galway with Lison, Hélène finally came out with it.

"I find it depressing, hearing about all your men."

"I like girls too," Lison replied, pulling a face that looked at once jocular and satisfied. "They're mostly just flirts, though. I probably only fuck about half of them."

"I mean it pisses me off to think that my turn is over."

"What? You're crazy. You have so much potential. They'd go wild for you on Tinder."

"Oh, stop it. If you're just going to make fun of me..."

But Lison was serious: the world was full of lust-crazed guys who would sell their own mothers to get a woman like Hélène in their bed.

"That's flattering," Hélène said, heavy-lidded.

Of course she'd heard about that kind of dating app before. The internet watchdog sites that she consulted were always waxing lyrical over these new models that enslaved millions of singles, monopolizing the dating market, their algorithms redefining elective affinities and intermittences of the heart, their direct channels and playful interfaces appropriating everything from broken hearts to the possibility of love at first sight.

In no time at all, Lison had, just for a laugh, created a profile for Hélène using photographs taken from the internet, two shot from behind and the third a little blurred. As for the About Me section, she kept it minimalist and slightly risqué: Hélène, 39. *Come and get me if you're man enough.* She then explained how the app worked.

"It's simple. You see the guy appear on your screen: a headshot, two or three other pics. You swipe right if you like him. If not, swipe left and you'll never hear from him again."

"And they're all doing the same with me?"

"Exactly. If you like each other, you get a match and you can start chatting."

With their elbows on the bar, Hélène and her intern looked through the region's collection of single guys and compulsive cheaters. This parade of poseurs mostly made them laugh;

attractive men were a rare commodity. The men of Nancy seemed to consist mainly of fake gangsters taking shirtless selfies in front of their Audis, single men in rimless glasses, divorcés wearing soccer jerseys, real-estate agents with slicked-back hair, or gauche-looking firefighters. Lison's thumb pitilessly sent all these poor fools leftward into hell, occasionally rescuing from the flames a guy who bore a vague resemblance to Jason Statham or some total misfit they could snigger over. No matter who she chose, she instantly got matched because, while girls could be picky, the boys on the site did not seem to turn their nose up at anything, casting their net wide and sorting through their meager haul later. At each new profile, Lison would make a stinging remark and Hélène, increasingly drunk, would laugh.

"Hang on, that one's not even eighteen."

"Who cares? You're not a general election."

"And look at that haircut!"

"Maybe that's the fashion in New York."

Lison, of course, had used Tinder in New York and London, which is why she'd had such amazing results. Because in places like that, with sky-high property prices and the pressure of competition, you had to work nonstop to keep your head above water, which left you with little time for stuff like buying groceries or dating. So people used online apps to fill their bed just as they did their shopping cart. A connection, a few words exchanged at lunchtime, an insanely expensive cocktail around seven, and before you knew it you were stripping naked in some minuscule apartment to have a fast fuck while thinking about all those urgent messages that kept filling your inbox. That was how those dagger-sharp lives were lived: quick and cutting, continually acted out on social networks, without tears or wrinkles, in the sinister illusion of a perpetual present.

Whereas here, in the small towns of northern France, it was obviously not the same.

"And you show your face on this thing?" Hélène asked. "It doesn't bother you that someone might recognize you?"

"Everyone does it. If you spread the shame around, it doesn't exist anymore."

They'd been interrupted by a text from Philippe just then, killing the atmosphere. *The girls are in bed. Where are you?* Hélène had paid for the drinks, dropped Lison off at her place, and deleted the app before going home.

The next day, she reinstalled it.

She quickly got the hang of the system, expanding her search zone to a radius of eighty kilometers and embellishing her profile with actual photographs of herself, but ones that did not allow her to be identified. The pictures highlighted her long legs and her seductive lips, which sometimes, when she woke very early or when she was in a bad mood, made her look like a duck. Another shot of her sitting on the edge of a swimming pool gave a glimpse of her hips, her big, toned ass, her tanned skin. She had thought about showing off her eyes, which were honey-colored but turned a kind of almond-green in summer, but in the end she opted against the idea. Romance was not on the agenda.

Within days, she was spending all her days swiping photos of men, each match restoring some self-assurance, each compliment making her feel taller and more beautiful. And yet, all this anonymous desire did not assuage her anger. She was still left with that what's-the-point feeling, that impression of being damaged goods. Now, however, she had these tiny, almost automatic compensations, and the satisfaction of knowing she had other choices. All these strangers wanted her, and their avid attentions put some color back in her life. She felt alive again and she forgot the rest. Even if, now and again, some poor over-polite, ugly guy would make her wince at her own behavior.

After a while, though, one of these men did manage to hold her attention. He was hiding too, but behind a panda mask. And at least his description dispensed with the usual bullshit. *Manuel, 32. Seeking beautiful, intelligent woman to come with me to my ex's wedding. If you're right-wing and you wear the same perfume as my mother, that's a bonus.*

Amused, Hélène asked him what perfume his mother wore. *Nina Ricci*, he replied.

Maybe we can come to an arrangement.

After that, they'd started chatting regularly. To start with, Hélène had adopted a distant and vaguely sarcastic attitude. Then Philippe went to Paris for a training course and she found herself alone for three nights. Their conversations evolved from playful banter to shared secrets and then to sensual insinuations. In the darkness of her bedroom, Hélène's world was reduced to a blue-lit face, and the hours sped by silently. She experienced hot flashes, insomnia, and red eyes as she squirmed in the sheets of their endless discussions. When she woke the next morning, she looked a fright and her first reflex was to check her messages. Two new words were all it took to fill her heart with joy. An hour of silence and she would start catastrophizing. Her feet no longer touched the ground. At last she agreed to meet him.

But now that the time had almost come for their date, Hélène was getting cold feet. Inside the Cube, on the mezzanine, she felt the fear take hold of her. What if she ended up regretting this?

Lison remained upbeat: "It'll pass. You're just out of practice."

"No, I'm going to cancel. This kind of thing just isn't me."

"Is this because of Philippe?"

Hélène turned to face the window. Outside, the overcast sky loomed miserably over the city and its motley swarm of buildings. On opposing railway lines, high-speed TGVs passed half-empty regional TERs between graffiti-strewn walls. Erwann had wanted offices with a view of the city. You had to build high, see the big picture.

"No, it's not that," Hélène lied. "It's just bad timing. I've got that meeting at the mayor's office. I mean, we've been working on it for three months..."

"Just wait. You can always cancel at the last minute. This guy doesn't know where you are, he doesn't know anything about you."

Hélène looked at Lison. She was so young, her whole life ahead of her... Hélène wanted to hurt her, to avenge herself on all that possibility.

"You're starting to piss me off with this thing. I'm not a kid anymore..."

Lison took the hint and disappeared without another word. Alone in the Cube, Hélène contemplated her reflection in the window. She was wearing her new Isabel Marant skirt, a pretty blouse, her leather jacket, and a pair of high heels. She had made herself beautiful for Manuel, for those idiots at the mayor's office. She noticed the thinness of her chignon at the top of her head and was suddenly mad at herself. Had she struggled through her whole life for this?

This was the moment Erwann chose to burst into the Cube, tablet in hand, unshaved, ginger hair disheveled, his senatorial belly straining against the gorgeous fabric of a blue twill shirt.

"Did you see Carole's email? They're really screwing with us. Honestly, I forwarded it straight to the lawyer. Fuck them. Anyway, are you still okay for the big merger meeting tomorrow?"

"Yeah, I confirmed yesterday."

"Cool, I didn't have time to check yet. What about the mayor's office—everything on track?"

"Yep, I'll be there at four."

"You're sure—no problems at all?"

"Nope, it's all good."

"We can't fuck this up. If we can just get our foot in the door, we'll clean up. I had lunch with the service manager. They want a total restructuring. If we ace this one, we'll be in pole position to bid for contracts in the future."

"We'll ace it, don't worry."

Just for an instant, Erwann stopped gazing intensely at his own navel and turned his small golden eyes on her.

At the ESSEC business school, he and Philippe had managed the student office together. Two decades later, they still bragged about how they'd siphoned money out of the treasury to buy themselves a weekend in Val Thorens. So Erwann knew all about Hélène, from her education to her Parisian burnout: her daughters, who prevented her working late in the evenings, her past glories, her past mistakes, maybe even some intimate details.

"I'm putting my trust in you," he said.

"We need to talk at some point too."

"About?"

He knew perfectly well what she was alluding to. Hélène did not lose her cool. Ignoring his fake ignorance, she said calmly: "You remember—my role within the company."

"Oh yeah, yeah. We should review that. It's absolutely one of my priorities."

Murderous thoughts ran through Hélène's head. She had been bugging him for months now to be promoted from the position of senior manager (which did not mean much at such a small company) to partner, and while Erwann had agreed in principle to this request, he had done nothing at all about it.

"Listen," she said. "I've been working like crazy all month, and I know you want to sell up to a bigger firm. But I'm warning you, there is no fucking way I'm going to let myself be tossed on the scrap heap by a branch of McKinsey."

"Absolutely not!" Erwann agreed, abruptly enthusiastic. "You know how I feel about that. Keep your best talent. You have zero worries."

If he was bullshitting her, Hélène thought, she would punch him in the mouth. Not that she really would, of course, but just thinking it made her feel better. Still pulsing with aggression, she went back into the open-plan office, where other consultants were sitting at their desks, scattered across various parts of the room, wearing earbuds and staring at screens. All these people who earned between forty and ninety thousand euros per year and didn't even have their own office. God, she had to get out of this swamp of mediocrity. She'd been telling herself the same thing forever. She had to succeed.

THE MEETING WAS supposed to take place in the basement of the mayor's office, a windowless room with fluorescent striplights, composite tables arranged in a U, and a whiteboard. After getting there first, Hélène checked that the projector worked, connected it to her computer, ran through a few slides to make sure it all went smoothly, then sat there waiting, legs crossed, tapping mechanically at her phone. Manuel had sent her three new messages that all meant essentially the same thing. *Can't wait. Thinking about you all the time. Tonight can't come fast enough.* It was sweet, but pointless. She didn't want him getting all worked up. She thought about writing a reply that would cool his passion but wasn't sure what exactly she should tell him. Just then, two men entered the room, leaving the door open behind them. Hélène instantly got to her feet, all smiles. She vaguely knew the first guy, who was already bald despite being quite young and who wore a fitted jacket and a pair of Church's. Aurélien Leclerc. He claimed he was the assistant communications director, but rumor had it he was actually just the communications director's assistant. In any case, he had graduated from Sciences Po. Everyone knew this because he generally reminded them every ten minutes.

The second man was in his fifties, tall and sharp-eyed with an even smoother skull than the first. He wore a white shirt and a crewneck sweater, and when he thrust forward his hand, Hélène saw a Brazilian bracelet dangling from his wrist.

"David Schneider. I'm head of IT."

"Ah," said Hélène. "Pleased to meet you."

Leclerc began churning out useful information. It would just be the three of them at the meeting. Monsieur Politi, who ran the communication and digital center, could not make it. He had a meeting with the prefect. But never mind, they could manage fine without him.

Hélène smiled again. Of course she understood. After all, it had only taken her a hundred fifty hours to straighten out this town's appalling IT mess, a labyrinth worthy of a Russian novel, wasting money and energy in the ludicrously complicated decision-making process that involved no fewer than three distinct organizational charts. All the way through her audit, she had been amazed that this Tower of Babel was still standing. The ingrained idleness, the blurred hierarchies, the ancient hatreds between bureaucratic chiefdoms had given rise to a digital Chernobyl. To think that the city's inhabitants entrusted their credit card numbers to this tottering, Soviet-style system so they could pay for their kids' school meals or their residency cards . . . it was alarming, to say the least.

"We can do it without him," Schneider agreed, utterly unruffled. "It's not a problem."

"Anyway, we're just starting out on this project," added Leclerc. "We can put together a methodology with a series of milestones that the director can validate afterward. That's how we generally operate with our service providers."

"Of course, but that's not exactly what we agreed with Monsieur Politi. We're already pretty advanced in the planning."

"That's how things work now," Schneider said decisively.

Hélène considered the two of them in turn: the self-satisfied assistant and the overconfident IT geek. She knew these types of men so well: they spent their lives showing off in meetings, carelessly managing bureaucrats with stagnant careers, dispensing municipal manna to a rotating wheel of subcontractors under orders, putting the pressure on whenever they felt like it, and giving empty speeches all day long.

"Okay," she said, "we'll do it your way."

She began her presentation in the standard way, with the organization's strengths and weaknesses, then listed the threats (four of which turned out to be critical for the entire system) before ending with the opportunities, which took hardly longer than a minute. She spoke in a composed voice, playing with the remote control and sometimes going over to the screen to point a finger at a particularly important detail. Her commentary was sprinkled with statistics not mentioned on the PowerPoint, figures that she had memorized for that express purpose, a method that was generally quite effective. After that, she dwelled on a few examples, did a bit of benchmarking, discussed the social elements of organizations. Leclerc and Schneider, attentive at first, soon grew distracted, forsaking her explanations so they could check their emails and send texts. At one point, Hélène even suspected that Leclerc was watching videos on YouTube. Just before moving on to her recommendations, she deliberately dropped the remote control for the projector on the floor. The back of the remote came loose and the batteries spilled out with a clatter of metal and plastic. The two men looked up, startled. Leclerc blushed bright red.

"What's gotten into you?" Schneider demanded.

"We're listening," said Leclerc in a more conciliatory tone.

Hélène stood straight, a few meters away from them, her jaw tensed. She was calculating the pros and cons of submission versus conflict. She thought about Elexia's turnover, about the close connections these two undoubtedly had with a number of their peers in various local institutions: the departmental council, the regional health agency, the board of education, and other local communities.

"Sorry," she said. "Just an accident."

She fixed the remote before concluding her presentation in an atmosphere of mutual reticence. Leclerc left before the end, saying he had an emergency to deal with. Schneider congratulated Hélène on her work but said he did not fully agree with her conclusions, which struck him as unnecessarily alarmist.

"We had an audit last year. Their recommendations were far less drastic. What matters in complex systems such as ours is to implement measures that enable a gradual improvement. You can't just knock everything down and start over."

"Of course," said Hélène.

She had seen that audit. It had been conducted internally, and its deferential tone and specious arguments were reminiscent of something the police's Internal Affairs department might produce: a complete travesty.

"Anyway, thank you," Schneider went on. "I'll go through this with my team. It's good work, especially the overview. For the strategic recommendations, I think we can improve things."

"Of course," said Hélène.

When Schneider told her that they would have to arrange another meeting to review everything, without fixing a date, she knew the project was dead in the water.

SHE RUSHED OUT of the mayor's office, walking quickly on the newly laid cobblestones, her head like a salad spinner. While she climbed the stairs to the parking lot, she checked her watch. It was too late to go back to the office. She thought about her daughters, the babysitter, Philippe. She would have to call Erwann and explain the situation. In reality, the decision had clearly been made prior to that meeting. Schneider had managed to sideline her even though that whole shitshow was his fault. For years he had been having endless conference call meetings, incapable of organizing his team, an omnipresent manipulator who intoxicated his superiors with technical jargon and showered his subordinates with disjointed directives that had no clear purpose and never achieved anything. He must have dealt with this particular problem over lunch with Politi or the CEO, between the sea bass and the fruit carpaccio, probably expressing a few polite reservations about the Elexia report and using the word "policy," which in those circles could justify the most jaw-dropping inertia, the craziest convolutions, could paralyze good intentions in a second. Soon his gas plant appeared to be the result of a series of complex and necessary decisions that could be disturbed by the smallest movement, leading to considerable disorder, first among the staff, then from an operational point of view, and that would end up annoying the users—never a good idea, particularly since the press had just unearthed that story about embarrassing subsidies granted to religious charities that had taken over some abandoned allotments near Laxou. Executives like Schneider spent their time covering up the chaos for which they were responsible with sophistries incomprehensible to the layman, making their mistakes seem necessary, disguising their cowardice under a diplomatic exterior. He'd totally screwed her, in other words.

A few sparse raindrops speckled the asphalt. Hélène sped up, encumbered by her skirt and heels. Immediately she was drenched with sweat, the strap of her purse digging into her shoulder while her raincoat slipped from her arm. But she didn't have time to make it back to her car. The rain lashed down on the city and she began running unsteadily through the suddenly empty streets, phone in hand, head lowered. Around her there was nothing now but the glistening ground, rain hammering onto car hoods and rooftops, the clean smell of the air and, above it all, the invisible sky.

Inside her Volvo, Hélène could only inspect the wreckage. Her long hair had taken on a wretched appearance, like a floorcloth or overcooked noodles. As for her clothes, they were sticky, waterlogged, too tight. With every movement she could feel them impeding her, and the skin on the underside of her thighs was sticking to the leather seat. She took some tissues from the glove box and tried to mop up the worst of the mess. Soon the windows were steamed up and she could see nothing outside but blotting-paper shadows. She was alone with her exasperation and the rumble of the rain. She couldn't do anything right. In the rearview mirror, she caught sight of her makeup running down her face.

"Shit," she groaned, tight-throated.

Desperate for some air, she pulled her blouse open and two buttons went flying. She'd paid two hundred euros for this floral-pattern silk blouse and now she may as well toss it in the trash. Seized by a crazy urge to smash everything, she gripped the steering wheel with both hands. Her lips were white. The rain was still pounding hard on the roof, filling the car with that constant drumming noise. Around her the city was just a vague pattern of greens and grays. She was alone.

So she pulled her skirt up over her damp thighs. She was breathing fast, on the verge of sobbing, her back wet and her neck hot. As soon as her legs were open, her right hand slipped beneath her cotton underwear and found the slick folds of her labia. She worked quickly, with two fingers, buttocks stuck to the car's leather seat, pressing down and circling precisely on the swelling with stubborn persistence. Her pussy grew soft and loose, and soon she had that delicious feeling inside, like a bubble, the warm possibility moving through her belly. All it took was a minute. She sped up, sure of herself, determined as a child. She had been doing this for so long; over the course of her life, she had perfected it. It was her haven and her right. Of course, she loved sex with men too. Their heavy bodies, their hairiness, their smell. The way they flipped you over, wrapped you in their arms, made you feel all small, bursting with happiness under their weight. She loved that, and even the disappointing ones generally gave her some little thrill. All the same, she would not give up this—the manipulation of her sex, the easy activation of her pleasure, so personal, delicate, shameless—for anything in the world. She often touched herself, even when she was in love, or pregnant, or happy, in the shower, in the morning, at work, sometimes on airplanes...and in her car, if she felt like it. From time to time, the desire would seize her so strongly and un-expectedly that she was tempted to pull onto the hard shoulder.

In the sultry atmosphere of the car that day, she masturbated quickly, closing her eyes occasionally, watching out for possible figures through the steamed-up windows, mentally replaying a situation that always worked for her, and suddenly she came, a clear, precise pleasure that spread outward, anesthetizing, leaving her almost at peace, or a little less agitated anyway.

At least she would be relaxed for her date. Then, having pulled her skirt down, she started the engine and set off. She didn't give a fuck anymore.

2

CORNÉCOURT WAS NOT much to look at. It was a peaceful little town with a church, a cemetery, a seventies-built mayor's office, a business park that acted as a buffer zone to the next town, residential estates that were mushrooming around the perimeter, and—in the center—a square lined with the usual businesses: a bar, a baker's, a butcher's, and a real-estate agency, where two men in short-sleeved shirts were moving about.

The birth rate in Cornécourt was low, the population ageing, but the local government was well funded, thanks in particular to the abundant taxes paid by an enormous pulp mill with a Norwegian name that nobody here could pronounce. This prosperity had not prevented the far-right Front National from topping the polls in the first round of voting; nor did it prevent the town's inhabitants from deploring a rise in incivility, always attributed to the same people. So it was that a damaged side mirror could give rise to prosecutable comments, and the graffiti sprayed nightly on the walls of the cultural center could provoke thoughts of vigilante justice. At the bar on the corner, Le Narval, violence was not rare, but it remained purely rhetorical. The customers there drank Orangina, glasses of Stella, and rosés on the terrace when the weather was fine. They also scratched off lottery tickets as they chatted about politics, horse racing, and immigrants. At five in the afternoon, the bar would be invaded by house painters in white-splattered clothes, anxious local business owners, Turkish bricklayers who had never seen a pay slip in their lives, and apprentices from the nearby employment training center, all eager to have a drink and wash away the cares of the day. Women were a rarer sight, and almost always accompanied by a man. In addition to these passing customers, a few majestic drunkards decorated the bar, along with some tropical plants. On the walls, photographs of Lino Ventura and Jacques Brel lent the place a sort of old-school, working-class glamour.

Cornécourt owed its name to the ponds north of the city, scattered across the land like a handful of change, producing a landscape of water lilies and bulrushes that extended over several kilometers. Under the low sky, their still waters looked like mercury, reflecting the passage of clouds, migratory birds, international flights. Fishermen haunted the ponds almost continually, diagonal rods signaling their presence from afar. In the spring, the place swarmed with kids on mountain bikes and families with picnic baskets. It was the ideal spot for teenagers to smoke their first cigarettes, make out in secret, drink booze around a campfire. Dog-walkers liked it too.

Fifteen thousand people lived in that average town, among the remnants of nature, a few failing farms, pointless traffic circles, a soccer stadium, a yellow-walled doctor's office, and the canal that split the town in two. Three generations of the same family could live there only two streets apart. The nights were quiet, even if the local police wore bulletproof vests. The years all followed the same pattern, punctuated by the St. Nicholas parade in December and the fireworks for St. Jean in June. At Christmas, the strings of lights gave the streets an opulent, joyous air. In summer, repeated heat waves caused panic in the geriatric wards. Here, everyone knew one another by sight. The mayor was not affiliated with any political party.

And it was with the mayor that Christophe Marchal had an appointment that day. Every month, he would deliver the same supply of dog biscuits—at least three bags. He and the mayor had known each other forever, and the old man called him "*tu*," as he did with all the kids who had been born and grown up in the area. Christophe, on the other hand, always called the mayor "*vous*." And when he parked his car, he chose a space some distance from Monsieur Müller's Range Rover, out of some kind of respect. The old man came out of his house just then, wearing rubber boots and a baseball cap advertising a home improvement store.

"Ah, there you are!" he said, lifting up the cap to scratch his head.

Christophe smiled. The two men shook hands while the mayor looked him up and down.

"Well, look at you! Are you off to a wedding?"

Christophe was wearing a white shirt and brand-new shoes, which did make him look like he was dressed up for something. Monsieur Müller, presuming that Christophe must have a date, told him he was right to make the most of life. Every word he spoke was wrapped in the heavy accent of local places—Les Hauts, Bussang, Le Tholy, La Bresse, cold spots, flower-bright meadows, vowels with circumflex accents—but no one should be fooled by such rustic appearances. During his five terms in office, he had crushed more than one ambitious man in J.M. Weston shoes. Christophe listened to him in silence, still smiling. Then he opened the trunk of his Peugeot 308 station wagon.

"I brought you a fourth bag this time."

"Oh?"

"On the house."

"Ah, that's good of you. I'll give you a hand. We need to take all this to the kennel."

While Monsieur Müller went behind the house to fetch a wheelbarrow, Christophe looked around. Next to the main house was another building, almost identical but on a smaller scale, where the mayor's friends—often hunters—could stay when they were in the area. Farther off, he could see the kennel with its rendered walls, and beyond that—two hundred meters away—the dark line of woods that marked the estate's boundary. When Monsieur Müller returned, the two men tossed the bags into the wheelbarrow.

"So, how's business these days?"

"Can't complain."

"And the hockey team?"

"Slowly recovering."

"What a shitshow... I haven't been for a while. What happened was disgusting."

"Yeah, it's a shame."

"You're not kidding... All the good ones have left. They'll probably call you up again at this rate."

"It's not impossible," said Christophe.

The mayor laughed and they set off, Christophe pushing the wheelbarrow while Monsieur Müller hopped along beside him.

For more than fifty years, the neighboring town had enjoyed some special moments with its ice hockey team. Through various ups and downs, the Épinal club had risen from the local divisions to elite level, forever in the limelight for its stunning victories, its brutal defeats, its hard-core supporters remaining loyal through thick and thin. During hockey season, the bleachers at the rink were full for every game. There, town councillors in overcoats mingled with families wearing strings of onions, and teenagers from affluent neighborhoods rubbed shoulders with toothless drunks who downed pints of Picon beer at the bar. Then there were the local businessmen in their private boxes, and the ultras, faces painted in the team's colors, who would line up from three in the afternoon to make sure they got the best seats. In that town, the skating rink was a sort of crucible, bringing people together in a way they never were anywhere else, in the cold air and the harsh echo of blades on ice. Four thousand eyes followed the same black dot as it shot around at a hundred fifty kilometers per hour. For two hours, everyone was gathered around the oval rink, hoping for goals, speed, and violence. The same desire filled every chest.

"Have they really asked you to go back?" Monsieur Müller asked.

"They're talking about it ..."

"And you can still see yourself playing at your age?"

"Maybe ..."

Two years before, the club had been relegated following financial problems—the result of an overambitious recruitment policy that had taken the team to the top of the table but left the club crippled by debt. After it went into receivership, all the Czechs, Slovaks, and Canadians hired at massive expense had disappeared. The reserve team was now trying desperately to stay afloat in the lower reaches of the second division. Why not me? Christophe thought. His years as a hockey player had been the best of his life.

"You might struggle," said the mayor of Cornécourt. "Your game was based on speed ..."

"There are ways of compensating. Experience is important too."

"And physique."

Monsieur Müller gave a cruelly mischievous wink. Christophe had put on quite a bit of weight recently. Life as a delivery driver was not much help when it came to staying in shape: always eating in restaurants, ass wedged in the driver's seat of his car eight hours a day. The forty-year-old clutched the wheelbarrow handles in his big fists and managed another smile.

"You need a few burly guys on a team."

This reminded the old man of a trip the two of them had taken long ago, with some other teenage hockey players and their parents, to a training camp in Canada.

"Remember the monsters?" Monsieur Müller asked.

Of course Christophe remembered. In Canada, every team had its own appointed brute who was there to protect the more technical, less physical players. Being a fighter wasn't easy. For quite a few players from poorer areas, taking on this role of enforcer was the only way they could reach the highest level. He could still see that guy, born in deepest Ontario, who had grown up in a small town in the middle of nowhere: two thousand souls and three ice rinks. At the age of twenty-five, the guy had lost all his incisors and had a metal plate under his right cheekbone. Before every game, he would kneel down to pray in a corner of the locker room. But when the time came to fight, he did not hold back: he threw off his gloves and hit hard. In America, certain enforcers had become true legends. Intimidation was enshrined in the rules there, and a large part of the crowd turned up for precisely that—the electric shock, the impression that, at any moment, the game could genuinely become a matter of life and death.

"You were never a tough guy, though," said Monsieur Müller. "You can't suddenly start playing that role at forty..."

"Depends," said Christophe.

He wasn't smiling as he said this, but the old man gave a hearty, proprietorial laugh, the laugh of someone who for the past fifty years had always felt certain he was right.

A brief volley of barking greeted them when they reached the kennel. Monsieur Müller whistled and the dogs calmed down. The only sounds now were the scraping of their claws on cold concrete, the jingling of collars, the damp huffing of the animals' breaths. There were about twenty hounds there, each in its own pen, with white tiled walls and high barred windows, the whole place very clean despite the heady smell. The two men went to the back, where the hermetically sealed bin for storing food was located. They divided the work without a word, Monsieur Müller opening each bag with a box cutter while Christophe poured the biscuits into the bin. When they'd finished, Christophe dusted off his clothes and took the invoices and a receipt from his pocket.

"I'll just need a signature…"

Monsieur Müller read the papers diagonally, then, without looking up, asked Christophe to bend down. The younger man thought this was a prank at first, but the mayor was serious. So Christophe leaned forward from his hips, hands on his knees, and waited while Monsieur Müller signed the documents on his back. The mayor finished up with two dots that stung his spine. All the time this was happening, the closest dog sat staring at Christophe with its beautiful, glistening, vaguely melancholic eyes.

This unpleasant episode did not prevent Christophe uttering a few kind words. He could tell that these dogs were well cared for. That wasn't always the case.

"I look after them. What do you expect me to say?" Despite this gruff outburst, Monsieur Müller was obviously flattered.

He lifted his baseball cap to scratch his head again, then added: "Come on, I've got something to show you."

The two men left the storage building and headed toward the woods. Soon Christophe spotted two tiny chalets surrounded by a wire fence.

"Is that new?"

"I gave myself a little treat," the mayor explained, patting Christophe's shoulder.

They continued across the meadow, under a slate-colored sky where the possibility of rain was ripening. The countryside spread out around them, with the gray ribbon of trees up ahead, and in the air the musky odor of the dogs mingled with the sharper smell of humus and fresh air. In the tall grass their footsteps made a pleasant, intimate swishing sound, almost as overpowering as a lullaby.

"You'll see," said Monsieur Müller, opening the fence.

In reality those little chalets were just spruced-up doghouses. Outside them Christophe saw bowls filled with water and with biscuits. The two men crouched in front of the entrance and, once his eyes had gotten used to the dark, Christophe made out two soft shapes inside: two beautiful puppies sleeping on plaid blankets.

"What are they?"

"Tibetan mastiffs."

"No!"

"Move closer."

Squatting on their heels, the two men began petting the two heavy creatures. Beneath the dogs' unbelievably soft fur, the men could feel their hearts beating, fast and stubborn. They truly were magnificent animals.

"Where did you find them? You don't often see them around here."

"My Spanish network."

"How much?"

"Two thousand each. Plus transportation costs. Their father was a real champion."

Christophe whistled. This breed had become fashionable recently, and with a good pedigree it was possible to sell them for dizzying sums. One dog had even gone for more than a million euros somewhere in China. Christophe glanced at his watch.

"I can keep one for you if you want," said Monsieur Müller, apparently serious.

Meanwhile one of the puppies had stood up and lazily paced around in a circle before collapsing onto the floor again and gazing at them languorously.

"That one's Jumbo. He'll be about seventy kilos when he's fully grown."

"He's a real beauty," Christophe admitted.

Nothing could touch him the way animals did. Apart from his kid, of course. Although, now that he thought about it, the kid had some of the same innocent mannerisms as an animal, a sort of sniffing, primal existence. Sometimes, watching his son as he lay on the couch, in front of the TV, his feet bare and his head lowered, he would think, that's it. His little guy, his little boy. Then he would think about what came after, about the kid's mother. All that hit him so hard that he had to leave the room.

"They're not the easiest pets though," Monsieur Müller said. "Incredibly pigheaded. If you want a guard dog, you can't do better. And to think I'm going to sell him to some stuck-up bitch in an SUV..."

"I read somewhere about a Chinese guy who bought a mastiff like that. The dog wouldn't stop putting on weight. It'd just guzzle food all day long. Astronomical quantities. And then one day, the mutt stands up on its hind legs. And that's when they understood."

The mayor turned to Christophe, frowning, awaiting the punch line. Up close, Christophe could see the network of tiny red and purple veins on his nose and cheeks. He was always tempted to look for his way home, there among the spreading arteries, to find a route beneath the leathery skin.

"They'd been given a bear."

"You're kidding!" the old man chuckled.

"I swear it's true."

The mayor's face looked suddenly childlike. He said, "Ah!" and slapped his knee. "Those idiot Chinese!" They were priceless, those billions of yellow, small-dicked men who lived over there. Impressively efficient though. He imagined them, with their bear, and he basked in the glory of that image. In his mind, the anecdote had taken on the neat and amusing outline of a scene from the Tintin book *The Blue Lotus*.

ON THE PATH that took them back to the house, Christophe looked at his watch again, then up at the gray, swirling sky. It was more humid now, and big drops of sweat had appeared on Monsieur Müller's forehead as he pushed the empty wheelbarrow. Twice, Christophe offered to help him, but the mayor of Cornécourt shook his head. So they went on, the young man and the old, over that vast stretch of coarse grass: two black silhouettes on the horizon, under the oppressive immensity of the sky. Halfway there, Monsieur Müller stopped for a rest. He patted his forehead with a handkerchief. He looked good like that, sweating in the open air. His face was red, he was breathing hard, and there was a shrewd gleam in his eye despite the way the pupils were starting to fade. Christophe wondered how old the mayor was. It seemed to him that he had always been like this: elderly, bald, a badly dressed despot, rich but discreet, relentlessly cautious, part of that race of hustlers who produce flattened heirs and turbulent successions.

After catching his breath, Monsieur Müller asked him if he'd heard about the last town council meeting.

"Vaguely. My father mentioned it."

"Marina doesn't have long left."

"Ah…"

During that meeting, the assistant head of leisure and communication had collapsed and been taken to the hospital. For some time before that, there had been whisperings in the corridors of the mayor's office about her repeated fainting fits. On several occasions, people had seen her turn suddenly pale and begin to shake. During a cheerleading exhibition, she had even had to stop mid-speech, looking glassy-eyed, before taking her seat with the excuse that she'd had a dizzy spell. These symptoms led to various diagnoses, all of them made by amateurs and all of them absolutely categorical. And yet she had been only sixty-two, a fact that provoked metaphysical musings and rekindled ambitions among her colleagues.

"I thought you might be interested in that post," said Monsieur Müller.

Christophe's eyebrows rose in unison. "Me?"

"Well, yeah. You've lived here since you were a kid. Everybody knows you. And your name brings back good memories around here."

The mayor's heavy accent wrapped each word in a familiar thickness that was both reassuring and persuasive. Christophe nodded. It was true: he was famous in his own way. The 1993 final remained engraved in people's minds.

"And your face would look good on an electoral poster," the old man added, chuckling.

Christophe smiled despite his embarrassment. He hated this kind of situation. He was so used to agreeing with others. Saying no remained an ordeal for him.

"So?" Monsieur Müller said.

"I don't know what to say."

"Just say yes. It's not complicated."

"I've never done that kind of thing before."

"It's not rocket science. As soon as someone comes up with an idea, you tell them it's brilliant. You watch out for the socialists, and the rest is always the same: living together in harmony, democracy, promoting local business, lifeblood of the community, blah blah blah. And most important, always nod in agreement when someone complains."

"I don't think I'd have time," said Christophe.

The old man turned away and seemed to sniff the wind that was blowing harder now, pressing their clothes against their skin.

"Do you really intend to start playing again? At your age?"

Christophe lowered his chin to his chest, abruptly pensive. Nobody understood what it was like. Every game made you want to play the next one, every goal gave you the desire for more. It was there, inside his body, pure muscle memory. People imagined sports careers with an exit at the end, medals on the wall, the feeling of a mission accomplished, but it was the exact opposite. Seven years after retiring, he would still sometimes dream about it at night: the sensation of sliding, the relief of hitting the puck, arms tensed, bodies jostling all around, the roar of the crowd. His shoulders, his arms, and his hands in particular were still full of those old habits. It almost hurt sometimes.

At last he raised his head and dared to look the old man in the eye.

"I'm sorry. I can't give you an answer right now."

Monsieur Müller shrugged and shook his head, as if in response to an amusing joke.

"Fine. We'll talk about this another time, then." And he took hold of the wheelbarrow again before adding: "But are you sure they actually want you to play?"

Thankfully, Christophe felt his cell phone buzz inside his pocket. It was his father.

"Sorry, I have to take this. I'll catch up with you in a minute."

The mayor continued alone toward the house, he and his wheelbarrow shrinking as the distant sky loomed closer to the earth.

"Hello?"

On the other end of the line, Christophe's father began stammering vehemently. Something to do with the kid, how late it was, the teacher, and some other kids at the school. Christophe listened as best he could, covering his other ear with a hand and lowering his head to shelter from the wind. He said yes several times, then okay, and promised to call back in five minutes. His father finally relaxed then, and he was able to catch up with the mayor of Cornécourt, who was waiting for him, leaning against his Range Rover.

"How is your father?"

"He's fine."

"Tell him hello from me."

"I will."

They shook hands. The mayor told him the offer still stood. For now, at least. Christophe thanked him and promised to think about it. As he left, he saw in his rearview mirror that the old man was still standing there, watching him leave, worse than a judge.

———

THE FIRST RAINDROPS spattered against the asphalt just as Christophe came to a stop by the roadside. He pulled on the handbrake, then looked at the sky through the windshield. Then came the deluge, a wall of water that drowned out the entire landscape. Before he called his father, Christophe took a few drags on his vape.

"Hello, Dad?"

"Didn't you try to call me back?"

"I *am* calling you back."

"I had to go to the school to fetch the kid earlier today."

"What happened?"

"Same thing as always. He's being bullied."

"What did they do to him?"

"I don't know. He was crying in the car."

"Did they hit him?"

"I don't know. Anyway, he doesn't want to go to school anymore."

"Did you ask him what happened?"

"He doesn't want to talk about it."

"I'll arrange a meeting with the teacher."

"You've done that before. You know it does no good."

"So what am I supposed to do?"

"He's your kid. If you don't do anything, I'll take care of it."

There was nothing visible beyond the car windows except for the relentless downpour of rain. Christophe felt his right eyelid twitch and with two fingers he touched the tiny scar just beneath his eye, the small part of him that had lost all feeling after a trauma.

"There's one in particular," his father explained. "A little shit in red sneakers. If he keeps doing this, I'll take care of him. He won't forget that in a hurry."

"Let me speak to Gabriel please," said Christophe.

A few seconds later, he heard that thin, little lisping voice.

"Hello?"

"Hey, sweetie. How are you?"

"I'm okay."

"How was school?"

"Okay."

"Grandpa told me you'd been crying."

"A bit."

"Were they bothering you?"

The boy did not reply and Christophe found himself alone in the car with the muffled echo of the rain. He sucked hard at the end of the vape. He wanted to feel it burn.

"Will you be okay?"

"Yes," said the small voice at the end of the line.

Christophe did not have time to say another word, because his father had already taken the receiver.

"Are you coming home late tonight?"

"Yeah, a little bit."

"What time, roughly?"

"Around midnight, I think. I told you, remember? I've got a meeting with his mother."

"What does she want this time?" his father grumbled.

"Nothing, we just need to go through a few details—vacations and so on."

"All right. Well, I'm going to make doughnuts. With blueberry jam. That'll make him feel better."

"Okay...I'll try not to be too late."

"All right. Well, good night. Have fun."

"Yeah, right..."

He should perhaps have gone home before driving to see Charlie. Since their separation, he had been living with his father, and with his son when he had custody. But when he thought of returning to the large, cold house with its peculiar smell of age and habits, of having to hear the muted sound of

Business FM from the end of the hallway and to see the ice skates in the entrance hall, his courage failed him.

He set off again, vaping as he brooded over the same old thoughts. All his life, he had felt caught between two stools like this. As a kid, he'd been the mediator between his father and his mother. Then he'd found himself torn by the other big dilemmas: sports or academics, Charlie or Charlotte Brassard, and now this—the cold war between his father and his ex, particularly since she had announced her intention to move.

"I'll never let her do that," his father had warned him.

Christophe replayed the scene in his mind. The old man watching TV, a cable show about some home improvement guys who could renovate your house from top to bottom for peanuts. He hadn't even bothered taking his eyes off the screen.

"I don't understand how you can let her say stuff like that."

It was something to see, the way they got along, the old man and the boy. In the evenings, when Gabriel tried to avoid his bedtime, he could always count on his grandfather's support, and pretty often the two of them would end up falling asleep on the couch together, the kid with his cheeks bright red and the old man snoring loudly. Christophe worried what his father might do if the boy were ever taken away for good.

Christophe reached Marco's place at six precisely. Marco lived at his parents' house too—but alone, since his father had died and his mother was in a retirement home. The house was fairly isolated house despite being less than ten kilometers from the highway, midway between the center of town and the back of beyond. Real estate had not been expensive back then, and Marco's parents had been able to build the cabin of their dreams for a modest sum. A thousand square meters of lawn, two floors, three bedrooms, and two bathrooms. In the evenings, when Marco was feeling optimistic, he would think about having a swimming pool installed.

Marco's friends were always welcome at his place. The cupboards were full of aperitif snacks and in the cellar there was a keg to keep the beer cold. You might know what time you were arriving, but the hour of your departure was generally less certain.

"Oh," said the master of the house when he opened the door, "what brings you here?"

Marco was a gentle giant: he might have weighed a hundred kilos at fifteen, but he had never thrown his weight around. Seeing his kind face and curly hair again, Christophe instantly felt better.

"I was in the area. Saw your car."

"Just in time for aperitifs," Marco observed.

"I can't stay long."

"Chill out, you just got here."

"Are you on your own?"

"Yeah."

Marco earned his living driving a taxi for hospital patients, so he spent his days inside a white Passat with a blue star on either door, racing around at top speed, with the car stereo tuned to Fun Radio. All year round, he transported people with kidney failure, leukemia, and diabetes who needed the high-tech medical services offered by the university hospital in Nancy. He knew every square kilometer of the department, the cheapest gas stations, the location of every speed radar. He was only one point away from losing his license. He had not had a single accident since 2007.

"What are you drinking?"

"Nothing . . . or whatever you're having."

The two men went through to the kitchen, where nothing had changed since Marco's mother had been moved to a care center. On the dresser was a painting of two lumberjacks and a sled on a mountainside. There were piles of bills and Daxon catalogues on the table. A lamp with a fancy shade cast a light with Andalusian accents over the table.

"Hang on, let's go outside. I've got something new out there. You'll like this . . ."

"We'll freeze."

"Nah, it'll be fine, come on."

Marco grabbed two beers from the fridge and a pack of pistachios from the cupboard and the two men went out onto the terrace, which was sheltered by the upstairs balcony. Marco had set up two heated parasols there, along with some new garden furniture. He turned the heaters on and soon it felt like Brazil.

"Pretty hot, eh?" the giant said, his face lit up. "With these, you could have a barbecue at Christmas if you wanted."

"You're unbelievable," said Christophe, laughing as he took a drag on his vape. "It must cost a fortune in electricity."

Marco made a little sound with his mouth that was the equivalent of shrugged shoulders, and they sat down on the plastic chairs.

"Cheers."

"Here's to you, big man."

The two friends took a long swig of beer and then sat there like that for a while, not saying anything, just enjoying the warmth and the peace. Then Marco stood up to turn on the yard spotlights, which revealed the bushy shapes of trees and, about ten meters away, a washing line suspended between two poles, with clothespins hanging from it.

"Watch this."

Marco grabbed an air rifle that had been propped up in a corner of the terrace and held it against his shoulder. There was a small pneumatic popping sound and immediately one of the clothespins began spinning around the line.

"Whoa, cool!" said Christophe. He had already put his beer down and wanted to have a go.

"See?"

"You're right—that is genius."

Marco beamed. He broke the barrel, inserted a new pellet, and handed the rifle to Christophe, who took three attempts before he managed to hit a clothespin. It fell to the ground, where it lay on the lawn among other corpses. Apparently Marco had been having fun with this activity for quite some time.

"How did you get the idea?"

"I found my little brother's rifle in the cellar. It's just a great way to unwind when I get back from work."

"It's perfect."

The two men continued to take turns shooting. They each drank another beer, occasionally exchanging a few words, and enjoying themselves like a pair of kids. They had known each other since seventh grade, and you could tell. When Seb Marcolini had arrived at the Collège Louise-Michel, Christophe was already on the junior team, and it was he who convinced the new boy to play hockey. The problem was, there were three children in the Marcolini family and only one wage-earner—the father, who worked as an odd-job man at the nursery school in the center of town. So Christophe's parents had had to provide the cash to buy little Marco's equipment. It was only cheap Artis gear, but it still forged a connection.

Later, the Marcolinis won a tidy sum in the lottery, almost seven hundred thousand euros, enough to make the front page of *L'Est républicain* and a lot of jealous neighbors. This jackpot had enabled them to build the house where Marco still lived and to reimburse the Marchals, among other things. Soon afterward, Marco's father had gone off the rails a little, buying a Chevrolet and becoming a regular at local hostess bars, where he got into the habit of buying rounds for all his new friends. He had been fired by the nursery school and had ended up crashing his car into an embankment one New Year's Eve. Marco's mother, who narrowly escaped with her life, had been left with a permanent suspicion of lottery tickets and fast cars.

Anyway, since the junior team already had two Sebs (Seb Madani and Seb Coquard), the new kid was called Marco and the name stuck. As a hockey player, he was always pretty slow and ungainly, and despite his big frame he never managed to intimidate anyone. But he was one of those easygoing, sweet-natured guys who help with the atmosphere on the bus and at the postgame party. Twenty-five years later, he played the bass drum for the supporters' club, the Cannibals. And then there was the third man, Greg, another former hockey player and schoolmate. The three of them never went a week without seeing each other.

"Oh shit," said Christophe a little later, handing the rifle back to Marco. He had just noticed the time. "I have to get going. I've got a meeting with Charlie."

"Oh shit."

"Nah, it's just bits and pieces this time."

"Now I understand why you're dressed up like that."

Marco had never been very fond of Charlie either. In fact, he wasn't very keen on any of his friends' girlfriends. As for his own romantic life, it was a mystery. He had gone out with a woman once, a nurse from Meurthe-et-Moselle. But that relationship had quickly mutated into a friendship with benefits—the benefits in question being that Marco had mowed her lawn and lent her a van to transport an Ikea wardrobe. No one knew anything more than that.

When Christophe and Greg talked about Marco, they liked to imagine that he had a secret life. So they would often come out with lines like: "I'm going to phone that faggot Marco and we'll meet up at my place" or "Have you heard from that big queer Marco lately?" But none of that really mattered. The three friends would go to one another's houses regularly: brief visits, for no real reason, just long enough to have a drink and a chat about sports or work, family and memories, sometimes the news. Hardly ever about politics. On Friday evenings their aperitifs would often turn into a marathon drinking session. And then, very late at night, tongues loosened by booze, one of them might mention a woman's name, an affair whose scars had never healed, a vague hope for the future. Even so, love remained taboo, hidden deep inside, inexpressible in words.

"Where are you meeting her?"

"Les Moulins Bleus, next to the bowling alley."

"Seems a bit weird."

"It was her idea."

"Well, at least it's cheap."

"I guess so. I wouldn't have minded spending a bit more and going somewhere nice though."

Christophe was finding it hard to leave. He would have gladly taken another beer, for the road, as they say. But Marco turned off the spotlights and the heated parasols, and night fell once again upon the lawn.

"Well," he said.

"Yeah."

In the entrance hall, before saying goodbye, the two men stood for a moment in front of the glass display case containing the lead soldiers that had belonged to Marco's father.

After watching a TV ad for Éditions Atlas, Monsieur Marcolini had bought the first three soldiers, then been sucked into the endless spiral: grenadiers, cavalrymen, hussards, dragoons, the emperor himself... They were all there, standing tall, every detail present, with their little cannons, their badly drawn faces, their colorful feathers, at once ludicrous and impressive. The collection had made Christophe and Marco laugh hysterically when they were fifteen-year-olds, smoking weed in Marco's bedroom.

"Oh, so did the coach ever call you?" Marco asked.

"No, not yet."

"Shit."

"I don't know if I'd have time to go to practice anyway, to be honest. I'm already flat out as it is, with work and the kid."

"Yeah, right," Marco said mockingly.

Christophe grinned too. They both remembered vividly games played in distant places, parties at seedy hotels in Nantes or Chamonix, the fear that gripped you in the locker room before the puck drop, fifteen boys rigged out like riot cops, the muffled roar of the crowd. *Come on, boys, let's do this.* Nothing could beat that feeling.

"All right, I'm off."

"See ya."

They kissed cheeks and Marco wished him a good night in his ex's bed.

"Ha, no way..."

Before setting off, Christophe sat for a moment in his car, blowing vape smoke through the half-open window, savoring the quietness, the darkness, the air still humid from the storm. In the distance, a dot of light flashed from the top of the pulp mill's tall chimney. The mill was the biggest source of employment in Cornécourt. Greg worked there, although less often these days since he had been elected to the works council. Norske Tre had tried to fire him on several occasions, on the basis that he spent his delegation hours at the local bar. Greg enjoyed telling his friends about the summonses, the letters with acknowledgment of receipt; it made him laugh. There was something mysterious about his optimism when you considered his lifestyle: single, debt up to his eyeballs, not even a driver's license. At the last New Year's celebration, he had turned up in a suit and cowboy boots, with three crates of Mumm. Given the state of his finances, that was practically suicidal. But Greg didn't give a fuck. His father had died young, a diabetic with an addiction to Paris-Brest patisseries. Greg liked a drink himself and smoked two packs of Camels every day. *No worries for the rest of your days . . .*

At last Christophe decided to leave and he twisted the knob on the car radio, searching for a good song. Often, when he was driving through the familiar streets of this town where he had grown up, fallen in love, and was now growing old, he liked to let himself be swept away by one of those crappy old hits that were on constant rotation on the FM stations. The roads were empty, the streetlamps punctuated his route, and, little by little, he started feeling those big emotions brought on by hearing the lyrics of songs etched into his memory when he was a kid. He had despised Johnny Hallyday when he was younger, but that voice pierced his heart now. Old Johnny sang about cruel twists of fate, men in pieces, the city, loneliness. The passing of time. One hand on the wheel, his vape in the other, Christophe rewrote history, a man all alone with his memories. The bus shelter where he'd wasted half his childhood waiting for the school bus. His old school, the kebab stalls that had sprouted up everywhere, the skating rink where the best moments of his life had been spent, the bridges from where he used to spit in the Moselle to kill time. The bars, the McDonald's, and then the emptiness of tennis courts, the local swimming pool with the lights off, the slow glide toward suburbia, countryside, nothingness.

That night, he stumbled upon the old Michel Sardou song "Les Lacs du Connemara" and once again saw his mother in her flower-patterned apron, shelling peas one Sunday morning while he drew a castle at the kitchen table, this song on the radio and springtime through the window. Then his cousin's wedding, when he vomited behind the village hall, an ugly tie around his head, "color the land, the lakes, the rivers"... His father had picked him up at dawn and, at a stoplight, had said: "You look like you're on a roller coaster, kid." At twenty, he'd heard the same martial drumming—*tatam tatatatatam*—in a nightclub on the edge of Charmes, Marlboro smoke and Charlie in the misty glare of pink and blue lights, before going out to the biting cold of the parking lot and the dull drive home on the expressway. Ten years later at the café, seven in the morning and the singer's voice quiet in the background while he drank a coffee at the bar, fatigue pooling under his eyes, wondering how he would ever find the courage to get through yet another day. Then, finally, at forty, one New Year's Eve after dropping the boy at his mother's house, the voice echoing around the lakes, "it's for the living," and him alone at the wheel, with no idea where he would eat dinner or with whom, and finally ending up there, his hair thinner and his shirt too tight around the waist, surprised by that wise old man who, out of the blue, picked him up in a company car, and this song rolling out its travel-agency heroism. Christophe thought about that girl he'd wanted so desperately, and whom he had left. About that kid who was everything to him and for whom he could never find the time. The feeling of waste, weariness, the impossibility of going back. He had to keep living, though, and hoping, despite the countdown and the first white hairs. Better days would come. That was the song's promise.

3

HÉLÈNE HAD LEFT that first date in a total daze, even if the date itself was probably not the main cause of her confusion. Anyway, instead of heading toward Nancy so she could go straight home, she had given in to old habits and had, without even realizing, ended up on the road to Remiremont, the one they used to take when she was a little girl going to see her grandparents. A few seconds of distraction had been enough for the memory of this old itinerary to take over. The past was quick to take over, given half a chance.

She made a U-turn as soon as she realized her mistake, but then she got lost somewhere between Dinozé and Archettes. Strange, because there were no surprises on that stretch of road. In the end, she stopped by the roadside to check her GPS, but she had no signal and finally, losing her patience, she got out to smoke a cigarette in the dark, leaning against her car. At one point, another driver slowed down to stare at this woman in skirt and high heels, smoking at midnight in the middle of nowhere. What was she doing there? Was she a whore? Hélène texted Lison: *A disaster. I'll tell you later.*

———

TO START WITH, however, the situation had seemed fairly promising. Manuel looked like his photographs, which was in itself a pleasant surprise. Early thirties, plain shirt, New Balance sneakers, a slightly bewildered look, like a teenager who'd just been dragged out of bed, but he had gentle eyes and a flat stomach, which changed things. They met at a café terrace in the center of Épinal. They had a drink there and chatted about everything and nothing.

Even so, Hélène found it hard to relax. She didn't like Épinal, and she couldn't shake the fear of bumping into an old acquaintance. That was the problem with little dumps like this: they were always full of familiar faces, friends from another lifetime who could collar you without warning, how are you, it's been too long, how are your parents? Not only that, but these acquaintances lived barely three kilometers away so they always found it a little odd that she had come to town without bothering to pay them a visit.

At first, she and Manuel went over, in person, several subjects that they had already discussed online, as if to check. They would finish each other's sentences during this strange phase when every word felt like a sort of password. On the other hand, the somewhat risqué conversations they'd had online seemed never to have existed. Sitting face-to-face, they kept to a cordial respectability, making small talk about their work, that storm a few hours earlier, a movie they'd both liked—that romance with Vincent Cassel; on the other hand, he'd found the latest Tarantino annoying, too much dialogue, and she was happy to take his word for it. In any case, she didn't really like that kind of thing: locked-room narratives annoyed her almost as much as stories based on misunderstandings.

More than once, though, Hélène sensed something disturbing beneath Manuel's words, which left an unpleasant wrinkle on the surface of their conversation. For example, he did not think it was really so absurd that the British wished to withdraw from the EU. Not that he had anything against Europe of course. He also had a tendency to overuse the pronoun "they" to describe the media, lawmakers, and the occult forces responsible for weather forecasts. Hélène did not really take offense at this, but soon she began to feel uncomfortable, her skin warm, as if she were wearing one of those tight synthetic sweaters. She wasn't sure if her discomfort was caused by the situation or by the sultriness left behind by the storm. She told him she was going to the bathroom to freshen up and, when she got in there, took a moment to stare at herself in the mirror. She examined her own face, noticing a wrinkle here, a few white hairs at her temples, maybe a slight sag in her cheeks... Her gaze, on the other hand, was steady, deep, sparkling. What the hell are you doing here, woman? she asked herself silently, then thought about that guy, wondering if he was worth it. In truth, she did not have any strong feelings for him. Maybe she ought to keep trying. No doubt that was the price of adventure.

With a confident, helical gesture she retied her chignon before going back to the terrace and ordering another drink—a spritz this time—which helped her better appreciate Manuel's gray-blue eyes, his sexy forearms, and a thousand other details that had been invisible ten minutes earlier but had now becoming pretty tempting. A splash of prosecco and he had ceased to be a stranger.

Unfortunately, sensing this change in his fortunes, Manuel had imprudently grown emboldened and had started sharing secrets. This was how she learned that he had been preparing to try out for a spot on the *Survivor*-style reality TV show *Koh-Lanta* for the past two years, something he had not thought to mention before. He went running three times a week, and attended a gym near his home as often as he could to focus on cardio exercises. He had learned scuba diving, started yoga. On sunny days he went hiking in the Vosges mountains, and he fasted every month in anticipation of the hardships he might have to endure on the island. Hélène listened to his account of this toughening-up process with dwindling amusement. Next, he told her his body mass index, his maximum aerobic speed, and the comparative disadvantages of various immunity tests. But, all things considered, the most important thing was mentality. And he had nothing to fear on that score.

During the third drink the situation took another turn for the worse when Hélène recognized a girl on the terrace who had gone to the same middle school as her. Sonia Mangin, a blonde with pinkish skin, had lost her father at twelve, was already smoking in seventh grade, and had four older brothers, all of them completely crazy. Back then, the rumor was that she had done it with the entire subdivision. And now here she was, sitting only ten meters away, looking almost beautiful, or at least well-off, in the company of a tall guy dressed in a striped shirt and imitation suede loafers. Hélène sensed those prying blue eyes fastened upon her and she felt certain that Sonia had recognized her. In the end, the woman waved at Hélène and started trying to talk to her, in the middle of a clandestine date. All of this was so disturbing that Hélène almost forgot about her apprentice survivalist. Just then, he decided it would be a great idea to unbutton his shirt and show her his Maori tattoo. Hélène, feeling suddenly very sober, stared at him with wide eyes and burning cheeks.

"What the hell are you doing?"

"Huh?"

"Stop it, we're not that drunk..."

Her date appeared very upset by this reaction, his eyebrows sending several surreptitious distress signals before he quickly buttoned up his shirt.

"Chill out," he muttered. "Who cares what other people think?"

It took him five long minutes to emerge from this sulk, while Hélène searched desperately for a way out, checking her watch, her phone, the sky above their heads. Philippe had not tried to call her, so that was something at least.

"I think I should probably get going," she said.

"No, listen..."

He told her how sorry he was. Surely they weren't just going to separate like that. He wanted to invite her to dinner, as friends, so they could end their date on good terms. Meanwhile, Sonia Mangin had started whispering and her boyfriend had even turned to stare on a couple of occasions. Hélène had to move quickly before her former schoolmate came over for that dreaded class reunion.

"Okay, listen, I'm happy to go somewhere for dinner, as long as it's quick and simple."

"We could try L'Étiquette."

"I'd prefer somewhere quieter."

"Oh, it's really quiet during the week."

"Less central, then."

"Well, I'm not going to take you to Flunch..."

And as Hélène dropped her pack of cigarettes into her purse, Manuel played his trump card.

"Listen, I know where we can go. It's really chill."

And so they found themselves at Les Moulins Bleus, a chain restaurant that had the twin advantages of guaranteeing fast service and being fairly out of the way.

INSIDE, THE LAYOUT reminded Hélène of her open-plan office, with the islands of tables and the low dividers decorated with fake plants. The waitstaff hurried through their trajectories, flashing smiles and bursting through the swing doors that led to the kitchen, from which emerged a mixture of smells. As soon as they entered, Hélène began examining the customers, on the lookout for a face she knew, a profile liable to turn and smile at her. Then, despite reassuring herself that all these people were strangers, she chose the most remote table in the room. Screens high up on the walls showed a slideshow of photographs of the restaurant's owner in the company of various minor celebrities: Michel Cymes, Frank Lebœuf, Véronika Loubry. The very long menu offered everything from pizza to grilled shrimp, not forgetting the inevitable *café gourmand*.

"Happy?" Manuel asked.

"I'm actually not very hungry."

"You could get the carpaccio. Or the Caesar salad."

"Yeah."

"Yeah what?"

"The carpaccio. That'll be fine."

After ordering, they found themselves alone with the undeniable fact of their failed date. He stared at her now like a basset hound anxiously inspecting its food bowl. She didn't dare move. The conversation was like Morse code. Hélène took refuge in looking at the tables around them.

To their left, three middle-aged women were drinking cocktails and swapping tales from the teachers' lounge. Behind Manuel were some tipsy men in loose suits—sales reps, she reckoned—who were ordering pitchers and taking turns to go outside to smoke. Farther off, a table of eight had already started on dessert. You could tell from the clothes they were wearing, and the children's clean faces and neatly combed hair, that they had made an effort. This must be a special occasion, thought Hélène; someone's birthday, perhaps. Elsewhere, she spotted a fiftysomething couple trying the veal Milanese, a girl with a French manicure being chatted to death by a boy who could hardly breathe in his fitted shirt, an elderly man with a flattened face who was eating kebabs with his son. And over there at the back, near the parking lot, a woman with attractive, regular features and yellow skin, having dinner with a man Hélène could see only from behind. She began to stare at this woman, fascinated by the nonstop flood of words that was bursting from between her lips, admiring her combative expression, and surprised by the way the man seemed to be simply taking it all. She was curious: What was going on between them? What was the cause of this simmering public storm? How much of it was love and how much rage?

The waitress came over to ask how their meal was and Hélène abruptly returned to reality. On the other side of the table, Manuel was scowling. They had been eating in silence. From time to time she glanced over at the couple again and saw the same attitudes: the woman pretty and imperious, the man's heavy figure remaining motionless. Then, just before he stood up, the man turned toward her and Hélène's heart split in two inside her chest.

"Something wrong?" Manuel asked.

"No, no, I'm fine."

Within her, however, the scaffolding of adulthood had just collapsed. Hands trembling, she poured herself a glass of wine.

Her date, tight-lipped, asked: "What exactly is the problem?"

Hélène had tried to distance herself from the past, through schools, diplomas, and good habits. She had left this town to become the woman of her own dreams, efficient and ambitious, a woman of consequence. And now, in a chain restaurant stuck between a cemetery and a parking lot, she had, like an idiot, experienced a hot flash at the merest glimpse of Christophe Marchal. Twenty years of hard work, all for nothing.

After that, she was incapable of swallowing a single morsel. Her adolescence had overpowered her, constricting her throat, filling her head with vague impressions of rules and laughter, tears over nothing, friends and boys, the skating rink on Saturdays, sheets of graph paper and folders that clicked shut, and those high-flown little words written on a desk between a chaos of insults and the drawing of a dick spurting cum.

"All right, maybe we should go."

"What?"

"You look miles away."

"I'm just a little tired."

"Bored, more like."

Manuel's tone had turned abruptly cold and Hélène felt almost afraid. On the other side of the restaurant, Christophe Marchal was coming back from the bathroom. He didn't even bother sitting back down at the table. He and the woman exchanged a few more words, probably logistical, although she sensed some dark emotion behind their eyes, and then they left without a backward glance. It cost Hélène an effort not to run over to the window to see if they were getting in the same car.

A little later, in the parking lot of Les Moulins Bleus, Manuel made one last attempt at reconciliation.

"Listen, we got off to a bad start. But we both know why we're here. We're not going to just leave it like this, are we?"

"Oh, yes, I think I'm done," said Hélène, unlocking her Volvo.

Manuel grabbed her by the arm. "Who the fuck do you think you are? You're not some twenty-year-old model, you know."

"Asshole," hissed Hélène.

And she was out of there.

Ten minutes later, the asshole in question was sending her abusive texts and messages on Tinder, calling her an arrogant bitch, telling her to go fuck herself. Hélène kept blocking him, without even bothering to slow down. Then she took a wrong turn and now she was smoking a cigarette on the side of the road, her mind overflowing with feelings more than two decades old. On her phone, she googled the name Christophe Marchal, but the signal was too weak and the information remained hidden behind a whirling circle. So she decided to go home, and if the inhabitants of that little Vosges village had not all been staring at their TV screens or in bed or just too old, they might have seen a black Volvo speeding through the only street in their village at close to a hundred kilometers per hour. Inside it was a woman high on crazy daydreams, anxious, in a rush, her heart full to bursting.

BACK AT HOME, Hélène climbed the staircase from the garage to the first floor on tiptoe, high heels in hand. Philippe had left a note on the table. The babysitter had not been able to make it, so he had looked after the girls himself. An exclamation point signaled his pride at finally acting like a father. This was followed by some unimportant practical information and an affectionate sign-off in which he called Hélène "pussycat." While she read this, she took a bottle of sparkling water from the fridge and drank several mouthfuls, before going upstairs, her skirt hitched high up her thighs to make it easier to walk.

She loved the quietness of the house at night, after everyone else had gone to bed. It was a building of sharp edges with an almost horizontal roof; the windows were large and somewhat exhibitionist, and to reach the second floor she had to climb black stone steps with no handrail, which always made her fear that she would fall and break something. It was, in other words, a house that a real-estate agent would undoubtedly describe as "modern." Outside, the two family SUVs were parked on the gravel driveway, like a pair of static cows, sheltered by the perfectly pruned trees nearby with their sheep-like forms. There were houses like this in every town in France, their serenity inspired by Japan and the California hills, enclosing within them the secret of their possibility, the essential chaos of business and money required to pay for these monoliths of fake eternity. Comfort came at the price of blood and hours, but late at night, as it was now, with the town sleeping below, Hélène could enjoy being at home.

She took a quick—and very hot—shower, then went into the bedrooms to watch over her flock. Philippe was asleep, one arm under his pillow, and the girls were sleeping so deeply that they might have been dead. Hélène hurried back to the kitchen, in bathrobe and slippers. Less than a minute later, with her laptop on her knees, she searched the internet for this guy who had just reappeared in her life.

After typing his name into the search bar, she was bombarded with names, dates, places. She had not even taken the time to put on her reading glasses, so she had to lean down, her nose close to the screen as it buzzed with old memories. Now and again, a drop of water would fall from her drenched hair onto the keyboard and she would wipe it away with the back of her hand. Scrolling through a blog by some hard-core hockey fan, she came upon some old newspaper articles about the 1993 final. A photograph showed a cloud of black-and-white dots, and yet it was clearly identifiable as Christophe. The headline was a quote from Christophe's postgame interview: "This defeat is not the end."

For more than an hour, she entertained herself stirring up the past with the churn of algorithms. On the website Copains d'Avant, other names resurfaced. John Morel. Magalie Clasquin. Virginie Comte. Jean-Didier Trombini. Marc Lebat. She had forgotten all of them, and here they were now, their class photos neatly lined up, revealing those ghostly features, those improbable haircuts, those big multicolored sweaters, that peculiar fashion where grunge met the French provinces and tried to find some sort of compromise. There was a chalkboard showing the year for each class, and there, in the last row, was that guy she used to think was so cute but who just looked like a jerk to her now. As for Hélène, she had always regarded herself as clumsy and awkward-looking, but in fact she looked pretty good with her long hair and that Oxbow jacket that had cost her three weeks of family negotiations. At the time, she would have gladly sold both her parents to wear that brand.

Her best friend, Charlotte Brassard, was right there next to her. The two girls wore the same clothes, more or less, the same hair clip; they even chewed the same flavor of gum—passion fruit. It was strange, seeing Charlotte again, with her perfect little face and her Benetton sweater. And yet the pixelated face on the screen did not match the one in Hélène's memory. Curiously, it was the photograph that seemed blurry, and the memory quite precise. It was all there though: the decor, and the distribution of a moment when everything changed, a moment that still mattered even now—old friends betrayed, the new bestie, and the others forming the mild hell that she had wanted to escape, come what may. Ultimately, that photograph was merely a monument for the dead, a lie set in stone, the gravestone for her thirteen-year-old self.

She checked the Facebook profiles for various people to see what had become of them. Plenty had put on weight, the men losing their hair . . . some of the women too, in fact. They all appeared happy. They were accountants, bakers, assistant managers, visual merchandisers, English teachers, house-wives and proud of it. Some had put together photo albums to show off their success. Each time, Hélène found the same children, the same vacations, the picture of a big motorcycle or a Labrador with a bandana around its neck. In the end, it was all rather depressing.

She concentrated for a moment on Charlotte, who had a LinkedIn account and now lived in Luxembourg, where she worked as a transfer agent. She had studied economics and management in Lille. But there were no recent photographs and no other details. She was not on Facebook, Instagram, or Twitter. Hélène was reduced to guessing at her existence, somewhere on the other side of the border. To think that they had slept in the same bed, had even fooled around once—during a party at Sarah Grandemange's house. She could still remember the wrinkled skin of her fingers afterward.

"What are you doing?"

Philippe had just appeared at the top of the stairs. He was wearing boxer shorts and his hair was disheveled.

"Nothing. Did I wake you?"

"It's two in the morning. What the hell?"

She took care not to close her laptop, because that would have looked suspicious. Instead, she showed him the results of her search.

"I grabbed something to eat and then went down this rabbit hole."

Philippe put his hands on Hélène's shoulders and bent down for a better look.

"Look," she said, scrolling down the page.

"What is it?"

"A website where you can find your old high school friends. It's crazy seeing all those faces again."

Philippe's face lit up and reverted to his usual mocking expression.

"Oh yeah! I got sucked into this one day at the office. Wasted a whole afternoon on it. It's a nightmare, this kind of thing."

Shoulder to shoulder, they spent a while laughing at those ridiculous faces, the surprising transformations, the stories that people told, the whole drama of lives spread over social networks.

"Then again, we're not much better, are we?"

"What do you mean?"

"We take pictures of our desserts. We show ourselves on the beach or on skiing trips. You did almost a whole album on our yucca."

"True," Hélène admitted.

Philippe went over to the sink and drank some water from the faucet.

"Shall we go to bed?" asked Hélène, closing her laptop.

"Yeah, I'll be there in a minute."

But she knew that he would spend ten minutes going through his emails before joining her. There could be a message from the United States or Amsterdam and he would answer it right away, as if he still belonged to that caste of twenty-four-hour people, the white-shirt tribe, mercantile princes using planes and computers to plot the invisible takeover of the world with products and services. Hélène had wanted that too once, a satellite life set to GMT, no longer having to lug the enormous suitcase to vacations in the Balearic Islands, but instead speeding through airports with her sleek, rigid Samsonite, catching planes the way others catch trains, knowing bars and hotels all around the globe, having a beautiful apartment that you hardly ever use, never complaining, never feeling tired, a super-productive proton surfing the waves of the Zeitgeist.

Instead of which she was thinking about Christophe Marchal.

Under the duvet, she wondered what he was doing, what his life was like, whether he had kids. Tomorrow, she would continue her little investigation. He can't have been very successful, she thought, if he's still living around here. He had probably married some local girl, failed his exams, and was now living a life pretty similar to his parents' before him, a life of dignity, the life of a schmuck. Whatever, there could be no doubt that their positions in the great pecking order had been inverted. The champion was now a loser. The class dork had changed.

She didn't sleep much that night, but her dreams were sweet.

4

AT THIRTEEN, HÉLÈNE is a stuck-up little bitch.

At least that's what her mother thinks, because she refuses to help out in the house, she is rude, she corrects her parents every time they make a grammatical error, gets angry for no reason, and lives in a bubble where Jim Morrison and Luke Perry are her gods.

Most of all, her mother hates Hélène's snooty attitude, the way she acts like some princess who happened to wash up in the home of these peasants. Even as a little kid she would lecture her parents. And there's not much chance of that changing, since, around her, all language is starting to unravel. So many things that she used to take at face value have become suspect. Kindnesses now look like manipulations. Honesty disgusts her. When her mother says *Not everyone can become an engineer*, for example, or when they tell her to finish her meal because there are countries where people have nothing to eat. Not to mention those clichés that are like the wisdom of the poor: *A bird in the hand is worth two in the bush*, *Don't think your shit doesn't stink*, *Money isn't everything*. When her parents beat the drum for a simple life, using her cousins as an example, when they criticize ambitious people, nouveau-riche types, people who flout their success, when they exult the merits of hard work, manual labor, home improvement, people who know how to do things around the house, people who slip between the cracks, people who live from day to day, from hand to mouth. When they say we're going to pack you off to the countryside, that'll teach you to live, when they use the definite article in front of someone's name—le Dédé, la Jacqueline, le Rémi—then Hélène feels something go taut inside her. Instinctively, unknowingly, she rejects all of this. Every sign of that lifestyle is a slap in the face. She would rather die than live like that, modestly, knowing her place. Yep, she's a big-headed, stuck-up little bitch.

Every Wednesday afternoon, she borrows her mother's bicycle, even though she's not allowed, and rides to the local library. The bike is too big for her, even with the saddle down, so she has to stand on tiptoe when the stoplight turns red, and for the whole of that journey, which is not very long, she is scared that she will crash into something and mess up the beautiful mountain bike. Her parents are at work; there is no way for them to know what she's up to. So she leaves the little house like a tightrope walker, her imitation Doc Martens on her feet, and rides through the subdivision, down Rue Jeanne-d'Arc, her huge backpack strapped to her shoulders. Near the mayor's office, she remembers to fasten the blue antitheft device to the bike, then goes into the tiny library that Cornécourt has haphazardly put together out of donations and bequests. A tall, tomboyish, very young woman, in a striped sweater, hair cut in a bob, says hello and calls her by her name. Hélène replies hello, ma'am. She doesn't know this woman's name despite the important role she plays in her life. Because the librarian lets her rummage through the aisles, she allows her to borrow twenty books when the maximum is ten, and she never gets upset if Hélène is late returning them.

She has even recommended a few of her own favorite books. *Matilda*, for example. Hélène was eleven when she read that— and it was a shock. Ever since then, she has read like crazy, storing away knowledge, just like Matilda in fact. She reads in defiance of the whole world, her parents, other people, life.

She usually follows the same itinerary. She starts with the comic books—the candy aisle of the library. She adores Iznogoud—those books about the history of France with King François I and the assassin Ravaillac—and Yoko Tsuno. Next it's novels: the Bibliothèque Verte collection, the 1000 Soleils collection, Jules Verne and Emily Brontë. She ends with the magazines. Of course there are old editions of wholesome, educational magazines like *J'aime lire*, *Géo*, and *Historia*. But one day Hélène comes across a pile of weird magazines that smell musty and turn out to be way more interesting. They probably came from someone's cellar after a death or a house sale. Whatever their provenance, she is immediately drawn to them. Sitting cross-legged on the floor, she begins flicking through them, one after another. She soon feels a little scared and...lots of other things. The pages are filled with naked people, disturbing science-fiction characters, adventures with big breasts, and even sometimes men's things. She can't stop turning the pages. She grabs five to start with and puts them on the counter, at the bottom of her pile. When she is about to note down the titles, the librarian says:

"Are you sure these are appropriate for your age?"

Hélène feels her face change color. She says yes and the librarian laughs before copying down the titles on a large index card. Twenty books and five editions of *Métal Hurlant*.

"Okay, you're all set."

Back home, Hélène hides the magazines under her bed and waits until the lights have gone out before devouring tales of John Difool and Thorgal while she lies on her stomach, pillow between her thighs. For a few days she squirms as she reads, afraid that someone will walk in but unable to stop. At the faintest noise in the hallway her heart races and she hurriedly turns off her bedside lamp. But, irresistibly, she returns to those old magazines that smell so bad and make her feel so good. Back at the library, she will borrow all of them and the librarian will stamp them all without blinking.

It is around this time that she discovers some books that her father hides in the drawer of his nightstand: *Amok in Bali*, *Gold in the River Kwai*, *Requiem for Tontons Macoutes*. These books all have the same sorts of covers: women in underwear wielding large guns and looking cool and sexy. The stories are stupid and repetitive, but at least she learns some new vocabulary. "Vulva," "member," "tumescent." Very quickly she adopts the habit of skimming the pages in search of the good stuff. Clearly, books and desire are closely linked.

And then one Wednesday in November, the librarian says come and look. Together, the tall, boyish woman and the stuck-up little bitch wander through the aisles until the librarian bends down to scan the books on the lowest shelf, her fingers caressing the spines, then stopping at three volumes, which she drags from their sleep and hands to the girl.

"You'll like these, I bet you anything."

They are three novels by Judy Blume. Hélène has never heard of them before. But the librarian is right: she adores them. Stories about the first time, about love, about all sorts of great stuff that makes her want to really live. Hélène devours these first three Blume books in no time. Then she reads all the others.

But it is *Forever* that makes the biggest impression on her. This novel tells the story of Katherine, a seventeen-year-old girl who meets Michael at a New Year's Eve party. It's all a bit cornball, but it has a power that circumvents logic. From the opening page, she is completely captivated and her sole wish is that those two morons will fall in love. And then some serious things happen to the heroine. Hélène reads these passages with her heart pounding: the first steps, the mutual shyness, her breasts, his dick, it's all so freaky and glorious.

Sometimes she wonders how it will go when her turn comes. She thinks about love the same way she thinks about a driver's license: everyone does it, but she is somehow persuaded that she won't be able to. She'll never manage to change gear, look right and left, check the mirror, she's too clumsy, too daydreamy, her mother is always telling her for God's sake look where you're going. Every time she washes the dishes, she breaks a plate. She can't help it—she's in her own little world. Occasionally she will still put her T-shirt on back to front or leave the house with toothpaste on her chin. She feels unfinished, and she can't imagine herself in bed with a boy. She'll never manage it, she's certain. And just like that, she hates them, which isn't difficult. They're so immature, so stupid. Big, aggressive babies with wobbly voices. And their zits, their Adidas Torsions, their too-short jeans, their scooters, and the off-putting peach fuzz on their upper lips.

But she rereads *Forever* and the story does something to her, leaves its American imprint on her. Hélène dreams about going to university, about all those conveniences Katherine enjoys, the father and his two pharmacies, the skiing vacations, life with a giant refrigerator and air-conditioned cars, the attentive mother and her good advice, a cocooned existence that leaves space for everything else, the important stuff: cultivating within herself that curious something that swells like a huge carnivorous plant, spending all day thinking about the boy who goes to the nearby high school, inviting him home, waiting, daring, saying yes, being scared, he'll be kind, it will be beautiful and with a curtain that barely stirs in the afternoon breeze, will she bleed on the sheets, apparently not always. She borrows this book four times and the librarian makes no comment. She is a discreet, diligent accomplice.

Meanwhile, at home, it's not exactly America.

ONE DAY, CHARLOTTE Brassard has a birthday party at her house. The whole class is invited. Charlotte arrived at the start of the year with her father, who had just been appointed to an executive position at the pulp mill. Before that, he used to work in Germany and Norway, as Charlotte is constantly reminding everyone. Her mother is an economics teacher, although she has ended up a housewife because her husband has a career and they have three children.

Anyway, fourteen is an important age and a party will undoubtedly help Charlotte make friends in her new class at the Collège Jeanne-d'Arc in Épinal. Consequently, everyone is invited, without exception. When Charlotte hands the invite to Hélène, she doesn't even look at it. She's too busy chatting with her best friend, Camille Millepied, acting like Little Miss Perfect: smooth as a sugared almond, with her neatly bobbed hair and the gold chain hanging over her sweater and her bitchy little face. The classroom, however, is in uproar. Because the Brassards' place is amazing. Some of them have been there already and claim they even have a pool table. The party will take place on a Saturday: the invitation says to get there at two in the afternoon and not to bring a gift. Hélène's family panic when they see this, because they aren't fooled by this polite convention. Obviously they will have to buy a gift—but what? What could people like that possibly need? What would they enjoy? Jeannot, Hélène's father, suggests flowers: they're simple and everyone likes them.

71

"It's not her mother's birthday," says Hélène, instantly losing her temper.

"What about chocolates?"

"Ugh, chocolates are crap."

"Oh là là!" her mother exclaims angrily.

Mireille is an energetic, short-haired woman, incapable of putting on weight. Her pale eyes are permanently ablaze with exasperation, aimed at anyone who is not lucky enough to be as energetic as she is, at clumsy people, at her daughter. She left school at fourteen, worked at a cotton mill, then took evening classes until she was promoted to the rank of office secretary. At twenty-five she was able to join a notary's office, a fact that gives her great pride, even though her days consist mostly of sorting through papers and answering the phone. At least she understands legalese—"notwithstanding," "given that," "willful misrepresentation"—which is some distinction. Based on this fact, she is more or less convinced that she is the intellectual of the family, and looks upon her husband, Jean, in a slightly condescending way.

Not that he cares. He accepts this domination, which has its compensations and means he can avoid getting lumbered with anything related to paperwork (a category that takes in everything from Hélène's notebooks to the family tax return, from Redoute catalogues to renting a place at the beach for their vacation). For his part, Jeannot likes mushroom hunting, pottering about in his workshop, going to hockey games at the stadium with his brothers, and cycling. He's a wonderful cook: in the kitchen, he always has a Gauloises cigarette dangling from his mouth, and when he's leaning over the stovetop, working on a blanquette or a soufflé, following the recipes, handwritten in purple ink, from a notebook he inherited from his great-aunt, Hélène can see the bushy tufts of hair emerging from the collar of his blue T-shirt, the same hairs he has on his biceps, while his head is already bald, and haloed by a cloud of gray smoke.

Jean is a good guy who has his limits; a pleasant-enough man as long as you don't push him too far. He has also worked in the textile industry, at La Gosse, the same factory where Mireille used to work, but the factory was shut down, and after a few months of unemployment he had to accept a new job at a store selling paints, wallpaper, and flooring run by his brother-in-law—his sister's husband. It's not so bad there, even if his brother-in-law is a bit of an interfering busybody who spends more time posing in his Audi than he does actually working.

At the home of the Poirot family—at thirteen, the surname is a source of endless embarrassment to Hélène—there is always a hint of electricity in the air. Before, Hélène didn't notice it. But now it really bothers her, the way her parents are always kissing, making out, making lewd remarks. Hundreds of times she's seen them go to their bedroom in the middle of the day and lock the door. When she was little, she would scratch at the door and her mother would yell at her to go play. At night, she hears them sometimes. She covers her ears. It generally doesn't last very long. They're one of those strange couples who never weary of each other, still filled with lust after fifteen years of living together, despite the constant repetition, despite knowing each other's bodies by heart. It's kind of odd, when you think about it, that they never had more children. But Jean was too worried. How could he bring another child into the world when his job might be moved to Morocco or Turkey at any moment? And anyway, they were already quite old when they had Hélène—both in their thirties. Never mind; Hélène would just have to shine as brightly as several kids put together.

"I can't turn up with some crappy gift," she moans now.

"We're not rich," her mother snaps, although Hélène does not see the relevance of this statement. "If you're going to be like that, you just won't go."

Hélène weighs the pros and cons: the shame of handing over some shitty present versus the horror of missing out on that teenage nirvana. Then again, what does she care? That Brassard girl is just a snooty snob. Hélène and her friends Béné and Farida can't stand her.

"You could just take her a scarf," suggests Jean.

"That's not a bad idea," admits Mireille, who knows they will be able to find something at Prisu without having to dip into their savings.

"All right, that's settled," says her father. "We'll go on Saturday. I'll have time then."

"Do that, then," adds Mireille, in a definitive tone that could be taken different ways.

All week long, Hélène and her friends talk about nothing else. This party is the event of the year. In class, everything is turned upside down. Charlotte's popularity, of course, rises dramatically: everyone's ultra-nice to her, even the boys make an effort, and for a few days class 4B is like Cape Canaveral just before a rocket launch.

"What time are you going?"

"Not too early," says Béné. "I don't want to be stuck there alone with her."

"Oh yeah, I hadn't thought of that!" exclaims Farida, who is often exclamatory.

"The best thing would be to get there just before three. That way, you don't look like you've been waiting outside the door."

They all imagine the party in their own way. For Farida, this birthday takes on the sparkling, dizzying appearance of a ball, halfway between *Madame Bovary* (they're reading it in class) and *Cinderella*. Hélène sees it more like a chic, *Dynasty*-style cocktail party, while Béné mostly thinks about the sodas and candy, hoping inwardly for Curly peanut puffs and M&M's, treats strictly rationed at home since the doctor diagnosed her as being overweight. Anyway, the excitement is so high that on Friday afternoon, at the end of their math class—the last of the week—even the teacher tells them he hopes they all have fun. At four o'clock they go their separate ways in a state of almost painful agitation. They all sleep restlessly that night.

At last the big day arrives. Hélène is still eating lunch when her father looks up at the kitchen clock, yawns, stretches, and says: "Well...we should get going soon."

"What?" asks Hélène.

"To your friend's house. Where is it, by the way?"

"But it's not time yet."

"Well, that may be. But I have other things to do, you know."

"But I'll be the first person there!"

"I have to stop at the Depétrinis to check out a leak. And then to see Doctor Miclos—he's got a problem with his water heater. So we need to leave now."

Jeannot can do a bit of everything. So much so that the Poirot family rarely calls for a tiler, a bricklayer, or a plumber. He gardens too. The proof of this lies behind their little house: a hundred square meters of onions, tomatoes, green beans, rhubarb, and parsley. Quite a few weeds too. In summer, Hélène has to kneel down and tear them out one by one, something she does grudgingly, with her Walkman blasting "Who Wants to Live Forever?" Who indeed. Anyway, all Jean's little extras help them stay above water, so they are obviously more important than some kid's birthday party. Very soon the discussion grows heated.

Mireille cuts it short: "It's that or nothing. We're not your servants."

Hélène thinks she can always wait outside, hidden in a corner somewhere. On that November day, the TV weatherman forecast temperatures ranging between 43 degrees Fahrenheit in Strasbourg and 64 degrees in Bastia. Not unbearable. She puts on her fake Docs, wraps a scarf around her neck, picks up the gift, and puts on her coat and hat.

"You look like you're on an expedition to the North Pole."

"Whatever," mutters Hélène. Her mother advises her to pipe down—she's not at her friend's house yet. The teenager grits her teeth and stares at the floor, seething. She is always being told to shut up, stay on the straight and narrow, keep her moods and her desires to herself. But they're always there; inside her, they orbit like planets. Hélène wants them to burst out of her, but everything conspires to hold them in: school, her parents, the straitjacket of the world. Jean swaps his old shoes for a pair of loafers, the same horrible and hyper-comfortable ones that he wears when he's gardening—well, he won't be getting out of the car anyway—then puts on his velvet, sheepskin-lined jacket.

"All right, let's go!"

He lays a heavy, fatherly hand on Hélène's shoulder, and feeling that weight upon her she is briefly reassured. It'll be okay, she tells herself, before suddenly being overwhelmed by an inexplicable sadness. She hates being like this, her feelings like clothes in a washing machine, her heart riding a roller coaster.

A little later, inside the red 309, Jean whistles along to the radio and his daughter loses herself in contemplation of his hands, which keep moving from the gearshift to the steering wheel and back, oblivious and thick-veined, the exorbitant curve of the thumb, the thin black line under the fingernails, their simple steadiness, then she turns to look out at the unchanging city beyond the windows. November is gray, from buildings to sky, and even the Moselle has lost its colors. The river flows under bridges with the slowness of oil. Like tears, she thinks. From time to time, an advertising billboard breaks this monotony with the gold flash of a perfume, the acid green of a meadow filled with cows. At last they come to their destination, outside a big house in the old suburbs: on a hill, looking down on things. Hélène kisses her father goodbye and thanks him. She breathes in his odor: aftershave, the skin still smooth, tanned like leather by the blade that slices off its hairs every morning.

"All right, off you go and have fun, I have work to do."

"Yeah."

"What's up?"

"Nothing, I'm okay."

"Don't forget the gift."

THE 309 DISAPPEARS and Hélène finds herself standing like an idiot before a long row of chic houses, the wrapped present under her arm. It's not really cold, but she's shivering a little bit anyway. She walks around the neighborhood for a while and gets the impression that everyone she passes is suspicious, that even the houses are staring at her. A little girl observes her from her bedroom, forehead glued to the second-floor window. Time passes slowly and Hélène's hands and feet start to feel cold. Finally, she decides to go back to Charlotte Brassard's house. Who cares if she's early. She presses on the round golden doorbell and listens, shivering, to the two notes that echo bombastically within.

Charlotte herself comes to answer the door.

"You're here already?"

Her classmate is wearing a *Never Mind the Bollocks* T-shirt, pink eye shadow, and lip gloss. Hélène thinks, is this a costume party or what? She also thinks, in her most secretive depths, that she wishes she could be like that too: pretty, classy, and a little bit punk. She hands Charlotte the gift. Charlotte says thank you and invites her in. Whoa, the ceilings are so high. Hélène walks through the house. There are frames all over the walls, on top of furniture: quite a few family photographs, with people smiling, living their lives happily, often on vacation. It kind of looks like a catalogue. Hélène notes a pair of twin boys, whose growth she can follow from diapers and pacifiers to black runs on ski slopes.

"Your brothers?"

"Yeah."

Hélène manages not to say that she thinks they look a little odd. Then the two girls enter a sort of old-fashioned veranda overlooking a beautiful garden full of neat flower beds and gray-green trees. There are two long tables piled high with drinks, cakes, and candy, and in between them there's a dance floor. To the side, the hi-fi awaits its moment on a pedestal table.

"That's cool," says Hélène.

"Yeah."

"Ah!"

Madame Brassard appears behind them, also in T-shirt and jeans, her wrists bare except for an ultra-slim watch. On her right hand, a thick silver ring is the only ornament.

"Mom..." groans Charlotte.

"Oh come on, can't I even say hello to your friends?"

Hélène quickly understands that Charlotte has negotiated her parents' confinement during the party. But Madame Brassard is curious to meet her daughter's new schoolmates, and this is her home, after all. Hélène barely has time to greet her before Charlotte drags her away.

"All right, let's go up to my room until the others get here."

Hélène follows her, eyes wide, through a hallway, up two flights of stairs, down another hallway. If she ever has to find her way out of here alone, she might well be in trouble. Then Charlotte's bedroom. Above the bed, a magnificent bullfighting poster. One whole wall is covered with postcards: Jim Morrison, Rimbaud, Gainsbourg, Duras, only the coolest people. And some others she doesn't recognize.

"Who's that?"

"Yeats."

"And her?"

"Virginia Woolf."

Hélène leans in for a closer look and examines each image: the shadows, the hooked noses, the identical gazes. Each time, the same expression of desirable melancholy, of sadness melting on the tongue like candy cane. She, too, wishes she could belong in this black-and-white world, could write poems, novels, have fateful love affairs, find the right setting for a life with meaning. It is in these photographs that she would feel most at home, in these exemplary lives, these atmospheres that she finds difficult to describe but where she would, she feels sure, be happy. She has the same impression as she does when leafing through *Madame Figaro* at the dentist.

Meanwhile, Charlotte sits cross-legged on the carpet and relieves her boredom by braiding the threads of the shag carpet. This should make Hélène feel uncomfortable, but her curiosity overpowers her concerns for her host, so she continues her inspection, looking through the CDs, the knickknacks, evaluating her book collection: Jack London and Roald Dahl, Balzac and *Little Women*. On those shelves she discovers things that fill her with yearning like the thought of patisseries after school. American road novels, Cocteau, Anaïs Nin's little pink books. She takes one from the small wicker bookcase.

"What are you doing?" Charlotte asks irritably, fearing that this guest will make a mess.

"What's this?"

Henry and June. Hélène has come across that title somewhere before and she retains an impression of something pleasant, all-enveloping. She often feels attracted in this way to obscure things that she feels sure have some personal connection to her, even though she knows nothing about them. For example, she had that impression when she saw a photograph of Marlon Brando in the TV guide. Or when she hears the voice of Jean Topart at the end of *The Mysterious Cities of Gold*. These vocations at first sight, these mysterious affinities, leave a mark upon her, like a fingerprint on a clean window. It is both exquisite and torturous, because it eludes and tempts. She has to keep digging. All her desire is there, alert, ready to sweep her away.

"Nothing," replies Charlotte.

But she makes the effort to get up and come over.

"Give it to me," she says.

She takes the book from Hélène's hands, puts it back in its place on the bookshelf, which once again looks implacable and forbidding. Then with her index finger, she pulls out another volume, also with a pink spine, close to the first one.

"This is her journal. It's amazing. She tells all."

"All what?"

"All."

Charlotte hands the book to Hélène, who immediately turns to the back cover.

"She writes about her life, her meetings with loads of other writers. How she pisses everyone off."

"Really?"

"There are some that are worse than that one. My mother's got the whole collection."

Charlotte has gone back to her bed. She sits down on it and opens the drawer of her nightstand.

"Here."

She shows Hélène the cover of a slim little volume: a woman sitting, back to the camera, naked to the waist, wearing a hat adorned with a single feather. The thick font of the lettering makes her think of sex-shop windows. Beneath the woman's raised arm, a few tufts of hair are shamelessly exposed.

"I stole this one," Charlotte whispers.

Hélène sits next to her on the bed. The two girls are shoulder to shoulder, faces leaning over the book, their hair suddenly entangled.

"What's it about?"

"They're short stories. About sex," Charlotte says in a low voice.

Hélène leafs through it. Certain words leap off the page. Suddenly it seems very hot in the room.

"Can I borrow it?"

Seeing the expression on her guest's face, Charlotte recognizes the seriousness of a fellow reader. She should say no, obviously. She herself is not allowed to have that kind of book. She took this one from her mother's personal hell, a corner of the large bookshelf where she hides forbidden texts behind her collection of art books. There are others there, even more terrible than this one. Charlotte will soon explain all this to Hélène. The two of them will go there to rummage through this treasure, laughing and red-cheeked, and will come up with a brilliant scheme to smuggle them out. In this way they will read Pauline Réage, Régine Deforges, Henry Miller, and a little bit of the Marquis de Sade, not to mention *Lady Chatterley's Lover*, which will inspire them with nothing but a stodgy feeling of boredom.

But for now, Hélène is hanging on Charlotte's every word. Her mother could come and knock at the door any second. The thought thrills them. Charlotte nods.

"Okay. But give it back to me in two days."

"I promise."

Hélène slips the book under her sweater. It is there now, cold and hard against her stomach. She can't wait, and at the same time she does not want it to end, this moment between them, electric, on the verge of laughter, her chest full.

"I got you a really crappy present," she admits. "I'm sorry."

Charlotte bursts out laughing. She's so cute, so precious, like an object. It's like they've fallen in love, then and there, till death do them part, or at least until the end of the school year.

Soon afterward, the other guests start turning up and Hélène has to abandon her new friend to hang out with Béné and Farida.

"Whoa, this place is incredible."

"Yeah, the thieving bitch."

Hélène and Farida turn to Béné, mystified. But she just shrugs, and they will never know any more than that.

A little later, the entire class gathers on the veranda. The buffet is picked clean in no time. Charlotte opens the gifts that no one was supposed to bring, and then it's time to dance. Boys and girls get a little frisky, but since Charlotte's mother opens the door to check on them every now and then, nobody dares go too far with the slow dancing. Hélène does not dance. She and her two friends just watch. It's strange seeing all these people that they've hung out with for so long, away from the context of school. The boys look even more childish, whereas the girls, who have made an effort with their appearance, seem at times like miniature adults. The afternoon passes in a haze of brushed skin, sideways glances, sarcastic comments, and brief moments of boldness. Like when Romain Spriet comes over to ask Farida if maybe she'd like to dance, and she refuses, even though she kind of wants to. But Béné is watching, and friends still count more than boys. At nightfall, Laurence Antonelli suggests they have a séance. So it is that most of the guests end up sitting on the floor around a few candles and a handful of Scrabble letters arranged in a circle. For several long minutes, they vainly try to summon spirits, caught between hysterical laughter and terror. Then suddenly all the lights go out. There are screams, a scramble of groping, a table is knocked over, and shards of glass stick into shoeless feet. There's the sound of sobbing and Charlotte's mother comes running. But it was all just a prank. They don't have time to work out exactly what happened before the first parents arrive to pick up their offspring. It's seven in the evening. The party is over. Oh well...it was good while it lasted.

It takes Hélène only three hours that night to finish the book she borrowed from her new friend. She finds it as beautiful as it is horrible. She is so shocked by certain pages that she reads them twice to make sure of her disapproval.

HÉLÈNE'S PARENTS DECIDED she would attend a private school because it was located close to the notary's office where Mireille works and her bosses' children went there. This speculative investment does have a few minor inconveniences, however, including the daily commute from Corné-court, going to Mass four times a year in the school chapel, and hearing her parents go on about how much it costs. Other than that, it is not really any better or worse than anywhere else. Her mother drops her very early every morning, then she meets up with Béné and Farida in the yard around a quarter to eight, on the side near Rue des Passants, not far from a secondary door, less used than the main entrance, which makes them feel as if they are free and can escape anytime they like.

After that birthday party, though, Hélène starts acting differently. She now waits for Charlotte under the covered playground on the Rue Clemenceau side. Sometimes, her friend will bring her a new book or Hélène will return the one she has just finished. Most of the time, the two girls are happy to just chat. These are rushed moments, almost clandestine. With a vague feeling of guilt, they retreat to the back, near the trash cans, away from prying eyes. The friendship is like a love affair, a secret.

When the bell rings, Hélène runs over to join Béné and Farida. But they have seen what's going on.

"Why the hell are you hanging around with that girl?"

Béné doesn't mince her words. Farida treads more carefully, but this doesn't stop her agreeing vehemently.

"Totally. Who even is she? She's nobody."

"Calm down, we're not in prison."

"You're the prison," replies Béné, looking all disdainful.

And she walks away, hips swaying as she carries her backpack. She's wearing jeans and a track jacket in the colors of Olympique Marseillais inherited from her older brother, which is already too small for her. Last year, a guy who sat behind her in biology pulled at her bra strap, and Béné spat at him.

Even so, Hélène is a little bummed at seeing her friendship with Béné and Farida going down the tubes. The three of them have known each other since elementary school. They went camping last summer, the best vacation of her life—three days by a small river near Plombières—and Farida had a crush on Béné's older brother; it was funny. They were together all day long, swimming, having barbecues. It felt like freedom.

She doesn't know what's going on, why what had been so precious yesterday has suddenly become so boring. She feels like that all the time these days. When her parents talk to her, it's like her eyes roll up on their own, she's not even controlling them. After dinner, she locks herself in her bedroom with her Walkman and her books. But even that room, the decor for which she's spent years perfecting, gets on her nerves now. Two weeks earlier, she tore down the big poster of Madonna and pinned up some photographs of old Hollywood stars in its place; you can get a pack of a hundred for ten francs at the newsstand. She gazes at the beautiful gray faces of Warren Beatty and Marilyn, even though she's never seen any of their movies. And there's Brando too, of course. Inside her, something is changing. Little by little, Hélène grows more distant. She would like to know why, to understand what's going on. Sometimes she breaks down and weeps, out of rage and impatience, desperate for life to speed up and at the same time sad that everything is changing. When she thinks that she still has four years before the end of school, she gets so pissed she wants to destroy everything. She counts the days to her eighteenth birthday, when she'll finally be able to say *I'm an adult now, so fuck you*. Her life is like a pressure cooker. She can feel it building toward an explosion. She'll never make it, she thinks, it's too much, it's not enough, and tears fall from her eyes even though she's not even all that unhappy.

IT TOOK A lot of cunning, and a long time to explain, but they've done it.

Hélène and Charlotte are holding hands, like two little Bambis on the ice, trying to keep their balance. They're both wearing big wool hats, even if Charlotte had originally planned to wear a beret, before deciding that she'd look trashy. From a distance, they look like sisters. From close up too, in fact.

Their parents dropped them at two-thirty and will return to pick them up at five. It's not much time, but they have to start somewhere. Outside the entrance, Charlotte's mother shook hands with Hélène's father. They were both friendly, smiling, obviously relieved that the other was a responsible person. We're trusting you, because you're big girls now, but move out of the way if it's not going well. Already the two girls can't take their eyes off the skaters inside.

To start with, they chose a quiet corner near the railing, to which they clung for quite a while, like two barnacles. Their cheeks turned pink and their noses dripped. They didn't dare do much, unsure of themselves this first time, content to watch the others and listen to the music blasting from loudspeakers. It was cool.

"Apparently they turn the lights off at some point," says Hélène.

"Yeah, there are spotlights. It's like *La Boum*."

Hélène giggles. She adores Sophie Marceau.

"Look over there..."

"What?" Hélène says.

"Those guys, look."

There are three of them, no gloves or hats, chatting with two trashy-looking girls with big hair and blue eyelids, both of them plump but pretty. Sluts.

"They're the guys from the hockey team," Charlotte explains. "My dad takes me to the games sometimes—he gets free tickets through his job. The smallest one already plays for the first team. He's sixteen."

"Oh yeah?"

"Christophe Marchal."

Hélène and Charlotte are at an age when a face can become a feeling. This happens to them with Christophe, but also with Mathieu Simon and Jérémy Kieffer, who are older, cute, and above all cool, because wanting to be kissed is also wanting to be part of a clique. The ones who matter have a bike or a scooter, they wear nice clothes and are invited to exclusive parties. Later, Hélène and her friend will spend delicious hours suffering on their bed, listening to Whitney Houston or Phil Collins, desperate and languid. They will learn the words by heart, sing them at recess, smoke in secret. Love songs were invented for precisely this, to dwell on intimate sufferings, to bring to life this shadow theater of grand emotions, a boy brushing up against you, the back of someone's neck in biology class, whatever.

"We have *got* to go and see some games," says Charlotte.

"Yeah, totally."

"I'm warning you, I saw him first."

Hélène laughs. "You can keep your little dwarf-boy."

And they hug each other, falsely welded together by the little romance novel Charlotte has started to invent. For now, Christophe is not really a person. He is more like a poster, his distant perfection placing him among the stars pinned to their bedroom walls. In any case, it is delicious to want him, like viewing the world through 3D glasses.

Hélène gasps. The boy has just torn himself away from the little group with a graceful backward movement, and after a no-less-elegant U-turn, he heads toward two girls in puffer jackets standing at the other end of the rink. He flies over the ice, brushing past other skaters with diligent disdain, then brakes abruptly in front of the two girls, producing a jet of ice that sprays them in the face. They give him a perfunctory telling-off as they dust off their coats, but nobody is fooled. Hands in the back pockets of his jeans, his whole life ahead of him, Christophe swaggers around, alone in the world, intolerable and super cute.

"Who are those ugly bitches?" Charlotte asks with a pout of disgust.

Hélène snickers. But they don't have time to chat for much longer. The lights go out and they hear the first piano notes, echoing deeply in the vast space above the rink. Then colored spotlights begin to sweep the ice. Immediately, couples start to dance, hand in hand, and while the glitter ball sprinkles its shards of light all around, Bonnie Tyler's hoarse voice sings the first sad couplet. And then it's always the same story, the same sense of urgency. The slow-dance section is soon over, like everything else. Tomorrow it will be Sunday, and boredom. They have to seize the moment. At the far end of the rink, Christophe Marchal has grabbed one of the girls by the arm and is pulling her along with him. She is blonde in that way only seventeen-year-olds can be, and it is weird and painful to see that glamour couple pass by them only two meters away. Hélène watches them and wants to die.

"Ugh, this is horrible!"

"Yeah, it sucks."

Charlotte drags her friend away from the railing and they start to skate, unsteadily, arms outstretched, together in the blue-striped darkness. Hélène feels Charlotte's hand squeeze hers.

5

CHRISTOPHE LOOKED AT his father and wondered how he was going to break the news to him.

The two men were still sitting at the table, lolling in the warm lethargy of habit and digestion. Christophe had put on a real spread that night. On his way back from work he'd bought two slices of beef tenderloin from the meat section at Leclerc and chosen a bottle of Saint-Joseph at the wine store. When his father had seen him unpacking his provisions on the table, he'd asked what they were celebrating.

"You'll see," his son replied.

And he had taken the new jersey out of his bag, with the number 20 printed on the back, just like the old days, except the shirt was green and white now, and there was a stylized wolf's head on the front. His father's eyes, normally pale as a lake, lit up.

"Why a wolf?" he asked.

"You know, it's the name of the team. The Beast of the Vosges, I imagine."

"Oh, yeah."

Gabriel, who was looking through the shopping bags, gave a cry of joy when he saw the Apéricubes and a box of ice pops, which sent their cat, Minousse, running for its life. The poor animal knew from experience that it was best to watch out when the child was happy.

Gérard Marchal did not say much after that, but he helped set the table and draped his fleece jacket on the back of the chair, his way of getting the party started. Then he served aperitifs—Coke for the kid, beers for the men—while Christophe busied himself in the kitchen. The boy asked for some paper and crayons so he could draw the skating rink and his dad winning games. At one point, they made a toast.

"To us?"

"To your season."

And they drank, three generations under the same roof, no wife or mother, just men illuminated by the stark fluorescent light, in the warmth from the oven and the squeaking of chairs on the tiled floor.

Then the kid got started on the Apéricubes, stuffing the little squares of flavored, processed cheese into his mouth at such a rate that his grandfather finally told him to calm down before he ruined his appetite. When he didn't obey, the old man brought down his big hand with its bruised skin and latched hold of Gabriel's small, round hand, and the child stood there for a second without moving, arm extended, mischief sparkling behind his glasses, as his grandfather gazed at him lovingly. Christophe watched them. Behind him, butter sizzled in the frying pan and spread its delicious smell through the kitchen. The old table, the deep white sink, the cupboards, the hum of the refrigerator. That unchanging decor. And yet all things must pass. Charlie was going to move. Their life here was over.

That evening, though, they ate heartily, and not only because of the bottle of Saint-Joseph. The grandfather even did a few of his magic tricks and, while Gabriel no longer believed that his nose had vanished, the part where the coin appeared from behind his ear left him dumbstruck once again.

After the kid had gone to bed, the two men lingered at the table a little longer. It was barely nine o'clock and Christophe was listening to the dishwasher behind him. He was waiting for the right moment. As for his father, he was in a wonderful mood, a little tipsy, and he was recalling the good old days as he scratched the head of the cat that had jumped onto his lap. The strangest thing with that condition was seeing how the brain would regurgitate memories as its cells slowly died.

Gérard Marchal had lived a fairly average boomer life, which became a sort of epic in the retelling. School until he got his certificate, an apprenticeship with Cugnot as an electrician, moving around France during the Trente Glorieuses, that period of economic growth between 1945 and 1975, going from one construction site to another: Grenoble, Tulle, La-Roche-sur-Yon, Guéret. The country was busy constructing hospitals and new office buildings back then, creating a swarm of happy, insignificant young people in their wake—plasterers, bricklayers, electricians, heating engineers, tilers, elevator technicians, painters, roofers. Those carefree men were put up in hotels and they treated work like a summer camp. The pay was good, they got raises almost every month, and when they got sick of their boss they just handed in their notice, knowing full well that another job would fall into their lap the next day. In the evenings they would eat at a restaurant and after nightfall they'd play belote for money in rustic-looking hotel dining rooms, with plaid tablecloths and clocks on the wall, drinking small glasses of the local eau-de-vie. Around one in the morning, the owner would say, *All right, that's enough*, and the men would grumble half-heartedly in their thick, male voices before scraping their chairs back and going upstairs to their rooms, laughing loudly. Lying in bed, they would listen to the sports results on a little Braun transistor radio, smoking a Gitane and reading a few pages of a short thriller, the back cover vaunting the manly merits of Balafre aftershave or Bastos cigarettes. Then they would sleep the sleep of the just, a whole happy generation of proles who had finally gotten lucky and who thought that this moment was just how things were now, that there would be work and progress in perpetuity.

Gérard remembered in particular the month of May 1968, which he spent in Corsica, where he was installing electricity for the new hospital in Furiani. While mainland France was caught in an uproar of strikes and riots, workers were able to forget for a short time their blackened hands and imagine new political tomorrows, while everywhere you looked the rich and the powerful were in a panic, taking refuge in Switzerland or the countryside or in reading Chateaubriand. Amid this bedlam, Corsica had grown even more insular and, in the absence of materials or instructions, the construction work at Furiani had abruptly ceased. And so Gérard and his colleagues had found themselves, like a gang of Robinson Crusoes, living by the sea with nothing to do.

Of course, they had been worried, stuck on that island where they didn't know anyone and they were no longer receiving their pay. But the owner of the Beau Rivage hotel—a calm, potbellied man—had allowed them to continue to stay and eat their meals there, and had even given them each a bit of pocket money to keep them entertained. This little interlude did not last long, but it remained in Gérard's memory like an oasis of pure happiness, at the intersection of youth and springtime, with its endless days spent at the beach, the tipsy haze of anisettes, evenings on the terrace, and the dark-haired girls there who were, curiously, more liberated than the mainland girls—or so, at least, he would recount fifty years later, smiling wanly under his gray mustache. He still kept in his wallet the photograph of a long-haired girl from Bastia. He'd forgotten her name, but not the hours they had spent together in those coves. By the end, this would perhaps be all that remained to him: the image of a beauty spot below a woman's navel.

Later, having grown tired of this semi-nomadic existence, Gérard had found work at Rexel, where he'd been promoted, and then he'd married Sylvie Valentin before opening his own sporting goods store. A grocery store for rackets, as he put it. Gradually, as their situation had improved, his mood had soured. Therein lay the tragedy of shopkeepers, that gnawing anxiety, the daily headache of supplies and logistics, stocks and deliveries, the customers—always too few or too irritating—and those two wily, idle employees of his who were always asking for more. The last remnants of his good mood had been utterly destroyed in the mid-1990s by an especially severe tax audit. He and Sylvie still had a beautiful house, two cars, three televisions, a full fridge, and two kids who were a source of pride despite the misdeeds of the elder. But it wasn't enough. Time had passed and that bilious torment had become a sort of background noise, an endless headache.

It was also true that Sylvie never really had much appetite for life. Once she gave up work after Christophe's birth, something inside her had died. When the boys were older, Gérard had advised her to find a job, to volunteer for a charity, or take up cycling. But his recommendations had inspired in that underappreciated woman nothing more than a warily raised eyebrow.

"Or I could just jump in the Moselle," she said carelessly, taking a drag on her Winston.

As a child, she had been a very good student, as attested by the school report cards she kept in the attic. Not to mention her famous IQ test, which she'd taken at sixteen and which she invariably brought up as indisputable proof that her life had been wasted, her brilliant mind left to stagnate. She could have gone to university if anyone had encouraged her a little, but in her family nobody saw the point in higher education. Her parents believed in pay slips, multiple pregnancies. Her mother had never bothered signing her report cards.

"You could go to university now," Gérard suggested, without truly believing it.

Sylvie rolled her eyes. Why bother? She was hardly going to become a lecturer or an engineer at her age, was she? She'd rather go out to smoke another cigarette and stare at the little pond, the fruit trees in the garden. So this was their daily life: this battlefield bereft of any real fighting, just a few unchanging skirmishes and sulks. Julien, Christophe's elder brother, had taken his mother's side early on. He was just like her, in fact: oversensitive, moody, incapable of expending any effort to make things easier, self-assured and yet full of hang-ups, with that razor-sharp wit that could cut you to the bone. Christophe, on the other hand, was more like his father, even physically. Anyway, the four of them had taken up their positions and their roles, hostile and loving, antagonistic and prisonlike, as families tend to be. Thankfully, ice hockey had allowed them to agree to a sort of truce. There, at least, they were all on the same side.

For a few years, Gérard had been a team sponsor, giving him access to a private box and free tickets. He'd been able to invite suppliers, customers, and friends, and they'd had a great time there. Even Sylvie was unrecognizable during the games. When a player on the opposition team sent Christophe flying into the barrier, you could hear her from the other side of the rink. The supporters, who had made her their mascot, would sometimes chant a caustic, invigorating *"Allez, Maman!"*

And then, at the end of the first period, the mayor would make the rounds of the sponsors. He would shake hands with them and exchange a few polite words. Gérard appreciated that kind of gesture.

"You remember?" his father said.

Christophe remembered. His father always repeated the same old stories, so there wasn't much likelihood of him forgetting.

"The kid'll be happy to see you play."

"I think so."

"We'll go to the games together."

"I don't know how much playing time I'll get. I'm mostly just there to fill a hole."

"We'll see."

Christophe smiled, but he knew where he stood. Madani, the coach, had been clear on that point when the two men had met three days earlier.

"I'm not going to lie to you. You're too old. You've already missed the preseason and five games. You'll have to get in shape. We're playing Vaujany next week. Do you have any idea what they're like?"

Vaujany was the team used by Grenoble to mold its future players—snot-nosed kids with too much energy, desperate to impress. They lacked maturity, but toward the end of the game it became impossible to keep up with them.

"I've only got one Slovak left. And with Pavel in goal, the average age is thirty-one," Madani went on. "Most of the players have work on Monday. It's a shitshow."

Madani and Christophe had played on the same team for almost ten years, but they had never liked each other. This, though, was nothing personal. The coach was right.

Of course, the club president had presented things in a very different light: that was his job.

"I got in touch with the communications director at Norske Tre, he's a friend of mine. The Norwegians have more money than they know what to do with. Unfortunately they're not too eager to sponsor us after all our troubles in the past few years. But I talked to my friend—the two of us went to the same business school, and his son plays tennis with my eldest. I think we can figure something out."

President Mangin was one of those pink-skinned, nicely groomed entrepreneurs who wear Ted Lapidus jackets and are always about to rush off somewhere. He owned a restaurant, two bars, and the bowling alley in town, and he also ran the shopkeepers' and artisans' union in Épinal. He had contacts at the chamber of commerce and the mayor's office, and people said he was left-wing because his sister had run for office on a socialist ticket. Wherever he went, this affable, energetic man left behind him the same trail of jovial bonhomie and the lingering scent of aftershave. However, nobody would go so far as to consider him an honest man.

"We're going to sell them a comeback story. If you put your skates back on, it'll really capture people's imagination. The journalists will be happy. The return of the prodigal son. You'll wear the colors of the pulp mill. That way, everyone can forget about the compulsory liquidation and all that crap. The legend returns. You see what I mean, Christophe?"

Christophe saw exactly what he meant, this total stranger who was already talking to him like they were best friends.

The next day, the two men visited Norske Tre, where they were given a warm welcome—cookies and fruit juice—followed by a tour of the property. The Norwegian company had kept a factory there for more than three decades, and yet there was still a residue of hostility toward its semi-Viking presence, despite the fact that the factory employed more than three hundred people and kept Cornécourt prosperous. The smell of rotten eggs that it emitted on certain nights, to the disgust of people in the nearby residential areas, probably had something to do with this negative attitude, which gave rise to rumors and petitions. According to Greg, the emanations in question were completely safe, and the whole controversy was just a conspiracy theory. Anyway, he couldn't smell anything, and he lit a cigarette to underline his skepticism.

"We're very happy to have you here," said Monsieur Gailly, the communications director, the kind of handsome gray and blue man that you can find in image banks.

He pointed to a photograph hanging on his wall that showed the whole expanse of the site: seventy hectares, a billion euros' worth of buildings and equipment, close to three hundred million euros in annual revenue. Monsieur Gailly spent most of the visit bouncing up and down on his heels.

"We want to change the company's image. People are already well aware of our economic impact, but they continue to regard us as foreigners."

The club president had nodded obligingly. He understood: mentalities, habits, a certain narrow-mindedness. But they could fix that. The locals wouldn't mind the smell so much after they'd won a few games.

As they left the factory, Christophe saw Greg in the parking lot, leaning against a workshop wall, smoking a cigarette. He was easily recognizable with his long legs, his cowboy boots, his prominent belly. The two friends waved to each other. It was good to see him, even from a distance.

Two days later he touched his new jersey, with the number 20 on the back. But no sooner had fate lifted him to his feet than it kicked him in the balls again. At the restaurant, Charlie had made the announcement abruptly, in a voice that mixed sympathy with absolute determination: she would be moving in January.

"This can't have come as a surprise. I told you before that I wanted to leave."

This was true, but Christophe had never believed her. He'd thought it was just another passing fancy, a girlish whim; they were fine where they were.

"I found a job as artistic director. In Troyes."

"Troyes? Are you serious?"

Troyes was more than two hundred kilometers away.

"Yeah, in a small agency. GrazzieMille Communication. They've got some big clients. The champagne fair in Troyes, some institutional clients, the BNP bank. I'll be earning almost six hundred euros a month more. It's a huge opportunity."

"What about your boyfriend?"

"It's not a problem for him."

Of course not. Speech therapists could find work anywhere; she had told Christophe that often enough.

There, at the restaurant, eating his steak with pepper sauce, Christophe had tried to digest this news.

"And the kid? Have you told him?"

"Not yet," Charlie replied, her face suddenly closed. "And I don't want you to tell him. I'll do it in my own way."

They exchanged a few tense words during the remainder of the meal, but Charlie was immovable. She reminded Christophe of his own past misdemeanors: his absences, his friends, his whores. When his plate was empty, he stood up to go to the bathroom. What could he say? Words never conveyed what he wanted them to, he wasn't going to cry in public, and a slap in the face was out of the question now. He had no way of processing the hurt. He thought about his father.

IN THE END, Christophe couldn't find the courage to tell him. He cleared the table, then went upstairs to check that his son was asleep. By the time he went back down, his father had moved to the living room and was already snoring in front of the television, the cat in his lap. He had taken his teeth out and he looked so frail and elderly then, so deeply sunken in old age, that he almost resembled a small child. His mustache was all that remained of the man he had once been. Christophe tucked the blanket over his shoulders, then considered him for a moment. Sometimes he wondered if his father wouldn't be better off dead. He looked at his watch. It wasn't very late, and Marco had sent him a dozen texts telling him he had to come visit. He and Greg had something to show him: Christophe should get his ass in gear and drive over there pronto. Christophe weighed the pros and cons. But did it really matter if he had one drink more or less? Besides, it was Friday. He gave the cat one last stroke before leaving, taking his new jersey with him.

WHEN HE REACHED his friend's house, Christophe was not surprised to find all the windows lit up. Those two freaks must already be completely smashed, a supposition confirmed by the bass line booming from the terrace. Before ringing the bell, he hid the jersey up his sleeve, then breathed in the evening air. It was a little chilly, but not too bad, and everything around was quiet. He could barely even make out the rumble of the highway in the distance. He glanced at his watch and promised himself he would not stay late. In two days he was going to start team practice again, and tomorrow he would go running, to try to lose some weight.

"Ah! The handsome prince is here," said Greg, opening the door.

Christophe laughed. His friend was dressed in a camouflage jacket and had a thick black line of soot on each cheek.

He looked like an American football player or a hunter. Above all he looked like a guy who'd had way too much to drink.

"What the hell are you up to?" Christophe asked.

"We're growing in power," explained Greg, deadpan.

In the kitchen the table was littered with empty beer bottles and torn-up junk-food packaging. The fridge door hung open. Greg grabbed some more beers and beckoned Christophe to follow him. As they moved through the house, the music grew louder and heavier. Christophe thought he recognized a Rolling Stones song. Before going onto the terrace, Greg whispered: "It's crazy, just wait and see..."

With that, he laughed between his teeth: *tsss tsss tsss*.

On the terrace, Marco was pointing what looked like a PVC pipe in the direction of the yard. He had the same soot stains on his face, and he was dressed in a Sepultura tank top under a khaki shirt. Meanwhile the gas parasols were blasting out heat and the speakers, balanced precariously on a windowsill, looked like they might fall and explode at any moment.

"What is that thing?" Christophe asked, gesturing at Marco's weapon.

"Just wait," said Greg. "You'll see."

He took it from Marco, wedged it against his hip, holding the handle and aiming straight ahead, then pressed the little red button. There was a huge *BOOM* and the tube spat its invisible projectile into the darkness with unexpected ferocity.

"What the hell is it?" Christophe asked again, moving closer to get a better look.

"A potato launcher!" boasted Marco.

"Oh my God, you two are like Dumb and Dumber..."

Feigning dismay, he grabbed the homemade weapon so he could try it himself. All dark thoughts were pushed out of his head.

"The only problem," Greg explained, "is that you have to recharge the gas after each shot."

"Did you make it yourself?"

"Yeah, there's tutorials on YouTube."

"You are seriously nuts."

Christophe quickly gathered that his friends had had the idea during the week, after a particularly alcoholic air-gun session. For the past two hours they had been guzzling beers and shooting spuds like crazy, which explained both their euphoric mood and their military getup. They fired another kilo of potatoes into the Vosges night, unconcerned by the amount of energy being consumed by the heated parasols, as excited and brutish as children. At last there was a lull. Marco turned down the music and Christophe took advantage of the quiet to show them his new jersey.

"Fuck me!"

Marco whistled. "That's beautiful, dude. Let me see."

The jersey was passed from hand to hand. They praised the color, the material, the design. Greg even howled at the moon, like the wolf emblazoned on the front. Christophe, who couldn't help feeling thrilled by this reaction, accepted a second can of beer. Then, things being what they were, he drank another three. Just after midnight, they collapsed onto the lawn chairs and, elbows resting on the plastic table, began to chat. Their heads were heavy, their shame had mostly evaporated, and Greg was in deep shit.

He'd been going out with this girl for a while now. He'd met her at his mother's place; the girl worked for a charity offering personal assistance and she would deliver meals there every day. She was younger than Greg, a fake blonde who did her job with an indefatigable spirit, and she had immediately caught his eye. Before daring to make a move, Greg had talked to his two friends about her for a long time, in a bawdy, falsely indifferent way, and both Marco and Christophe had done their best to encourage him. For weeks, Greg had turned up at his mother's house whenever he could, at the time when her meal was delivered, about ten in the morning. He had even asked to go on night shifts at the factory just so he could have his mornings free. His relations with Jennifer Pizzato—that was her name—had initially been limited to quick hellos, polite evasions. The young woman put the vacuum-sealed dishes in the fridge and talked to Greg's mother using the third person—had she slept well? was she eating well?—in a loud, clear voice, which irritated the old lady, who was not deaf, thank you. After that, Jennifer hurried out on her white Reeboks, her formidable behind swaying as she made her way to the next address. From the balcony, Greg would watch her get in her van, which she would then drive through town, to feed other helpless old people.

Of course she had eventually realized what Greg was up to, unless his mother had slipped her a note. Anyway, she started speaking a little more quietly and applying her makeup with a little more care. Greg bought some coffee and, while his mother watched game shows on Channel 2, they stirred it with their spoons in sandstone mazagrans, sitting face-to-face in the tiny sixth-floor kitchen. Light fell from a very high window that overlooked a cornice where some pigeons came to shit and fuck. In spring, three eggs had appeared in a nest. The day the baby birds hatched, Greg finally took the plunge.

Until then, his love life had not amounted to much. From time to time he would go dancing at Le Pacha, or turn up to one of those tea dances at Le Panache so he could bring home a fiftysomething who wasn't too fussy, but that was about all. With Jennifer, on the other hand, he had access for the first time—despite being over forty—to a proper romance, with trips to the movie theater, breakfast in bed, introductions to the in-laws, and all that shit. He had even tried yelling at Bilal, the kid Jenn had had from a previous relationship, a bit like that guy on TV who went to strangers' houses and told them what to do. But at thirteen, the kid was already five-ten and he'd been through this routine many times before. Son of a bitch, he had replied, you're not my dad, and Greg had left it there. In any case, he and Jennifer had slipped into that routine of cozy restaurants and peaceful evenings spent watching TV. Their life as a couple had gradually solidified, and presumably it was going well in bed too, even if Greg, normally a braggart and a bit of a compulsive liar, didn't talk about it, which was perhaps a sign in itself. So anyway, everything was going fine, and nobody was bringing up any dangerous subjects, like marriage, living together, vacations, or joint bank accounts.

And then, a few days earlier, he'd found out Jenn was pregnant.

She told him this on the phone and Greg was lost for words. I know, it's a pain, she admitted. But what are we going to do? Greg had no idea. Or rather, his idea was to run for his life, to drive along Route 66 under a false identity. He went to see her the next day and drank a beer without even sitting down. He was cold as ice, a stranger. Jenn got the message. She was the kind of woman who always has to understand, to appease angry men and forgive cowards, to carry kids around and wipe the asses of old people, to always get paid less and never make a fuss. The same stoicism, passed down from mother to mother.

"Why, what do you want to do?" Greg asked her.

"I don't know."

Which strongly suggested that she wasn't sure she wanted to get rid of the future human growing inside her womb.

Bilal's father had disappeared years before and she'd had a hard time holding her life together, working extra hours and dealing with her difficult kid. She'd made it through, fierce and smiling, without ever completely giving up on the idea of life as part of a couple, the only other life she could imagine. She didn't have any great hopes about the kind of man she could get, and she harbored very few illusions about love after all these years. For her, it was no longer a question of love at first sight, or even of raw passion, heart racing and hands clammy. Where that stuff was concerned, Hollywood and the Harlequin collection could go fuck themselves. At thirty-two, Jennifer wasn't kidding herself anymore.

In her life, she had known nice boys and weed-smoking temps, Xbox crackpots, violent brutes, and zombies, like Bilal's father, who could spend hours in front of the TV without speaking a word. She'd had guys who fucked her quickly and badly at 2:00 a.m. in the parking lot of a Papagayo somewhere. She'd fallen in love and been cheated on. She'd cheated and felt guilty. She'd spent hours sobbing into her pillow like an idiot over liars and jealous boyfriends. She'd been fifteen and, like anyone, she'd had her dose of love letters and hesitant flirtations. They'd held her hand and taken her to movies. They'd said I love you, I want your ass, by text and in a whisper in the intimacy of a bedroom. Jenn was a big girl now. She knew what to expect. Love was not that symphony that people always went on about; it was not a TV commercial or an enchantment.

Love was a shopping list stuck to the fridge, a slipper under a bed, a pink razor next to a blue one in the bathroom. Schoolbags spilling stuff on the floor, a chaos of toys, a mother-in-law who takes you to get a pedicure while her son transports some old furniture to the dump, and late at night, in the dark, two voices warming each other up, barely audible, saying simple things without intonation, there's no bread left for breakfast, you know I'm scared when you're not there. But I *am* there.

Jenn couldn't have said it in so many words, but she knew all of this. It was in her body and in her skin. A baby was coming, a baby that would be warm and would block out the thought of death.

Greg, for his part, did not have any real opinion on the matter. So Jennifer gave him a few days to think about it, which he managed to avoid doing as much as possible. This night with his friends was yet another opportunity to escape the need for reflection. Unfortunately, late at night and after lots of alcohol, Marco had a tendency to overstep the mark.

"But do you love her, at least?"

"I don't know," replied Greg, who found the question almost insulting. "She's nice."

"That's not enough for a kid."

"Why not?"

Why not, indeed? Christophe and Marco brooded on this for a moment before Greg spoke again.

"I feel like I've fallen into a trap. I don't know what to do anymore. My life will never be the same again..."

"Maybe it won't be worse, though."

"I don't like arguments."

"Yeah, it's true that when you have kids, you do tend to get more arguments..." observed Marco, who, like everyone who is not a parent, could never resist the temptation to give his opinion on the matter.

Christophe listened. He thought about Gabriel. He didn't get to see him much as it was, just one week out of every two. Time would speed up again after he'd left. He would know only scraps of his son's childhood, brief summaries of the latest news. A sketch of a life.

Marco went to find another drink and the other two remained sitting under the parasols in silence, both slightly dazed by alcohol and tiredness. On the radio, Nino Ferrer was singing about time passing slowly. Night stretched out around them like a sea. By the time Marco returned with three more bottles, the atmosphere had lost its lightness.

"I received something strange today," said Christophe, using his lighter to open his beer.

"What was it?"

He took his phone from his jacket pocket and showed them a message he had received from a stranger on Messenger.

"Who's she?"

"A girl from our old high school."

"You stud, you," Marco snickered.

"She's not bad-looking," said Greg, scrolling through the woman's photographs.

"Yeah, although it's hard to tell from those."

Greg and Marco took turns rereading the message and looking through the woman's profile. She was called Hélène and she wrote briefly that she had spotted Christophe at Les Moulins Bleus and that it had been a strange experience for her. She said she hoped he was doing well.

"She wants you, it's obvious," said Marco.

"No doubt about it. She's hot for you."

"Don't be stupid, she's got two kids."

"So?"

Christophe held out his hand so they could give him back his phone, but Marco had already begun typing something on the screen.

"What are you doing?"

"Nothing," said Marco, getting to his feet.

"Hey, stop that."

"Shit, yeah!" shouted Greg, his face lighting up. "I remember this girl."

Christophe's arm was still outstretched across the table. His face, though, turned toward Greg.

"What do you remember?"

"A girl who used to come to the games. She was best friends with Charlotte Brassard."

Christophe did not bother confirming this, but he remembered too, and that message had left him feeling strange. It had brought back so many memories: songs by the Pixies and Mano Negra, the way everything felt so easy, the whole town at his feet, the games, his final. It was far away and cruelly close.

"There you go, I sent a reply," said Marco, handing back the phone with a satisfied grin.

Christophe grabbed it, but he must have touched something on the screen because he accidentally closed the app. It took him a few seconds to find the message from the girl and the reply that numbskull Marco had sent. "Shit," he said, when he saw the damage.

I'd love to meet up for a coffee. I really felt something, the other night.

This was followed by his phone number.

"You're such a dick," said Christophe.

"Ah, it'll be fine," said Marco. "You'll get along like a house on fire."

"If I remember right, she wasn't all that hot," said Greg, frowning doubtfully.

"Oh, people change," said Marco, with an unexpected flash of wisdom.

WHEN HE WOKE, Christophe was hungover and had no memory of how he'd gotten home. He turned over in bed, grabbed the bottle of water from the floor, and drank it all. Apparently he had been too tired to close the shutters before going to bed and daylight was pouring through the blue tulle curtains, hurting his head like a loud noise. Then there was a noise: he recognized a familiar *tum tum tum tum* in the hallway, and the door opened to reveal Gabriel's face.

"Hey, sweetie." His throat was still sticky despite all the mineral water; his voice sounded rusty. He had to swallow a ball of phlegm before adding: "Up already?"

"Are you sick?" the child asked, without sounding particularly concerned.

"Nah, I'm fine. Didn't sleep too well."

Dressed in only his underwear, the little boy jumped onto the bed and quickly burrowed under the sheets, close to his father's warmth. Christophe kissed his head, the kid's hair, light as air, against his lips.

"You smell bad!" said the boy, pinching his nose.

The alarm clock on the nightstand said it was already ten-fifteen. So much for going for a run.

"Can we play something?"

But Christophe had collapsed back onto the pillow and was lying there like a statue, one arm folded over his closed eyes.

"What do you want to play?"

"Would you rather have a tongue made of poop or be followed around all your life by ten ducks?"

"Okay, I get the idea."

A deep sigh, time to think, then Christophe said: "Would you rather have knees made of whipped cream or an eye at the back of your head?"

"That's no good," the child said, disappointed.

"I'm tired, sweetie."

So Gabriel threw back the covers and straddled his chest like a horse.

"Giddyup!"

"Oh fuck," Christophe moaned.

And he held his son in his arms, eyes still closed, hugging him tightly to his chest. The child started laughing and struggling to free himself. His skin, against Christophe's stubbly face, was unimaginably soft. Christophe squeezed him even harder, then suddenly let go, and the boy rolled to the side.

"Did I hurt you?"

"No, I'm okay."

The small hand resting on his arm. A foot, cold from the floor, touching his leg.

"Dad?"

"Yeah?"

"Is it true that we're leaving?"

"What makes you say that?"

"Mom said it."

Of course. Children always overhear stuff. Christophe cleared his throat again and rubbed his temples, still unable to open his eyes.

"It's not happening yet, anyway."

"I know."

Then he put his arm around his son and brought him closer.

"You're not going to cry, are you?"

"I can't help it," the boy replied.

"I'll come to see you. And you'll come here too. You'll come and watch me play."

"Yeah, but still!" the boy cried out, suddenly angry.

Christophe could feel the small body shaking with sobs against his own, then the wet warmth of tears through his T-shirt. He kept saying: "It's okay, sweetie, it'll be fine." The tears continued for a while. Then, when his son had calmed down, he said: "Don't tell Grandpa yet, okay?"

"I know," the boy said.

And Christophe hugged him again, but this time for himself.

6

THEIR PARENTS HAVE not spoken a word to each other since morning.

This is not unusual, especially on Sundays. At this time of day, their mother must be in the living room, peeling clementines in front of the TV, while their father does stuff in the garage, listening to the radio. Later, he'll go out to visit one of his brothers or one of his friends. He'll be more relaxed when he comes home, smelling strongly of dark tobacco, his mouth full of news that Sylvie will pretend to listen to while she makes dinner.

"Well, well," she'll say to bring the story to an end. "Dinner's ready."

In the meantime, she sent her sons outside, first of all because she can't stand their fighting, and secondly because it can't do them any harm. She told them: "You're driving me crazy—get out before I make one of you kill the other one." Out in the yard, Christophe and Julien tried playing soccer, but soon gave up. It was boring with only two of them, and the ball was flat after spending the whole winter outside. So now they're sitting on the fallen tree trunk that their father varnished to turn it into a bench, hands in pockets, steam exiting their mouths. There's no way they'd be outside in this weather if they had any choice in the matter. The two boys sniff, staring at the trees, the gray earth, the small pond covered with ice. Nature's ugly when you're cold and feeling sad, especially during February in Cornécourt. Every time Julien spits on the ground, Christophe copies him. In four years he will be fifteen too, so obviously he needs to get ready. Above their heads, the sky is a dirty white, and behind them stands the big, warm, forbidden house. Christophe feels his eyes getting wet.

"Ugh, don't start crying again."

"I'm sick of it..."

Julien shoves his brother's shoulder.

"Come on, who cares? Fuck them."

Christophe nods and grits his teeth.

"Listen," says his big brother. "I've got an idea."

He jumps to his feet and strides over to the pond. Christophe wipes his eyes on his sleeve, his nose with the back of his hand. He knows Julien doesn't have to stay here. He could be out with his friends somewhere. He's stayed here for him.

Julien reaches out with his right foot, touching the ice that formed on the surface of the pond a few nights before. Their father dug this pond to decorate the yard and in the spring it's full of rushes, wild grass, water lilies. You can even hear frogs sometimes and see water spiders drawing circles on the surface of the water. Their father tried to breed trout and carp there, but found them two days later, floating belly-up. Christophe is a cautious kid and he doesn't like seeing his brother tempt fate like that.

"Stop!"

"It's okay, just let me do it."

Julien takes another step forward, arms outstretched like a tightrope walker. Suddenly the ice cracks under his weight.

"Stop!" Christophe yells again, then rushes forward.

But his big brother isn't listening. He keeps walking ahead, and with each step of his big feet, the ice emits the same deep, crunching sound. In a few seconds, he has reached the farthest point from shore and he turns back to his younger brother, grinning triumphantly.

"Now you," he says.

He's dressed in jeans and a denim jacket, and the red scarf wrapped around his neck stands out against the gray landscape, the albino sky.

"Come on, don't make me say it again..."

Christophe feels a sudden urge to piss. It's always the same thing when he gets scared. One day he was down in the cellar, rummaging through some old stuff—photographs, his father's things—and he was so scared that someone would find him that he pissed his pants. His mother didn't even bother yelling at him that day. She just said: "What is wrong with that kid?" Christophe did not take offense. His mother says things like "I wish I was dead" if there's a pile of laundry that needs ironing.

Meanwhile, Jules is still there on the ice, waiting.

Christophe reaches out a foot. Under his shoe, he can sense the immense fragility of the ice and, beneath it, the terrifying mystery of the black, freezing water. A shiver runs down the back of his neck despite the thundering of blood through his veins. He can hardly breathe anymore.

"Come on, it's easy."

Julien crab-walks back to the shore and grabs Christophe's hand so he can drag him toward the middle of the pond. Christophe shuts his eyes. He hears a bird fly above them, leaving nothing in its wake but a quick flap of wings and the sky. Little by little, fear gives way to something else, a feeling of ease under his feet that rises up through his legs, and still that urge to piss.

"Open your eyes," says Julien. "It's okay now."

He feels Julien's hand let go of his, then his brother moving away.

"Don't be scared. Don't move."

Christophe opens his eyes and sees his brother leaping through the air. Every time his foot hits the ice, there's a thunder crack that resonates through the surface of the pond and vibrates inside his chest.

"Stop! What's wrong with you?"

But Julien's silhouette is now nothing more than a sliding blue blur cut across by the red line of his scarf. Christophe contemplates his movement through space, unhindered, fluid, gloriously fast. It's so beautiful. He pisses himself.

THAT NIGHT, IN bed, Christophe struggles to fall asleep. He can still feel it in his legs, that gliding feeling, that dizzying flow, his head finally empty, despite the cold and his soaked corduroy pants. Not that he was able to enjoy it for long. Julien made him get changed before their father came home. When their mother found them whispering in the laundry room, she just said: "You're washing your own clothes? Now I've seen everything..."

The next day, he wakes very early and quickly gets dressed before tiptoeing downstairs. Outside it's still dark but he knows he can find his way from the dot of light made by a wall lamp on the front of the house. In silence he puts on his boots, his hat, then slips out the back door. It's not seven o'clock yet, and the cold burns his eyes and nostrils. He hurries across the crisp grass toward the pond and breathes in the good smell of frost, so clean in the new morning.

Out on the ice, he instantly feels the same pleasure of the movement under his feet, the sliding ground. He does it again—runs, skids, arms out for balance, the speed of the start, and then the feeling of something so right that rises up from the soles of his feet through his entire body. Soon, dawn appears above the horizon, pale pink and blue, rounded at the surface, and the boy sees it spread delicately from the ground, infusing the sky with its tender touch. Tiny in that nascent landscape, he thinks: one more time and then I'll stop. A dozen times he tells himself this same lie. But the pleasure is too great, ending it impossible.

Standing in the front doorway, his father has been watching all of this. He blows on his hot coffee, without taking his eyes off his son. He could yell at him, punish him. But instead he smiles. He finds a strange comfort in the sight of that child's body as it erases the resistance of ground and air. That night, at bedtime, he goes to see Christophe in his room. He sits on the edge of his bed.

"I saw you this morning. On the pond."

Christophe does not have enough time to invent an excuse, and his father does not ask him for an explanation.

"I don't want you to do that again. It's dangerous. This isn't the North Pole, you know." The boy promises, and then his father says: "We'll go to the rink, if you like. But I want you to swear you won't go out on the pond again."

"I swear," the child says.

He watches his father's lips, barely moving under his mustache. In the darkness, the voice seems to come from nowhere.

"You'll see," his father says. "It'll be even better with ice skates."

Christophe imagines. His brother played hockey a few years before. Soon he will find his elder brother's equipment in the attic. He will put on the sweat-burned leather gloves, the helmet, and his blue and white jersey, and he will search for the stick, in vain.

IT'S TOUGH AT first. Christophe has just turned twelve and he feels cold all the time. Plus he's one of the smallest players on the team, a late developer, and he hates the locker-room atmosphere. It stinks in there, the mingled smell of sweat, feet, rubber, and burned coffee too, because there's a machine gurgling constantly to supply caffeine for the coach, Monsieur Lukic, unmistakable in his red puffer jacket, his red, white, and blue hat, and the steaming cup he always has in his hand. He wears shoes with crepe rubber soles on the ice, which is strictly forbidden, but he doesn't care. In fact he sometimes even smokes out there, when he's sure none of the management are around, keeping his cigarette hidden inside the palm of his hand. Not that anyone is fooled, with the reek of the smoke.

Not only that, but quite a lot of the kids already know each other from skating class. They shoot across the rink's perfect oval like missiles. Christophe struggles to put his skates on, his feet hurt, and he feels slow and clumsy.

"Marchal!" yells the coach. "What the hell are you doing? You're slow, Marchal. You're too slow."

Lukic says "slow" in English. He speaks a sort of pidgin French, full of Slavic words and other foreign borrowings. And the less they understand, the more incomprehensible he becomes.

Practice is on Tuesday and Thursday evenings, after school. For Christophe, the pleasures of the lake are just a distant memory. After a few weeks of hazing and stupidity, he tells his parents that he wants to stop so they can save their money. But given the price of the gear and the license, they tell him that's not going to happen. "Unless you lose a toe or something," his mother says, "you're going to keep playing."

115

All things considered, the most annoying part of hockey is that scumbag Madani. Every time Christophe bends down to tie his laces, that bastard smacks him over the head with a glove. It's not really that painful, but everyone laughs. The asshole won't stop making fun of him. And on the ice, he's like a bulldozer. Christophe has bruises all over his body.

"Well, he's two years older than you, what do you expect?" says Julien. "You just have to be faster, more aggressive. That's the only way you'll beat him."

To motivate his little brother, Julien has the idea of a special training session, which begins with a bit of brainwashing. They watch *Rocky*, *Chariots of Fire*, *Karate Kid* and *Slap Shot*. In every movie, it's the same story: bare-chested actors and training scenes set to music, during which they are transformed from total losers into winning machines.

"When I played," Julien says, "The best player was the Adam kid. He had thighs like tree trunks, muscles like electric cables. It's the legs that matter."

So, whenever he isn't training with the team, he goes running near home and exercises in the garage with a foam puck. On Saturdays he goes to the rink with his friends Greg and Marco, whom he has convinced to join the team.

At least hockey brings the two brothers closer, because apart from that Julien isn't around much. He's too busy drifting moodily around town, showing off the depth of his boredom, proving that he's smarter than most mortals. And maybe he is. He did find a way to empty the parking meters around the basilica with a screwdriver, after all. This source of income didn't last long, but the legend was born. At home, things are less glorious. During meals, Julien sits with his nose in his plate and communicates only in onomatopoeia.

"We need to do something about your hair," his father says.

"I can't believe I gave birth to that thing," his mother adds wearily.

Pretty often, Julien leaves the table before dessert.

"He'll get over it," says Gérard hopefully. "Anyway, how was practice?"

After that, the evening is always spent same way at the Marchals' house: in front of the TV. Gérard falls asleep during the weather forecast and Sylvie takes advantage of this to grab the remote and change the channel. This wakes her husband up and gives rise to endless arguments about sexual equality.

There is love in that house, but it's expressed clumsily, irritably. They don't say much, but they make up for that by spending a lot. Well, if Gérard is going to bust his ass twelve hours a day at the store, they should at least enjoy the money he earns. So, at birthdays and Christmases, or whenever they're about to go on vacation, no expense is spared. They often go out to eat at a pizzeria called La Gondola, or at Le Tablier, a restaurant that overlooks the Moselle. Julien even bought himself a four-wheeler. As for Sylvie, she would give her right arm to make her children happy. She also cares deeply that they are successful at school, not that it always works.

"I'm not going to let you screw up like your brother," she tells Christophe.

"As soon as I'm eighteen, ciao everyone," Julien replies.

Christophe hates it when he says that. He does not dare imagine this house once his brother has flown the nest. Probably better not to think about it. Better to clear his head with hockey practice, running, skating, and—every night—push-ups and sit-ups in his bedroom. Afterward he always poses in the mirror to check on his muscles' progress, of which, for all his efforts, there is as yet little sign.

"That's good," says the Serbian coach with his thick accent. "In a hundred years, you will be a real champion."

It sounds like mockery, but coming from him it is more like a compliment.

Thankfully, there are also those little scrimmages that the coach organizes at the end of each practice session. Eight against eight, three periods of three minutes each, the players buzzing around at top speed.

"Passing—that's what matters."

And they hear Lukic yelling "Patch! Patch!" under the rink's echoing dome. From a distance, the kids look like armored dwarves, the puck ricochets from one stick to the next, you hear *tshak tshak* and the sound of the blades digging into the ice. Usually, Madani is the one who scores the most goals, but it's here that he's at his most impressive, passing without looking, sending the puck behind him yet always finding a teammate.

"He looks beforehand," Julien explains. "You always have to know where the others are, even the ones you can't see."

Christophe will not forget this lesson.

He also adores the Saturday afternoon ritual when he and his friends go to the rink. The teenage wildlife seeking each other out, the girls huddled together, the boys in little gangs, the way they pile on top of one another, then scatter like birds before the storm. The families too, who come to have fun and always look happier than his own family. It's always the same here too. Around four, the music is silenced while the Zamboni smooths over the ice. Everyone waits as the machine moves back and forth, leaving wet stripes behind it. Then comes the "minute of speed."

This is the highlight of the afternoon, much better than the slow dances, only for the toughest skaters. About twenty guys and a few girls line up at the starting line, the announcer says go, and they all set off, skating faster and faster, forgetting risk, ignoring pain. Most of them do not wear gloves or hats, the craziest ones in just T-shirts and jeans. The rink turns into an enormous centrifuge then, filled with no sound but the hiss of skates, that big sharp wheel slicing through ice, and occasionally a roar of encouragement from the bleachers.

Christophe and his friends are in the front row, and every time the peloton passes, they can feel the air displaced by the mass of moving bodies, the intoxicating disturbance in the air produced by speed. But time is running out and soon a few leaders emerge from the pack to jostle for first place. When those sixty seconds are over, just one among them crosses the imaginary finish line. Christophe stares hungrily at the winners. He imagines himself with arms raised, soaking in the adulation of the crowd.

THAT SUMMER, THE boy and his family pass a boring vacation on the Giens Peninsula. His brother didn't want to go in the first place, and he made this clear during the eight hundred kilometers that separate Cornécourt from their holiday resort. They made the trip in a Renault 25 with no air-conditioning, which gives some explanation for Julien's reaction when he found out he was going to have to share a room with his little brother.

"Screw it, I'm going home."

"Of course you are," replied Sylvie, biting into a peach.

Gérard did not react at all, having decided he was going to relax come what may, a resolution that was in itself a little tension-inducing.

Thankfully, they soon hit upon an enjoyable routine. Christophe goes swimming early every morning with his brother. When their parents show up at the beach with towels, parasols, and all that crap, Julien disappears. Nobody really knows what he's up to, but Gérard has made it clear that they should let him get on with it. As long as his elder son turns up for dinner and does not spend the night outside, he doesn't care. After that, Christophe waits until his father has finished looking through *L'Équipe* so that he can read it himself. For him, pro sports is like a huge soap opera, with its own heroes, plot twists, and bubbling intrigues. That year, the French rugby team wins the Grand Slam, Lendl triumphs at Roland Garros and Flushing Meadows, and the great French soccer star Michel Platini retires. Christophe reads every word of the tributes, with their lists of trophies and records, that the newspaper devotes to this sporting idol. Every day brings its harvest of faces and role models. Should he be passionate like Senna or meticulous like Prost, infallible like Lendl or punk like McEnroe? Christophe tends to favor the hotheads; the sensible ones remind him too much of his parents.

During that trip, the boy spends a lot of time in the water and makes friends with some boys in the apartment complex. They play soccer together and hang out in the parking lot until ten at night. But he likes it even better when they nose around near the beach volleyball court, which attracts a whole pack of young people, bringing together locals and tourists. The boys all wear swimming shorts, and Christophe feels a bit of a dweeb in his Speedos. He talks about this with his mother, who resolves the problem with a single phrase: "It's not a fashion show."

He sits on a wall and watches them play for hours. Arrogant, muscular guys make rocket serves and then rush the net; they high-five each other every time they win a point. Their shoulders are peeling, their smiles dazzling, and around their necks they wear heishi beads like surfers in Malibu. But it's the girls whom Christophe is there to watch, with their round butts and their ponytails that bounce up and down when they run, their feigned indifference, the way they sit chatting in little groups on the rocks that lead down to the sea from the road. Some of them even go topless. Christophe's favorites are two Dutch sisters, the taller of whom has huge breasts and swaying thighs and who reminds him of a brioche still hot from the oven, while the other one is more willowy, with thin lips and a series of beauty spots on her back in a pattern he has learned by heart. They come quite late in the afternoon, walking slowly after their siesta, and, each time, it takes them ages to go back into the water because they're so sensitive to the cold. They splash around half-heartedly, wetting their shoulders and neck, pulling faces. Everyone knows that afterward they will return to the beach to dry in the sun and smoke a cigarette after first undoing their bikini tops. All the boys wait, while pretending not to, for that second when their breasts will appear, and Christophe is just like the others, his legs dangling, eyes staring. It's a pain in the ass having to wear a pair of tight blue Speedos when you want to make space in your life for two hot young Dutch girls.

Sometimes, when he gets too hot, Christophe rushes back to the apartment. His mother gives him the keys, raising her eyebrows knowingly. His flip-flops make that ridiculous slapping noise as he runs up the staircase. He opens the door, grabs a magazine—*VSD* or *Voici*—from the kitchen countertop (they always have some useful photographs of naked women) and sorts himself out in the bathroom in five minutes flat. This sometimes happens three times a day. Afterward he feels guilty and embarrassed: there has to be something unhealthy about it. But he can't help it.

One day, a girl from the famous gang of volleyball players comes over to talk to him. He hadn't noticed her especially before this. She's an unremarkable-looking girl, topless, with freckles and long dark hair, and she chews gum as she talks. She sits next to him on the wall and asks him what he's called, what he's doing there. Christophe looks at her shyly from the corner of his eye, but she seems less and less insignificant as time passes. This is how he discovers that people's faces can change depending on how nice to you they are. When she catches him staring at her breasts and asks him what he's looking at, the mischievous sparkle in her eyes takes his breath away. He doesn't answer. She says she doesn't mind. As if he can do what he wants.

"How old are you?"

"Fourteen," Christophe lies.

"Have you been out with a girl before?"

He blushes. Thankfully he's tanned and she doesn't notice. He doesn't really understand what she means by "been out with." Out where? To do what? Amused by this, the girl explains it to him.

But it's starting to get late and as the heat fades, they see families on the beach taking down their parasols, packing up their things. Sand squirts from the sandals of suntanned, exhausted children as they shuffle away. The sea, meanwhile, has turned the color of dark metal. And that girl is sitting close to him. She makes fun of him a little and her nipples are a shiny, pretty brown color that makes him salivate. She says: "If you were older..." This is how Christophe learns that he is cute. It's a strange feeling, but it's good news.

The next day, however, she doesn't even glance his way. The worst thing is that he never even dared ask her name.

One night during their third week, Julien is picked up by the police. He got drunk and pissed on one of the boats in the Hyères port. Nothing too bad, but it's enough to transform the family into a prison camp. After that, the boys are ordered to remain within shouting distance and Christophe is no longer allowed to go out alone to the beach volleyball courts. Lying on his front, he has to make do with spying on the players from a distance, looking for that nameless girl whom he can't stop thinking about. "Don't you move from there," his mother tells him. "You've done it enough already."

On the way back, Christophe is submerged in an immense wave of misery. A ten-hour drive, being passed by reckless idiots, the car like a furnace and his father chain-smoking in the front, his elbow leaning out of the open window. While they're stuck in traffic jams at Orange and Vienne, Christophe has time to think things over. And he realizes: this year, he was no longer young enough and not yet old enough. At one point, the Marchals stop by the side of a mountain path for a picnic. Christophe feels distant from them, even his brother, although he's always miles away. Back at the house, Julien runs straight up to his room without even helping the others empty the trunk. This will be their last-ever family vacation.

IN AUGUST, THANK God, Christophe spends three weeks at a summer camp where he plays golf, judo, and Clue, and sails an Optimist dinghy. Best of all, he makes some friends his own age. He tells them about the bare-breasted girl on the beach; their jaws hit the floor and they beg him for details. He gives them plenty, inventing some new ones when he runs out. They ask him what it feels like to touch a girl's breasts, and Christophe shows them, although he doesn't have the faintest idea, by getting them to feel the fleshy swelling between their thumb and their index finger: a tit is just the same, he promises. The others reach out their fingers respectfully. True, it's really soft and squishy. All these innocent boys squeeze their fists shut and fondle themselves, straight-faced. Is that really what it's like? A terrifying mystery. Christophe says nothing more. Anyway, it's snack time. They sit in a circle on the grass and eat some bread and fruit paste. Below them, the lake smells of mud and the windsurf boards await a breeze that never comes.

The rest of the day, they laugh and swim; the food is disgusting and the guy in charge of the stables is a thug, but the female instructors are nice. Not like the male ones, who are all show-offs and flirt with the girls, even the underage ones.

The coolest thing is that Christophe gets along well with Myriam, the instructor in charge of the morning dance class and the quiet games in the afternoons, activities that he chooses to attend every day. Around three, when the sun is still hot, they meet up with a few friends in one of the little chalets with a terrace overlooking the lake. They play Mikado and belote, and in between games they chat. Christophe and Myriam sit side by side and he can feel the closeness of her arm, their skin magnetized, even if she is seventeen and he's only thirteen. She's blonde, with a little layer of puppy fat, round cheeks and a crease in her neck, her buttocks spilling out of her pale cotton shorts. Sometimes, to make him laugh, she will tickle him or hug him. One day in the middle of August, while the temperature is in the nineties and the lake is as still and shallow as a big puddle, Myriam sits in his lap during a game of kemps. The night before, she took part in a big drinking session with the other instructors and now she feels weird, hypersensitive, her body languid and her head like it's trapped in a vise. Christophe feels his weight on her, rounded and mobile; the back of her neck smells sweet. When he dares to put his arm around her waist, she says: "Hey, watch it." But with each movement, he experiences once again the elastic softness of her flesh. The unbearable heat beats down on them all, on the whole country, and Christophe tries to think about something else so he doesn't get hard, but he can't help it, he's tortured by the need for her to swallow him up, to close up around him like some sea animal, like hot algae.

"I can't stand it anymore," she says.

She lays her head, which weighs a ton, in his open hand, and crosses her ankles under the wooden bench, then starts rocking back and forth on her soft, damp, fleshy ass. As she leans back, he glimpses some blonde, downy hair in the gap between the top of her shorts and the bottom of her tank top. He swallows his spit. Karim Dahbane is watching them with mocking eyes. Christophe can tell he's tempted to say something, to turn it into a joke. He's a scrawny, fidgety kid in a Fido Dido T-shirt who's constantly clowning around. There's always one. Christophe glares at him: say a word and you're dead. Then Myriam gets up and sits next to him again.

"It's too hot," she says. "Your skin is sticking to me."

Christophe presses himself against the table, holding his cards tight in both hands. Karim giggles. That's it— Christophe punches him in the shoulder, right in the spot where it really hurts. It's like giving a dead leg if you aim it just right. Christophe got hit like that several times in the hockey team's locker room. Seb Madani was a master at those punches.

THAT SUMMER—THE summer of 1988—Christophe kisses two girls. The first behind the cabin that smells of mold and socks, where the boys get changed after going swimming. Her name is Émilie Costa. A bold girl, always falling in and out of love. Her pale blue irises remind him of sled dogs' eyes. She made the first move, slipping him a note in the cafeteria. As soon as he turns up, she pushes him against the wall and kisses him. In all honesty, it's not particularly pleasant at first, that tongue rummaging about inside his mouth, not to mention the fear of being caught, the splinters in his back from the cabin's wooden planks, the smell of piss. They keep twisting their heads in all directions. They're at that age of acrobatic French kisses followed by shy muttering. In the end, though, Christophe starts to enjoy it, and that evening they sit together at the back of the bus and she lets him grope her a bit. By the next day, it's all over. She's fallen for someone else and Curtis, her big brother, tells him: "Touch my sister again and I'll smash your face in."

He kisses the second girl at the final-night dance. A tall, unattractive girl in shorts who comes on to him while he's gawking idiotically at Myriam. He lets her, to get revenge and because this girl is two years older than him. They go outside to make out under a poplar tree.

"You're not too bad at this for a virgin."

At least, after that, there's no doubt that he's one of the lucky boys—the fast learners, the ones that girls like. He's grown up.

AT THE FIRST practice session of the next season, he's surprised to discover that his gear is now too small for him. And when Madani comes to find him in the locker room to fuck with him as usual—"What's up, dickless?"—Christophe stands up and his tormentor realizes right away that he will have to find someone else to bully. He laughs despite his surprise.

"Chill out, pencil dick." But things have changed for good.

As far as practice is concerned, however, the basics remain as they were, except that Coach Lukic has returned to his native Serbia and the under-sixteens are now coached by Anthony Gargano, a first-team player idolized by all the kids. He has two caps for the French national team and, even more impressive, he drives a Ducati. But he, too, is obsessed with passing. Pinball, he calls it.

"Whenever you're in their half, your passing should be as fast as the bumpers of a pinball machine. You shouldn't even see the puck, it's moving so fast. The secret is: don't think. As soon as you start thinking, it's already too late."

Once, Gargano even takes his players to the little café opposite the rink and shows them a real pinball machine, the Diamond Lady. With the boys standing around him, he shows off his skills and they start to howl with excitement.

"See? Don't think."

He gets them to skate forward and backward, to slalom between cones, the puck glued to their stick. He shows them in blue marker on his whiteboard what he expects from them: automated movement. To achieve this, he sets them up in lines of five, and each line has to reproduce combinations of his own invention as fast as possible before leaving the ice so that the next line can take their turn. To start with, they make stuttering progress and Gargano bawls them out a lot. Gradually the instructions are internalized, transformed into muscle memory. The puck speeds up. Each line becomes a wave, and there is something implacable, almost musical about the way they crash over the ice.

"Come on, faster! Go, go, go!"

They're like dwarves in helmets now, thrashing around so quickly that soon all you can see is a complex ribbon of passes. *Tshak tshak tshak*. Goal.

CHRISTOPHE HAS DEVELOPED a new routine to put on muscle. Every evening after school, he rides his mountain bike down to the center of Cornécourt, then heads toward the Suprema 2000 zone until he reaches Firefighters Hill.

Seeing that, you have a better understanding of what people mean when they say the town was built in a basin. For a kid his age, that slope is like the Ventoux. So he sets off, speeding downhill before the stoplight and then climbing as far as his legs will take him. At first he can't get past the bus shelter and he collapses, wheezing, onto the ground. But day after day, meter by meter, he keeps setting new records. It's a depressing sort of adventure, because the hill offers no surprises, no mercy. But it teaches him the arithmetic of progress, where you add only small numbers. And when the weather is so bad that he can't ride up the hill, he feels as if he's losing some of his strength, as if he's missed out on the most important meeting of his life. Every day, he repeats this necessary torture, and sometimes all of life seems to be summed up in that tableau: a steep slope in a small town, a kid on a bike, riding one centimeter farther before dark. The hill keeps pushing back but he refuses to give up. He has to hold firm. To change.

At last, one Saturday afternoon while he's with his friends at the rink, the announcer's nasal voice informs them once again that it is time for the minute of speed. Christophe decides to try his luck.

"You'll get smashed to pieces," Marco warns him soberly.

All the same, heart pounding, Christophe skates out onto the ice and is soon joined there by the regular crowd: hockey players, old-timers, and Gainz (named after Serge Gainsbourg because of his cauliflower ears), an inveterate weed-smoker and projects rebel who skates in a T-shirt, one of those ghetto heroes who live with their parents until they're thirty-five and respond to the slings and arrows of outrageous fortune by punching people in the face.

The Zamboni has departed the ice, leaving it as impeccably smooth as ever. The announcer, with his fairground voice, whips the crowd into a frenzy. A rink employee arranges a few orange cones to mark out the racing track.

"It's almost time. Are you ready? One minute. Just one minute!" the voice blares through the loudspeakers.

Christophe gets into position, deaf to the trash talk of the men beside him, his body tensed like a bowstring.

"Hey, kid!" He turns to see a big guy in a sheepskin jacket calling to him. "Don't do that—you'll end up on your ass."

But the front row is already moving slowly forward.

"And here we go..." the announcer screeches as the skaters elongate their movements.

The race starts calmly, the competitors surreptitiously eyeing one another. Then the peloton becomes gradually stretched out. At the third bend, the leaders start to accelerate. Christophe speeds up too, well balanced, his arms pumping wide to either side. And without warning he starts moving through the pack.

Behind the barrier, a wave of surprise stirs through the crowd, everyone wondering who that kid is, what he's doing there. The first lap is already over and Christophe is still making up ground. He comes up alongside the second-placed racer. Generally the best skaters don't really hit the gas until the end of the second lap, because the third lap is usually the last one. So the boy's attack looks like what it is: brave, impossible, suicidal.

But he keeps putting distance between himself and the pack, driving forward with his thighs, fluid and spare in his movements, almost silent, following the ideal curve he has set for himself, the shortest distance to the finish line. Behind him, a burst of pride. The pack shifts into top gear.

"Come on! Faster!" shouts the man in the sheepskin jacket.

But Christophe can already sense the disorder of the other skaters, the displacement of air at the back of his neck. He knows the ice by heart. He could almost close his eyes, let his momentum carry him through the bend. He lets them come for another second and then, to a collective gasp, accelerates again.

People start whistling, yelling encouragement, clapping.

"Only twenty seconds left," announces the voice from above them.

After that, everything speeds by in a blur. Christophe finishes the second lap in the lead. He can see nothing now but the crowd. All those faces merged in a single vague blur. But his pursuers are still there. He can practically feel their breath, their hostile speed. They are hot on his heels. Guillaume Papeloux, who also plays for the first team, outflanks him to the left, crashing into his shoulder. Christophe wavers, feels the ground giving way beneath him, then Gainz shoves him before two other anonymous bodies, stronger and faster, knock him completely off balance. For an instant, his speed carries him forward through the air, levitating above the rink, until he falls flat on his stomach, his chin smashing hard into the ice.

Twenty other skaters cross the line without him, like a flock of sheep.

When the boy gets up again, leaning on one knee, he immediately recognizes the copper taste in his mouth, almost pleasant, then brings two fingers to the skin below his right eye, where it stings. Blood. The race is over.

"You okay?"

Papeloux is already standing in front of him, helping him up. Christophe nods. He smiles, exposing his teeth. One of his incisors has broken clean off, at an oblique angle strangely reminiscent of a guillotine blade.

7

VARIOUS EXPRESSIONS PASSED over Lison's face, like clouds in the sky.

"Meh," she said, handing the phone back to her boss.

"Really?"

She shrugged. "He's just not my type, you know."

Hélène had to admit that none of the photographs of Christophe really did him justice. Family portraits and shots on the beach, stolen from his Facebook account, an old blurry photo showing him as a very young and fairly dumb-looking hockey player. Nothing very convincing.

"He was like the It Boy at my high school . . . All the girls wanted him."

"I guess he's changed, huh?"

Not only that, but he had only sixteen friends on Facebook. Lison looked apologetic.

"Are you going to meet him?"

The two women had been sitting in Le Galway for some time by this point, assessing the problem while each drinking a pint of Kilkenny. Outside on the sidewalk, customers in hats and scarves were smoking cigarettes, hopping from foot to foot. It wasn't crowded inside the pub, thank God. Hélène took another swig of her beer and zoomed in on Christophe's lips, which had grown thinner over the years.

"It'll be better than your Tinder guys."

"I don't know about that," said Lison.

Hélène stared at her intern, whose wrists were jangling with red, orange, and yellow plastic bracelets, and who was wearing chunky wedge shoes, a blouse covered with birds of paradise, and a jacket with shoulder pads bought at a cool thrift store in Le Marais. What the hell would she know about it?

Anyway, Hélène had already made up her mind. She wanted to see him again. She wanted him. She wanted to treat herself to this shot of adolescent adrenaline, to be carefree and reckless like she had been back then. Above all, it was the reversal of fortunes that excited her, seeing how the idol of her teenage years would react when he saw the woman she had become. It felt all the more necessary since Erwann had played one of those tricks on her of which he was a master. That very day, he had come out into the practically deserted open-plan office and swooped down on her, his perfectly ironed shirt looking like it was about to burst.

"Can we talk?"

No hello, no how are you. He hadn't even looked at Lison as she moonwalked out of shot to avoid this unpleasant scene.

"In your office?" Hélène asked.

"Yeah, it'll be quick. I've got a meeting in twenty minutes."

Inside the goldfish bowl, Erwann had closed the door and begun pacing around, breathing hard, nervously playing with his beard while his leather soles squeaked on the laminate floorboards.

"Is this about the mayor's office?"

"Yes. I just talked to Schneider on the phone. We were supposed to have lunch, for something else. He told me he couldn't. And then he told me that you behaved like an idiot the other day."

Hélène told herself to stay calm, not to make herself look like the office hysteric.

"Go on," she said. "I'd rather hear their version first."

"Their version is that your report was completely biased and that you acted like some strict, man-hating German teacher."

"Is that it?"

"Who the hell do you think you are?" the fat man shouted, springing toward her. "They're our clients, for fuck's sake. They're the ones forking out for this."

"Schneider's a loser," said Hélène, unfazed. "He's incompetent and the IT department at the mayor's office could collapse any day."

"So?"

"So, it's my job to tell them that."

This time, Erwann took two steps back, as if appalled by the staggering stupidity of his employee's words. Raising one hand tragically into the air, he revealed a large dark stain in the right armpit of his shirt.

"Your job is to satisfy them."

"At the beginning, I was dealing with the service manager. They squeezed him out so they wouldn't have to deal with any headaches. They don't have the faintest clue what they're doing."

"Now wait just a minute," Erwann interrupted, on the verge of apoplexy.

But Hélène kept talking, pinning him to the wall like a beetle.

"Let me finish. Afterward, I'll bend over backward as much as you want. I'll go and belly dance for them. I'll resign if necessary."

This last phrase seemed to reassure Erwann, who magnanimously waved at her to continue while he collapsed into his leather chair.

"Politi gave us the green light to carry out a system audit. I spent two months on it. The report I wrote was irrefutable. Their IT system is ridiculously overcomplicated. It's full of security failings. The organizational charts are insane. Politi gave us carte blanche to expose all of that. And that's what I did. I looked at it from every angle. And when I turn up there, Schneider and his little yes-man tell me Politi isn't coming. Before I even begin delivering my report, I know it's dead and buried. Those bastards screwed me over. They were on their phones while I was talking to them. And at the end, it was all great, we'll call you. I didn't go to a top-five school to be treated like a maid. So, if you want me to hand in my resignation, that's fine. Just give me the word and I'll be out of here in fifteen minutes."

While she was saying all of this, Erwann smiled appreciatively and swiveled his chair from side to side.

"Such pride..."

He spoke these words in a soft, vaguely admiring voice, almost as if she were his favorite pet. Hélène felt simultaneously flattered and sullied.

"Listen," her boss said, interlacing his hands over his enormous belly. "I have a business to run. With those kinds of clients, seventy-five percent of the work is political. That's their bread and butter—covering up their own mistakes. If you go in there to sort out problems that they spend their lives trying to hide, they're obviously going to be suspicious of you. Fearful."

"I know that."

Hélène had gradually started to relax. She liked this sort of smooth complicity after the storm. Now that her master had

134

calmed down, she felt an irrepressible urge to sit in his lap and purr, to make him happy.

"You can't destroy them because they're not as smart as you or because they swagger around like gods just because they once showed up to a class at Sciences Po fifteen years ago. I deal with people like that all the time too—bullshit merchants, jobsworths who treat people like shit to prove to themselves that their lives have meaning, assholes who have not had an original idea since 1981. And you know what?"

"You bow down to them."

"Yeah, I grovel at their feet. You know why?"

"Your company, your money, your house."

"Exactly!"

Erwann wobbled cheerfully on his chair like a Weeble, perked up by this barrage of cynicism.

"Deep down, they know that we earn more money than them, that we have cooler lives. Those guys would kill both their parents for a raise, a promotion, an office with a door, an annual bonus. Forget them. Think about your bonuses. Be a doormat."

He accompanied his conclusion with a horizontal hand gesture that signified the drawing of a line. Hélène smiled, fully on board despite the disgust she felt at this little tactical demonstration.

"I know all that. We're selling servility as well as expertise. I don't have any illusions about this business, believe me. I screwed up, simple as that."

"Good. And you're going to go back there. You have to make this work. Suck them off if you have to. I don't give a fuck."

Hélène did not flinch at these crude remarks. She'd been used to it since business school—the schoolboy humor, the moronic jibes, the jockstrap fraternity.

"I thought they didn't want to see me ever again."

"I'm going to call Politi. One of his kids goes to the same music school as mine. I think he plays the tuba. Anyway, we'll work something out."

With that, Erwann glanced at his large plastic watch, an indestructible model no doubt designed for marine commandos and cosmonauts, and jumped to his feet.

"Anyway, who cares. With the regions merging, we'll be selling organizational charts by the ton, we'll have warehouses full of matrixes, whatever we want. Michael and Nath are coming up with just-in-time proposals. The Vosges and Moselle health agencies both called me yesterday. They're all so at war with each other, we could sell them anything. You're going to have to get on the case fast."

"The simplest thing would be to offer the same thing to all of them. Do the job once, sell it ten times over."

"Yep, that's the secret."

"One size fits all," she said in English.

"True, although that doesn't mean we can't do made-to-measure too."

"And deliver it on time."

"And in compliance with CSR."

"Not to mention QC."

"AFNOR!" he mock-sneezed, before grabbing her shoulder and steering her toward the door.

It was always the best way to patch things up, laughing about how much easy money you were going to make together.

"For us, this regional merger is a godsend."

"Not for the poor regions, though," said Hélène, feigning sadness.

"God no, it makes no sense at all for them. It won't save them a cent and it'll take ten years to get over the shock. Manuel Valls is a genius."

They then exchanged a few pretty, healing words before going their separate ways. Erwann went back to his desk and began typing on his computer keyboard. But as soon as she left the office, he called out:

"By the way..."

Hélène froze.

"We hired someone new."

"Ah?"

"A rising star. Jean-Charles Parrot. He went to HEC, maybe you know him. A really nice guy. You'll see."

Hélène could not bear to hear more. Seeing Erwann's sudden, beaming smile, she realized that his online meeting had begun. She rushed out of his office and told Lison: "You're coming for a drink with me tonight. And that's an order."

Lison gave a military salute. In the meantime, she suggested, Hélène should have a cup of green tea. "It's a diuretic and an antioxidant."

IN THE DAYS that followed, Hélène barely had time to think about Christophe, and he didn't message her in any case. As Erwann had predicted, there was a wave of new business and with the new recruits (among them that worrying big shot from HEC) taking time to settle in, Elexia was struggling to absorb this boom in activity.

To remedy the situation, Erwann organized a series of meetings aimed at reviewing workloads and streamlining processes. Hélène picked up several cases relating to the merger of regional agencies and to the regional directorates of cultural affairs. She was soon buried under work.

Because, before the establishment of the new Grand Est mega-region, expected to make a fortune for the consulting industry in general and Elexia in particular, the old regions obviously had to get rid of their own organizations, the result of years of plastering over the cracks and local idiosyncrasies. Above all, at the head of each of these organizations was a boss who had no intention of stepping down. At first, no one had considered it worthwhile paying for external experts to carry out this Paris-ordered merger, since there were clearly enough resources available internally. But after six months of unproductive meetings, of dirty tricks played by steering committees, and confronted with the threat of the administrative authority taking matters into their own hands, they had finally farmed the problem out to a third party.

Consequently, Hélène found herself in the crossfire of these paltry little internal wars. In each organization she visited, she found employees who hated one another and a handful of executives on the verge of a nervous breakdown. The scale of the damage came as no surprise. Many times before, she had witnessed the devastating effects of these overhauls ordered on the basis of the latest economic theory to spring from some prestigious business school. These managerial manifestos changed with the passing seasons, but the havoc they wreaked remained consistent.

So, depending on what was fashionable at the time, they converted to lean management or decided to decentralize support functions, before reintegrating them into the main organization, in order to prioritize organic management or silo management, to knock down walls or rebuild them, to horizontalize verticals or square circles, to invert pyramids or refocus the hierarchy on core values, to devolve, to rearticulate, to raise by increments, to highlight operations or value creation, to model functionality on a quality-focused approach, to intensify reporting or establish a collegial leadership style.

The employees, constantly grappling with these abrupt reinventions, were left disoriented, no longer sure where they were or what they were supposed to be doing, floundering in a sea of chronic incompetence. Within these agencies and administrations in a state of perpetual mutation, asking for a raise became practically a firing offense. As for the unions, they were left trying to cling to reality as the ground kept shifting under their feet, with no resources other than good intentions, a vague nuisance value, and a glorious past like a flag flying proudly outside a bombed-out building.

This regional merger was a long-held government dream, an attempt at achieving the kind of political efficiency that had not been seen for almost fifty years. But that meant disturbing some ancient strongholds of power. The result was every bit as disastrous as might have been expected. Everywhere, quasi-prehistoric habits crashed against the necessary homogenization of practices. Small human communities united by a few objectives, a workplace, a wage policy, and meal vouchers were suddenly presented with some fellow human beings with whom they had to come to an arrangement, whether by mutual agreement or by force, and the friction produced by this impossible need to pool resources led to irritation that occasionally sparked into hate. A secretary burst into tears in her office because she had just received a threatening email from some faceless executive. An assistant manager in suspenders developed ulcers after a particularly heated video conference. Every little detail became an opportunity for a fight, every privilege accepted here but unknown there a cause for fury. The slightest nonconformity became an excuse for wiping the enemy from the face of the earth.

Because before starting work on the reorganization, they first had to draw up the cruel inventory of specific local features. Special privileges, abuses of power, minor gratuities, regulatory incongruities allowing people to take a day off here, a benefit in kind there...it all had to be accounted for.

Of course, the point of all these practices—outside the law and yet untouchable—was not only to smooth things over and make life easier, but above all to give employees the feeling that they were fortunate. Once payment had been made, everyone compared themselves to others. Then the most privileged were put on trial. Resentment grew quickly between managers. People talked about it at the cafeteria, in office corridors, their voices thick with outrage. The discovery of all these regional privileges and peculiarities inflamed the passion for equality that characterizes the French.

The hierarchy's response to this discontent was always the same: some would lose and some would gain, but ultimately, mathematically, based on the median results, everyone would be better off. But there is nothing mathematical about bitterness. As soon as a worker saw his territory threatened, he demanded the destruction of the enemy's benefits. And the workers' anger was stoked even more strongly by the sense that, in this time of redistribution, the only way to avoid being wronged was to bring down someone else. Without meaning to, the masterminds behind this plan had set off one of those leveling storms that periodically grip the French nation. In fact, some wondered if they had done it deliberately.

In this imbroglio of grudges and emergencies, Hélène's task was to put out fires and heal wounds. First she had to organize a meeting between management and unions, and to promote an online questionnaire that would gather the opinions of all stakeholders. After that, she identified expectations, sticking points, opportunities, and problems. Three graphs and two pie charts later, she returned to give her presentation to a plenary meeting of the workforce. There, watched by men and women sitting with their arms crossed, staring suspiciously up at her, she introduced herself, projected her results, made remarks about the data she had gathered, laser pointer in hand, speaking too fast and pacing around as if she were in an episode of *The West Wing*, adroitly dropping in Anglicisms, proper nouns, and quotations from experts. Often, an engineer or an IT technician who knew how to count would point out an error in her calculations, a dubious interpretation. Hélène put those mistakes in there deliberately, to lure the wolf from the woods. Once she had identified her most dangerous opponent, she would speak only to him, her words as sharp and precise as a rapier. The rest of the room, identifying with the heckler, was gradually convinced along with him.

In reality, this little piece of stage-managed democracy was there only to demonstrate her competence and to make her audience trust her. Statistics were just one form of support. She could just as easily show a film or a PowerPoint with quotations from Gandhi and Milton Friedman; it was all artifice, pure and simple. Hélène was not fooled by her own pseudo-science. Behind the mathematical framework, the managerial theories, the organizational principles (which could sometimes prove remarkably efficient), her job was in many ways not so different from that of a snake oil salesman. For preachers of her kind, failing administrations were like a new Wild West, with government-led reorganizations acting as churches for these confused congregations. What she sold was the same bullshit that had once fleeced cowboys in Tombstone and Abilene. It was a job. Offering miracle cures, bringing news of the economic Zeitgeist, and acclimatizing the latest creatures from the neoliberal menagerie to these fragile ecosystems. To acquire this indisputable expertise, it had taken her six years of higher education and several tough semesters at private firms that had ended in severe burnout.

Today, she continued doing the same job, quickly and competently, but she no longer found any pleasure in it, and her faith was all gone. And often, while she was trying to fall asleep, or driving along some road in Meurthe-et-Moselle, alone, music blasting from the car stereo, she would think about her life, her undeniable success, and wonder sourly: Did I really go through all of *that* just for *this*?

ONCE A MONTH, Erwann organized a small drinks party. It was a team-building exercise and a chance to share the latest news. It was at these parties that the Elexia employees found out about the company's impressive growth. Each time, Hélène saw new faces there, people she didn't know and to whom she took an instant dislike.

Late one Tuesday, as she was passing by to pick up her meal vouchers, she found flyers scattered all over the office, decorated with a unicorn and announcing one of these monthly drinks parties—for the evening of November 10. There was even a brief agenda:

- Update on the latest results
- New developments planned
- Introducing new recruits
- Surprise gift

"Guess who designed the flyer?" Lison asked proudly, appearing from behind her.

"I recognized your style. What's the surprise?"

"A bottle of Veuve Clicquot. The boss wants everyone there."

"Smart."

Turning toward her, Hélène thought that her intern looked different, as if she'd grown taller. She was wearing a white T-shirt tucked into a pair of 501s that came down to just above

142

her ankles. She wore Vans on her feet and a sumptuous Burberry trench coat from the 1980s.

"Were you leaving?"

"I was going outside to smoke."

"I'll come with you. So how are things?"

"It's nonstop at the moment. Erwann's monopolizing me. He thinks I'm his personal graphic designer or something."

Hélène did not like this idea. After glancing at her watch, she changed her mind. "Actually, I'm running late. I should go. I'll see you Thursday."

"Yeah, it'll be great. I'm organizing the whole thing."

And to illustrate this, Lison mimed an old-fashioned waitress, hand in the air, palm horizontal as if carrying a tray. Hélène hurried home. The nanny would be leaving soon, and she still had to work to finish for tomorrow morning.

ONCE THE GIRLS had been fed, bathed, and put to bed, Hélène calculated that she still had a good two hours' work ahead of her. Philippe was on a business trip in Bordeaux and she had not even had time to eat dinner. Inside the house, a perfect silence reigned. She savored it for a moment, standing there in her stainless-steel kitchen. After the rush of the day, it felt as peaceful as if she were on vacation. She hadn't had a second to breathe since waking up at six that morning. She was so exhausted that her head was spinning.

She decided she should have a drink—just a small whiskey to give her courage. As soon as she swallowed her first mouthful, her whole body relaxed, and Hélène began producing slides without any effort at all, almost without thinking. There was a kind of exhilaration to that quasi-automatic activity. Later, she thought, she would treat herself to some stracciatella ice cream, with whipped cream. She always tended to put on weight when she was overworked. Oh well. God knows she deserved a treat now and then. And, wouldn't you know it, just then she received a message from Christophe.

It didn't say much. He was fine, and he hoped she was too. He apologized again for that other message, the one his friends had written as a prank. He said he'd been thinking about her.

Hélène felt tears come to her eyes. It was so sudden, so unexpected, so silly that it made her laugh. Alone at the table, in front of her laptop, completely shattered. This man had been thinking about her.

"Mommy?"

The little voice was coming from upstairs. Hélène closed her laptop.

"Why are you still awake, sweetie?"

From the stool where she sat, she could see only Clara's bare feet and ankles, standing on the top step of the staircase. There was a brief hesitation, then the girl said:

"Mommy, I forgot."

"Forgot what? It's really late, you know."

"My English. There was a poem for tomorrow."

"God, no..." Hélène moaned.

"Yes. The poem about the boy who falls up."

"It's too late, honey."

"We have to know it for tomorrow."

Sighing, Hélène got to her feet. She walked upstairs and took Clara by the hand.

"Didn't Claire get you to do your homework?"

"I forgot to tell her."

"Doesn't she look in your folder?"

"No."

Back in her bedroom, Clara took a large blue folder from her schoolbag and began rifling through it.

"Here," she said, handing a notebook to her mother.

Hélène looked at the duplicate of the famous poem.

"It's okay, it's not too long. So you haven't learned it?"

"I did. But I haven't recited it."

"You could have done this on your own..."

"But what if I got it wrong?"

"All right, go on then," Hélène said impatiently. "I'm listening."

"Didn't she do her homework?"

Mouche had just appeared in the doorway, dressed in her underwear, her face hot and creased from sleep.

"What are you doing here?"

"Is she going to be punished?" Mouche asked.

"Get out of my room!" her sister shouted.

"Whoa, calm down."

The younger girl, whose hair had gone all frizzy in the warmth of the sheets, shrugged before turning back toward her own bedroom.

"Okay, I'm waiting. Get a move on."

Clara closed her eyes, chin pressed against her chest, and began to recite.

"'I tripped on my shoelace'..."

"Good. Go on."

"'And I fell up.'"

"Excellent."

She remembered the first five verses perfectly. At least this would soon be over, Hélène told herself. She found herself thinking about Christophe's message. She couldn't wait to get downstairs and reply to it. But Clara got stuck on a word.

"'Blend in the sounds.'"

"Not 'in.' 'Into.'"

"What's the difference?"

"The difference is that 'into' is right and 'in' is wrong."

"I don't understand."

"You have to recite a poem the way it's written. You can't just change the words if you feel like it. Now, try again..."

"'Blend into the colors.'"

"'Sounds.'"

"What?"

"It's 'sounds,' not 'colors.'"

"Oh yeah..."

Clara seemed to rewind a tape inside her head, took a deep breath, and calmly repeated: "'Blend into the colors.'"

"All right, that's enough. We'll try again tomorrow morning."

Hélène snapped the notebook shut and pointed imperiously at the bed. Clara's face fell.

"But the poem..."

"Tomorrow, sweetie. It's late."

Already the little girl's chin was trembling in anticipation; her big eyes were glistening. Torn between her impatience and the sorrow she felt at seeing this pathetic yet sincere display of emotion, Hélène grew even more irritated.

"Bed," she said. "Now!"

She pulled the sheets back, but still Clara resisted. School was important—her parents had told her that often enough. She was only in seventh grade, but a poor grade in math could make her cry.

"I have to recite it tomorrow," she stammered.

"Listen, do what you want, but I'm done."

And Hélène left the bedroom, slamming the door behind her. Clara immediately burst into tears and rushed into the hallway. Seconds later, Mouche came out too, enthralled by this spectacle and grateful for an excuse to get out of bed.

But Hélène had had enough.

"I don't want to hear another word out of either of you! Go to bed."

Back in the kitchen, she felt an immense weariness steal over her. Upstairs, the drama continued for another minute or two, then the shouting and the stomping ended. Hélène poured herself another drink. How long had she felt like she had to do everything herself, alone against all the worries of the world? Obviously, she and her partner earned enough money that they could just hire a nanny and a cleaner, they could take Monsieur's laundry to a dry cleaner's and let a private firm take care of the gardening. But ultimately that didn't change anything. Philippe's life was superior to hers, clearly more important in every respect, so she was the one who had to deal with the nitty-gritty. Sure, once a year he would unclog the sink or mow the lawn, and then that's all he would talk about for the next ten days, but the rest of the time he didn't bother with all the little tasks required to keep the family ship afloat. They had talked about this, of course, because they were a modern, open couple, and Philippe had always acknowledged that she was right. It wasn't difficult to find evidence of his efforts, his empathy. But in the end, she was on her own. Tonight was the norm, not the exception. And each time, she got mad and then regretted it. She mistreated the ones she loved and there was nothing she could do about it.

Mouth twisted in a snarl of bitterness, she opened her laptop, clicked on Facebook, and wrote to Christophe. She was fine too, and thinking about him. She hoped they could meet up one of these days. Soon, if possible. Then she went back to her slides, finishing them as quickly as she could before going upstairs around eleven to check on her sleeping daughters and kiss their warm foreheads.

"OH, GRAND EST!" declaimed Erwann, arm outstretched like some Roman senator.

The whole company was watching him, champagne flutes in hand, smiling at the boss's buffoonery as he addressed them from the mezzanine.

"Oh, Grand Est!" he said again, before making that line of mock poetry rhyme with others ending in the words "incest," "blessed," and "molest."

What a sight he was with his far-reaching captain's gaze, his belly threatening to burst the buttons of his blue twill shirt, spit frothing from his lips as he spoke, his hair red as an Irishman's. Hélène soaked up the glory of this moment. Opportunities for laughter were rare in the Elexia office.

After this lyrical ode to the new, expanded region, Erwann gave a rundown of the business opportunities it afforded and the excellent results the company had posted during the previous few weeks. Cue applause. He then thanked his employees, naming some of them, and Hélène was granted a particularly effusive tribute, describing her as a pillar of the firm, an indispensable asset, and so on. She nodded, feigning modesty, as the occasion required. Standing next to her, Lison was sucking a cranberry gin fizz through a straw. Hélène asked her where she had found that drink, and the intern replied that she had been in charge of supplies for the party.

Becoming more serious, Erwann explained that this merger of the old regions represented, for Elexia, an extraordinary moment.

"Let's be honest. We all know that the regional authorities are freaking out. They are up shit creek without a paddle and they don't have the faintest idea what they're doing. The path is clear. It is up to us to step into the breach. And, for now, we are doing that superbly!"

With these rousing words, he raised his glass and everyone in the office, looking up at their boss, did the same.

Hélène, staring through the window at the low, static sky, thought to herself what a foul month November was. Particularly in this part of the world. And she seriously doubted whether the advent of the Grand Est would make fall in Lorraine any less depressing.

What arrogance it must have taken to invent a new region! What ignorance of people's lives, their weary anger, the grim moods spreading through all those towns and villages, all those millions of people grumbling endlessly, unhappy at being misunderstood, sidelined, disrespected, menaced by the prospect of their monthly bills, management and foreign competition, their national pride and dreams of progress eroded for at least half a century.

Of course, Hélène no longer belonged to that griping world in which she had grown up, and in fact she found it a little repulsive these days. She visited her parents only when she had no choice—for Christmas and New Year's, and once during the summer to show them the girls and leave them there for a week in the fresh air of the Vosges. Despite herself, however, somewhere deep inside she still had the reflexes of a poor person, a sort of cuckold's instinct that enabled her to see straight through the stupidity of vertical orders, the fundamental mismatch between the good intentions of elegant people and the heavy desires of average lives. And in this climate of universal mistrust, where everyone clung to his own little patch of land, his name, his race, his flag, some politicians had thought it a good idea to delete with a single pen stroke centuries of identity to create a...territory. Erwann was well aware of all this, yet he celebrated it with cynical laughter. On the rare occasions when he relaxed a little, it was his habit to regale his audience with these little odes of his.

"Now it is time to introduce you to your new colleagues," he announced.

Hélène scanned the crowd for Parrot's face. She had not yet met him in person, but his features were familiar to her, since she had carefully examined his LinkedIn profile. Though he had just turned thirty, this guy had already worked for two of the biggest consulting firms in the area, won awards for some innovative scheme, and enjoyed a meteoric rise to the Ministry of the Environment. Apart from that, his profile did not provide much information beyond a few links to inspiring articles about his friends' achievements, empathic human resources management, and combating climate change through charities and Corporate Social Responsibility. Below these articles were stupid hashtags like *#soproud* or *#letsbuildabetterworld*. As for his contacts, it was just the usual mass of young people in the same mold, with the same neat, competitive smiles, using job descriptions such as "founder," "CEO," "senior manager," even "global strategist," wielding their business English like a sword.

Hélène was not even a decade older than these people, but it already felt like they belonged to a completely different world, both ludicrous and disturbing. She had spent a long time looking at Parrot's profile photograph, vaguely searching for some flaw, but there was a robotic perfection to his face, except perhaps for the faintest hint of a squint in his eyes. What the hell was a guy like that doing in Nancy? The profile told her nothing worthwhile.

She was dragged from her thoughts by a smattering of applause. Erwann had just compared Elexia to Barca and assured them that the company was fully able to compete with bigger firms like Capgemini, Arthur Andersen, and the rest. Because what distinguished Elexia, of course, was its *agility*.

"So, new guys, please raise your hand so we can see you. And thank you, everyone, for giving them a warm welcome."

Erwann introduced Ninon Carpentier and Karim Lebœuf before it was Parrot's turn. Hélène saw a hand raised a little farther off, but Parrot was facing away from her and all she could make out of him was his slim build, his thick and impeccably styled hair, and the fitted blue suit he wore. Meanwhile, Erwann was talking about him like he was the messiah...

"Some of you will already have heard of Jean-Charles. He was co-president of the student association at HEC during a rather punk period, from what I've been told. Back then, he also created a very smart little startup, Alalouche.com, which offered local authorities a tool to measure the popularity of their service in real time. The idea was that you could find out, with a simple click, if there was a line outside the administrative center or if the municipal swimming pool was packed. Well, that was the plan, but perhaps he will tell you himself how it ended up being tanked by our wonderful French bureaucracy. All that to say, by hiring Jean-Charles, we are focusing on ideas, on creativity. So he will lead our new 'innovation' team. For a long time, I think, our growth has been based on us adapting to our clients' needs. But if we want to keep moving forward, we have to start anticipating or even creating those needs."

These words were applauded too and Erwann concluded his speech by inviting everyone to drink and have fun as if the world were ending, because they deserved it. Flutes filled with lukewarm champagne were raised once again, but half-heartedly this time. The employees' minds were weighed down with work problems and looming deadlines. Unfortunately, the world was not ending just yet.

Hélène had had enough. She pushed her way through the massed bodies to meet the new prodigy. They shook hands and smiled until their faces ached, and he told her how pleased he was to meet her, how much he'd heard about her. He couldn't wait to work together, blah blah blah. He was handsome, she thought, in an almost unpleasant way. Behind the affability and the pretty face, she sensed something far less cool.

At this point, Erwann, perhaps dreading the first face-to-face encounter between his little firm's two stars, trotted over to join them, oily and tactile, his face even redder than usual, laughing at everything they said.

"I didn't know we were going to have an innovation team," said Hélène.

"Actually, that was just decided today," Erwann explained. And, arms tensed and legs bent, he moved his hips like a surfer atop a wave.

"How many people will there be in this team?"

"We're still thinking about that."

"And from an organizational point of view?"

"Transverse, of course."

Hélène, who could churn out organizational charts in her sleep, was immediately able to draw conclusions from this annoying news. Parrot would inevitably occupy an ambiguous position in the company's hierarchy, since his team would be involved with everything and could create strategic orientations that everyone else had to follow. He would report only to Erwann and would have his own budget and employees. Depending on their negotiations, he would be in a position to make his own rules. Given that he was head of a team and had been to HEC, his salary would probably be 150K even before bonuses. The newbie smiled angelically as he buried a stake deep into her heart.

So she smiled back brightly, clinked glasses with him, and wished him success from the bottom of her heart.

The next day, she would give Erwann a simple ultimatum: if she wasn't a partner by the summer, she was out of there.

8

EVERY YEAR, HÉLÈNE'S parents take off three weeks in August, two of which they spend in a small rental apartment at La Grande-Motte. It's a cramped, stifling one-bedroom flat on the ninth floor of one of those 1960s apartment buildings that proliferate along the coastline with their wavelike concrete architecture, their brown and orange awnings. The location costs a fortune, and Mireille keeps repeating that they should make the most of their vacation, given how much they're paying for it.

Hélène has her own room. It's tiny and has a view of the parking lot, but it does have bunk beds, which makes a change. Naturally she sleeps in the upper bunk and from there, if she looks through the square window, she can see the starry sky and hear the *shush* of the sea, the voices of passersby, the ceaseless rumble of traffic below.

For the Poirot family, vacations are sacred. The reason for this is both political and existential. The time here in summer makes amends for all the rest: the school year, with its repetitive rhythms, up at six-thirty, classes on Saturdays, the interminable winter, annoying bosses, weekends that fly by in a blur, the marathon of weekdays. And they think, too, of their ancestors' sacrifices; if people had to die to obtain the right to vote, imagine the slaughter required to amass five weeks of paid leave every year.

By the seaside, the annual routine gives way to other habits. Every morning, Jean goes down to the newsstand, Le Grand Pavois, in shorts and sandals, before he even washes and shaves. The eight o'clock sun is warm on his stubbly cheeks. He buys two packs of filtered Gauloises and a copy of *Midi Libre*, which he reads while drinking his coffee on the terrace of Le Miami, an unpretentious little bar where they play Radio Monte Carlo. He unfolds his newspaper, smokes his cigarette, and sips his coffee, taking his time. The simplest things make him happy. Just before nine, Mireille joins him, her shopping bag filled with apricots, peaches, and a fresh baguette, which she bought at the market on her way here. She orders a coffee too. There's no rush. They tell each other this as they watch the comings and goings of summer tourists.

Hélène wakes up later and has a Coke and two pains au chocolat for breakfast while she leafs through magazines. Around ten or eleven she meets up with her parents and they go to the beach together. Under parasols, they unroll their pleasant-smelling straw mats and spread out the brightly colored bath towels. They each do whatever they want. They can read, go for a swim, or walk along the beach with their feet in the water, take a nap, dig holes, or buy an insanely expensive pan bagnat from the street vendors who shout out their wares under the sky as clear as a Hollywood swimming pool. They don't worry about money while they're on vacation, even if they are still outraged by the liberties taken by local storekeepers, calling them thieves and swindlers.

Mireille and Jean often hold hands as they walk into the sea. As soon as they are chest-deep, they hug and kiss. Hélène leans on her elbows and watches them from a distance, vaguely repulsed. The sun is reflected off her father's bald head and her mother's swimmer's shoulders, the almost too-muscular body revealed by her bikini. She prefers not to know what they're up to; they're too old, and for Hélène love is still a sort of mirage untouched by wrinkles or baldness or hairs on its back. And let's not even talk about sex.

Late in the afternoon, exhausted from the heat, the family goes back to the apartment, which is relatively cool because they took the time to close the shutters and the two big fans are spinning nonstop. This is the time of showers and tan lines. On the balcony, hair wet and skin taut, Hélène flicks through *Femme Actuelle*. Her father smokes a cigarette at the guardrail, and all her life the smell of dark tobacco will remain associated with those deep sensations of six in the evening, when—relaxed and radiant, her legs stretched out and her skin clean—Hélène savors the slowness of time and the sea breeze.

Sometimes her mother turns on the TV in the next room to keep her company while she makes a quick snack for supper—tomatoes, cured ham, chips, cheese, maybe some pasta. The sound of plates being put on the table, the jingle of silverware, the *ssshhh* of soda bottles being opened, the murmur of people strolling along the street, watching the boats float and sway. They eat supper while the light fades, turning the sky orange and pink, the sun casting mercury reflections on the Mediterranean as it sets. These hours are the most precious of all, even better than the evenings when they go out to a pizzeria or a seafood restaurant.

SO WHEN HÉLÈNE announces that Charlotte has invited her to the Île de Ré and that she is planning to spend the summer of her fifteenth year there, the family is immediately plunged into crisis mode.

"Absolutely not!" Mireille yells, in the middle of washing the dishes.

In her apron, she looks like Medea, her eyes flashing angrily and her lips curled back in incredulity. Hélène stands in the kitchen doorway, ready to retreat, while her father, elbows resting on the plastic tablecloth, slowly smokes and waits to see what will happen next. She has chosen the moment carefully: a Saturday after dinner, in May. The sky is overcast and later that day she is supposed to go into town to meet her best friend, to whom she hopes she will be able to announce the good news.

"I'm old enough!" she barks.

"No you're not," replies Mireille, abandoning the sink to better confront this new monster, her daughter.

"We never do anything bad. I've had perfect grades every quarter since sixth grade. I always do what I'm told. I should be allowed to do what I want with my vacations!"

"I don't believe this," her mother laments, putting a hand to her heart.

"Why don't you want to come with us anymore?" her father asks, knocking ash into his ashtray.

He looks up to hear her response, and the smoke escapes through his narrowed nostrils. As always, he's wearing a T-shirt that emphasizes his narrow chest, his muscular arms, his tiny waist. Whenever he moves, the muscles in his body are as expressive as those in his face, and to judge from the tension in his neck, Hélène senses that he is not happy about this situation either.

"It's not that," Hélène explains. "I just want to be with my friend. I'm allowed to see something else, aren't I?"

"You won't see anything at all."

Hélène doesn't bat an eyelid. This is just the first skirmish in a long battle. She has to keep control of herself, hold back

156

the anger she can feel stinging her nose, contain her eagerness for victory. She must watch out for surprises too.

"Why don't you ask your friend to come with us?" suggests her father, before taking one last drag on his Gauloise, which he then crushes meaningfully in the ashtray.

"Don't be ridiculous!" Hélène shouts, suddenly panicked.

"Why not?" her mother asks, sensing a weakness in her daughter's defenses. "Explain it to us."

"No reason. They've got a house down there. They spend all their vacations there. That's all. I'm not going to ask her that, it's stupid."

"So? You've always spent your vacations at La Grande-Motte. Just invite your friend."

"She's perfectly welcome," Jean adds, arms crossed and biceps bulging.

"Yeah, why not?"

Hélène doesn't know what to say. She feels like she's on shifting sands. Obviously she doesn't want her friend to see them, the way they behave in private, her father, who farts at the table or makes little noises while he sips his coffee, her mother, who is always in a state of anxiety. She wants to hide their small-mindedness, all those modest joys and obsessions that now make her feel so ashamed.

Because her friendship with Charlotte has become a way of measuring her own existence. Not only that, but her new best friend never hesitates to correct her and is pitiless when it comes to any departure from the rules of good taste. When they are strolling around town, Charlotte takes aim at those around: blonde women with dark roots, men in sports socks, people in shorts, too much makeup, bodies bulging from too-tight clothes, girls from difficult neighborhoods with that gray, unclean look, old men at bus shelters, hunchbacks, people with limps, fake thugs in sweat suits, inbred yokels, guys in badly made synthetic suits...anyone deviating from her golden rules is fair game.

Charlotte's family has clear ideas about table manners and bouquets of flowers. They know how to set the table properly and to get dressed for an evening at the theater. How to be at ease and act the right way. In their home, it feels as if happiness itself is the product of a certain knowledge about life. Hélène absorbs it all. She mimics it, then goes home with a laser eye. Two years before this, her parents struck her as unquestionable, as almost transparent. Now she sees only their faults. Her mother talks too much, her father drags his feet, they get mad for the wrong reasons, laugh too loudly, and when they "relax" they let themselves go to a degree that makes her want to hide in a cupboard. And all those awful expressions that drive her crazy: "Each to his own," "It takes all sorts," all those crude pseudo-philosophical platitudes that she hates, praising tolerance through weakness, aggression through submissiveness, those sayings that sound like demands but only ever take up a subordinate position, fists clenched, taking pride in their lowliness. And, in hunting out these faux pas, Hélène ends up becoming this contemptuous, anxious little prosecutor who no longer knows what to do with her parents. But even if she does not yet dare put words to these feelings, her mother has no qualms.

"You're ashamed of us, aren't you?"

Hélène protests, vehemently, on the verge of tears. Oh, they never understand anything.

In the weeks that follow, she returns to the fray on several occasions. She promises to be good, to work even harder in school, but these arguments do not have much weight given that she is already a straight-A student. So she goes on smiling strike. At the kitchen table, she stares at her plate and responds only in grunts. The mood at home quickly sinks. In the small, one-story house, the atmosphere grows as cold and gloomy as a morgue. Mireille polishes every surface as if her life depends on it, even cleaning the locks with Q-tips. Jean finds work with a friend who is renovating an old farm near Cheniménil. He goes there with his tools whenever he can and comes back, tanned and happy, before being discouraged by the miserable faces of his wife and child. It gets so bad that Mireille tells him "Not now" when he kisses her neck.

One evening, Jean Poirot makes a decision. He goes to find Hélène in her bedroom. It's still a little girl's room, with posters of New Kids on the Block on the wall, a few stuffed animals on the duvet, the flowered wallpaper, a pitch pine table and the swiveling office chair from Conforama. And a standing mirror in which Hélène likes to watch herself giving imaginary interviews or making herself cry. But that night, she is simply stretched out on the bed, reading *La Mare au diable*. When her father sits beside her, she doesn't even bother looking up from her book.

"Well, I talked to your mother."

Hélène keeps her mouth shut, but the words on the page are now nothing more than a procession of unreadable insects. She raises her face a little, listens. And, above all, hopes.

"It can't go on like this."

She sees his big hand lying flat on the blue sheet, the thick veins like slow worms under his skin, climbing like ivy up his forearm. Her father's working hands, which carry and protect and frighten, and which she used to watch whenever they set off on vacation, gripping the steering wheel lightly so that they could hold a cigarette while shifting gears.

In his low, nicotine-coated voice, Jean reminds her briefly of Mireille's past, her five brothers and sisters, the father taken by cancer when she was six, her own mother placed in a nursing home and never the same after that, the madness that menaced her home, the sadness of that little girl now become a woman's insomnia.

"It's not easy for her."

Hélène sees it coming. Her father is playing on her emotions—it's textbook. But it's also too late. She has already reached that cruel age when only one thing matters and the suffering of others becomes purely fictitious. Her mother's depression is not going to win out over her own fantasy. She wants the bikini, the white beach, the blue sea. She wants bicycle rides, the big life she senses waiting for her on that island at the other end of the country.

"So we're going to find a compromise."

Her father explains the situation to her. She will spend a week with them at La Grande-Motte and then she will go to stay with her friend. They'll figure something out for the train journey. Hélène grabs her father around the neck and kisses him. Thank you! Thank you, Dad. Before he ruins everything.

"But we want to talk to those people first. There's no way we're sending you over there without knowing who'll be looking after you."

"But you know them."

"We've met them three times. We want to talk to them. It's only normal."

Oh shit, thinks Hélène. She can imagine the scene, the intersecting circles, the false notes, her mother's suspicions and complexes: Who do these people think they are? And that one with her two-thousand-euro watch, did you see it?

All the same, she tells Charlotte the next day and her friend is thrilled—she doesn't see the problem. Unsurprisingly. The bitch. Her parents are super cool, her mother looks like a model, and her father has two horses and a Mercedes.

The negotiations go on for two weeks. First, the Brassards invite the Poirots to dinner at their house, an invitation that

160

Hélène does not pass on. Ambitions lowered, they suggest drinks and snacks. Hélène, who cannot imagine her parents in her friend's enormous pad, dodges this too. Consequently, it is now up to the Poirots to invite the Brassards. Hélène vetoes this plan too.

In the end, the two families meet on the terrace of Le Narval in Cornécourt. And curiously, the Poirots and the Brassards don't look that dissimilar when you put them side by side. Both women wear little dresses; the men are in polo shirts and jeans. They smile and stand in the same way. The two men order a beer, Mireille a tomato juice, and Madame Brassard a Badoit. To get a sense of what separates them, you have to examine the small details, the watches, the shoes, the skin, the teeth, the jewelry, the calluses on their hands, and then more intangible things—a gesture, an intonation, a roundness here, a firmness or a softness there, the movement of their bodies, what might more generally be labeled attitude, a thousand nuances that implicitly signal their different diets, their disparate activities, schedules that do not overlap, contrasting lifestyles and destinies.

Even so, the gulf between them is not unbridgeable. Charlotte's father is called Jean, after all, just like Hélène's. They were both born in the provinces, they speak the same language, they have the same vaguely affectionate feelings toward France, and a vision of the State so exalted that it gives them excessive expectations and causes them to criticize it bitterly when those expectations are not met. They are not racist, but. They believe in the value of work, celebrate Christmas without attending Mass but go to church for baptisms, weddings, and funerals. Both couples judge people according to the car they drive, love pot-au-feu and local pâtés, and drink Bordeaux, which they consider the best wine in the world. Mireille Poirot and Nicole Brassard are equally adept at making fruit tarts, even if the former prefers plums and the latter cherries. In front of the television, Jean Brassard and Jean Poirot both watch the news, World Cup soccer games, and documentaries about nature and extreme sports. Mireille and Nicole could talk about the TV news anchor Christine Ockrent, whom they both admire, or about the upmarket entertainment show *Le Grand Échiquier* because they are fascinated by Karajan and they adore Pavarotti. They are all agreed that it's better not to talk politics.

And so the two couples get along famously from the start, obviously helped by the fact that drinking aperitifs at seven in the evening is not the most stressful of activities. Instinctively, the two women sit next to each other, and the men start talking about Formula 1. Hélène and Charlotte drink diabolos through a straw and try not to show how happy they are. All this is very promising. For now, there is no fear of the vacations becoming contentious. After the first round of drinks, Monsieur Brassard suggests they are having too much fun to stop now, so they all agree to share a bottle of rosé. The glasses arrive, they make a toast, and since the Poirots of course do not wish to be outdone, at nine o'clock, as it's starting to get dark, they order a second bottle. Laughter comes easily now, and Nicole Brassard puts her hand on Mireille's wrist to whisper something into her ear. Charlotte's father suggests organizing a visit to the pulp mill where he works.

"It's pretty impressive, you'll see."

They would like to believe it. Anyway, all factories still in existence are clearly worth visiting, as a matter of principle. Here, everyone is still haunted by the crimes committed against the textile and steel industries. One day, the people who sold off those family jewels will have to explain themselves. Or at least, that is what Jean Poirot believes. Charlotte's father does not argue the point. He has the fatalistic view of well-informed men, ready to admit anything since they have understood everything. Soon, it is time to say goodbye. As cheeks are kissed, they all promise to arrange something—a dinner, maybe at a restaurant, sounds good, we'll work out the details later. The question of their summer vacations never arises. But it is there all the time, between the lines.

On the drive home, Hélène's parents are in a wonderful mood. Not only are the Brassards very nice, but they are simple people: they don't think their shit doesn't stink.

"Although... did you see her watch?" Mireille says.

"I didn't notice," Jean admits.

"They're obviously not short of money."

As they talk, the word "executive" keeps cropping up. Charlotte's father is an "executive" and Hélène would like to understand what that means. Apparently, it's not about money or what he does or his precise job title, like lawyer or minister. But the term haloes Jean Brassard with a curious prestige, conferring upon him a position that is both enviable and vaguely reprehensible.

"What's an executive?" Hélène asks finally.

"It's complicated," her mother replies.

HÉLÈNE WILL FIND out the answer two months later, on the road from Gillieux to the supermarket in Ars-en-Ré. That morning, Charlotte's father said *Come on, we're going to buy groceries*, and she did not feel this was an invitation she could refuse. Charlotte and her mother had gone to the market, and perhaps he had a particular reason for not wanting Hélène to stay in their vacation home on her own.

Hélène has been here a week, and from the start she has felt slightly uncomfortable. She thought she knew these people, having eaten dinner with them and slept over at their house dozens of times, but after only twenty-four hours she no longer recognizes the relaxed yet classy atmosphere she had gotten used to. Every family has its hidden sewers, and—with mother, father, and daughter all in close company—the Brassards' begin to emit some unexpected odors. For example, when Charlotte's parents talk to each other, their conversation is laced with malicious innuendos that she has never noticed before. And Nicole Brassard is incapable of addressing her daughter without criticizing her for her behavior, the food she eats, the clothes she wears, the way she stands, even if she delivers all these reproaches in a jokey tone. Hélène had already observed this tendency to disparage Charlotte, but it takes on completely different proportions when they are living under the same roof for an extended period. She begins to understand why the twins prefer to spend their vacations somewhere else.

But, worst of all, the Brassards are constantly badmouthing other people. After passing a bare-chested man in the street, they bitch about him for twenty minutes straight.

In such circumstances, it is difficult to feel at ease. Particularly since her friend's parents do not follow a fixed schedule when they're on vacation. The time they eat their meals varies from day to day; sometimes they go to the beach in the morning, sometimes in the afternoon, and sometimes they don't go at all because they decide they would rather hang out on the terrace, reading magazines and sleeping in the shade. Quite often, Hélène has the feeling that she is spending all her time waiting. She is lost in an alien landscape. At dinnertime she haunts the kitchen like a ghost, in search of clues to when and where they will eat. Her own family eats dinner at seven every evening, and she finds herself craving that kind of certainty.

At least she can depend on the breakfast routine, though. Jean Brassard loves going to the neighboring village very early to buy fresh bread and a newspaper. When the girls come downstairs from their bedroom, still sleepy and surly, the table is already set. From the stairs, they can smell the delicious odors of coffee and toast. Hélène also recognizes the smell of her friend's father waiting for them on the terrace in shirtsleeves, his hair still wet: that clean, male, bourgeois scent of aftershave that she likes so much. Sleeves rolled up, a pair of battered boat shoes on his feet, Jean Brassard pours coffee into bowls and asks the girls if they've slept well. Then Nicole appears, usually in a striped sweater. For the vacation, she has tied to her wrist a little red cotton bracelet that absorbs the salt and sunlight—and the smell of their sheets, Hélène thinks to herself.

They chat distractedly while they eat. The adults flick lazily through newspapers, glancing only at the headlines and photo captions. Nicole enjoys crosswords. The house is littered with books and women's magazines, yet Hélène senses that the Brassards don't really read much. For them, books are just objects. Like the linen couch covers, the paintings on the walls, they are nothing more than knickknacks intended to give the room a touch of soul.

"What are your plans for the day, girls?" the mother asks.

"La Conche," Charlotte announces, making the decision for them both.

Or maybe Trousse-Chemise, or La Couarde. One of the local beaches, anyway.

"Okay," says Nicole. "What about us?"

Jean shrugs. He'll do whatever she wants, he doesn't care. He is difficult only when it comes to eating.

There is one thing here that Hélène adores, however: the advantages of island life. There are very few criminals in the area and abductions are extremely rare. And even the influx of summer visitors does not alter the atmosphere of mutual surveillance and luxurious confinement that characterizes the Île de Ré. So the girls are free to wander unchaperoned, even after dark. They ride bikes, go swimming, and meet up with friends whom Charlotte has known since childhood. Among these friends is Boris, a boy in a white Lacoste polo shirt who is, thinks Hélène, quite good-looking, even if he's on the short side and talks about himself all the time.

They go home around seven, riding along the little paths that crisscross the salt marshes with their strong smell of sulfur. They're tired and dirty, their bodies full of sun, hair full of sand, the down on their spines and the backs of their necks dyed bright blonde. Inside the house, they take forever to get showered. Sometimes they go out for an ice cream or dinner at a restaurant. Hélène always chooses the cheapest thing on the menu. She tastes the wine that Jean Brassard pours into her glass. It's lovely to be drunk after three mouthfuls when she is caramel-colored and far from home, pinching her nose to stop herself bursting into laughter because her best friend's father is imitating the bellowing of a stag in the woods. It's so good to have enjoyed the whole day and to know that tomorrow will be the same.

The two teenagers are allowed to stay out until midnight, so they go to the carnival. They lock up their bikes and, sunburned shoulders highlighted by their pale clothes, they walk in espadrilles among the rides and the stalls that smell of hot sugar, waffles, and candy apples. Charlotte always has money to buy something sweet or hire an electric scooter. They stare at boys, meet up with their friends, ride home just before curfew, laughing, imagining that they're drunk because they've had two beers, then stampede upstairs to their room and leap onto the beds, hair flying, giggling into their pillows and not even brushing their teeth.

But despite these pleasures and these parent-free hours, she is still bothered by a corseted feeling, a weird tension that Hélène can't quite put her finger on and that disturbs her all the more because the limits of the constraint are spectral, the thresholds invisible, all the rules unwritten.

In short, she feels pressured to behave correctly.

But in what way? Certainly not when it comes to choosing her words. Charlotte's father often says "shit" and points out assholes at every intersection. Nor is it about clothing. Nicole goes topless at the beach, and all Jean's clothes are frayed, stained, sometimes full of holes, and he seems completely indifferent to the fact. It's not a question of politeness either, or the sort of conventional respect that children are expected to show adults. It's something else, something more subliminal.

Once, for example, Hélène collapsed a bit too heavily onto the living-room couch and she felt disapproval stir the air like a breeze. Since then, she has been living in a state of anxiety, trying to copy everything Charlotte does. She imitates her movements, the way she sets the table, lies in the sun, laughs. She apes her intonations. She has even adopted the little tongue-click that her friend makes whenever she's annoyed. And yet the Brassards are so kind to her. They give her oysters to eat in the middle of summer, and melons so sweet that they taste like candy. Hélène tries to make herself worthy of such generosity.

Thankfully, after a few days, she settles into a comforting little role-playing game with her friend's father. Jean likes to tease her and pretend he's her humble servant, going to comic lengths to be considerate, asking her if everything's okay, if she wants to call her parents, if she feels fine, not too hot, not too cold, treating her like a capricious princess whose moods are feared by all below her.

Hélène giggles, thrilled and embarrassed to be the center of attention.

When Nicole announces that they should go to the dining room, for instance, Jean says: "I don't know if Hélène will agree." She blushes. He kids her like this, always kindly, never pushing it too far, until there is a sort of hazy complicity between them. At least now she has a role she can play. The best friend, the little protégée. The girl they want to make laugh.

That summer, Hélène also discovers a new power. Before this, she has always gone unnoticed. Now, suddenly, seeing her reflection in the windows they pass on their bicycles, she notices a change in stature. At fifteen, she is five foot six tall and her legs, which a year before had been nothing more than a graceless means of locomotion, have now become an attraction. When she pedals, runs, or walks, when she crosses them on café terraces, when she stretches them out after eating too much, when she sits cross-legged on the sand and counts the folds in her belly, when she strolls along the beach, men in their twenties and middle-aged fathers with potbellies ogle her shamelessly. For now, she doesn't really know what to do with this new interest she has aroused. It makes her head spin, hollows out her stomach with fear. She wants to disappear and, at the same time, wants the spotlight all to herself.

One day, when she is about to put on her bikini in the little upstairs bathroom, she catches sight of her reflection in the large mirror fixed to the door. She turns to the side, admiring her left profile and then her right, poses with her chin on her shoulder, then contemplates her tan lines, the contrast of brown and white so pronounced that even naked it looks like she is wearing underwear. At the base of her spine, she is almost surprised to find that new behind which stretched her skin during the spring and left welts on her hips that she still hasn't gotten over. She checks her breasts too, but they have not grown much. So she goes back to eyeing her ass with base indulgence, trying out a few hip thrusts. She seduces her reflection, which is beautiful and carries no risk. She wishes she could take a photo. Soon she will have to go home and all this will disappear, the freckles and metamorphoses of July; she will return to Cornécourt and her daily life in its various shades of gray.

One day, she tells herself, she will have to earn loads of money too. Then she'll be beautiful all year round and she'll be able to live like these people who don't have to count their pennies and who know how the world works. But the fluorescent light above the mirror denounces a cluster of zits on her right temple. She leans over the sink, on tiptoe, to squeeze them. Then moves back. Red marks, a pinprick of blood, she's ruined everything. There are a few toiletries on the glass shelf, among them the father's shaving soap. Recognizing its familiar aroma, she opens the pot and breathes in. A strange sensation. Then she brings the bottle of Habit Rouge to her nostrils and inhales the smell of morning; all that's missing is a man's rough skin, the veiny hands, the hairy arms. She is overcome by a peculiar feeling, a mix of desire and disgust. She sprays some of the perfume onto her wrist to understand it better. Suddenly she freezes. Someone has knocked at the door.

"Hey...Charlotte and her mother have gone to the market. I'm going to the Super U to pick up groceries. Do you need anything?"

She quickly turns the tap on and rubs at her wrist with soap. The blood has rushed to her face and in her panic she can feel her forehead pouring with sweat, her hair becoming electric.

"Hélène?" says the big voice behind the door.

She tells him she doesn't need anything. She'll be out in a minute.

"So you won't be long?"

"No, no."

169

"Well, you can come with me then."

Yes, okay, she'd like that.

And so she finds herself in the Mercedes with the AC on full blast and goose bumps all over her skin. And that's when she asks the question that has been bothering her for so long: "What's an executive?"

Jean laughs. "Just someone whose job is to supervise other employees, his subordinates if you like. It's about having responsibilities, going to a lot of meetings, and being up to the task. What about you ... what do you want to do when you're older?"

"Like the baccalaureate, you mean?"

"No, after. At college."

Hélène has not really thought about this. The AC is making the air so cold now that she crosses her arms tight across her chest, presses her thighs together. Charlotte's father keeps his eyes on the road.

"I don't really know. Maybe law."

"Law can lead anywhere, but it's pretty useless. Everybody does law."

She is not entirely sure what he means by this. Where she comes from, the strategies are simple. If you work hard, you'll be successful. If you get good grades, you may be lucky enough to go to college. As far as her mother is concerned, notaries, court bailiffs, lawyers ... these are the best careers imaginable, because not only are they highly paid but they inspire a sort of awe in ordinary people.

Jean Brassard sweeps all these assumptions away with a few words. Even now, at high school, she needs to choose the right stream. The Bac L, with its literary slant? Forget it. Unless you want to be a teacher, of course. Afterward, you should avoid state universities at all costs. Unless you want to waste three years of your life doing nothing among a bunch of nobodies.

"My sister is an English teacher," he explains. "She's highly qualified, so she does okay financially, especially if you consider how few hours she works. But even so. She's been on anti-anxiety meds for the past two years. Earlier this year, one of the students called her a whore."

Hélène listens demurely as her friend's father tells her how things are. The first thing she needs to do is find an exclusive career path: competitive exams, preparatory classes, prestigious schools.

"You should take Greek and Russian. You'd be in a class of smart, hard workers. Emulation is important."

Later, in the aisles of the Super U, he continues to explain what she should and shouldn't do with her life, while she pushes the cart and he fills it. The conversation drifts naturally toward his own youth. From time to time, Hélène feels his arm touch hers and she hopes the contact is accidental, even if it is not exactly unpleasant. He grew up in Neufchâteau. His father was a civil engineer, and his grandfather a grammarian and high school teacher. There was no joking around for young Jean when it came to schoolwork. In fact there was no joking around in general. He took a preparatory class at the Poinca in Nancy, then went up to Paris. Like in that Barrès novel that no one reads anymore. He took law, of course, but luckily he was accepted at Sciences Po afterward—only it was Sciences Po Grenoble.

Hélène is completely lost. Poinca, civil engineering, grammarian, Barrès, Grenoble's inferiority to Paris...she has no idea what he's talking about. What she discovers in that supermarket full of tourists in flip-flops is a new language with a curious syntax that ranks and orders everything, its grammar carefully weighing every word.

Once the groceries are in the trunk of the car, Jean asks her if she'd like a drink. They still have a little time. He checks

171

his watch to confirm this. The brown leather wristband makes his hand look more adventurous, like something from an advertisement. Hélène knows that their new closeness is not altogether welcome, but she can't help enjoying this little bubble in which she is elevated to a queenlike status. They head toward a little café on the other side of the road, behind which is a stretch of sun-browned grass where some exotic animals are grazing, freshly released from the cages of a circus that has just set up camp there. Charlotte's father orders Perriers with slices of lemon and the two of them sit staring at the traffic, no longer saying much.

They sit there in the shade of an Orangina parasol, caught in eddies of heat, under the unrelenting hammer of noon, in the dust raised by passing cars. Nothing else is possible. Hélène doesn't dare look at him anymore. She feels like she's waiting for something. The moment lengthens. Finally a cloud moves in front of the huge sun, long enough for her to take a breath. The teenager feels her body relax a little and notices that her back is drenched with sweat.

"They should be back from the market by now," says Charlotte's father.

"Yeah."

"Ready to go?"

He's already on his feet, car key in hand. Hélène finishes her drink, then stands up, and, as they cross the road, Jean takes her hand. It lasts only a few seconds, and he does have the excuse of the busy road. As soon as they reach the other side, he lets go. But in Hélène's head, everything is muddled, unrecognizable.

"You okay?" he asks.

She nods. Abruptly she wishes it were December and she were wearing a thick sweater and boots, but the sun is at its zenith, on the most perfect day of the hottest month of the year. She gives a weak smile and gets into the large black sedan.

On the way back, they listen to the news. Michel Rocard, the penalty points system, and those names that she hears constantly and mixes up: Serbia, Bosnia, Montenegro, all these things that neither of them could give a shit about. Charlotte's father changes the station and they end up listening to religious music on France Musique. Hands joined in her lap, Hélène stares at her feet while sepulchral voices fill the car's refrigerated interior.

THE REST OF the vacation is passed pleasurably in the waves, each day the same, amid the growing melancholy of something coming toward its end.

Hélène begins avoiding Jean, who is clearly put out by her change in behavior. She can't stop thinking that she must have done something wrong. She fears he will trap her somewhere and give her a piece of his mind. One ugly word keeps bothering her: "cocktease." And yet she didn't do anything. Or let anything happen. Since there is nobody she can talk to about this, all these thoughts churn endlessly in her mind, producing waves of anger and traces of guilt.

Thankfully, she and Charlotte escape whenever possible, meeting up with the little gang on the beach every day. They spend their days playing paddle tennis, swimming in the sea, and laughing a lot about nothing very much, in a sort of intoxication. Occasionally, Angélique—a tall Parisian girl from the sixteenth arrondissement with ultra-short hair—turns up with her tarot cards and reads their futures. Often they don't even bother to eat. Cigarettes have replaced food, and Boris—the short guy who wears white polo shirts—continues to flirt lightly with Hélène, which she finds flattering and relaxing.

She and Charlotte spend hours lying on their towels, tanning their backs and then their fronts, and chatting away. Charlotte has just finished *Zoo Station: The Story of Christiane F.*, and is still in a state of shock. Hélène, meanwhile, is obsessed with *Belle du Seigneur*. She hasn't actually read it, but she loves the idea. Their French teacher had talked about it during the school year, making it clear that they were too young to read it, that the book was too difficult, too long and dense, too experimental for them. That was all it took to make her borrow it from the library. She has gotten stuck halfway through: some of the passages are completely incomprehensible. But it is so beautiful, all that passion, all that cruelty. In her mind, love is now partly associated with death. Which does not exactly encourage her to take the plunge.

On the last Friday of Hélène's stay, the two girls come back from the beach later than usual to find Charlotte's parents slumped in the living room. An empty bottle of white wine stands on the coffee table.

"So where did you go?" Nicole asks, her gaze slightly unfocused and a big smile plastered across her face.

There are snacks on the table too: anchovies and red mullet, cherry tomatoes, some bread and salted butter. Charlotte sits cross-legged on the carpet and butters a slice of bread.

"We lost track of time," she says before biting into her snack.

"Want a drink?" her father asks, grabbing the bottle of Viognier.

The two girls swap a look, both smiling. Nicole makes a show of protesting, but she doesn't really care.

At home in Épinal, among her books and plants, Charlotte's mother looks like one of those women in ads for anti-wrinkle creams, chic and healthy, a fifty-year-old woman shot in soft focus, gold bangles on her wrists, an eternal schoolgirl. But during this vacation, Hélène has noticed cracks in the veneer.

On several occasions after dinner, Nicole has downed so many glasses of white that she's had to be helped up to her bedroom. Each day, the morning after, she's looked like a freshly dug-up corpse, her skin a spiderweb of lines. But more strikingly, Hélène has caught the look on her face when she listens to her husband bragging, elaborating the theories he has about everything, making the same jokes he's been making for twenty-five years. It's as if an invisible rain clears away her usual expression, leaving behind an arid, bitter landscape. For the past two days, she hasn't even bothered going to the beach. She has stayed inside with her white and yellow books and her Marlboros, lying on the couch to read and listen to music.

"What's up with your mother?"

"Nothing, she just likes peace and quiet."

Both her daughter and her husband leave her to it. Hélène has looked at some of the books that Nicole spends her days reading: they are all novels, most of them French, many about unhappy women, motherhood, melancholy. It can't be that bad, she thinks, to be sad and rich, to lie on your couch and read stories about someone just like you.

"Anyway, we're not going to bother making dinner tonight," the father says.

"Maybe we'll take a shower first."

"Yeah, you go get freshened up and I'll open another bottle."

The two friends rush upstairs, Charlotte going first and stripping off in the hallway so she can beat Hélène to the bathroom.

Hélène is excited. She is eager to drink wine, to get drunk, even if she is a little fearful of the father's presence.

"Hey, don't take too long!" she shouts through the door at her friend.

Then she goes to their room and collapses onto the bed. There, she looks up at the ceiling, listening to the sounds of the shower on the other side of the hallway, before turning onto her stomach, knees bent, and breathing in the smell of the sheets, which have not been changed since the start of the vacation. Under Charlotte's bed, she spots an open bag and some books. She gets up to take a look at the books her friend has brought with her. And comes across a large, soft-cover journal. The lower corner of each used page has been torn off along a dotted line. Hélène flicks through it, hardly believing her eyes. Then her heart stops.

April 14: "Christophe came here yesterday. We did it again in my bed. Mmm. I think about him all the time. We watched *Dead Poets Society* while Mom was out. I think he liked it. The video is getting worn out. I told him I'd wear the same panties to his game and he laughed. I love him so much. I didn't do my math homework until really late. Exhausted and happy now."

Hélène keeps leafing through. The pages are filled with Charlotte's large, round handwriting. There are lots of exclamation points. She notes a sentence here and there. She's looking for her own name, but she's barely even mentioned.

March 19: "Today, I can say I feel comfortable in my own skin. I don't want to be someone else anymore. I don't care as much about being the best and I'm not constantly wondering what other people think of me. Christophe is always paying me compliments. I am filled with joy. It's just having to keep it secret that annoys me. That and his whore."

Below this, in red marker, is a couplet from the Salt-N-Pepa song "Let's Talk About Sex" and a big blue heart.

She can no longer hear water running in the bathroom. Hélène tries to tear herself away but the urge to keep reading is too strong. Her friend's journal is like a pack of candy that you eat in one go while swearing to yourself that each mouthful will be the last. She keeps turning to the next page, and then just one more ... A world has opened up before her, so luxuriant in its jungle-like horror, its malarial beauty, that it makes her head spin. She feels everything at once: wet, excited, lost. Suddenly she laughs. One page contains only the words: "Christophe is a bastard!" Written in three different colors of marker, at least it has the virtue of being clear.

Farther on, a day in May: "I've made my mind up: I'm not going to see him anymore. I'll express how I feel, think about myself. Have a HAPPY sex and love life. Say what I think, even if it hurts." And below this: "Thinking about Hélène's birthday. Ideas: the little bracelet from L'Oiseau Bleu (expensive), or chocolates (basic), or take her the VHS of *Rain Man* (Tom Cruise—heart)."

On the other side of the hallway, the bathroom door opens. Hélène rushes to put the journal back under the bed. Kneeling on the floor, she slips it into the bag where she found it.

"Your turn."

Charlotte has just come into their bedroom, accompanied by the pleasant smell of shower gel and clean hair. She finishes drying herself in the doorway, her torso wrapped inside a long pink bath towel, her feet bare, no longer innocent. Hélène looks at her with a curious mix of admiration and bitterness.

"Get a move on," says her friend, who has already sat on the bed to put her panties on.

"I'm going," says Hélène.

"What's wrong?"

"Nothing."

Hélène is a really bad liar. She becomes instantly embarrassed, shifty-eyed. She rushes out of the bedroom before another question puts her on the spot. In the shower stall, the hot water pours hard on her salt-encrusted hair. Ideas whirl around her head. She is furious with herself for not having guessed, for having been so naive. She is furious with Charlotte too. But what she feels above all is an all-consuming curiosity. She needs to find a way to keep reading that journal.

"Come on, girls! If you don't get downstairs soon, the bottle will be empty."

THEY OPEN THREE more bottles that evening. Soon, the light-filled living room grows blurred and cocoon-like, and Charlotte's parents become different people, charming and unfiltered, full of anecdotes and opinions. Above the bottle-strewn table they exchange *Do you remember when*s and *Oh that reminds me*s. The wine makes them more loquacious, but it also provides them with a very easy audience. Hélène laughs too much and stuffs herself with bread and anchovy paste, popping cherry tomatoes and cubes of Comté into her mouth one after another. Not to be outdone, Charlotte continually provokes her father, fills their glasses, raises her eyebrows knowingly at Hélène. Much later, Nicole decides to put some music on. She even dances a little bit, before suddenly going quiet and glassy-eyed. Around one in the morning, she says it's time to get some sleep and, after a few protests, the girls go upstairs to brush their teeth and get ready for bed. Charlotte, even more ham-mered than her friend, wants to keep chatting awhile longer. She laughs into her pillow a few times before falling fast asleep.

Inside the summer home with its white walls and blue shut-ters, everything is calm once again. Under the bedroom door, Hélène sees the hallway light come on, then go off. She recog-nizes the mother's footsteps, then Jean's heavier breathing, his weight making the floorboards creak. At last there is silence. Sleep descends upon her ten minutes later with the sudden-ness of a general anesthetic.

But around three in the morning, she wakes with a dry mouth. She feels as though she's barely slept at all. For a moment she just lies there, torn between inertia and the need to pee, then she gets out of bed. Standing up is even worse. The blood pulses under her scalp, her brain hurts, and her mouth tastes like something has died in there. Close by, Charlotte is practically snoring, like some hibernating animal. Hélène takes a step toward her and whispers: "Hey! Are you asleep?"

Leaning closer, she recognizes the scent of her friend's hair mingled with her stale, boozy breath. And the furnace heat rising toward her face.

"Hey," she says again.

When Charlotte does not respond, Hélène kneels down and touches her thigh through the sheet. Nothing. So she lies flat on the floor and reaches under the bed for the journal. She can feel her heart drumming against the floorboards. Her bladder is a knot of pain as her fingers grope around, finding nothing but fabric, dust, an indeterminate mass of stuff. And then she has it. She grabs the journal, clambers to her feet, and slips the book into the elastic band of her boxer briefs before draping the edge of her T-shirt over it and leaving the room on tiptoe. Then she goes silently downstairs, simultaneously meticulous and hurried, and shuts herself in the first-floor bathroom, taking care to bolt the door behind her. She turns on the light and, finally secure, sits down to read her best friend's journal and take a really long pee.

"Strep throat. I watched *The Umbrellas of Cherbourg*. Beautiful but depressing."

(in red ink): "Don't cry! Look at me. People only die of a broken heart in movies."

"Thinking about Christophe. His body drives me crazy."

"Mom told me to pick up my room even though I've got a fever and I ache all over. She was in one of those horrible moods that make me so sad. But I'm seeing Christophe tomorrow. At times I want him so much it makes me shake."

Farther on:

"I think I'm getting depressed. Christophe is cold and distant. He spends all his time at the rink or with his skank. I cried last night, and this morning too, when I woke. I feel so **TIRED**, I'm sick of it. Hélène has borrowed my red Lacoste sweater. She's always taking stuff from me and I'm too scared to say no."

Hélène flips backward, searching for the moment when it all started. On December 7, she finds this:

"At lunchtime I was alone in the lobby and Christophe Marchal looked me in the eye. I didn't know what the hell to do with myself. We bumped into each other three more times today. Hélène says I'm imagining it all. She's probably right. Anyway, I'm going to bed to think about it."

A few days later: "I kept nagging Mom and finally convinced her about the Docs. After three weeks! But she doesn't want Hélène to stay here next weekend because she came for St. Nicholas. That pisses me off."

The minutes pass and Hélène reconstructs the whole story, piece by piece. Christophe was prowling around her friend and she never even realized. Then one day, he went to her house. Charlotte knew he was dating that horrible punk girl, Charlie, but she let it happen anyway. No doubt she was flattered. And consumed by desire. Hélène herself feels something as she reads those pages that reveal what happened in plain language. The journal is full of short sentences with the power of detonators. "He tried to get in but it hurt and I said no," "His body is so beautiful." The words "hand job" repeated ten times around the edges of a page, like a garland, with hearts and miniature dicks in yellow highlighter. Conjugations of certain English words ("I lick, you lick, he/she licks, they lick, we lick..."), a photograph of Jim Morrison, *Paris sous les bombes*, "Chic lingerie, it's the snap of a suspender."

From late December, the same phrase keeps coming back: "I want to fuck." No frills.

Sometimes there are dramas, arguments, the end of the world summarized in four or five words. He's such a dickhead. He doesn't understand anything. He's going to dump her. His whore is manipulating him. And then the victorious hockey games, newspaper cuttings of results or black-and-white photos, *Cosmo* advice columns on how to achieve orgasm during sex, passages about Hélène, the best friend, adored or badmouthed by Charlotte depending on how she feels, Hélène, with whom she wishes she could talk about all this, but she's promised Christophe she'll keep it a secret. So she keeps her mouth shut, and the secret is the great wonder of her life, the pulsating heart of her sixteen-year-old existence. On every page there's desire, longing, schoolwork getting in the way, her unbearable parents, hearts, *I love you*s, *I'm crying*s, *sick of it*s, and *his whore*s, and pride at games won, in capital letters with rows of exclamation points. Most of all, though, there are detailed descriptions of his dick, his abs, his thighs, making out, sex that doesn't last long enough because he never has time, he always has to go to practice or see his whore. Or because he comes too quickly.

Forearms leaning on her thighs, her head buzzing, Hélène devours this multicolored chronicle. She creases the pages, goes back and forth in time. Her friend is there, recognizable in every line and, at the same time, horribly unfamiliar. Hélène hates her and envies her. As she reads, it seems to her that they are *her* hands, *her* mouth, on Christophe, that this love affair should have been hers.

But the spell is broken by a banal sound. Someone knocking at the door. Brought back to reality, Hélène presses the journal to her chest and holds her breath as she waits to see what will happen next.

"You okay?" murmurs a sleepy voice behind the door.

Hélène pulls up her boxer briefs and slips the journal into the back of them.

"It's me," breathes the voice that she doesn't recognize.

"It's occupied," she replies.

"Hélène?" says the voice.

A man's voice, very quiet.

The handle turns and, from the sound the door makes in the doorframe, Hélène guesses he's pushing it with his shoulder. It's all so quiet, but he is there, with his strength, his weight, his owner's rights.

Hélène turns to look at the small window. But she can hardly start running through the streets in the middle of the night...

The handle turns again. The floorboards creak, then she hears the heavy presence move away. After a moment, she takes two steps toward the sink and turns off the light switches. The hallway is plunged into darkness. Not a sound. A few more seconds pass, stretched out and speculative, and Hélène feels something brush past her back. She presses her hands to her mouth to stifle a scream and turns on her heels, her body shuddering, but finds nothing behind her but the darkness and the silence. She thinks about her parents then. She thinks about her parents, but they are so far away and she feels so small all of a sudden. Perhaps this is what growing up is—discovering that you are just a kid and that the world is a frightening, dangerous place. A minute passes. It feels like an hour. Motionless, Hélène gradually reassures herself. She even dares drink some water from the tap, in the dark, and it's crazy how much better the coldness of the water makes her feel.

In this house that has grown so strange, she listens out for the slightest sound, seeks the smallest sign of a presence.

But there's nothing, nothing but her fear, which is starting to fade now. So she slides the bolt across, steps timidly into the hallway, and begins to chide herself for being such a fool. What was she so afraid of? Like a mouse, she quickly, quietly climbs the stairs, hunched up small in the darkness. She opens the bedroom door, which emits its treacherous diagonal creak, then rushes to her bed and buries herself under the sheet. There, in that bubble of safety, in that cotton tent, she can finally catch her breath. There's a creaking noise in the dividing wall, rising up to the roof, as if the room around her has a cramp and is stretching its muscles. She jumps, then snorts at her own cowardice.

It is then that the bedroom door is quietly opened.

Once again, fear pins her down, as heavy as cement. Barely two meters from where she lies she can make out the shape of that adult body, its strength, its gaze. Her heart is pounding so hard she can almost hear it. The girl hugs the journal to her chest, reflexively praying to it, begging its forgiveness, making every promise she can think of. Then, at last, the door closes and she is left with nothing but a dizzy nausea, a breathlessness, a buzzing between her temples. She weeps into her pillow then, with relief, the journal still clutched to her chest.

The next day, none of this is mentioned. Hélène slips the journal into Charlotte's bag, then eats breakfast with the whole family, feeling oddly numb. There are croissants and baguettes, and the coffee tastes the same as it did on all the other days. The only difference is that she sits at the other side of the table, as far away as she can get from her friend's father.

9

IT HAD BEEN a good day's work.

In the space of less than a hundred kilometers, Christophe had managed to visit three farmers, including two new prospects who had been happy to sign an exclusivity agreement. This was far from a sure thing, given the crappy freebies he had to offer them: a CaniGood jacket and two plastic food bowls. Another two like that and he would meet his quality target for the year. But his problem remained the same: the quantity target for cat food. A fifteen percent increase ... were the guys at HQ off their heads? All the salespeople agreed it was crazy. Some even suspected the figure was a trick, designed to prevent them landing the bonus that, in the best-case scenario, represented an extra quarter's salary. The staff representatives on the works council had stirred up discontent among the troops. But the only result had been a memo reaffirming the target, assuring employees that it was perfectly attainable, and announcing a new targeted advertising campaign to be launched in the coming weeks. They had two months to meet the expected figures and the sales manager, Serge Pelekian, was confident.

"Bullshit. They're going to screw us over like they did last year."

"Yeah, half the guys came up short. They don't give a fuck about us."

"And you, what do you think?"

"Well, yeah," Christophe said, more out of politeness than anything else.

Beside the coffee machine, in the warehouses, by text, the discontent grew. Some even talked about organizing blockades, work slowdowns, stirring up trouble for management. Christophe just followed the general drift, his mind elsewhere. In the end, whatever happened, he always managed to hit his targets.

CaniGood had two manufacturing plants on French territory, plus a sales force of almost two hundred people and a dozen distribution centers. It was in those centers that the traveling salesmen met, with their white station wagons, their cheerful dispositions, their bellies bulging from too many restaurant meals. Very few women worked this job—there was only one of them at CaniGood—and nobody over fifty. The men bumped into each other while working, went to the offices to say a quick hello and pick up the products and goodies they needed, then exchanged a few words in a corner, near the loading zone, smoking and vaping in a circle, hand in pocket, looking relaxed and confident, in shirt and jeans, sometimes in a suit but that was unusual. They used these chance encounters to catch up, talking about their families, the vacations they had planned, sharing recommendations—for a roadside restaurant where the salt pork was excellent—and, above all, to complain: about working conditions, clients, targets, management, logistical problems, strategic screwups, and all those shareholders in

Miami who didn't lift a finger while there they were racking up two hundred fifty kilometers a day easy.

Not only that but, since the regional merger, HQ had decided to reorganize their sphere of operation. Instead of covering two departments, a salesman would soon be stuck with four. Behind all these euphemistic expressions—"reorganizing spheres of operation," "pooling resources," "resizing areas of expertise"—CaniGood was only ever seeking to generate additional margins, since the business was barely growing. The employees moaned about it quietly, interminably, mingling the vocabulary of the hierarchy with ideas aimed at causing it harm. This was how they defended themselves, with their powerless, schizophrenic language, unable to comprehend that in a mature market they were now the only margin that could still be compressed, the only raw material whose price could go down, a cost doomed to erosion. So they kept driving ever greater distances, struggling constantly to meet ever less realistic targets, seeing their slender benefits stolen from them one by one in the name of justice and equality, progressing ever farther in that curious mechanism where every step forward was translated into a step back, where every innovation gave rise to more archaic relations, where future profits could be secured only by drastic belt-tightening.

But things weren't really all that bad, and Christophe had had a good day. After seeing his three farmers, he'd still had time to call on Gamm Vert in Corcieux to launch the final-quarter special operation. The woman at the store was nice: she'd bought him a coffee and given him a hand putting his signs in place. At four, he'd paid a flying visit to Dr. Désirant, a vet from Vittel to whom he had promised some hockey tickets. Veterinarians were still his best promotional outlet, since they were in a position to pass off any old dog or cat biscuits as a form of treatment. It was thanks to them that Christophe was starting to develop the CaniHealth range, an assemblage of vitamins, vegetables, and "best quality" chicken supposed to keep the animals in perfect health and to solve their kidney problems. This segment had seen a fifteen percent rise in sales over the last eighteen months, even though the price had gone up twenty percent. Proof that you could always hope to extract some unexpected profit as long as customers didn't read the small print. One day, he thought, they would eke out the last percentiles by selling the promise of degrowth.

But, whatever, it was with a feeling of having done his duty for the day that Christophe went to Épinal for his first date with Hélène.

They had been messaging each other a lot lately, swapping memories, sharing the image they'd had of each other when they were young. The past was their opportunity. She had stroked his ego. And then they had talked about their current lives, first in an overly positive and optimistic way, before confessing some less idyllic details. At their age—close to forty—it was hard to admit, but the truth was that the future no longer belonged to them in quite the same way, and that the passing years had left their mark. Without going into too much detail, they had surreptitiously shown each other their scars, the simple bruises and blows of fate that were a feature of almost everyone's life. Work, parents, kids, love, all the intimate crap that never goes well for anyone. And then, since Christophe could not make up his mind, Hélène had taken the initiative of organizing a meeting. It was obviously not a good idea to meet in Nancy, and she insisted that they find somewhere quiet and discreet where there was no risk of bumping into someone they knew.

Hélène's marital situation had never come up during their conversations, but her Instagram account did not leave much doubt on that score. There were numerous photographs showing her on vacation—in Dordogne, in Vietnam—with a man, always the same one. He was well-built, curly dark hair, not bad-looking, although there was a sort of mocking glint in his eye. You could also see two little girls whose growth could be monitored over time. Other images showed Hélène's favorite architectural styles, gourmet meals, some street art, big mirrors in gilt frames, several interchangeable friends, and a few brief indignant comments. In all honesty, though, Christophe had spent the most time looking at a photo of her in a swimsuit. Hélène seemed to have nice legs and a great ass. He was starting to really like her.

So Christophe went to Le Casque d'Or, a cheap restaurant located in the shadow of the basilica in Épinal, where the air smelled faintly of grease but where you could still buy a beer for less than two euros. It wasn't exactly chic, but it met all Hélène's criteria and Christophe went there pretty often. He had a satisfied feeling as he walked into that familiar decor, the mosaic floor and Formica tables, the industrial-sized percolator and the upside-down bottles of spirits. Not to mention, in front of the enormous mirror, the row of classic Monin syrups like a rainbow-colored pipe organ.

He chose a table at the back. He usually came here to fill out his expenses claims and client reports. Joss, a tall, stringy woman whose voice sometimes reminded him of Claudia Cardinale's, called out her usual "What will it be?" and Christophe ordered a coffee and a glass of water.

It was Joss who kept the heart of this half-dead dive bar beating, with her tireless zeal, her constant hygiene obsession (which explained the faint odor of bleach and the relentless wiping of surfaces), and her dictatorial authority over the regulars—mostly old men whose drinking habits and medications she kept a close eye on, a few lawyers from the nearby courthouse who came here for a quiet drink, some street peddlers on market days, a thirsty mailman or two, and, of course, a handful of genuine drunkards, anxious wrecks who knew they could take refuge there on their thirstiest days. Sitting at the bar, or at a table in a dark corner, these men would order golden-colored drinks, glasses of wine or something stronger, quickly knocking back two or three, in their crumpled jackets and their shining skin. She watched over them like those spectral, touching creatures that you see in aquariums. From time to time, one of the stools would remain empty for a few days. A regular was no longer with us.

Christophe had been coming to Le Casque d'Or for years, always alone. He had discovered this haven just before Gabriel's birth, and it had become his womb while Charlie's expanded. Many was the time she had asked to come with him, but he had always refused.

It was funny, thinking back to that now. He had been crazy for that girl as soon as he met her, infatuated like a kid, his love for her drowning out everything else and making him do the stupidest things. God, he had worked so hard to get her. Charlie was older than him, and at the time she had seemed to belong to a completely different world. At fifteen, she was already going to gigs, hanging out with a whole tribe of weirdos that included skinheads and punks, all of them lefties in leather jackets or bomber jackets who listened to the same grunge rock. She had been smoking since seventh grade and in the playground she would read books by dropout American writers like London and Kerouac. And while most kids her age had to fight for the right to be allowed out until midnight, she was already in the habit of going to clubs and sleeping at friends' houses whenever she felt like it.

Between fourteen and twenty-five their relationship had been on-again off-again, but, through it all, everyone considered them a couple. She lived in one of those little houses in

Saut-le-Cerf, with her grandparents, who were easygoing and spent their time playing French tarot at a neighbor's house. There had been afternoons in her attic room, the first unbridled sex sessions, that stunned amazement at all the stuff they could do, the other's body as new as a PlayStation under the Christmas tree, licking each other from lips to legs, the sweat, the fluids, the twisted sheets, take me, bite me, don't let me go. And then after two wild, obscene hours, during which he never lost his hard-on, they found themselves in surprise, soaked with sweat, staring at the ceiling, with her smoking a cigarette and asking: "How are you feeling?" And of course he was feeling horny so they went at it again until they heard the front door opening downstairs and they just had time to get dressed, the clothes sticking to their salt-scented skin, and to turn the TV on as if all they'd done was watch it. "Haven't you even been out in this lovely weather?" the grandmother would ask. And: "Are you hungry?" Yes, they were starving, and in the kitchen they would stuff themselves with supermarket-brand pains au chocolat and look at each other with sparkling eyes.

Overall, though, they probably spent more time fighting than fucking. He had his practice sessions; she had the friends she didn't want him to meet. They were grown men who drove crappy cars and took her to gigs in remote villages in the Vosges or Haute-Saône, to weird parties in warehouses or under bridges. He'd even found Ecstasy tabs in the pocket of her jeans. Once, while he was on a hockey trip to Prague, Christophe had gone to a whorehouse with some other players and of course Charlie had found out. In retaliation, she had headbutted him and given him the silent treatment for two months.

But what distinguished Charlie above all back then were her depressions. There was something dark inside that girl that blotted out all the light around her.

"What do you want to do?"

"I don't know, what about you?"

"Nothing."

And then, after ten minutes of silence and sighing, while she pretended to tidy up her room, she would tell him to fuck off. He would take his scooter and ride home, sulking, knowing full well what was going to happen next. She would call her friend at the café, Natacha, to arrange something with those other sons of bitches—Keuss, Karim, little Thierry—those unemployed guys who were permanently drunk or stoned and who spent all day spouting their stupid losers' wisdom. Christophe imagined them in a Renault 5 by the side of a road, smoking weed, laughing, squeezed close together, the windows steamed up. Maybe they were even making out. Or worse.

Back then, Christophe was also involved with little Charlotte Brassard, so cute and clean in comparison. She worshipped him, and her constant availability compensated him for Charlie's ever-changing moods. With hindsight, it seemed to him that he'd had a strange youth, like the view from the window of a train, one of those landscapes blurred by speed where you can't really focus on anything. Hockey always came first, anyway.

After taking her baccalaureate, and passing it at the first attempt, Charlie had gone to Dijon, where her father lived, to study sociology in college. He'd had to retake his year and they hadn't seen each other except by chance, often during the holidays, when she came back to visit her grandparents. The two of them would stop then, on the sidewalk or in an aisle at Monoprix, and look all embarrassed. *How's it going? Great. What are you up to?*

Those haphazard reunions always left Christophe vaguely troubled. He felt only irritated by what remained of the teenage girl she had been: her eyes like little stones on a river-bed, her perfect skin, almost yellow, the ebullient, mischievous part of her personality, her small breasts under her T-shirt, hardly ever confined inside a bra. But what had changed hurt him even more: the high-heeled shoes that had replaced her Converse sneakers, the jewelry, the polite friendliness that had smoothed over that deep furrow between her eyebrows, the way she seemed like a woman now, an adult mostly rec-onciled to the way things were. Each time, he learned a little more about her life. She had gone to college, dropped out, worked here and there, then gone back to school to become a graphic designer, like everyone else. When they went their separate ways, it took all the willpower Christophe had not to turn around in the street and check out her ass.

And then one day she came back to Cornécourt for good, to be closer to her grandmother, who was not getting any younger. After that, things moved forward easily. They were not yet thirty, just starting out in their careers, had a bit of money, each with their own car and apartment, a life that seemed free. They went out to restaurants and movies, they made love and found, in each other's presence, a sort of peaceful com-fort that needed no words, where one moment smoothly gave way to another. They would simply make a quick phone call at the end of the day to decide whether to spend the evening together or not. Often they would just eat lasagna or a salad in front of the TV. They would watch American cop shows or travel documentaries. When her car broke down, he started driving her around. In winter they went snowshoeing in the Vosges, ate hearty potato dishes in mountain restaurants, be-fore emerging hours later, red-faced and half-drunk. The bal-cony of Charlie's apartment overlooked the Moselle and they would invite friends there, eating plum tarts in fall, spending the winter playing *Crash Bandicoot* on an old games console that Christophe had found at his dad's house. Charlie listened as he told her about his working days at the Renault garage near the exhibition center, then his problems with the staff at the Hotel Campanile, where he briefly worked as a manager. She was there to support him when he bought the old café in the Galerie Saint-Joseph, which had of course failed, since nothing lasted long in that tunnel of doomed businesses. In fact, all the stores in the city center appeared as if they were caught in a heat haze; you expected to see them vanish at any moment, leaving a gap, an empty storefront, while customers rushed to the signs proliferating on the periphery, with their shitty products and their infinite parking lots. During that period, Christophe went through job after job, almost one per year, until he decided he'd had enough. He then used his unemployment benefit to support him while he did some thinking, taking the time to consider his future.

Money worries soon arose, however, and Charlie solved the problem by finding them a two-bedroom apartment in Cornécourt, where they moved in together in May. The night of their housewarming party, she didn't drink and everyone understood why. Marco took Christophe in his arms to congratulate him. The idiot was close to tears. Happiness had sneaked up on them. He had to look at old photographs to see it again now.

It was soon after this that Christophe got a job at Cani-Good and began spending his evenings at Le Casque d'Or. This place became his sanctuary. He didn't drink, just passed his time contemplating the destinies that had washed up there. They were all so happy to sit on a stool, to lean their elbows on a bar, to find an ear into which they could pour their simple thoughts about the weather or the Rio-Paris flight that had crashed in the ocean. Christophe listened to those husky or reedy voices, the rattle of dice and the questionable jokes, the silences like a pause in the too-brief day; it was a conservatory of pain, with a deep calm at its core.

Elsewhere, everyone urged him to be a man, soon a father, to be punctual and meet his targets. All day long, he felt like an instrument in someone else's hand, a device that made things work. This yoke was something he could neither name nor escape. But one thing about it was sure: it was the opposite of youth. At least at Le Casque d'Or, there was no road map. The machine ceased its clatter for an hour. It left him in peace.

Even so, when he saw Hélène come through the door, the bell ringing cheerfully, Christophe was seized by doubt. Maybe this wasn't exactly the kind of place a woman like her would appreciate. And the cloud he saw pass over her face did nothing to reassure him.

"Will this do?" he asked while she sat down facing him.

"Yeah, yeah, it's good."

And she gratified him with a big smile that swept away his anxiety.

"Did you find it okay?"

"Yeah. I know my way around here, believe it or not."

It was his turn to smile, although he didn't know what he could say to that. Joss had already come over, hands on hips, an amused expression on her face.

"So what will it be?"

"A Coke Zero," said Hélène, raising one eyebrow politely.

Joss repeated the order aloud and went back to the bar. It was warm in the café and Hélène seemed at ease. Behind her, a couple were drinking hot chocolate. At the bar, the lawyer Cécile Clément ordered a glass of white wine to recover from a particularly rough hearing, which she recounted in minute detail to two other regulars. The first of them, Nénesse, lived close by and hardly ever left the café. A skinny man who wore too much cologne, he had graying, slicked-back hair and baggy pants. The other was younger and wore his shirtsleeves rolled up; he kept sniffing and nodding vehemently in agreement. He knew the courthouse well. Bastard cops, corrupt judges. Nénesse was content to listen while taking tiny sips from his glass of Anjou.

All of this formed a useful backdrop. Silences could pass for curiosity. Hélène made a few complimentary remarks. For her, this place was pretty exotic.

"I don't have much time," she said then, still smiling.

This was not wholly true. The girls had a babysitter and Philippe was spending the night in Strasbourg. But by looking at her watch, she was preparing an escape plan.

All the same, she felt quite relaxed in this place. It was six-thirty. Soon they'd be able to drink an aperitif without having to make excuses. And Christophe was eyeing her with evident pleasure. When he asked if she would like something else to drink, she nodded happily and he ordered two Chouffes. The beer's generous flavor went well with the mood of the bar and, as soon as she took her first mouthful, Hélène felt lighter. The door opened every few minutes, revealing new customers, and behind her the other conversations created a warm, cushioned background noise. Turning around, she noted a few faces. There was an ogre-like salesman with a garnet nose, a service manager with a gleaming face whose physiognomy reminded her faintly of a cephalopod, two court ushers who might easily have been sisters, and a man on his own, as tall and stooped as a Giacometti, well-known to everyone in this town, where he worked as a drawing teacher. He attended all the exhibitions for local artists and in June he organized some curious viola da gamba concerts in the ruins of the old castle. He was an artist, in other words, who lived with his mother and whose only escape was Le Casque d'Or. Hélène felt as if she were inside a Flemish painting. Returning her gaze to Christophe, she noticed that he was still staring at her.

"What?"

"Nothing."

But she felt beautiful and his answer told her all she needed to know.

"And Charlotte?"

"What about Charlotte?"

"Have you seen her since then?"

"Never," Christophe replied.

She admitted that she'd known about their affair at the time. In saying this, she sensed she was luring him to the other side, to the side of secrets and skin. Le Casque d'Or was becoming their island. They were castaways.

"She was supposed to keep that to herself," Christophe grumbled.

"She never told me about it, the bitch! But I found her journal."

Christophe burst out laughing and took another swig of beer.

"And what did it say?"

"Lots of things. It was pretty detailed, actually."

"Really?"

She responded with a raised eyebrow heavy with insinuations, and Christophe looked thrilled. In the smile that lit up his face, she saw again the teenager he had once been, so cute and fought-over.

"I was madly jealous at the time."

"Oh?"

"Yeah, I mean it was *really* detailed. It turned me on."

"What sorts of details?"

"About her coming..."

196

She accompanied this revelation with a vaguely orgasmic expression and Christophe, flattered, pretended to be embarrassed.

"I wasn't fucking at all back then. I was really uptight."

"That's not how I remember it," said Christophe.

Now it was Hélène's turn to playact. Of course she remembered that night after the exams, at the Stade de la Colombière.

"Hey! Hello?"

Hélène and Christophe turned at the same time toward the bar owner, who was shouting at them and snapping her fingers, a telephone in her other hand.

"Your wife's trying to get hold of you."

"My wife?" Christophe said.

He rummaged around in his bag for his cell phone and saw that Charlie had left several messages.

"Sorry. It's my son's mother."

"Problem?" asked Hélène.

"I don't know."

He stood up to grab the phone from the owner and everyone in the bar saw his face fall as he listened to the voice at the other end. When he handed the phone back to Joss, his hand was shaking slightly.

"I have to go. I'm sorry."

His whole appearance had dramatically changed. He was pale now, hesitant, and as he picked up his bag he knocked over a glass, which smashed into pieces on the floor. Everyone was staring at him. He began searching his pockets in the hope of finding his wallet, so Hélène took his wrist in her hand.

"Leave it. I'll take care of it."

"I'm really sorry," he said again.

"It's fine, don't worry."

And he left the café without another word, without a smile, clutching his bag and his coat to his chest.

IT TOOK CHRISTOPHE more than twenty minutes to drive the five kilometers that separated him from his father's house. It was the worst possible time: right in the middle of rush hour. Every day, the same traffic jams blocked the same roads. He kept honking his horn and at one point risked his life in a bend just to save a few extra seconds. He didn't know what made him feel more pressured, the situation itself or Charlie's reproaches about it.

As he came closer, he recognized the Golf parked outside the house. Even from a distance, he could tell that his ex was furious. He parked the station wagon close by and heard a door slam. Then he went out to meet her in the evening cold. Wisps of steam flew from their mouths. Even the wind seemed tense.

"So?" said Charlie.

"I don't understand. They should be here. I told Gabriel this morning when I dropped him at school. And I left a note for my father."

"I've been ringing the bell for ten minutes. I called him on his cell phone about twenty times. He's not answering. I didn't even understand the message on his voicemail."

Charlie's arms were crossed and she was shivering.

"They must have gone for a walk in the woods," said Christophe.

"In November? At night? What the fuck."

"I'm sure they didn't go far."

"How many times have I told you not to leave him with your dad anymore?"

Christophe fell into a sheepish silence for a moment. Above them, the sky was empty, and the only source of light was the dim ceiling lamp in the 308. They were scared.

"Well..." Charlie said.

"Wait here, I'll be back in a minute. We can take my car."

Christophe ran to the house and came back soon afterward carrying a big flashlight. Then they got into the station wagon and set off. The child and his grandfather liked going for walks in a nearby part of the forest. They got there in less than ten minutes and Christophe parked on the patch of gravel that served as a parking space for hunters. He had hoped to find his father's van there, but it wasn't.

"They must have come on foot."

"But what the hell would they be doing here at this time of night?"

"They scatter corn, to attract game."

"Ugh, hunting again!"

"The kid loves it."

"I know. We've talked about that before too."

They walked along the narrow dirt path through the trees that the old man and his grandson usually took. Christophe went first. His father liked to teach Gabriel the names of mushrooms, animals, and birds, and how to recognize a creature by its tracks; Christophe had no idea about any of that stuff. As soon as the season began, the two of them would start to hunt game. In his younger days, Gérard had been part of the hunting club, but his financial situation no longer allowed him to pay his yearly dues. Shopkeepers, as everyone knew, did not have generous pensions. On top of that, he had suffered several setbacks with the rental property he had invested in to give him an income in his old age.

Gérard had poured most of his savings into an apartment building on the edge of Cornécourt, on the Chantraine road, midway between the Leclerc supermarket and the municipal swimming pool. The location was good: a former office building transformed into two one-bedroom apartments and one two-bedroom. He had chosen his tenants carefully, opting for young couples who were solvent with promising careers. Unfortunately, appearances could be deceptive, and two of the three apartments had been occupied for three years without his receiving a single euro in rent. Meanwhile he still had to keep paying property tax and overheads every month. He had done everything he could think of to pull himself out of this mire: letters sent by registered mail, bailiffs, visits to the police station, threatening phone calls. He had even had the outside shutters removed, hiring some tough travelers to carry out this task. None of it had worked. In the end, he'd had to start a fire. The firefighters had arrived quickly, but the insurance company lawyers had found some clauses in his contract that damaged his case. By the time the dust had settled, he had lost close to two hundred thousand euros, not to mention all the rent that the apartment building had been intended to produce.

There had been a series of other misfortunes, then a cascade of catastrophes when Sylvie was diagnosed with cancer. After a life of unremitting hard work, he now found himself choosing the cheapest laundry detergent at the supermarket or calculating how many liters of heating oil he could afford to keep him going through the winter.

All these tribulations had left him embittered toward his homeland. Politicians, cops, judges, insurance companies...he considered them all untrustworthy. Same thing for social security, pension funds, government welfare, all of which seemed designed to help only work-shy slackers and immigrants, even if all they knew how to do was burn cars, rape girls, and beat up bus drivers. And every day, he would fan the fire of his resentment by watching certain news channels that confirmed his intuitions and drove his ideas toward the extremes. His life felt pleasureless now, choked with disappointment, stretching out interminably into growing darkness, and yet he clung to it all the same.

Because of the kid. The two of them had fun together. Especially when they went hunting in the woods or played card games.

"Maybe we could try calling out to them," said Charlie. "We're not going to find them like this."

She and Christophe had been walking for quite a while, not speaking, listening to the cracking of twigs under their feet, eyes scanning the beam of light ahead of them. Charlie called out her son's name now and it echoed through the trees. Christophe did the same. Then he called out to his father:

"Da-ad!"

He sounded pathetic, he knew, as if he himself had become a kid again, calling out for help. Around them the forest seemed to grow bigger, darker, alive with menace. He kept staring into the flashlight beam. When he tried calling again, Christophe felt his voice die in his throat. Charlie's shoulder pressed against his.

"Where the hell are they?"

"They can't have gone far. It'll be okay."

"We should go to the police station."

But they didn't. They kept walking, shouting out "Gabriel" and "Dad" on a regular basis, despite the forest's stubborn silence. As they advanced, the black smell of earth grew more intense, as did the squelching sound made by the drenched leaves underfoot, the dull plop of raindrops falling from tree branches onto their shoulders. Now and then they would feel the cold at the backs of their necks like a stranger's gaze.

Charlie nestled into him and he put an arm around her. Both of them were thinking about their son, imagining his little body amid the dark disorder of the woods, his tears in the night, all alone. They imagined his snowballing fear and then it was theirs too. Christophe hugged her tight.

"Did you hear that?"

They froze, listening, staring into the darkness for a sign. Was that a voice behind them? Or perhaps it was just the wind, playing tricks on them. As soon as they paid attention to it, the silence broke down into an infinity of tiny noises, deceptive whispers. Christophe swept the flashlight through the darkness around them. But it was Charlie who spotted them first. Gérard was holding a small flashlight in his right hand and Gabriel's hand in his left. A plastic bucket hung from his arm.

"Where the hell have you been?"

They rushed over. Fear was already giving way to anger.

"What do you mean?" replied the old man, pouring out the rest of the corn at the base of a tree.

"We've been looking everywhere for you. Do you know what time it is? What the hell were you doing in the woods at night? And I told you his mother was coming to get him."

The old man stood silent, waiting for the storm to pass, then shrugged before tapping the bottom of the bucket to make sure it was empty. Charlie, meanwhile, had knelt down and was holding Gabriel tightly in her arms.

"Are you okay, baby?"

The child, who was hugging his mother back, kissed her on the forehead as if blessing her.

"Yes, I'm okay."

"Are you sure?"

"Of course, everything's fine," the grandfather replied cheerfully.

Even so, Charlie could see traces of tears on her son's face. Gabriel sniffed but smiled reassuringly. Everything was fine.

"Well, come on then. We're not going to stay here all night, are we?"

The old man led them back toward the gravel parking space. Christophe, bringing up the rear of their procession, wondered what would have happened if the batteries in his father's flashlight had gone flat... Better not to think about it. At last they reached the station wagon and Christophe asked his father what he had done with his van.

"It's at the house," the old man said.

"No it's not. It's not at home and it's not here. So where is it?"

His father's mouth trembled silently. Then, unable to find an answer to this question, he turned to the boy.

"Come on, he's exhausted. Let's just go home."

It was true: Gabriel looked pale and drawn, and his teeth were chattering. Christophe sighed and they all got in the car. On the way back, nobody spoke, but everyone knew where they stood. The boy fell asleep, head tilted sideways and mouth hanging open, and Charlie, unable to stand it any longer, leaned toward the passenger seat and asked the question that had been gnawing at her.

"Did you get lost?"

She pronounced these four words as calmly as she could, almost in a sigh, but the accumulated fear behind her anger was clearly audible.

"What?" the old man asked, turning so that she could speak into his good ear.

"Did you get lost? Is that what happened?"

This time, she could not suppress a hint of aggression.

"No, no. We were scattering corn."

The lie drew an exasperated sigh and a scowl from Charlie.

"Well, this won't go on much longer anyway."

"What does that mean?" the old man asked.

"Shhh," Christophe said, "you'll wake the boy."

He drove slowly and carefully, in no rush to get to the house. Because as soon as he did, he would have to do something he'd been trying to avoid for months: explain. And then he remembered Hélène at Le Casque d'Or, earlier that evening. And the thought blew him away.

AFTER CHARLIE HAD moved the sleeping child to the back of her car, she sat behind the steering wheel and Christophe thought he had gotten away with it. But the driver's-side window slowly lowered, and he had no choice but to go over there.

"I'm warning you now," Charlie said, "I don't want any more of this. I mean it. Don't force me to take away your custody."

"Come on, it's not that big a deal..."

"Yes it is. Your father's ill. I don't want him being left alone with Gabriel anymore."

"I know."

Forearms resting on the roof of the Golf, head hanging down, Christophe waited for the verdict to be delivered. The whole weight of the night pressed down on his shoulders.

"Have you seen a specialist at least?"

"Of course. We went to a neurologist."

"When?"

"Two or three weeks ago. We're still waiting for the results."

"Well, there's no mystery. We know what's wrong with him. Have you told him about the move yet?"

"Not yet. I'm afraid he'll take it hard."

Charlie leaned her head through the open window and said: "Tell him, or I will. Understood?"

Christophe nodded. Then she raised the window, and he watched in silence as they left, mother and child inside the black car. This girl he had known in middle school, with whom he had made love and racked up debt, with whom he had fought and separated. And now this. She was taking his son away. He became truly aware of the fact for the first time. What the hell was he going to do, with this huge hole in the middle of his life?

10

THE FIRST TIME Christophe sees Charlie, he's in ninth grade and she is being slapped in the face.

She has just arrived at the Collège Louis-Armand in Cornécourt in the middle of the school year after being expelled from a private school in the city center and, from the start, she has made no attempt to disguise the fact that she considers herself far superior to the rest of them. It's obvious in the way she walks, the company she chooses, the way she stares at the little kids around her, the way she almost always walks into class with her hands in her pockets.

There are few distractions at that small-town school and no sooner has Charlie come through the gates than she is the center of attraction. Since she was born at the start of the year and she is having to repeat ninth grade, she is sixteen years old and she looks so much more rebellious than her classmates, with her bangs and gray eyes, her swaggering air, the Converse sneakers she wears even in winter, and her black bomber jacket lined with orange canvas. Within days, the rumors are rife. It's said she was expelled after being caught in a toilet stall with a school monitor, or because she was selling hash, or because she insulted a teacher. It's also said that she had a fight with a guy who pulled her pony-tail on the stairs. It took three people to drag her off him and the guy broke his coccyx when he fell. That very word, "coccyx," seems to hover above the girl's head like a heroic, disturbing halo.

She always sits at the back of the classroom, often alone, slumped on her chair or asleep with her head on her crossed arms. Seeing her like that, so young, so female, so masculine, so dangerous and pale, Christophe can't help wondering. Even the teachers appear worried about her, as if hoping she will be rapidly transferred to another school, one better suited to her needs. Marco quickly notices the curiosity Christophe feels toward this unusual creature, and he is happy to share his own opinion of the new girl.

"She's a bitch," he says. "And she's full of herself."

The first time Christophe sees Charlie probably coincides with her first day at Louis-Armand, although it's hard to know for sure. Memory is capricious, and easily overtaken by legend. Anyway, she is facing Monsieur Juncosa, a monitor in his early forties who wears burgundy blazers, creepy transparent pedo glasses, and loafers with a small metal crest on the side, and who has made the surveillance of middle school kids his life's work. The ink stains on his back testify to the way those kids feel about him.

Christophe spots him lecturing Charlie in the playground and, even if he can't hear him, he can easily imagine his tight-assed voice and his verbose vocabulary, because Monsieur Juncosa likes to use words such as "flagrant" and "contravention." Abruptly Charlie frowns, wrinkles her nose, and says something that makes the monitor's face turn pale. That's when he slaps her hard in the face before striding away, rummaging in his pockets, and finding nothing to help him. After that, he will never go anywhere without a box of Tic Tacs.

That's how Charlie is: a trouble magnet. Over time, it always finds her. And if she ever gets bored of waiting for it, she does something to bring it down upon her. She seems to be constantly on the lookout for walls she can crash into. Christophe is still only fourteen and when he looks at her, he feels tectonic movements inside his chest, over which he has no control at all. Often, it feels as if these inner quakes will smash his body to pieces. At hockey practice he loses his ability to focus. He thinks about Charlie all the time. She is present, like background music, even when his mind is elsewhere. At home in the evenings, he is miserable as sin, refusing to set the table, neglecting his homework, and sitting there in front of the TV like he's taken too much Xanax. At dinner, his mother asks him why he's not eating and he doesn't even bother answering. What a pair of sulky teenagers they are, he and Julien.

"Well, this is cheerful," says Sylvie as Gérard slurps down the remains of his soup.

One day in November, after a particularly soporific math class, Christophe stands next to one of the windows on the fourth floor while he waits to go into German, his forehead pressed to the glass, and drifts into bitter thoughts as he looks down at the ant-like children below. Greg is there too, looking far less despairing, even if he is equally bored by this endless afternoon that will come to an end only after two hours of history and geography. Christophe sighs. And then he sees Charlie walking across the playground. Fucking hell, even from above, she looks bigger than everyone else. He watches her quick, warlike march, her legs like compasses, her ponytail swinging, the Gotcha bag slung over her shoulder. He is powerless to resist.

"All right, let's go," he says.

"Huh?"

"Come on."

Greg doesn't need a second invitation. He hurtles downstairs after his friend. Unlike Marco, who has an English class at that moment, Greg is not annoying or jealous. And since his parents run a bar and he often steals from the cash drawer, his pockets are always stuffed with money. Consequently, when Charlie dives onto a Line 11 bus, it is Greg who coughs up for two tickets so they can follow her.

Christophe quickly spots her. She's sitting by the window at the back, headphones covering her ears, watching the landscape flash past. He wonders where she will get off. Greg wonders the same thing.

"How far are we going?" he asks, one hand hanging from a ceiling strap as his body sways gently from side to side.

"I dunno."

"And what are you planning to do? Ask her out?"

"Shut up..."

The bus moves through pedestrianized streets, across the covered bridge, out toward Saint-Laurent, and as it gradually empties it becomes harder to disguise their voyeuristic presence. Finally, Charlie stands up and her gaze passes over them unseeingly. Leaning against a handrail, she waits for the bus to sigh to a halt. The doors open at last and she jumps off, leaving the two boys standing there like idiots, too cowardly to follow, watching meekly as she enters a bar on the street corner, Les Mousquetaires. They get off at the next stop and walk back toward the bar. Outside the door, Christophe hesitates. Neither of them is old enough to go into a bar. Thankfully, Greg doesn't care about stuff like that. He lights a cigarette and opens the door, as if this is his parents' place. Christophe has no choice but to follow him.

"Good afternoon, gentlemen!" the bar owner calls out.

There aren't many customers, so the owner was always going to notice them. He is a middle-aged man in a V-neck sweater and a striped shirt that make him look like a catalogue model. Greg orders a coffee and a glass of water, and Christophe says, "Same." Through the serving hatch behind him, the boys can see a smoky game room where customers armed with pool cues are coming and going amid the clicking of balls and the electric clatter of pinball machines. They drink their coffees and wait. Then Greg climbs off his stool.

"Come on, let's take a look," he says.

"Where?" asks Christophe, already anxious at the fact that he's under age.

Without answering, Greg walks around the bar and, impassive as a gunslinger, pushes through the saloon-style swing doors to the game room. Christophe smiles at the bar owner, swallows his saliva. Then he in turn gets off his stool.

"Hey, young man..."

The teenager freezes, already imagining the worst—police, parents, scandal—but the man just gestures to the wallet Christophe has left on the countertop. He gives an awkward little laugh and picks it up.

"Thanks."

Of course, the owner knows full well they are too young to be there, but since his bar is halfway between two high schools, one public and the other private, he sees youngsters coming in all the time, pretending to be older than they are. Occasionally he will ask for an ID, just so he can say he's done it, but he can't spend all day checking people's birth dates and he would soon ruin his own business if he did. There aren't enough drunks in the area to keep the bar in business, so he's dependent on these high school kids ordering flavored beers and coffees, playing a bit of pinball and smoking a lot of cigarettes, chatting and flirting, with their long hair, scrunchies, and duffle coats. For twenty years he has been watching them with unruffled stoicism, the teenagers unvarying from one generation to the next, always making out, cramming for tests, yelling at one another, messing around. Making one drink last three hours while they put the world to rights. But from his observation point, the world does not seem to change that much. His customers are always seventeen years old and worried about their exams. The owner of Les Mousquetaires turns on the TV and lights a cigarillo, only his second of the day.

Christophe, meanwhile, has just discovered the miniature Las Vegas of the adjoining room: three pool tables, a flashing, beeping electronic dartboard, and an equally noisy Gottlieb pinball machine. A handful of high school students and a few older men stand nonchalantly around, cues in hand, cigarettes dangling from mouths, their voices curiously muffled by the green felt covering the walls. On the bar tables, half-empty glasses jostle for space with blue cue chalks and enormous Johnnie Walker ashtrays.

Christophe goes over to Greg, who has expertly assembled the red and yellow balls inside the triangle on a pool table. Straight from the break, he sinks a red in one of the side pockets. Two others follow before Christophe gets a turn. But Greg signals to him. Charlie has just appeared, accompanied by a cute blonde girl with a doll-like face, very long hair, and a black leather jacket, her hands invisible under its sleeves. The two girls walk past without glancing at anyone, almost in slow motion. All of this is engraved into the boy's memory: the light, Charlie in profile, her bangs, the perfect line of her face, her cool indifference, the flashing stars on the pinball machine behind her, and the cheerful *ding-ding* of darts thudding into the electronic board.

"Have you got a cigarette?" Christophe mutters to his friend.

"You smoke?" Greg asks, surprised.

He does now.

The girls go through the swing doors, then stop at the bar. The blonde asks the bar owner, who is her father, to give them two diabolos and they start chatting half-heartedly, looking totally bored, taking care to not even touch their glasses. Charlie is so pretty, and so obviously couldn't care less about how pretty she is, that Christophe would be willing to jump out of a fourth-floor window to get her attention. In the meantime, he takes a drag on his cigarette: always a good option.

"So, are you going to play or what?" Greg asks.

"Yeah."

But he doesn't. He has moved to get a better view through the serving hatch. He is separated from Charlie by maybe three meters, but it feels like the other side of the world. And then their eyes meet. A glint of mischief in the girl's look. He could swear she smiles, even though not a single muscle in her face moves a millimeter. Christophe blushes. It was hardly anything, just a glimmer in her eye. And yet it will last him twenty years or more.

THAT MOMENT IN the poolroom has various effects on the boy's existence, some happy, some less so. First of all, his schoolwork becomes suddenly insignificant. And he wasn't exactly a diligent student beforehand.

Next, he begins to cultivate a space inside himself where he can nurture his secret thoughts and obsessions, stuff he won't talk about to anyone, not even Greg and Marco. To start with, Charlie occupies that entire space, especially in the evenings when he is in bed with his headphones.

Lastly, hockey becomes an absolute necessity, a chance to purge his emotions, a release valve, and the source of big ambitions. Until then, what he liked most was skating, the feeling of speed, seeing his friends, getting away from his family.

But now that Charlie rules his heart, everything has changed. Christophe needs to shine, and since he can't really depend on his academics for that (not that she would care if he did), nor on his guitar-playing, hockey is the most obvious outlet. Christophe decides to become an elite athlete. He wants to play for the French national team, and one day perhaps go abroad to play in Germany or Canada.

The whole family joins him in this fantasy of sporting glory. He and his brother set up hockey goals at the back of the garage. That's where he has shooting practice when he's not training at the Poissompré rink. Pretty often, the pucks hit the back wall and leave a mark in the insulation panels. His father comes down occasionally to check the damage by sticking his finger into these tatty wounds, frowning and muttering.

"*Oh là là!* I don't believe it. You're destroying the house."

But he still lets them play.

One day, Julien has the idea of fastening saucepan lids to the top corners of the goals. The longer Christophe trains, the more often he makes those stainless-steel discs sing. It's muscle memory: he must bind his body to the puck's trajectory, repeating the movements so many times that they become subconscious, intuitive, drawing an unswerving line from his gaze to the nets. And during these hours of training, Christophe tells himself, over and over, the same dramatic stories of impossible comebacks and last-second goals. Inside his skull, crowds of strangers stand up and shout out his name.

Sometimes, Sylvie will come down in her bathrobe to watch her sons, the big one in goal and the younger one shooting. Her two boys... She blows on her herbal tea, smokes a cigarette, and—after reminding them yet again to be careful, because they don't want to end up at the emergency room— she goes back upstairs.

On the ice, however, things are not so easy.

"Head up! Look around! Look!" the coach yells.

Squatting on his heels, Gargano explains things to the players gathered in a circle around him. With a finger, he draws shapes and patterns above the ice. He tries to teach them dummy moves, combinations, vision.

Now and then, Christophe has the feeling that he's grasped some secret element of the game, and for a minute or so everything seems clear. Reflexes click into place, every movement makes itself, and, briefly, he feels like he could practically play with his eyes closed. But it is always a fleeting sensation, a momentary grace that is stolen away almost immediately, like a word on the tip of your tongue that vanishes before you have time to pronounce it.

In the winter of 1989–90, the players' parents spend a weekend organizing a small tournament in Morzine. Christophe and Marco make the trip, but Greg—who has dislocated his shoulder—stays home. The competition features six teams, among them the impressive Chamonix and Grenoble. Monsieur Müller, the recently elected mayor, rents vehicles to transport the players, among them his son Lionel. He takes the Mercedes MPV for himself, while Christophe's father finds himself driving the far less sexy Fiat Ulysse.

It's a six-hour drive to Morzine and by the time the Fiat arrives, the Mercedes has already been there for twenty-five minutes, which naturally results in a certain hostility between the people emerging from each vehicle. Not only that, but they have to play Morzine right away and the kids, who have spent the trip listening to the Red Hot Chili Peppers and No One Is Innocent while stuffing themselves with candy, are all on the verge of puking. They head out onto the ice in a daze, irritable, sullen, almost shivering, while the local families boo them for a laugh. Monsieur Müller and Gérard Marchal know they're in trouble even before the team has finished warming up, and any remaining hope is soon killed by the seven goals they concede in the first period.

In the locker room, Gérard tries desperately to galvanize the troops, but his B-movie speech goes down like a lead balloon. The players want only one thing: for this to be over as quickly as possible. When Christophe stands up to go to the bathroom, Madani deliberately leaves his stick lying across his path. So Christophe smashes it in two with his skate.

"Hey, what the hell's wrong with you?" yells his father.

"You son of a bitch..." hisses Madani.

The game continues amid an atmosphere of crumbling team spirit, ending with a score of 16–3. A thrashing.

The players are off duty for the rest of the day, and they take advantage of this by sitting at the edge of the rink, vaguely watching the other games, smoking cigarettes when the adults' backs are turned, and losing their temper over the smallest slights, to the point that they almost come to blows on several occasions.

For dinner, the mayor of Cornécourt has negotiated a set meal with the hotel management: a starter of grated carrots, a main course of roast pork with noodles, and chocolate mousse for dessert. Around the table, the morning's animosity has not faded. You can feel it in the air like gas fumes and, confronted with this ambience of prepubescent aggression, Gérard and the mayor decide to keep their spirits up. The former orders a bottle of Burgundy and the contents disappear so quickly that the latter asks the waiter for another one. The two of them are soon in a very good mood, two men making the most of the moment, just as they should, agreeing on pretty much everything: the benefit of sports for young people, how the Left and the Right are as bad as each other. Monsieur Müller ran for mayor as an independent, something he explains repeatedly to his dining companion, although naturally that position does not mean he lacks convictions. He needs people like Gérard on his team—sensible people well-known in the area. Christophe's father is flattered by this entreaty and clinks his glass against his new friend's. Then the two of them, with Carolingian expressions and a sparkle in their eyes, contemplate the table where ten exhausted young boys are sullenly stuffing themselves, looking about as athletic as a tapioca pudding.

"We should get them to bed, don't you think?"

"Let's have a digestif first," suggests Gérard.

"With pleasure!"

CHRISTOPHE IS SHARING a double room with Marco, who falls fast asleep without even brushing his teeth. He stands in the bathroom, staring at himself in the mirror. This is a new habit. In his own room, he spends a considerable amount of time examining himself from every imaginable angle. Thanks to all the physical exercise he does, he has manufactured a pretty good body: a V-shaped torso, muscular shoulders, thighs that are practically like a man's. On the other hand, he's not a fan of the zits that cover his jaw and the sides of his nose, and he squeezes them one by one. Leaning on the sink, he considers his reflection. He thinks about Charlie. About how badly his team played earlier that day. About his dad and Monsieur Müller. About fat Marco in the room next door. He finds all this abruptly depressing.

In the shower, the hot water crashes down on his head and shoulders and he starts playing with himself with his right hand, hardly even aware of what he's doing. At least this way, he can end the day with a pleasant feeling. His dick gets hard very quickly, as usual, the veins swelling, the balls retracting, and Christophe closes his eyes to summon the best images.

All that time he spends sniffing out sex at the newsstand, in magazines like *Lui* and *VSD*, a pair of tits, preferably big ones, an ass, ideally in a G-string, and the aisle of X-rated movies at the video club where he and Marco go to rummage around, giggling, the two of them belching weakly as they point out the dripping covers, the full-frontal images, the intimidating size of those mutant dicks, black or pink, all of them scary, this whole disgusting and magnetic display, and yet the desire keeps drawing him back, the beast inside him insatiable. He and his friends watch the VHS videos that Greg's dad hides in his nightstand. Greg even took out his cock once, couldn't help himself, and the other two yelled at him, *What the fuck, are you crazy or something?* In privacy, though, they're all the same, just wild animals, dreaming of women in fragments, constantly hard, the victims of urges that make them act like morons and always end in the same way, a sudden emptiness, the bleakness of paper towels, once the desire has passed and nothing remains but the shame of the open magazine and their sticky fingers. And then two hours later: rinse and repeat.

Christophe would never dare think about Charlie when he touches himself, though. For him, sex and emotion are still separate things. Love is a sort of bromide, and Charlie remains on a pedestal, reduced to perfection, an untouchable dream.

So, there in the shower stall, Christophe puts together the pieces of a jigsaw-puzzle woman… Let's say she lives in the house next door, wears a silk bathrobe with a dragon on the back like on those René Chateau covers, let's make her older, huge breasts, a redhead, or maybe a brunette, he's not sure about that, but he sees the deep shadow line of her cleavage, her throat, how soft and enveloping she looks, it's coming, he speeds up the movement, and just then there's a knock at the hotel room door.

He turns off the water and quickly dries himself while the knocking continues. When he opens the door, he finds himself face-to-face with Madani, Monsieur Müller's son, and Michael Santander, all of them red-eyed and in their boxer shorts standing outside the door to his room.

"What do you want?"

Madani has already shoved him inside and the three visitors crowd into the entryway while Santander closes the door behind them.

"Your father can go fuck himself," spits Madani, grabbing him by the back of the neck.

Christophe isn't sure how to respond to this somewhat enigmatic witticism. The intruders are clearly drunk, and all three are older than him. So he doesn't resist, only holds as tightly as he can to the towel tied around his hips. Madani squeezes his neck.

"You understand?"

Behind him, his two stooges are blinking in the fluorescent light. They are dry-mouthed and they instinctively turn their eyes from the light, looking like they have been dragged there against their will.

"Maybe we should go," suggests Santander.

"Shut your mouth!" Madani barks.

In a single movement he yanks away the towel. Christophe stands there completely naked, hands covering his crotch, at their mercy. Madani clumsily attempts to knee him in the balls, then grabs Christophe by the throat and slams him against the wall. The small painting hung on the wall goes crashing to the floor, where it breaks into pieces. The carpet is now covered with shards of glass. Christophe looks at the mountain landscape lying at his feet, its narrow sky and craggy peaks, its reassuring hideousness in which he can make out the tiny figure of a chamois staring into the distance. He feels Madani's fingers dig into his throat.

"Let me go," Christophe grunts, grabbing his attacker's wrist.

Madani gives him a little headbutt. But he and his friends don't really know what to do now in this brightly lit entryway. Their revenge mission is losing momentum. Christophe is still naked, defenseless, ridiculous, on the verge of tears.

"Well..." says Müller. "I think he's got the message..."

Madani raises a hand and slaps Christophe hard across his temple. The blow is so violent, so unexpected, that his two sidekicks look startled.

"All right, that's enough," one of them says.

But Madani's mind is made up. This time, he's going to hurt him. His resentment has been festering for a long time, imprisoned inside a jar of self-control. With his free hand, he is now trying to grab his victim's genitals, while Christophe— dazed, eyes glistening—does his best to evade him.

"Stop it," he gasps.

Madani does not stop. A strange desire is visible in his eyes. It's a pathetic sight: the wriggling naked body and that hand fishing for its most vulnerable part. Christophe's fear grows. He tries to catch the eyes of the others, who look as helpless as he feels. There's no heckling anymore. Something definitive is about to happen.

"Hey, what's going on?"

Marco has just appeared in the hallway, still half-asleep and wearing pajamas.

"Fuck off," hisses Madani.

Marco sniffs. He's over six feet tall, in his Red Bulls tank top. He sizes up Madani, looks at the two stooges. Then, throwing his head back, he starts to roar:

"Aaaaaarrrrgggh!"

"Shut up, you dick!" shouts Madani, suddenly panicked.

But Lionel Müller has already opened the door and is bravely slipping away, quickly followed by Santander.

"AAAAARRRRGGGH!" yells Marco, mouth wide open, neck tensed, like a hunting horn.

Voices are audible in other rooms, recriminations.

"What's going on?" someone shouts.

"You're a lucky little fucker," says Madani, giving Christophe a little slap on his forehead before escaping.

The two friends stand there in the room's entryway while, in the distance, they hear stampeding feet and muffled laughter, followed by a conversation between an angry adult and some boys trying to play it down. Christophe grabs the towel with one hand to cover himself and Marco locks the door.

"You okay?"

"Yeah."

Then the noise outside fades and the two boys go to bed without a word, in that boxlike hotel room.

"Good thing you were there," says Christophe in a low voice.

"No problem."

Soon the only sound is the rustling of sheets, the other boy's breathing, close by. Christophe listens to the strange silence that has fallen between them and that feels like a sort of waiting. His panic has gone, and gratitude has filled the space left behind, a soft and generous gratitude that rocks him like tiredness.

"Hey…"

"What?"

"You okay?"

"Yeah," Marco replies.

It must be late now. Their voices are mere whispers, the brushing of skin against the velvet of insomnia.

"I was totally freaking out."

"I know. Get some sleep."

And Christophe reaches out with his hand, through the gap between their beds.

"Hey," he says again.

The mattress groans as his friend shifts his weight. Marco's hand finds his. And they stay like that for a moment, in the silent hotel.

The next day, Épinal will lose to Saint-Gervais and Orléans. On Sunday they will be defeated by Megève before narrowly beating Grenoble. On the trip back, Christophe will pretend to sleep. As for Marco, he will always keep, in a drawer at home, a matchbook bearing the crest of the Hotel Alpina in Morzine.

11

THEY HAD BEEN driving less than ten minutes when Gabriel started crying in the back seat.

"What's the matter, sweetie?"

In the rearview mirror, Christophe saw the usual sorrowful expression: cheeks wet with tears, snot bubbling from nostrils, small mouth twisted, glasses steamed up.

"Huh? What's wrong?"

At the stoplight, he turned toward the child, who was still crying his eyes out.

"Tell me, honey."

He opened the glove box, pulled out a box of tissues, and handed it to his son.

"Here. Dry your eyes, my love. And try to stop crying."

The boy noisily blew his nose, then wiped the wetness from his cheeks. His whole face was bright red now. Christophe took off his son's glasses, then wiped the condensation away before handing them back.

"Is that better?"

Gabriel nodded, but his mouth was a horizontal figure of eight, heralding more tears. The light changed to green and the guy in the car behind flashed his headlights. It was eight in the morning: rush hour. Gabriel gave a little hiccuping sob and his body began shaking again on the booster seat.

"Calm down, sweetie. Tell me what's wrong..."

Christophe checked his watch. It was only a five-kilometer drive from home to the school, but it was the same crap every morning: endless traffic jams, every car filled with the same stressed parents, the same fresh-eyed women covering up their exhaustion, the kids trussed up in back seats in their parkas, the same employees listening to the news on the radio, staring vacantly ahead or picking their nose, all of them miles away from this weary work routine, in their own little worlds, trapped in the same daily commutes from residential areas to schools, from apartment buildings to office buildings, a flock of sheep herded from one place to the next, each of them dreaming of success and time off.

Christophe and Gabriel were no exception to this rotary existence. It was 8:07 a.m. and they were occupying their usual spot in the slow flow of useful lives. Soon they would be late, and the machine, in one way or another, would punish them for it. Christophe grew impatient.

"Is it because of Grandpa? Because we're not allowed to tell him?"

Gabriel shook his head, closed his eyes, the tears still pouring. Clearly, nobody had a clue what he was going through.

"Then what is it?"

"It's...it's..."

But the words were trapped in his throat, too big to come out. Thankfully, they had arrived. Christophe parked on the sidewalk close to the school, put on his warning lights, then turned to his son, one arm reaching out behind his headrest.

"If you don't tell me, I can't do anything to help."

"It's Kylian."

"What's going on now?"

"He hits me all the time."

"You have to tell the teacher, sweetie."

"I told her already!" the little boy shouts, and his tears pour more fiercely, running down his cheeks and pooling in his collarbone. His eyes are invisible again behind his glasses.

"Well, you'll have to learn how to defend yourself, then."

"I can't," says Gabriel. "I'll get in trouble."

"Yes, you can. Listen. You're allowed to defend yourself."

The child shook his head. He was sunk deep in his sorrow, the impossibility of life, the wall he was banging his head against. He started sobbing even harder. The clock was still ticking, and Christophe didn't see what more he could do. He'd arranged a meeting with the teacher twice before already, and she had promised to keep an eye on Gabriel during recess and to explain to Kylian that bullying was wrong. But it made no difference: that little shit was always attacking his son.

"Sweetie, he can't be doing this for no reason."

"He *is*!" Gabriel shrieked.

Automatically, Christophe touched the small scar under his right eye. It was growing ever warmer inside the car and the windows were steaming up. He opened his window and sighed.

That's life, he thought. You make kids, they catch measles and fall off their bikes, you put antiseptic on their knees and tell them stories, and then that miniature sumo wrestler's body, once small enough to be bathed in the sink, starts to disappear... Innocence is gone so quickly, and you haven't even taken the time to enjoy it. Of course, there were still photographs, that surprised look from the other side of time, and a baby monitor kept at the back of a drawer because you can't bring yourself to throw it away. Days without him, days with him, love in a discontinuous current. But the worst was yet to come.

Because some little thug, whom you imagined with a set of socioeconomic excuses and short-tempered parents, began bullying your kid. Violence had entered his life and you wondered how to deal with it. Because that was life, after all. He would have to learn to defend himself too. It was just the start of a long war. You tried to find solutions, taught him how to kick, had meetings with the teacher, only to end up here: wanting to beat the shit out of some kid you knew nothing about except that he was in second grade and wore red sneakers.

Just then, a man in a Clio honked his horn as he drove past the station wagon half blocking the road, and Christophe made a decision.

"All right, let's go."

"Go where?"

"I'm going to talk to your friend."

This news brought a smile to Gabriel's face and he got out of the car and took his father's hand. Once they were standing in front of the school, the boy searched for his tormentor among the crowd of kids running around in the playground, then pointed at a little boy in a puffer jacket with a pom-pom hat on his head. But this one was wearing blue sneakers.

"Are you sure that's him?" Christophe asked.

"Yes."

"All right, go ahead, sweetie. I'm right behind you."

Gabriel went through the school gates, his backpack strapped to his shoulders, while a female monitor shivering in a long cardigan flashed friendly smiles at the parents dropping off their progeny.

Within seconds, the boy that Gabriel had pointed out rushed over to him and began jumping around him, talking furiously. Gabriel hurried toward the covered playground, like a tortoise under his enormous backpack. He turned to his father. His mouth was starting to grow misshapen again. The other boy leapt at him. He was hitting his shoulder. Then he smacked the top of his head. It wasn't a hard smack, almost affectionate in fact, but Christophe's blood leapt. He charged at the boy.

"Monsieur!" shouted the woman in the cardigan.

Too late. Christophe was already halfway across the playground. A few children turned to stare at this half-running man, wondering who he could be. On the ground, the colors of old hopscotch lines were slowly fading.

"Hey!"

Christophe had grabbed the little shit by his arm and was shaking him angrily.

"You'd better stop that, you hear me?"

"He started it," said the kid. "I was just—"

"Don't lie to me," Christophe interrupted.

The child in the blue sneakers went limp, his eyes staring into thin air as he thought about the explanations he had not been allowed to give. Christophe's anger soon began to dissolve. This was not how he had imagined his son's tormentor would be. It was just a boy with pale skin and blond hair. The poignant freckles on his nose made hate impossible.

"I don't want you to touch Gabriel ever again," Christophe said. "Do it again, and I'll have to talk to your parents. You understand?"

The child tried to explain again, but already the monitor in the cardigan was running toward them, accompanied by Gabriel's teacher. Christophe let go of Kylian, who did not seem particularly disturbed by this encounter. Gabriel, meanwhile, had gone over to join his friends and wasn't paying any further attention to his father.

"Go have fun, Kylian," said the teacher, smiling but firm.

The boy danced away without a word, looking for another group of children to get mixed up with. In fact, he was probably two or three centimeters shorter than Gabriel.

"You can't enter the school grounds like that, monsieur."

The teacher was a slender woman who wore a quilted bolero jacket and a pair of Kickers. She smiled coldly, her eyes sparkling.

"Gabriel was crying again this morning," Christophe explained. "He can't take it anymore."

"Yes, but you cannot enter the school grounds. It's out of bounds for parents."

"The other kid's harassing him. I've told you that so many times..."

"He's very present, that's true," the young woman replied, still smiling calmly.

"Present? Are you kidding me?"

The bell rang then, and all the kids vanished in the blink of an eye. Only one class remained in the covered playground—the one taught by Gabriel's teacher. The young woman listened patiently to Christophe. Of course she understood what he meant. She had plenty of experience dealing with parents, and was well versed in obsessions and demands, the premature ambitions they nurtured for their kids, the way they were starting to treat their children's teachers as though they were their own personal servants, some of them even lecturing her on how to do her job. She had been dealing with them for some time now, and was no longer emotionally affected by their patronizing, intrusive behavior. She knew that behind it all lay an immense reservoir of anxiety.

"We'll talk to Kylian about it," she concluded after Christophe had gotten it off his chest.

"And his parents?"

"They're aware."

"And they don't care?"

"It's not that simple."

"This is unbelievable—it's happening in front of your eyes!" Christophe shouted, having used up all his reasonable arguments.

The teacher leaned close to him and explained the situation in a whisper. That little boy he had just been shaking did not mean any harm. True, he had certain behavioral problems, but that was not his fault. Had Christophe ever heard of autism spectrum disorder? It was true that Kylian was always grabbing Gabriel, but that was, for him, a mark of affection. Because of his condition, he did not understand the usual social cues.

"He finds it hard to grasp the idea that Gabriel is unhappy."

The bell rang again, an edgy, metallic sound perfectly matched to that cold November morning, the steel of the sky, and the weird fragility of Christophe's emotional state.

"I have to go," the teacher said, blinking rapidly.

"Of course."

They said goodbye and Christophe waved to Gabriel. Then he went back to his car, which was still half blocking the traffic. Two months from now, the boy would be gone, and he would never have to take him to school again.

AFTER LEAVING HIS car in the parking lot of the Hotel Kyriad in Ludres, Christophe ran upstairs to room 321. Hélène was waiting for him. She opened the door and he kissed her on the lips, then went into the room, looking around as if afraid that something would be missing.

"Are you okay?" Hélène asked.

"Yeah, yeah, I'm fine."

But she could tell instantly that something was off.

After their first aborted date at Le Casque d'Or, Hélène and Christophe had seen each other one more time, and then Hélène had suggested they rent a room on Airbnb; it was simple and practical, and since it was obvious that they both wanted it, what was the point in continuing to beat around the bush? Subsequently, they had hooked up in the spare bedroom of a house in Charmes—a village midway between Nancy and Épinal—belonging to a couple in their seventies who owned a pretty farm on the bank of the Moselle and who had not been impressed by their two-hour stay.

"Aren't you going to stay?" the old woman had asked, seeing them leave.

"We're in a bit of a rush," Hélène had explained, and the woman had looked disapproving.

Not only that, but the room they'd rented, which had looked quite cute in the photos, had in fact been as cold as an abattoir, since the insulation left something to be desired and the small convection heater emitted barely any more heat than a toaster oven. In the end, they just lay down together on the bed, in the pale light coming through the skylight, the curtain to which no longer closed properly—another reason why they did not feel entirely comfortable stripping off.

"We can't do it here," Hélène had said. "It's just too ugly. I'll find us somewhere nice and warm."

Christophe had looked up at the skylight, then back at the woman beside him. Her face was familiar to him now. She was part of his life.

"I'm still happy to see you again," he'd said.

"Yeah, me too."

They uttered these words with so much sincerity that they sounded slightly ridiculous. It wasn't easy doing this kind of thing when you were forty: the newness, the hesitant beginnings, the stealthy progress. They were beginners again, no longer very adept at their age, but that wasn't such an unpleasant sensation after all.

"Do you think we'll get there in the end?"

Hélène was leaning back on her elbows and he had leaned forward to kiss her. That feeling, all silk and speed. Soon they didn't know who was kissing whom. Eyes closed, they settled into it, fondling each other, their kisses soft, slow, searching. Then Christophe reached for her hand. She slipped her fingers around the thickness of his neck and felt his arms close around her. Something between them gave way, a sigh of relief rising while Hélène pressed herself against his crotch. They brushed noses, cheeks, foreheads. They forgot to think.

"You okay?" Christophe asked, catching his breath.

"Better than okay."

And that night, on her laptop, Hélène had not been able to stop herself giving a five-star review to the shabby little room in Charmes.

Three days later, they saw each other again at the hotel. There, Christophe wanted to do things right. He hitched up her skirt, slid off her stockings, pulled aside the fabric of her underwear—a pair of Eres panties that she had bought especially for their date—then, after throwing her onto the bed, gave her head for a long time. It was good. Here, at least, was a man who knew where the clitoris was. Hélène lay on her back to maximize her pleasure, despite the anxiety she felt over her pubic hair. With Philippe, she had never even thought about it, but after years of monogamy that worry did take the edge off her arousal. Because the fashion seemed to be for shaved pussies, and in porn movies at least—those American ones featuring girls with gigantic boobs—they always seemed to have slits like prepubescents. She'd talked to Lison about this, and her intern, who, that day, had been wearing leggings, jeans, and a shirt under a leather jacket, had told her in no uncertain terms: they can all go fuck themselves. To back up these words, she had unbuttoned her shirt and shown Hélène her armpits, which were exactly as nature had made them. Anyway, Christophe had not seemed to take offense. He had dived in, as deep as he could. Until, after a while, Hélène had lifted his chin.

"Come on."

"What?"

"I want to. Now."

She unzipped his pants, unbuttoned his shirt, kissed his belly, her hands eager, her mouth surprised not to find what she'd been imagining. Clearly, he was not a teenager anymore. Still, he had a man's body, its smell, its thick flesh, its hair. And she had actually felt quite touched by that little disappointment. He was hers.

"Come on, put a condom on."

Unfortunately, Christophe was in no fit state to fuck. Out of nowhere, Hélène felt the pitiful fear that she was no longer desirable. In moments like that, no matter how much she fought against it, the darkest thoughts would instinctively flash into her mind; the most idiotic reflexes were often the most deeply rooted. The male gaze as the benchmark. But she had quickly noticed that Christophe was looking sheepish too.

She had said "Come on" again, and this time they had gotten under the sheets together, in the warmth and the darkness, and kissed again. He felt her skin against his cock, her breasts against his chest. Her ass was even better than he'd imagined and he grabbed it in both hands, then bit her neck, feeling the flesh under his incisors. But it was his ears that had proved the ultimate erogenous zone. The rustling of fabric, her sighs, their breathing, the wet sounds of their kisses, the panting that grew louder and louder as Hélène rubbed herself against his thigh...all of this had finally worked its magic. She had even helped him put on the condom and finally, after so many years, they had done it. Even if it wasn't spectacular.

Thighs open and knees bent, she felt his weight on top of her, breathed in his already familiar scent, ran her hands over his body: his tensed arms, his huge shoulders, his back, the unbelievably soft skin of his butt, while he thrust himself into her. When he asked her if it was good, she nodded. *Look at me*, he said, and she obeyed. Then Christophe rolled to the side, having come too quickly and without really feeling anything.

So that was it. She had fucked Christophe Marchal. This idea pleased her so much that she giggled.

"What's up with you?" Christophe asked, frowning as he took off the condom and tied a knot in it.

"Nothing, it's just funny..."

"Thanks a lot."

"Not like that, you idiot."

When he headed toward the bathroom, naked, condom dangling from his hand, she enjoyed watching his movements, his tight little ass, his back, his enormous thighs. Who knew how things would go between them, but she was cheered by the thought of being able to enjoy it while it lasted.

Since then, they had seen each other twice in the same hotel, which had the advantage of being easily accessible and was only ten minutes from Nancy, in one of those places that existed only for motorists, caught between an urban development zone and the service road of a highway.

"Places like this blow my mind," Hélène had said.

Christophe had replied that everywhere was like this now. He spent his life driving and he didn't see a difference.

Even so, for their next date, Hélène came armed with two scented candles, a half bottle of Mumm, and a scarf to drape over the lampshade. They fucked again, less clumsily than the first time, patiently, tenderly, with eye contact, to the point where they might have started to wonder if this was something more than just sex.

"That was better, wasn't it?"

"Yeah, much better."

Christophe did not want to probe her feelings any more deeply than that. It was just then that she saw the little scar under his right eye.

"What's that? I never noticed it before."

"Nothing."

"Does it hurt when I touch it?"

With the tip of her tongue, Hélène pressed hard on the scar.

"No. Sometimes I feel something. But not then."

"When it's about to rain?"

"No. It's weird. It's like I don't feel anything at all there anymore. It's just numb."

"How did you get it?"

"I don't remember."

She kissed the little scar, then his nose, his mouth, his chest. She would have liked to suck his cock for a while, but after checking her watch, she said:

"Okay, I've just got time for a cigarette."

A second later, she was crouched in a corner of the room, rummaging through her purse. Sitting on the bed, Christophe asked her how tall she was.

"Ah, that's what's bothering you. I'm five-eight."

"You're taller than me."

"Well, yeah, I know."

She went to the window to smoke then, with his shirt over her shoulders, and he thought that he would be breathing in her scent all day long.

"When will I see you again?"

"Soon," she promised, looking at the cars in the parking lot, the stores spread around it like cubes on a play mat.

It was strange coming back to this kind of place. Every weekend, families would venture here to buy a Ping-Pong table or some wallpaper, to eat a T-bone steak with fries or go wild at an all-you-can-eat Chinese buffet. Hélène had experienced those weekly blowouts, the retail therapy that canceled out the identical weeks of earning, the balm of pointless little purchases. She too had spent hours with her parents drifting through these concrete archipelagos, from warehouses to parking lots, filling carts and taking home a plant or a cushion, some useless knickknack that seemed to make life more bearable. Now, whenever she found herself in a place like this, she was gripped by a sort of repulsion. She wanted to put as much distance as possible, as quickly as possible, between herself and these ubiquitous logos. But that day, contemplating the traffic circle that led to a Saint Maclou home improvement store, a gym, and a store selling bed linen, she felt a wave of tenderness. When it came down to it, everything was easy, and beauty could be found anywhere. And oh my God, she thought, it really is nice to get laid. And this expression was so foreign to her that it made her laugh quietly to herself.

SO CHRISTOPHE AND Hélène had become lovers. They had continued seeing each other, a source of satisfaction on the margins of life, carrying on their secret affair that could not be allowed to encroach on all the rest. For a few weeks, they had managed to maintain this boundary between normal life and their stolen hours together. And then one Thursday morning, Gabriel wept on the drive to school because he was being bothered by another kid in his class, and the dam broke.

"What's up with you?" Hélène asked, while Christophe stood in the middle of the bedroom, incapable of looking at her, hands in pockets and head hung low.

She had noticed his penchant for sulking even before this. When something was upsetting him, he would chew over the problem like a pack animal, with the same dull obstinacy, the same incurable stupidity. He seemed so distant from her then that he was like another person.

"It's my son," he said.

Hélène wormed it out of him and, once he had gotten his feelings off his chest, stole a kiss from him.

"It'll be okay."

"Yeah, I know."

He smiled weakly and kissed her again. But she could still sense the shyness in his lips, the distance that remained between them. So she pressed herself against him, a gesture that was both sweet and comical, and mimicked the seriousness of his expression, the sulky irritability of his posture. Seeing himself reflected like this, Christophe rolled his eyes, but she could tell the tension was easing a little inside him. She put on an innocent face then, like a Disney princess, eyes wide and gleaming, and ran her fingernails over his cock through the fabric of his jeans. Christophe was staring at her now with a poignancy that seemed to combine suffering with a hint of gratitude. There was another kiss—heavy with meaning this time—and she felt him relax against her as his dick grew erect. So she unzipped his jeans, went down on her knees, and swallowed him as eagerly as, on hungover mornings, she would devour bacon and eggs to settle her stomach. Her mind was blank as she sucked him off, intoxicated by the act, as he watched her, then touched her hair, stroked the back of her neck, her cheeks, her distorted lips. She gripped his thighs possessively, then grabbed hold of his butt, taking him deep inside her mouth until she could feel the smooth, gluey sting at the back of her throat, the sudden saltiness of the drops that had beaded there. Then, in a single movement, Christophe lifted her to her feet. They kissed again, their tongues shameless, the taste of semen in both their mouths, as their lower parts blindly sought fusion. They wanted to be dirty now, to do something bad. His anxiety was rapidly evaporating. They found themselves on the bed and he instantly slid inside her, hardly moving, feeling very big in the tightness of her pussy, because she was squeezing him, wanting to feel every inch of him. Hélène wrapped her arms around his back, her thighs around his hips.

"Shit, the condom..."

"Forget it. Look at me."

They kept staring into each other's eyes as they fucked, then Christophe supported himself on his forearms and thrust harder, again and again, the force disappearing inside her almost without appearing to affect her. Hélène held him by the shoulders and withstood the blows, her mouth half-open. When she closed her eyes, he said:

"Look at me. Stay with me."

For the first time they spoke metal words to each other, those white-hot words whispered into ears at night, in enclosed spaces, in darkness, far from policing and progress, insults better than any compliment, shameful expressions that create special connections, bonds of us-against-the-world. And, little by little, the lines became blurred. The sweat fell, drop by drop, from Christophe's forehead and Hélène opened her mouth, stuck out her tongue. She said bite me, harder, again. He said you feel that, you want more, squeeze it. They felt their nails dig into meat, pains and urgent desires that demanded other positions, the smell of the sea, of saltpeter, bland cosmetics running, acidic tastes that would normally have disgusted them, and—under their tongue—the texture of hair, smoothness, folds, the hell of physical matter, versatile and unimaginable, the other like oneself, wide-open, liquid, revolting, edible, all of it distilled in those spaces under arms, between legs. My God, your ass, your hands, your cock. There were pauses, of course, and remarks, the surprise of finding themselves there, panting on the shore, and almost immediately, sliding back in, the mechanical lapping starting up again. Suddenly a swamp-like languor, interchangeable ends, swapping roles, and that need right in the center, in the hot wet circle, her turning around, him falling back arms open, waiting for her to crouch down on him, and again and again the amazement of feeling a world that surrenders wholly. Thankfully, civilization reclaimed them. Christophe, after a while, admitted he couldn't take it anymore and he just lay there on his back.

"You haven't even come," said Hélène, leaning on an elbow, legs parted, not even bothering to pull the sheet up.

"I didn't want it to end."

"We could have brought it back to life again afterward," she said, watching his penis soften.

He frowned doubtfully and she kissed his shoulder. He looked at his watch.

"I should be going."

"I hate letting you leave like that."

"We'll see each other again."

"When?"

The sweat was starting to dry on their skin. The room no longer felt so warm, and Hélène jumped out of bed to find her cigarettes. Christophe, looking sad again, began picking up his clothes, which were scattered all over the floor. When he looked up, he saw Hélène lighting her cigarette.

"Are you sure you want to smoke in the room?"

The question felt like a slap, like being told off by a teacher. Hélène was speechless for a second, cigarette dangling from her mouth, lighter in hand, and she felt cold all of a sudden. As he walked into the bathroom, she called after him: "Listen. Let's not start talking to each other like that."

"What do you mean?"

"Talking to each other like we could get away with anything. Like a couple. Like assholes."

Christophe did not appear to understand what she was getting at, and incomprehension made his face look aggressive, almost ugly. But he forced himself not to sigh.

"I have troubles of my own, you know," said Hélène. "It's not easy for anyone. But I don't want that to screw us up."

Her last sentence made him shiver. It was the first time she had said *us*.

12

ON THE ADVICE of her guidance counselor, Hélène chose to specialize in science during her last two years of high school, despite preferring literature and history.

"Students of your ability should always go Bac S," said Madame Simon as they filled out the forms at the end of tenth grade.

In her junior year, then, she finds herself surrounded by all the bourgeois students, the children of people who know how things work and who planned long ago that their kids would end up in these classrooms preparing to apply for the best schools in the country, aiming for med school...or law school if there was really no other option.

Charlotte chose the same stream, of course, even if it took her father's intervention to convince the principal, who saw her as more of an economics and social science student.

Charlotte has changed. She's put on weight, her breasts and hips have grown bigger overnight, and her mother watches her like a hawk now, convinced that she must be raiding the fridge at night. The atmosphere in that big house on Rue des Murmures is not what it was. Charlotte's older brothers live in Paris and The Hague now, her father works nonstop, and

Charlotte has begun to suffer from a curious condition. Every time she gets her period, it's the end of the world. At first, Hélène thought her friend was just being a drama queen, but the same nightmare recurs every month. Pale as a corpse, Charlotte writhes in bed, sobbing. Her breasts ache. The pain goes down to her belly, spreads to her back, and she feels as if her ovaries have been replaced by big olives. She bleeds too much and sometimes the agony is so bad that she vomits. Nobody knows what to do. Her mother makes her infusions and hot water bottles. The doctors express surprise, but don't seem to truly believe her, especially the gynecologist, who prescribes acetaminophen and tells her to exercise more. Whatever it is, it's not going to kill her.

This monthly torture, which transforms her into a delicate porcelain figure, has created a distance between the two girls. Of course Hélène feels sorry for her friend, but it's a drag, seeing her lying in bed for ages, looking like some ghoul from a horror movie, and having to wait for it to end.

Anyway, Hélène has not felt able to talk to her openly since reading her private journal. She's started hanging out with other girls—Laurence Lefur, Magalie Conraud, Sonia Hadid— and, while Charlotte still has a place in her heart, she is no longer so central to her life. Their friendship has become less urgent; it has started to feel almost like an obligation, as if the connections they had forged have been replaced by the chains of memory and shared moments. Hélène wonders if her friend is still seeing Christophe, if they still have those hidden hours all to themselves. Sometimes, alone in her bed, she remembers the words in the journal, the ones in red ink, the exclamation points. All this envelops Christophe Marchal in a special aura of mystery and sex, as if he has become a sort of portable idol, associated with silent pleasures and secret encounters. And when she spots him in the playground, or passes him in the cafeteria, her face flushes crimson and she can barely walk straight. Not only that, but the fact that he failed his exams the previous year means Hélène imagines him as someone basic, simplified, a purely physical being. Bizarrely, this reduction enchants her.

The cool thing is that his bitch girlfriend, the haughty punk with the American name, is no longer around to get in the way. She's gone off somewhere to take her baccalaureate, and good riddance to her. Sometimes Charlotte and Hélène see Christophe passing the smokers' yard. He's often alone these days. His friends have left high school and headed off to Nancy, Metz, and Strasbourg, to technical colleges and vocational training courses. And he's stayed here, with his sweet little mouth, his sherpa denim jacket, and his Vans. He looks like he needs a cuddle. The girls don't talk about this. For each of them, Christophe is their secret.

One day, by chance, Hélène ends up on the bus with him, on Line 5, the one that goes from the city center to Corné-court, on the road that runs alongside the Moselle. When he turns in her direction, she makes herself small as a mouse. She has no desire to talk to him. She's not that interested in the reality. What Hélène loves is staring at him, making up stories about him. Eventually, though, he recognizes her and smiles politely. She blushes so furiously, it's embarrassing. The next Saturday, she tells her mother that there's no need to keep driving her to school.

"Oh really?"

Mireille is polishing the surfaces in her kitchen, as she always does at that time, between the end of lunch and the one o'clock news.

"Yeah, I'd rather take the bus."

"Hmm, that's new."

Mireille does not take offense. She dries her hands on a dish towel, which she spreads on a radiator, then carefully folds up her apron.

"All right, then, I'll give you some money for the fare."

Mireille has an odd habit of batting her eyelashes very quickly, as if she's blinking in dazzling sunlight. Arms crossed under her meager breasts, she spends a moment contemplating her only child, sizing her up like a horse dealer: this is her way of loving Hélène, practical, utilitarian. She's very tall for a girl now, not especially pretty, or rather let's just say that she's still at an awkward age, and she's looked a bit strange ever since she cut her hair short after that vacation she took with those rich folk on the Île de Ré, but she does have very long legs leading up to that giant ass, which she sometimes shows off and sometimes hides, depending on how she's feeling. Anyway, she's still shining at school and that's all that matters to Mireille. At the end of tenth grade, the guidance counselor told her: "Your daughter can go far, you just have to keep pushing her."

"Can I trust you?" Mireille asks.

Hélène rolls her eyes. This is her mother's mantra, trust. What does she think is going to happen? That she'll say no, I want to take the bus so I can have sex with some loser, get pregnant, and screw up my life?

"Ugh, of course, Mom..."

"*Oh là là*," Mireille says. "Calm down."

She isn't really annoyed, though. In fact, things are not so bad at home. She talks about it with Jean sometimes, late at night in bed. When their daughter told them she wanted to take the Bac S, they were against it at first. After all, Hélène's best results had come in literary subjects and they imagined her having a career as a teacher, or a notary, maybe even a

242

lawyer if she aced her exams. Mireille, naturally, was hoping for the latter possibility. But a Bac S with two modern languages plus Latin...where would that take her? To them, it is a grand, unfamiliar path, its destination unknown. Only two people in their family have ever been to university, both of them women. One cousin became a teacher, and the other works for the Transport Ministry. Those kinds of careers are easy to understand; you can easily imagine what those people do all day. But all that stuff about advanced math, then business or engineering schools, it's just baffling. In their anxious minds, those words have started to sound like traps.

"Are you sure that's what you want?"

They did the prudent thing, trying out every dissuasive argument they could think of. What if the level was too high? She'd be crushed, punished for not knowing her place. Maybe it would be better to choose something more attainable. And then the other students, all those rich kids, would she fit in with them?

"We're not trying to discourage you. But you can't go in with your eyes closed."

Besides, youth is for having fun. What was she going to put herself through in those long, dark tunnels, those years of intensive cramming, sacrificing her life, and for what? Just so she could make money? In the Poirot family, they have long known that money can't buy happiness.

Hélène hates them for this working-class skepticism, their philosophy of the eternally fucked that makes a virtue of modesty, sees servility as wisdom, ambition as arrogance. Hélène wants it all.

After a few days of hemming and hawing, Hélène's father ends up taking his daughter's side. He's naturally more trusting, something his wife often reproaches him for. And, well, you know what fathers and daughters are like...

From the very start of the school year, Hélène shines academically. Everything seems to come easily to this kid, who gets As in math and in German.

"It's funny when you think about it," says Jean.

But her brilliance worries them. They are trapped in the dilemma of parents who encourage their kids, who feel like every step forward their child takes will leave them farther behind. On the station platform, they see the train vanishing into the distance, gathering speed. Sometimes Mireille can't help wishing she could put a stop to that terrifying acceleration. When Hélène shows off her knowledge, correcting the way they pronounce certain words ("socialisT" not "socialiss," "eXperience" not "esperience," and let's not even talk about English—the way that kid makes fun of them when they try to say *"Dirty Dancing"* or *"Star Wars"*), or when she interrupts them or quotes Jean-Paul Sartre over dinner or reads Virginia Woolf in the living room, her mother loses it. *Who the hell do you think you are? You think intelligent people despise their parents?* Hélène says it's nothing like that, she just thinks things like the truth, accuracy, and education are important, and anyway she's allowed to express her opinion, isn't she? But every time she spits her superiority in their faces like that, she sees something vile in the lower part of her face: the jutted chin, the sneering mouth. Such episodes often end in tears, a slammed door. Betrayal is an ugly business.

Even so, Hélène's parents are proud, and things are not so bad. And Mireille does not have the words to tell other people what a pearl her daughter is, what a miracle, what a prodigy. At the office, her colleagues grimace behind her back whenever she begins a sentence with "My daughter." Maître Bienvenue, one of the firm's partners, told her: "You must introduce us one day to your little wonder..." Mireille felt her cheeks burning. One day, Hélène will belong to this world, she thinks, the world of orders and knowledge, people who casually command others and walk around with a folder under their arm, who laugh at incomprehensible things and act with others like adults with children. This revolts and thrills her.

Jeannot vaunts his daughter's merits too, although he has fewer opportunities at the wallpaper store where he works, particularly since his brother-in-law's kid is not exactly a straight-A student. But you should see him at dinner, the way he looks at her when she brings home her grades, those eyes of his like a tamed animal. Where did this creature come from, he wonders. And the words in her mouth, the ideas that pass through her mind, her constant dissatisfaction, her inflexible enthusiasm, that desire to see the world, to distance herself from her roots, that urge that sometimes borders on insult? Where does she go to find all of this?

So when their daughter needs money for a class trip or to buy books, Mireille and Jean do not hesitate. They dig into their savings. They do what they must. It is the terrible work of a parent to give their child the means to flee them.

However, this gradual escape does not happen without a few disappointments.

Hélène's decision to take the bus, for example. The bus stop is almost a kilometer from home, and she must walk all that way with her schoolbag on her back, at night and in the cold from October onward, and carrying an extra bag on Thursdays, when she has sports. For someone who dreams of strolling through life with her hands in her pockets, this is a real pain in the ass. Every time she sees those privileged little misses turning up to the high school—the ones who are lucky enough to live in the city center, who can get an extra hour's sleep before coming to classes, who never have to brave the crush of public transport, who can travel light because they go back to the house for lunch anyway, all those bitches with their big, chic tote bags—Hélène wonders if she made a mistake by giving up the daily car ride with her father.

Especially since Christophe, who has been given a scooter, never takes the bus anymore.

So, to kill time during those hours on buses and in bus shelters, Hélène reads. Plenty of classics still—Balzac, Zola, Flaubert. But increasingly, it's the Americans she is drawn to: Dorothy Parker, *Martin Eden, Beloved*. Then *Perfume*, which she devours in three days, so enthralled that she forgets to do her math homework, resulting in a mediocre grade that brings tears to her eyes. Charlotte is green with envy: she worked like a dog and got the same grade. Hélène promises herself she will never let this happen again.

ONE MORNING IN November, she arrives at the school just before eight, as she does every day, and immediately senses that something unusual is going on. In the playground, the students are gathered in excitable little groups, all of them staring at copies of the local newspaper. Hélène glances anxiously at these clusters of kids, hands hidden inside the sleeves of her Oxbow jacket. None of this means anything to her, all the more so since she is feeling self-conscious: her jeans are too short, revealing a flash of her fancy socks. She complained about this, but her mother didn't want to know.

"Your other jeans are all in the laundry basket. You're growing too fast, that's the problem—we can't keep up with you!"

She joins Charlotte in their usual corner, under the bell and near the red ashtray.

"What's up with everybody?"

"Haven't you seen?"

"What?"

Charlotte is semi-hysterical too, like she's just won the lottery or something. She takes the front page of *La Liberté de l'Est* from her coat pocket and carefully unfolds it.

There's a photograph of Christophe Marchal, hair drenched with sweat, smile as big as America, with his name in the headline above it.

"He was on the TV news last night too. It's unbelievable."

This is how Hélène learns that Christophe scored four goals against Caen in his most recent game. Of course, she already knew—as everybody does—that he has been playing for the first team since he was sixteen, an impressive feat in itself. But until then he has not really shone, and nobody's talked about him except in terms of the hazing he's gone through. For his first away game, he spent three hundred kilometers taped to the bus toilet, and when they arrived they had to use a box cutter to free him. But Christophe has proven himself a good teammate and eventually become a regular in the starting lineup. The 1991–92 season ended well too, with Épinal reaching the playoffs for the first time in years and finishing fourth in the D1 championship.

They're still a long way from the top, but for the first time fate seems to be smiling upon this hardworking, solid little team. At least that's what it says in the article in *La Liberté de l'Est*, which Hélène devours that morning. The team's core players have been working together for the past four years, and there is an almost telepathic connection between them now. In the past there have been some terrible defeats, but this season they seem to have found their groove. The article highlights a friendly game against Megève, during which Épinal was losing all the way through the game but did not give up. Instead, the team continued following its game plan, working as a well-organized unit, before winning the game in the last seconds by nine goals to eight.

The journalist also mentions the fate of Jan Pavlík, the Czech forward who joined the team in 1990. The poor guy played only three games before being diagnosed with testicular cancer. The Saturday after his hospitalization, there was a somber silence in the locker room. Apparently some of the players were in tears, and not necessarily the youngest ones. That night, Coach Villeneuve did not say much in his pregame talk. This wasn't a Hollywood movie. One of their friends was possibly about to die; he was young, and the father of a four-year-old boy. Under the circumstances, the game they were about to play did not seem very important. None of them felt like goofing around, or even winning. All the coach said was: "Come on, boys." In the sound of sticky tape being unrolled, a few sniffs, hockey sticks scraping the ground, something took shape.

Now, Pavlík is playing again. He scores in every game, without any big celebrations. He is composed in front of goal, works hard in practice, is focused and conscientious, not very talkative but always smiling. He has become a role model, his impeccable attitude shaming the shirkers who care only about getting drunk after the game. He has brought a professional-ism to the team.

Not only that, but Pavlík convinced the club management to hire two of his former teammates, Zlatko Kovar and Bruno Pelc, who played with him in Zagreb before the war. To reach Épinal, they had to travel through Hungary, Austria, and Germany in a Fiat Panda decorated with bullet holes, before finally being arrested at the French border. The club president was forced to abandon his wife and children during their vacation in Juan-les-Pins from July 14 to August 15 so he could rescue the Czech boys from their difficulties. When he saw those two scarecrows, neither of whom had washed for five days, he thought: shit, we've been screwed over here. The story spread quickly. At least it was something to talk about.

To celebrate their reunion, the three Czechs went on a three-day bender that climaxed with them swimming naked in the fountain at Place de la Chipotte. And then preseason training began, the dreaded fitness program designed to dust off the cobwebs of summer and build up muscle and stamina. And, right away, the coach sensed that something was happening. In their first friendly game against Dijon, the Czechs proved devastating. Nobody in Épinal had seen hockey like that before: so fluid, so fast. Dijon were completely dismantled. "A Team Is Born," ran the headline in the Sunday paper.

After that, everything went perfectly. At the Poissompré rink, the supporters were more fervent than ever, and those who had stopped attending games during the past few seasons of mediocrity swarmed back. The press sniffed a comeback story. Sponsors offered money. The VIP seats were packed. And on Saturday night, Christophe Marchal scored four goals in the victory over Caen. This is what everyone has been hoping for: a local boy—someone young, handsome, and gifted—to turn himself into a legend. The people here have so few reasons to be happy: they are miles from the sea and from Paris, God is just as dead here as He is everywhere else, and evenings end at eight o'clock on weekdays and in clubs on weekends.

So, when Christophe—"as seen on TV"—arrives at school that Monday morning, it's full-on Marchalmania. All the guys want to be his friend; all the girls find him even sexier than before. People want to touch him, hear him speak. He just laughs and scratches his head, but nobody is disappointed. At last the bell rings and he heads toward Building B, followed by half the teenagers in the department. On the way there, his eyes meet Charlotte's and his smile falters slightly. Charlotte takes a drag on her cigarette, as disdainful as a fallen star.

"What a moron," says Hélène.

Charlotte doesn't even bother responding. From that moment on, both girls go to see every game at the rink.

UNTIL CHRISTMAS, THE Épinal players win most of their games. They don't rack up huge scores, but they do enough. Everyone knows their strengths and weaknesses. Now that the element of surprise has been removed, the Czechs do not prove quite so irresistible, but they still play a brand of hockey that blends technique with aggression, and the coach knows he can depend on them. The older players bring their experience to the mix, in particular Papeloux, Giovaninetti, and the captain, Anthony Gargano, who—after a brief spell with Mannheim—has returned to Épinal to finish his career. His knees have gone and his back aches constantly, but a few injections and three physical-therapy sessions per week are enough to keep him on the ice. And in the locker room, everyone enjoys his deadpan humor, his concealed kindness. He is better than the coach at shutting up the big mouths in the squad: Madani, Petit, and the Russian goalkeeper Dimitriov, whom nobody really understands but who loves to grumble in Cyrillic. Gargano also knows how to galvanize the troops when fatigue sets in or when they have to get back on the scoreboard after letting one in.

When it comes to scoring goals, the team's most potent weapon is Christophe Marchal. Nobody knows exactly how the metamorphosis happened, but he has abruptly changed from being a promising but selfish little jerk into a prolific goal scorer whose elusive movements and laser-sharp finishing sometimes bring an awed hush to the rink.

Sadly, the team is already ageing. It is entirely possible that they will end the season by being promoted into the top division, but will they be able to maintain this level of performance?

For all these reasons, the 1992–93 season is unmissable, an epoch of potential greatness that is also a last-chance saloon. The weight of this expectation can be felt at every game. The greater the hope, the greater the devastation if that hope is shattered. When the winter break arrives, Épinal is in third place behind Megève and Strasbourg.

The games that take place during the holiday season always have a special atmosphere. In the middle of winter, the locals seem to flock to Poissompré in search of the warmth they are missing in their daily lives. They are off work, relaxed. They've been drinking mulled wine at the Christmas market, and by late afternoon you can see them walking in procession toward the rink, filling the streets, in their coats and scarves and hats, kids running ahead of them and sometimes starting brief snowball fights. When they get there, the strings of white lights that cover the building's façade are flashing, and the enormous Christmas tree is decorated with baubles of white and gold, the club colors. When Tino Rossi's voice emerges from the speakers, singing "Petit Papa Noël," almost a thousand people outside the rink sing along, shivering and red-nosed, stamping their feet to keep warm.

The first game takes place in Épinal on December 20, and their opponent is Strasbourg. Over the years, the local rivalry between the two towns has accumulated a long list of grievances: the usual mix of bad luck, injuries, and refereeing mistakes. The geographical proximity feeds into this, as does the stupidity of certain supporters. Not to mention the habit that Strasbourg has developed of helping itself to Épinal's best players once the season ends, nor the efforts of the local press to stoke the fires of this two-bit rivalry. In any case, sparks always fly when the two teams meet.

That night, Hélène and Charlotte have managed to buy a small bottle of rum from the local Monoprix and they drink its contents on the way to the game. At the rink, they meet up with a few school friends who are sharing a bottle of plum punch. The two girls link arms, their faces shining in the light from the Christmas decorations. After a while, Charlotte slips away with Fabrice Scandella, and when she returns she has red eyes and a dry mouth.

"What have you been up to?"

"Nothing."

"Were you smoking?"

"Whoa, chill out, you're not my mom."

Hélène refuses to drink when they pass the bottle of punch. She doesn't like making a show of herself when there are adults around. She can't help thinking about her parents. It's annoying, having to be so disciplined, so worried about tomorrow, such a goody-two-shoes. She wishes she could not give a fuck, like Charlotte, or like that slut Caroline Lambert who hangs out with college students in Nancy and goes clubbing every weekend. For her part, Hélène stays strictly on the straight and narrow; not that this prevents her parents from giving her a hard time.

"Come on, don't sulk," says Charlotte.

She takes her friend by the arm and nuzzles her neck.

"I'm not sulking," Hélène replies.

"Could have fooled me..."

Charlotte winks at her, then moves off toward the others. The little gang is growing more and more animated. That idiot Scandella has started singing "We Are the Champions," and now he's encouraging people to shout along with him: "Strasbourg! Strasbourg! Up yours! Up yours!" The crowd obediently goes along with this, the kids especially, happy for any excuse to repeat expressions that make their parents frown.

When the rink finally opens its doors, the crowd rushes in and two firefighters have to intervene to calm a few people down. Hélène and Charlotte have managed to sneak in before most of the others and, tickets in pockets, are running to the bleachers to choose their seats. Soon the rows are crammed, and the waiting begins. The whole town appears to be there, everyone looking around excitedly at everyone else.

At last, after a good half hour of this, the players emerge onto the ice to the sound of "We Will Rock You," amid sweeping searchlights and flashing spotlights. The crowd rises to its feet while the announcer's nasal voice reads out the team roster. Each player's name is met with applause and cheers. The bass notes vibrate inside their torsos. When Christophe Marchal's name is announced over the loudspeakers, Hélène and her friend lose it completely.

"You sound like feral cats," says Xavier Cuny, the gastroenterologist's son who already has a car and is famous for eating his boogers in class.

"Oh, shut up," says Charlotte, looking ecstatic.

"Yeah, shut up," Hélène choruses.

Xavier Cuny gives them the finger, but the arena is filled with the sound of booing now as the Strasbourg players come out onto the ice. You even hear a few insults—*assholes*, *Krauts*, *motherfuckers*, the usual stuff. Finally, the game starts and time speeds up.

In the third minute, the Canadian player Martial Maxwell scores against Épinal with a perfect shot into the top corner. Stung, the Wolves swarm around the opposition net, but a counterattack by the Schwartz brothers earns the Strasbourg team its second goal, quickly followed by a third, this one scored by a former Épinal player—a guy who had grown up in Épinal, in fact. Gargano's teammates look stunned. In the bleachers, a sickened resignation has replaced the earlier jubilation and the first break in play comes as a relief. Hundreds of people rise as one to seek consolation at the bar.

"I don't feel good," says Charlotte.

"What?"

"I think I'm going to hurl."

Hélène looks at her friend. She's pale, hair glued to her clammy forehead, eyes glazed.

"Come with me," Hélène says, grabbing her hand.

And she pushes her way through the mass of bodies to the restroom, where she pulls Charlotte into a stall and locks the door behind them. Charlotte falls to her knees and, hands gripping the edge of the bowl, pukes up her guts while Hélène holds her hair in a ponytail. When her stomach is empty, she slumps onto the floor and leans back against the plywood divider. Her teeth start to chatter.

Hélène hugs her and says: "It'll be okay."

She kisses her forehead, rubs her shoulders and her arms. Charlotte is whining and a trickle of saliva is running over her lips, which have turned a weird pinkish color.

"It hurts," she moans.

"Your stomach?"

Charlotte does not reply. In the distance, Hélène can hear the muffled roar of the crowd, hundreds of feet stamping in time. The game has started again, but the two girls stay there for a moment without moving, like an egg dropped on the tile floor. Charlotte dozes for a while on her friend's shoulder, and Hélène feels quite good in their shared bodily warmth, despite the smell of ammonia, the cold under their butts, the general filthiness, and the slamming of other stall doors.

Gradually, Charlotte starts to look better.

"How are you feeling?"

"Okay ... I'm sorry."

"Don't worry about it."

"Thank you," whispers Charlotte.

They look at each other almost like lovers, both of them thrilled to be close friends again. And even if it doesn't last, who cares?

IN THE FINAL period, Épinal is losing five to one and the crowd goes wild, aware though they are the game is almost up, particularly with Strasbourg defending as if their lives depended on it.

"What the fuck, they've got four goalies now!" Scandella shrieks.

Christophe comes on with his two fellow forwards to replace the Czech front line and the supporters barely have time to chant his name before he sends a shot rocketing straight at the Strasbourg goalie's mask. A shiver runs through the crowd, sickened by the precise thud of the puck, which sounds like it smashes against bone. After a brief interruption, the goalkeeper is ready to play again and the game restarts. Papeloux intercepts, passes to Christophe, he passes to Gargano...goal!

Little more than a minute later, Christophe scores, his shot so powerful it almost rips the net. Five to three. The rink is in uproar, packed to the rafters, the atmosphere pulsing with the crazed, unquestioning aliveness of Saturday nights. But Christophe's forward line has already been replaced. The Strasbourg players, momentarily disoriented, start to misplace their passes and once again lose the puck. The Épinal coach asks for a time-out. His players crowd around him and examine the drawings he's sketched in green marker on his little whiteboard. Then he says something to Christophe, who shakes his head. There's a brief altercation between them, with everyone watching, and in the end Christophe theatrically throws his gloves onto the ice before heading back to the locker room.

"What's he doing?" Hélène gasps.

"What a dick!" says Scandella.

The crowd can't believe it. A second before, anything had seemed possible, but now the magic spell is broken and fatigue seeps through their limbs. The supporters realize they've been yelling too loud and too long, the players that they are getting old and have nothing left to give. The game restarts, but everyone knows it's over.

IN THE NEXT day's *La Liberté de l'Est*, the incident is duly blown out of proportion. Christophe is criticized for his immaturity, his selfishness, his diva-like attitude. At the bar, people wonder who the hell he thinks he is. *The insolent little fucker*, says the club president, though he smiles as he pronounces these words in what sounds oddly like a tone of pride. Christophe does not apologize, but in the return game, won 12–7 by Épinal, he scores three goals. Thus is born the legend of that almost perfect season, with its bouncing Czechs, the rebellious but gifted young forward, the hard-drinking but reliable captain, a team on the verge of terminal decline and yet at the peak of its powers, going all out to seize this once-in-a-lifetime opportunity.

After finishing third in their pool, the Wolves move into the playoffs. There, good luck and hard work enable them to overperform, and despite their modest talent levels they are feared. They beat Caen in the quarterfinals, and Lyon in the semis. Each time, it takes them three games to make it through. In Épinal, everyone is starting to believe. The press has a field day, and some of the players are even asked for autographs out in the street. And then there is the final, against Tours.

The Épinal team is audacious and alert in attack, and extremely robust in defense. But Christophe delivers his worst performance of the season. He even gets into a fight with an opposition player and ends the game on the bench after being carded. From there, he watches his team lose. An opportunity missed.

So Épinal is promoted to the top division, but two of its most important players, Gargano and Papeloux, hang up their skates for good, while the Czechs are signed up by Chamonix, Gap, and Reims. The dream ends in all-too-predictable bitterness. Even so, at the end of June the club organizes a party to celebrate their semi-success. All the local bigwigs are there, various town councillors and representatives of the chamber of commerce, the sponsors, and the players of course, accompanied by their families and friends, not to mention the usual freeloaders and a few handpicked supporters.

Hélène and Charlotte, as cute young girls, have little difficulty getting into the party, where they knock back a few drinks while listening to bland thank-you speeches. The club president, however, after making the obligatory polite remarks, gets straight to the point.

"And now, I'd like to talk about the future!"

All the girls in the room are staring at Christophe, whom they have spotted next to the buffet, where he and two of his teammates are quietly plundering the food on offer.

"Next year, the Wolves will play at the highest level. Coach Villeneuve and I are already working hard on recruitment. And I have to say that it's looking promising. I can't tell you any details right now, but we have targets in Quebec and the Czech Republic. And other ideas, around Valenciennes in particular. But, most importantly, we are holding on to our young players—including this season's new star. Is he here? Christophe Marchal. Where is he? I know I saw him here earlier."

The guests look at one another questioningly and their eyes scan the room, but number 20 has disappeared. In the end, Papeloux goes off to search for him. And Charlotte follows, quickly telling Hélène: "I'll be back."

"Sure you will," says Hélène.

"I *will*."

Hélène watches her friend head toward the bathroom. The president's speech drones on for another minute or two with promises of great victories to come, a few touching tributes, and a toast to the club's health. Hélène raises her glass along with everyone else, feeling vaguely disgusted. It's not the first time Charlotte has played this trick on her. She goes outside to smoke a cigarette and sees that her friend's scooter is no longer in the parking lot.

WALKING BACK HOME, Hélène's heart is heavy. Five kilometers on foot gives her plenty of time to think. She will turn seventeen a month from now, and her mother is constantly telling her that these are the best years of her life. This does not seem promising for the rest of her existence. As far as she can tell, being a sixteen-year-old consists mostly of being bored out of your mind because you're not allowed to do anything. And even when her parents do let her go out, she has to be careful, keep an eye on the time. Pretty often her mother will sniff her breath after she comes home from a night out with friends. So, in the end, her pleasure is spoiled by an excess of fear and precautions. She was once grounded for two weeks just for smoking one measly cigarette.

And everything is like that: negotiated, arbitrary, whittled down. Apparently, it's for her own good. But Hélène no longer believes this. She senses something else behind the tight rein her parents keep her on. As if her mother fears what she might become: a beast, a woman, maybe a rival. Hélène doesn't make a fuss, though. She doesn't want to give them the satisfaction. She just slams doors and locks herself in her bedroom to seethe in silence. I'm going to get out of here, she thinks, just you wait and see. One day I'll be able to do anything I want.

This is why she spends all her time studying, why she's top of her class in every subject. Because she has a plan: get the best grades she can, then get as far away from this place as possible.

In class, while others crumble under the weight of all their work, Hélène sails through.

"Fuck me, we've got math homework, an essay to write, and the whole of the First World War to learn," Charlotte moans. "Are they literally trying to kill us or what?"

"I can show you my math if you want."

"Sure, but what about the essay?"

"Well, I can't write it for you."

"Are you sure?"

On her report card, the math teacher writes: "Hélène is a machine." And it's true. She's methodical, fast, organized, and she has an unbelievable memory. Her only problem is impatience. Sometimes she finds the teachers mediocre, her parents completely stupid. Now and then, she will sigh so loudly in class that the teacher, busy writing proper nouns or equations on the blackboard, will turn around.

"Is there a problem, Mademoiselle Poirot?"

"No, monsieur."

"Am I not going fast enough for you?"

"It's okay."

"You are not the only person in the world, you know."

"So it seems…"

"I am going to write to your parents about your attitude, young lady."

Hélène's attitude has already been brought up during the third-quarter parent-teacher night, and it is the reason she did not receive the best possible grade for behavior. Madame Collard, her French teacher, did everything she could to screw up Hélène's student file. She reproached her for her arrogance and described her and Charlotte as disruptive to the harmony of the class, and even "subversive." The two girls were thrilled by this last word, giggling over it for days. They found out about it from another teacher, who summoned Hélène to her office. Madame Clair is a small, round woman with very long hair who sometimes wears a tie and almost always a hideous, copper-buttoned blazer. She teaches math to the Bac S students, and is so highly qualified that the school allows her to get away with certain eccentricities, such as playing the musical saw in class, or forcing rowdy students to stand on their desk with their hands on their head. Anyway, she really likes Hélène.

"You know, I come from a very modest background too."

Hélène grimaces. She hates it when adults look at her as if seeing their own youth reflected back at them.

"For the competitive exam, you need a solid student file. Madame Collard is nuts, she's hysterical. I'm going to make sure she doesn't cause you too many problems. But you absolutely must stop behaving that way in class."

Hélène rolls her eyes.

"Yes, that is a very good example of the kind of behavior I'm talking about."

Madame Clair summons her on several occasions to her shabby little brown-and-yellow office full of moldering archives, far from the agitation of the school itself, almost in the basement in fact. At ten in the morning, when a beam of spring sunlight shines through the window, Hélène can see half a century's worth of dust shining golden in the air. Each time, her stomach writhes in anxiety as Madame Clair closes the door, sits down, and confides in her.

"I had incredible abilities too, you know. I finished second in the national schools competition."

Forty years later, she harps on about this almost-success and various others—taking the exam for the École Polytechnique, a brief appearance on the TV game show *Des Chiffres et des Lettres*—before discussing other frustrations: her difficulties with the administration, the growing stupidity of students, her aching feet. But the most important thing is that Hélène has a promising future, and she refuses to see it ruined. She also insists that Hélène should enter the national schools competition. Hélène does not see the point.

"It will be good for your student file," Madame Clair tells her, almost pleading.

Of course she understands that Hélène is bored, that she finds adults lacking and life too constrictive. And the copper buttons on her sleeves jingle in the pinkish-gold rays of that April morning.

"You're right," she says. "This place is too small for you. You'll be better somewhere else."

She simpers, sad-eyed, like a spaniel. Hélène promises to behave better and, in the privacy of her bedroom, continues to work hard every day, pursuing her studies with a seriousness that only increases as her friend gets on her nerves, as her parents bore her to tears, as boys seem more and more like a total waste of time. Hélène sinks into the consolation of effort. She normally starts with memorization—history, languages, the long lessons—but things stick in her mind as soon as she hears them and she has no difficulty reeling off dates and definitions, German vocabulary and grammar. Then she moves on to the sciences. In addition to the problems and exercises that everybody has to do, Madame Clair also gives her a few little treats that will not be on the curriculum until the following year. Integrals, derivatives, vector geometry.

"Whatever you do, don't get sucked into their nonsense about computers and calculators. This is where math happens," she says, tapping her forehead with an index finger.

Hélène takes an almost physical satisfaction from all of this. The possibility of establishing some kind of truth in this ill-conceived world is not only a comfort, but a pleasure. When she reaches the end of an equation, by calculating a derivative or by tracing a curve on graph paper with the tip of her Criterium, and at last comes up with an irrefutable answer, she feels euphoric. The temporary solidity of mathematics becomes her refuge.

Sometimes her mother finds her working late at night, bent over in the light from her desk lamp, hair scraped back in a ponytail. She sits on the edge of the bed, close to her, and watches.

"What are you doing?" Hélène asks.

"Nothing."

Mireille is prey to contradictory feelings: admiration and anxiety, a mother's amazement at seeing her baby become this tall, self-conscious teenager with a woman's hips and a child's reactions, with her fiery Mary Magdalene hair and her bitten nails, who lazes around in bed and has ambitions to go to a *grande école*, who quotes great writers and still can't manage to put her dirty clothes in the laundry basket, whose vocabulary is stuffed with obscure words and who sniffs her T-shirts to decide whether she can wear them for another day, who sometimes eats noodles with her fingers, her mind elsewhere, and who stretches like a cat at the end of a meal after wiping the sauce from her plate with a slice of bread, a kid who wants high heels and the pill. She watches her, caught in a mix of hopes and fears.

Because both she and Jeannot know they cannot do much more for her. They act as if they can, but in reality they can't make decisions for her anymore. They are reduced to trusting her, crossing their fingers, hoping that they've brought her up right and that this will be enough.

Adolescence is premeditated murder, planned long in advance, and the body of their family as it used to be already lies dead by the side of the road. Now they must reinvent roles, accept new distances, to deal with the horror and the sudden kicks. The body is still warm. It twitches. But what used to exist—childhood and its tender moments, the unquestioned reign of adults with the kid at its center, cocooned and protected, vacations in La Grande-Motte and family Sundays at home—all of this has died. It will never come back to life.

So Mireille watches her daughter. She envies her, resents her, she wishes she could touch her. The love inside her hurts. She thinks: little idiot, my love, stupid numpty, my darling, who do you think you are, don't leave us. She is so proud. Letting go is so hard. Her eyes well with tears. Oh great, this is all she needs. If only she could go back in time, follow the thread to its beginning. When Hélène was ten, six, three. Even before that: her little body wobbling on two feet, the tiny robot with a runny nose, the voice repeating each word, the chubby little fist holding the spoon and banging it against the tray of the high chair, the gap-toothed smile, the wrinkled nose, that other Hélène who was all hers.

"Are you working?"

"Yes," her daughter replies.

"That's good."

THE YEAR PASSES, easy and painful at the same time. Naturally, Hélène passes her baccalaureate with flying colors. In

263

the written section, she chooses to do the literary commentary on a boring Julien Gracq text and is given a score of seventeen out of twenty. At the oral exam, she gets Baudelaire's *L'Invitation au voyage*, and the astounded examiner asks her: "What do you plan to do after your exams?"

"HEC Business School."

"Ah... Well, I'm going to give you eighteen anyway."

Charlotte doesn't do too badly either: twelve for the written test, seventeen for the oral. The school year is over, just in time. In May, Hélène played hooky for the first time. Her academic abilities saved her, but the truant officer explains to her that life doesn't work that way. Arms crossed and chewing gum, Hélène barely listens. The truant officer holds the trash can in front of her and she spits the gum into it. He knows her type: super smart, already looking way past school and regarding her classes as supermarket aisles, taking whatever she likes and forgetting the rest. In five or six years, Hélène will undoubtedly earn more than he does. This does not make it any easier for him to admonish her.

That year, Charlotte did not invite Hélène to go on vacation with her family to the Île de Ré, and that's good too. They have been a little cold with each other since Charlotte left her friend in the lurch at the hockey party so she could sneak off with Christophe. And then Hélène got a job at a summer camp for young musicians. In the mornings, the kids have to practice their instrument, and in the afternoons they do the usual camp stuff: pony rides, rock climbing, archery, swimming in the Serre-Ponçon lake. She's heard the camp is full of little geniuses, rich kids who are often a little eccentric but very affectionate.

In the meantime, she is preparing for the big post-exam blowout. Charlotte has heard about a party organized by seniors near the Stade de la Colombière, in the hills just outside

Épinal. The two girls have decided to attend. When Hélène talks to her parents about it, they pretend to give her permission, but the truth is that they have no choice: if they told her she couldn't go, they know perfectly well she would sneak out anyway. And they can hardly tie her to the bed.

"You will be careful, won't you?"

"Of course."

"Protect yourself."

Hélène rolls her eyes.

When the big day comes around, Charlotte turns up thirty minutes late, looking gaunt, her shoulders slumped, shoulder blades sticking out like cuttlefish bones.

"What's up with you?" Hélène asks, grabbing her motorcycle helmet.

But she already knows the answer.

"I ache all over. It's like someone's stabbing needles in my belly. Honestly, I almost didn't come at all."

"Have you taken anything?"

"Advil."

"You'd better not drink."

"I don't think I'm even going to stay."

Mireille spies on this scene through the half-open shutters. Jean goes over and kisses her hair, caresses her arm. Below them, the scooter whines as it stutters into life. Hélène's parents watch as the two girls ride off into the distance, narrow-shouldered, long hair flying from under their helmets. Mireille feels very old. Her husband tells her it'll be okay, and this irritates her. Of course it'll be okay. It couldn't be any worse than this.

The girls ride through Cornécourt, deserted at that time of day. Already the setting sun is blurring edges, turning streets an oily golden color. It's one of those aimless weekday evenings when everyone stays home, enjoying their yard or watching the local news on TV, waiting for the winning lottery numbers to be announced. When a traffic light turns green, only one car sets off. Some young morons on a motorcycle have begun their usual patrol and, on the highway in the distance, the girls can hear the sound of 750cc engines, those catastrophic satellites that orbit endlessly around small French towns. Meanwhile Hélène and Charlotte continue sputtering toward their destination. On the back of the scooter, Hélène smokes a cigarette. Her heart feels so light. The school year is over and she has a week of total laziness before she leaves for the summer camp. She will do nothing but read and wait, masturbate whenever she feels like it, maybe go for a bike ride now and then, or go into town to see what Charlotte's up to. Together, the two of them will chill out on the terrace of Le Commerce, maybe head over to the skate park, share the usual complaints about how little there is to do in this shitty town. But Hélène isn't fooling herself: the future is wide open and just up ahead. And that evening, her chest is filled with the glory of an unending dawn.

A half hour later, reality slaps her in the face.

Charlotte, doubled over in pain, says: "I can't handle this anymore. I'm leaving."

Hélène is pissed. They've only just gotten here, and it took them ten minutes to find the place where this party is supposed to happen: a crappy soccer field surrounded by remnants of woodland with, at one end, an unimpeded view of the town's less salubrious neighborhoods. For now, there are only about fifteen high school kids drinking beer and trying to light a fire. Apart from Nirina, a tall girl in her English class, and a few vaguely familiar faces, Hélène doesn't know anyone there.

"Well, I'm staying," she says.

Charlotte stares at her for a moment, disappointed. Tiny beads of sweat are visible on her pale forehead. With a sigh, she slowly straightens up.

"If you see Christophe..." she begins.

Hélène tries to remain impassive. That pathetic secret, which has been between them for so long. But Charlotte changes her mind.

"No, forget it."

She just raises the seat of her scooter and grabs the six-pack of beer inside it.

"Here."

"Thanks."

Another moment, looking at each other, not saying anything.

"Well."

"Yeah."

"Bye."

"Bye."

Hélène watches her friend ride away, wobbling over the bumpy ground, half bent over with pain. Then she carries the six-pack over to where Nirina is standing.

Two hours and five beers later, Hélène drunkenly begins wandering from group to group, can in hand, feeling pleasantly lethargic, sweatshirt tied over her shoulders, barefoot inside her sneakers. She's happy. She feels free, enjoying this perfect little interlude, when the year is over and all that remains of it is this suspended moment, this temporary island of neutralized summers, days of pure relaxation, no kids, no worries, no wrinkles, nothing but her summer job and those two months of largesse that we think will always come back. Against the velvet canvas of the high sky, she sees constellations glinting only for her. Head thrown back, mouth open, teeth exposed, she feels like she could eat the whole universe. Her stomach would hold it, that's for sure.

Around eleven, Christophe turns up with his friends on motorcycles, the usual gang of macho show-offs, making too much noise and acting like the kings of the world. From a distance, Hélène watches them as they laugh around the fire that the others finally got burning between two cinder blocks. There's a hint of contempt in the way she looks at them, but behind it that other desire still pulses. The flames redraw Christophe's face in thick black and bright lines, and he becomes a sort of miniature sound and light show, with laughter, the sound of engines roaring and fading as people come and go, the rotating shadows that seek and sway. She finishes her beer, then makes a decision and heads straight for Christophe.

"Hi."

He turns to her, surprised, his friends snickering, but Hélène doesn't care.

"Can I talk to you?"

"About what?"

"A thing."

The boy turns to his friends, who feel they have the right to be even more stupid than usual.

"Who's that?"

"Does she want some sugar?"

Christophe shrugs and nods, though, and they walk off, leaving the taunts and monkey noises behind them. Hélène shivers slightly, although it's not really cold. After a while she feels the back of her hand touch the boy's skin and that sensation goes straight to her heart.

"So where are we going?"

The girl stands still. A little dazed, she turns to face him.

"I wanted to tell you..."

They are standing at the edge of the trees now, far from the others, reduced to two vague, faceless shadows. Her heart is pounding inside her chest. She swallows.

"Charlotte had to leave," she says.

"What?"

"Charlotte. She wasn't feeling well."

"Ah."

She needs to do something now or she will miss the boat. He's there, so real. All it takes is some courage.

"She had a stomachache."

"Okay."

Two seconds longer, then the boy takes a step to the side. Hélène grabs his arm and kisses him randomly, her lips finding only his chin. Without a word, he frees himself and she's left alone with nothing but the memory of her ridiculous move. Already he's rejoined his friends around the fire as it dances in the perfect night, silhouetting images that she will never forget. Hélène hears their laughter and the crackles of the blazing wood. Tomorrow she will be seventeen. The best years of her life.

13

THE TWO OF them went on with their lives, stuffed to the brim and blinkered, punctuated with occasional what's-the-point feelings. And now with this new thing that occupied the center of their existence: each other.

For Christophe, there were long days spent on the road, roaming the countryside, the interminable round of client meetings, the cold calls and the stupid sales conferences. And then, at eight o'clock, practice sessions at the rink.

When he had Gabriel, he would go to practice only on Tuesday and Thursday evenings. He came to an arrangement with Marco, who would pick the boy up at school and take care of him until Christophe came to fetch him around ten, when he would often be asleep. The two men would chat for five minutes in the kitchen and Marco would tell him how it had gone: homework and ground beef with mashed potatoes. Christophe would give Marco a kiss on the cheek, then carry his son out of the house and put him in the back of the station wagon, wrapped up in a blanket, the softest he'd been able to find. Back at home, he would take the child up to his bedroom, undress him, trying not to wake him, then pull the duvet up to his shoulders. He would murmur *I love you* into the pillow, breathing in the smell of his son's hair. For a moment he would stand there in the little bedroom and look at the pirate night-light, the collection of *Star Wars* figures, the tank with the broken cannon, the wallpaper where Gabriel had drawn ships in Crayola.

Charlie was moving in January, and Christophe still hadn't told his father. The decline in the old man's faculties seemed to have been on pause for a while, although that had not prevented him from losing his credit card again, nor from leaving the gas on under a saucepan for three hours the week before. And he kept having those terrible fits of rage that made him unrecognizable and terrified the boy, after which he would apologize profusely before retreating to watch TV.

For Christophe, things went on as they had before: nights of fitful sleep, days of physical exhaustion. Now and then he would feel as if the world's makeup had run, exposing its true face, naked and horrifying. These brief moments of lucidity were like deep dives into memory, bringing back flashes of the past, often while he was on the bus with the hockey team, his forehead pressed against the window, the landscape blurring past his eyes.

He saw himself again as a little boy in the school playground, the blackboard with its round sponge, rules of French grammar and the big chestnut tree through the window. He remembered Jacky and Corbier, the Orinoco and the smell of clementines, playing the Atari console with his brother, riding his BMX, and Christmases better than armistices.

For a long time he had swallowed every lie, taken each curve in the road without blinking. Then, starting with middle school, his life had suddenly accelerated. He'd had to carry a backpack weighing ten kilos, be cool and check out girls, listen to his ever-more-boring teachers drone on as each year passed, shorter than the one before. There had been hockey and the illusions that went with it, Julien acting so differently, that whole farce of their dysfunctional family life, even if it was still full of love. Trips to the fair with Marco and Greg, the Tokaido Express roller coaster and the smell of hot waffles, holding Charlie's hand in a city-center street one Wednesday afternoon.

And then the words that had cut his life in two: Mom is dead.

Everything had sped up then, until he reached the endurance race known as adulthood: the unending tiredness that nobody ever talked about, clearing one hurdle after another with another one always just ahead. Work, children, and—already—the hint of death, discreet but perceptible because it took him two days to get over a drinking binge, because sleep became a faint mist, blown away by the smallest worry, and because tomorrow it would all be over. This was how Christophe had realized that this life was not his. It had just been a bridge he had crossed, a pair of shoes he had borrowed, leaving him nothing from those first forty years but a string of blurred memories. Ultimately, all he had done was give his strength for a master plan he knew nothing about. The world had perpetuated itself through him, without ever asking him what he thought. When you looked at it objectively, it was enough to make you want to kill yourself.

Thankfully, from time to time, Épinal would win. And on the bus home they would sing and drink vodka until they blacked out.

AS FOR HÉLÈNE, she had her hands full too. The uptick predicted by Erwann had occurred: Elexia was attracting new clients every week, and the forecasts were for a year of stupendous growth. For weeks, everyone at the company had been working under pressure, and twice employees had broken down in tears in the middle of the open-plan office. Some of them had even threatened to form a union, but such rebellion was confined to whispers by the coffee machine or via personal messages, and nobody truly believed it would happen. Jean-Charles Parrot and his innovation team, meanwhile, were coming up with innovative solutions, and you could hardly blame them for that. Thanks to Parrot, Elexia would soon be able offer inclusive management training, transition advice, behavioral design modules, cognitive system audits, and tools for environmental and collaborative forecasting. Erwann was ecstatic, and the two men spent hours on end in his mezzanine office, changing the world with a lot of arm-waving and visionary Anglicisms. Erwann was expected to make an important announcement at the Christmas party, which would be bigger than ever that year—a somewhat disturbing prospect, given that the previous year there had been vomit all over the walls and ceiling of the women's bathroom.

But what most annoyed Hélène was seeing Lison get caught up in all this nonsense. That little jerk Parrot had even given her a benchmark mission: to find out what other regions were doing to help local authorities facing mergers.

"But do you have any idea what you're doing?" Hélène asked her.

"Oh, I'll just surf the web. It's not really that complicated: you start off by saying stuff like"—here Lison made air quotes—"'Now that the stakes have been raised,' and then you just use loads of words like 'creative,' 'agile,' blah blah blah."

"Yeah, although that doesn't really mean anything."

"I'll find a few examples, a bit of Rhône-Alpes here, some Aquitaine there, you know... Anyway, the main thing is coming up with a good triplet."

"Huh?"

"The three *B*s, the three *V*s, the three *I*s. Doesn't matter what it is, but there has to be a triplet or people start to worry."

"And what triplet do you have in mind?" Hélène asked, gazing in amusement at her intern, who that day was wearing platform sneakers, boyfriend jeans, and an impressively oversized camel coat.

"I'm thinking of going with the three *C*s. 'Collective,' 'concerned,' and..."

"'Complex'?"

"Nah, too easy."

"'Creative.'"

"Too clichéd."

"'Cooperative.'"

"I was thinking more along the lines of 'calamitous.'"

"That works too," Hélène agreed. "Although personally I would go with 'cretin.'"

"Yeah, and I'll use a slide of Parrot's face to illustrate it."

Despite everything, Hélène and Lison had managed to make their Thursday meetings at Le Galway a regular thing. Philippe knew about them and would go home early to look after the girls. Sitting in the pub with a pint each, the two women would have playful, feisty, in-depth discussions. Hélène's secret affair naturally took up a lot of the conversation. The day after she and Christophe had consummated their relationship, Hélène had proudly announced: "Well, it happened."

"Really? Come on then, tell me..."

Hélène had pulled a face, but a few minutes later she had told her friend everything.

FOR CHRISTOPHE AND Hélène, the Hotel Kyriad had become an island in the raging ocean of their lives. They went there once or twice a week, meeting briefly in the mornings or afternoons, never getting enough of each other, always wanting more.

Christophe usually arrived first. Spotting his station wagon, Hélène would park at a distance away from it, out of some inexplicable superstition. The hotel staff were used to seeing them now. Everything had become familiar, automatic. She climbed the stairs and scratched at the door. Christophe opened it, barefoot, then grabbed her hand and pulled her inside. And there, still standing, eyes closed, they kissed. At first he hadn't done it the way she liked, but they had gradually become attuned, finding their own style through trial and error. Hélène, too, had learned some new techniques. For example, unlike Philippe, Christophe was not a big fan of her being on top. He wasn't especially keen on foreplay either. He preferred to just grab hold of her, unzip her pants or hitch up her skirt, slide down her panties, and fuck, without bothering to undress properly. The clothes would come off later, in the middle of their lovemaking, when they paused to catch their breath or drink from a bottle of water. And then they would get back to it, licking, sucking, avid for new sensations. Christophe would hold himself back to make it last, Hélène gripping his shoulders, hanging on to his arms, holding his thighs and pulling him into her.

When they first started, she would always lower the lights to protect herself. It had been so long since she'd been completely naked in front of a man, and the thought of it brought all sorts of unpleasant ideas to mind. Would he like my pubic hair, my belly? Had my pregnancies changed something— would I be tight enough, narrow enough, smooth enough, young enough? She'd wanted to ask him for reassurance about all these things but hadn't dared. And sometimes, watching him walk to the bathroom after sex, observing the way he moved with the manly assurance of someone used to being naked in locker rooms, she would think: shit, I bet he never worries about this stuff at all, I bet he's never even wondered if he's fuckable or not. This thought made her angry. In that moment she wanted to hurt him, to grab a fistful of the fat on his belly, to yank out one of those hairs that grew from his back, and tell him: look, you're flabby, you're heavy, you're changing, your skin is less elastic than it used to be, and look what a mess your hair is—you're getting older too, so why do I obsess about it while you're totally fine?

They would hook up in the morning, or sometimes the afternoon, and they would have sex, trying to take their time despite the inevitable stopwatch, despite the world waiting for them just outside the door. And then, doggy-style across the bed, or forehead to forehead, their bellies making toilet-plunger noises, dark-eyed and sweat-soaked, they would make love. Christophe did not think too deeply about it all. For him, this girl, like hockey, was from his life before, from the glory years that he still yearned for, and—as was his habit—he had let himself be swept along by the current. And now here he was. He could depend on those two special hours at the end of the road, the cocoon of their room, this woman who cared about him, and whom he found ever more beautiful, familiarity acting like the best cosmetic in the world.

He liked going to the hotel, which she always paid for. He enjoyed the simplicity of the surfaces, the ergonomic efficiency of it all, the short distance between bed and shower, the absolute cleanliness of the towels, the neutral flooring and the television set hung from the wall, the plastic-wrapped cups, the precise click that the door made when it fell shut behind them, the Wi-Fi code printed on a little card next to the kettle, all this limited but unvarying comfort. To him, there was nothing anonymous about these interchangeable hotel rooms. On the contrary, they were a sort of refuge, a parenthetical setting where he and Hélène could fuck to their hearts' content, yell if they felt like it, and wipe themselves on the sheets afterward, where they could talk about themselves without inhibitions. All things considered, it was perhaps the last of these that Christophe needed most, a confessional. He griped about not getting enough game time, about his father, who was losing his marbles, while Hélène complained about her job and her partner, who, maybe because he suspected something, was absent even more often than usual.

Having said that, when Philippe did deign to grace them with his presence—on weekends, for example—things weren't much better. They slept in, spent a long time in the bathroom; the girls refused to go outside or eat lunch and instead spent hours glued to the TV. And she always had some work to finish up at home, as did he. Sometimes, sitting at the table, Hélène would catch her partner staring at her moodily, and with an aggressive jut of the chin she would ask him what his problem was. He never said anything. At bedtime, Mouche always wanted one more story. Clara had trouble falling asleep. It was probably just the accumulated fatigue of winter; the holidays would do them good.

All the same, Hélène did sometimes look at her daughters and think: What am I doing? In those moments, she felt like she was committing a crime. Then she checked her WhatsApp messages and found a short note from Christophe, and everything else faded into the background.

But Christmas was approaching again, and they had to plan their vacation. Hélène made her intentions clear.

"I can't take more than a week off this year."

"How come?"

Philippe was on the couch in his bathrobe, laptop on his knees. His hair was still wet from the shower. The girls were sitting on the rug in front of the stove, the elder one playing on the tablet while her younger sister waited her turn.

"Work is crazy at the moment."

"Same for me."

"I already explained all this. With Parrot around, I can't afford to let my guard down. It's as simple as that."

"Which days do you plan to take off?"

"From the seventeenth to the twenty-sixth."

"So we're not going on vacation?"

"We could."

"I don't see how. And I'm going to be stuck home alone for a week with nothing to do."

"You can look after the girls."

Philippe glared at her.

"Well," she said in a more pacifying tone, "we could get a rental place in the Vosges for a week. Saturday to Saturday. We could celebrate Christmas there. That way, we wouldn't need to travel far."

Hearing this suggestion, the girls pricked up their ears and awaited the verdict.

"The skiing there sucks," Philippe replied.

"I'm just trying to come up with a solution."

Clara and Mouche besieged their father then, and he finally gave way, though not without making a few unpleasant remarks. Hmm, the holidays should be fun, thought Hélène. Then she left the room and locked herself in the bathroom, where she wrote to Christophe:

Will I see you tomorrow?

Instantly those flickering dots announced that he was writing a response.

I miss you.

She smiled, her heart suddenly released from its knots of tension.

What time? Christophe added.

Eleven.

Can't wait.

Me too.

I want you.

Your dick..., she wrote, grinning mischievously.

The dots reappeared and she stifled a giggle. It always worked.

Your ass, he wrote.

Your hands.

Your breasts.

Your shoulders.

Your legs.

She sat there for a moment, thinking, then slyly played an unexpected card.

Your BIG brain (with a heart).

More dots.

Now you're just making fun of me, Christophe replied.

She laughed and quickly wrote a few dangerous words, which she deleted right away, seized by the irrational fear that he might have seen them.

WITH THE TWO of them swept along by the current of life, those brief encounters at the hotel became their raft. They clung to it and, in the process, learned about each other. Hélène discovered that he was gentle, a little cowardly, easily won over to her point of view, but at the same time there was within him a sort of black hole into whose depths she could not see. She was spellbound by this, the strange mystery at the heart of this apparently guileless man.

For his part, Christophe admired Hélène's abilities, the places she had been, the three languages she spoke, her eloquence, and the opinions she had on pretty much everything. Not that he was especially convinced by them, but their existence was enough to impress him. As was her aggressiveness toward men in general, which added more value in his eyes to the sweetness she showed to him. That a woman as classy and well-paid as her, with such beautiful hands, gold bangles around her wrist and a five-thousand-euro watch, could take care of him the way she did... Christophe found this deeply touching. When her skin brushed against his, he had the impression that she was rubbing off on him, that a little of her worth became his. To have her in his bed, even for an hour, even for five minutes, was to step into that privileged world. He just regretted that he had to keep these incursions into the wider world to himself; he had once tried opening up to Marco on the subject, but his friend's reaction had quickly cooled him off.

"Oh yeah, I bet she sucks like a Dyson."

Christophe gave up then and there.

Hélène was also one of those women who feel compelled to try to save everyone around them. When she noticed that something was wrong—if Christophe replied too abruptly, for instance, glancing at his watch and becoming a grumpy, obtuse stranger once again—she would disarm him with a word, lasso him back before he went off on one of his epic sulks. She gave him advice that he rarely followed, wanted to change him for his own good.

Watching him struggle sometimes, she would think: yeah, men like him get no respite at all. They were always working, uncomfortable in their dysfunctional families, without enough cash to treat themselves occasionally. With their love of soccer, their big cars, and their fat asses, they had become the lowest of the low. After centuries of relative dominion, these poor guys suddenly felt ill at ease in this world that had once seemed to fit them perfectly. The fact that there were so many of them made no difference. They felt cornered, outmoded, fundamentally inadequate, insulted by the Zeitgeist. Men raised as men, basic and cracked, relics of another age.

When he told her about the evenings he spent with his friends, getting wasted and messing around with Nerf guns, or playing hockey at forty, she couldn't help thinking of those poor fools who dress up to restage Waterloo on the weekends, or those middle-aged kids who love paintball.

Yes, Christophe upset her sometimes, and when that happened she would feel a terrible unease, a sudden shame. What was she doing with a guy like that? But he also made her feel almost unbearably tender at times. Maybe, ridiculously, he reminded her of her father.

"Guys are such a pain," she would tell him. "We always end up playing nursemaid to you."

"What are you talking about?" Christophe would reply, immediately on the defensive. "I never asked you for anything."

But Hélène was a good listener. And, with her, Christophe dared to open his heart, expressing in a handful of words his meager lot of frustrations and impossibilities, punctuated with mirthless laughter: well, that's life, you act like a dick and then you die, a great adventure my ass.

For example, he would tell her that his father called the kid Julien half the time.

"Why Julien?"

"Julien's my brother."

"You have a brother?"

He also talked to her about his friend who'd gotten involved with a home helper and was going straight from sworn bachelor to family breadwinner. The wedding was due to take place in the spring.

"It'd be funny if you came," said Christophe.

"To the wedding?"

"Yeah."

"You're losing it, kiddo."

But she gave him a kiss anyway.

Hélène was less talkative. Her meetings with Lison were probably enough to get her feelings out, even if she still preferred asking questions to confiding. That generation never ceased to surprise her. Maybe because they had grown up with the internet and social networks. Maybe because they were harbingers of the end of the world. Or, at least, that Hélène's generation was being evicted from the conquered land of youth. In any case, that odd mix of prudishness and passion, of commitment and I-don't-give-a-fuck-ism, of depression and total delusion still took her breath away.

Once, the two women had talked about that mindfuck of a contradiction that they found themselves trapped within sometimes, in intimate moments, when the great project of women's liberation collided with their strange desire to be abased.

"What contradiction?" Lison had asked, instinctively dialectic. "They've got nothing to do with each other."

"I'm not sure about that."

"You can't be serious!"

They each finished their second pint of IPA and the intern, loosened by alcohol, naturally took on the role of teacher.

"Take me, for example: I love it when someone spits on me."

Hélène's eyes went big and round and she burst out laughing, before asking her friend to elaborate. What on earth was she talking about?

"I don't know why, it just drives me crazy. I was talking about it the other day with my friend Robin—he's gay, a quality engineer in something or other, Irish roots, you know, a really cool and beautiful dude, you should see his house, it's gorgeous, plants everywhere, I don't know how he does it, I kill them within days, anyway he's a total slut—guys like that do anything and everything, I swear, the stuff they tell me, you wouldn't believe it. So anyway, spitting... he's totally into it, of course. But then there was our friend Laura. That chick gave me hell about it—it's a lack of self-respect, a man spitting on you, it's disgusting. She went on for ten minutes like that and I couldn't take it anymore. I just rolled my eyes in the end. What are you gonna do? Anyway, nobody gets to tell me what I should or shouldn't do in bed."

Later, Hélène shared this anecdote with Christophe, who was pretty turned on by the idea.

"We should try it."

"Okay, but I'm the one who spits on you."

He grinned. Their relationship wasn't so bad, really. They were close enough that their boundaries became blurred and sometimes, in the middle of a conversation, a dangerous declaration would make its way through.

ONE NIGHT, HÉLÈNE got a call from Christophe while she was driving. She answered right away, assuming something terrible must have happened, because normally he just messaged her on WhatsApp.

"Hi."

"Are you okay?"

"I had a little problem. Car accident."

"What happened?"

"I don't really know. Must have fallen asleep at the wheel. Anyway, I crashed the car. I'm two or three kilometers from Saint-Dié."

"You fell asleep?"

"Yeah, it's possible. I'm so tired these days."

The night before, practice had gone on until eleven, and work was always a nightmare at this time of year. He'd had to drive to Saint-Dizier and then Commercy, followed by an industrial zone near Metz, before going back down toward Lunéville, Baccarat, and lastly Saint-Dié.

"You're going to kill yourself at this rate."

"Yeah...that's not why I'm calling, though. I'm supposed to pick Gabriel up from school later. Nobody can do it. Marco's at work, so is Greg. And there's no point even thinking about my father."

"Okay. So?"

"I was wondering if you could go..."

Hélène was spellbound for a moment by the rhythmic ballet of the windshield wipers. She was stuck in the six o'clock traffic jam, watching the lights turn red then green then red again without advancing a single meter. She was trapped.

"I'm not your wife, you know."

A heavy silence. She began looking through her purse for her cigarettes, but of course they weren't there. She drummed her fingers on the steering wheel.

"I understand," said Christophe. "I'll figure something out."

He hung up and Hélène found herself alone inside the car. The rain was falling, as soft as snow, and the red taillights of other vehicles snaked in a long line ahead of her. She raised her index finger to her lips and bit off a flake of dry skin. Oh, fuck it.

"Hello?"

"Yeah, okay. I can pick him up. But it'll be at least an hour before I can get there."

"Oh my God, thank you! I'll call the school. You're saving my life here."

"And what am I supposed to do with your kid?"

"Take him for a Coke somewhere. I'll be as quick as I can. I'm waiting for the tow truck. The garage is going to lend me a car. Then I have to get home. It won't be long."

"All right..."

"Thank you," said Christophe.

"Yeah, yeah," Hélène said, trying to sound cold and casual. But they were both happy.

HE WAS A little boy with pale eyes, a round face, grime under his fingernails, and—like most kids in winter—a runny nose. He was about as normal-looking as a little boy can be, except maybe for the glasses he wore, which made his eyes look enormous and perpetually surprised.

"I'm a friend of your daddy," she told him outside the school.

"Okay," he replied, not looking particularly bothered either way.

Since he didn't ask for any more details, she explained that his father had had a problem with his car but that he would be there soon. Her name was Hélène. There was nothing to worry about.

"I'm not worried."

He held her hand and followed her, the hood of his coat pulled down over his face. She felt slightly intimidated and could not think of anything else to say until they were inside the café.

"Would you like a Coke?"

He thought about this for a moment.

"A Fanta, please."

She had chosen the first café they'd come across, a small place with bathrooms at the back of the room. The kid sat facing her and did not bother taking off his coat. His eyes were immediately drawn to a television screen showing a soccer game.

"You like soccer?"

"It's okay."

The café owner brought over the Fanta and a cup of tea. Hélène checked her watch, then looked at the boy.

"What grade are you in?"

The kid, absorbed by the images on the screen, did not reply. He had placed both his hands on the table, fingers interlaced, and this posture, and his serious expression, made him look disconcertingly grown-up. Hélène smiled.

"Do you have any homework?"

"No," he said.

"Could you look at me when I speak to you, please?"

He turned toward her and forced himself to smile. Then he drank some of his Fanta.

"So you're Gabriel, right?"

"Yes."

"I have two daughters."

"Oh?"

He did not seem particularly interested. She decided her attempts at conversation were going nowhere, but maybe that wasn't a bad thing. So she grabbed her phone and began looking through her inbox. There were four hundred seventy-six unread emails. Many of them would probably never be read.

By the time Christophe finally turned up, the little café was practically the only lit-up building on that quiet street. He stood outside on the sidewalk for a moment, taking the time to look at them—Hélène and his son, alone in the café, as in a display window, the walls behind them decorated with plates and pennants. What the hell were he and Hélène playing at, he wondered.

14

AT TWENTY-SIX, Hélène lives in a nice one-bedroom apartment in the ninth arrondissement of Paris. She earns two thousand euros a month gross, not bad for her age although it could be better. But to earn more, she would have to pass more competitive exams.

Because at WKC, the firm that hired her, what they sell is gray matter, rankings, awe. This means that a consultant fresh out of HEC can charge up to six hundred euros a day. His salary is calculated proportionally. Same for someone from the Polytechnique, or Paris Tech. Or for those rare few who managed to get an MBA at Wharton, Harvard, or the London School of Economics. Beyond those select schools, the drop is pretty steep. There are people who went to Parisian business schools or Supelec or Sciences Po. One notch below this are those who went to provincial business schools. And, finally, there are the "atypical profiles": occasionally, WKC will hire a graduate in organizational sociology or anthropology who has written a thesis on the business world or the spirit of capitalism or some crap like that. This is not as good as hiring someone from the École Normale Supérieure, of course, but these intellectual types are supposed to bring some left-field thinking to this monolithic corporation with its four thousand nine hundred six employees and its annual turnover of almost three billion euros on French territory alone.

Since joining WKC, Hélène sometimes feels as if the entire planet is in the hands of these little men in blue suits who visit every business, every corporate group and government body, to demonstrate the indisputable inadequacy of each firm's workforce and figures, to explain to the employees what their job consists of, how they should do it better, to support the constantly overwhelmed HR departments, and to offer their insights to decision-makers invariably doomed to efficiency gains, slaves to productivity, the damned souls of operating profit.

Hélène went to ESC Lyon. Not a bad school. She could have done worse—by going to Nancy or Strasbourg, for example—and at least this way she was still in the top ten. But if she hadn't given up German at the preparatory school, she would probably have done better at her exams and made it to a more prestigious institution, which would have completely altered the trajectory of her career.

Except that, up to that point, she had always rested on her laurels. She'd been the best student at her high school, had found prep school relatively easy because she was good at math, and then done plenty of partying after her baccalaureate. While they looked for an efficiency apartment, prior to Hélène's joining the Lycée Poincaré prep school, her mother had warned her: "You're a big girl, so you can do what you want now. But if you fail your exams, you come home right away, and we never talk about it again."

And Hélène *had* done what she wanted, relieved as she was to be free of Cornécourt, her parents, and Charlotte, with whom there was nothing much left to talk about. In their senior year, Charlotte had finally been transferred to the Bac

ES stream, which did not require such a high level of math, and the two girls had hardly seen each other. Hélène knew that her ex-BFF had been through difficulties at school and through several men too, that she had passed her driving test and now had a little blue Clio. Hélène, on the other hand, had mostly just stayed home, pinned there by boredom, lack of money, and a vague sense of disgust. In her small bedroom, she had dreamed of other places and read lots of books, notably Edith Wharton, who had become one of her favorite authors. One day, she had thought, she too would discover the beau monde, travel widely, be a free woman. The expression "international career" lit up her head like fireworks. During this period, her mother often criticized her for staying in her room, not getting any exercise, being gloomy and spiteful. But almost everything beyond the confines of her room caused her pain. No cash, no space, no openings. People who all knew one another and who interfered in your life. She nurtured a hatred for the provinces, for subprefectures and local roads, that would never leave her.

Hélène had passed her baccalaureate easily, while Charlotte had just scraped by. They saw each other one last time, the night the results were released, at Papagayo, a tawdry nightclub in the city center that changed its name every year after a brawl or after a customer disappeared, often taking the contents of the cash register with them. But the two girls barely spoke. Their friendship was practically dead: it was like a zombie, a half-extinguished fire. Hélène had stood on a balcony, chain-smoking cigarettes, and watched her ex-friend preening on the dance floor. I am so done with all this shit, she'd thought.

Anyway, prep school had not been difficult, and when she graduated from her business school, Hélène had immediately found a job, starting with an internship at Olympus. Soon after being hired, she was chosen by a program seeking out high-potential employees. It was only then that she found out what competition really meant.

For four months, she took part in an expensive and extremely selective training program in Levallois-Perret with a dozen other lucky candidates. The program was a sort of hothouse, designed by Olympus to find out which of the seeds they had planted would grow most spectacularly. Talent recruitment was clearly a major strategic initiative for the Japanese multinational.

At the prep school and in Lyon, the atmosphere had not been especially competitive—not that different, in fact, from her old high school—but this was something else. From the moment each candidate introduced themselves, it was easy to deduce from the exams they had passed and the degrees they had taken each person's market value. Hélène realized she was at the bottom of this particular ladder, and from that moment on she noticed that people didn't really listen to her, that even the instructors seemed to pity her. On dress-down Fridays, some of the students would wear a sweatshirt boasting the name of their American university or the famous letters *HEC*. On several different occasions, she felt like shit. But she didn't cry. She didn't crack. That was not her style.

As for the training program, it was pretty simple. The company's main aim was to identify the strengths and weaknesses of these elite students, and then to improve them. They were also taught to behave like real managers, not to move their hands too much when they talked, to speak calmly, avoid negative expressions . . . all that pop psychology made up of platitudes and cursory manipulation that passes for science in the upper echelons of management.

But most of the work was based on practical scenarios: human resources, crisis management, communication, team management, profitability. This last domain was, of course, the most important. The exercises consisted of managing a wide range of data in a minimal amount of time to produce the best decisions. Hélène was a natural at this game, and the only person who could better her was a tall and already bald guy who'd graduated from Paris X. Six-two, with an eagle's face and a tendency to spit when he spoke, this man could calculate an EBITDA rounded up to the second decimal after half an hour spent studying thirty pages of data. It was breathtaking to witness. After all those years thinking she was some kind of prodigy, Hélène now discovered, in that white-walled class-room, among that small group of over-qualified posh people, that she had simply never been exposed to any adversaries worthy of the name.

After that, she worked at Olympus's European headquar-ters in Hamburg, an incredibly wealthy and populist city rooted, with all its tonnage of ships and containers, at the mouth of the Elbe, full of fat pink busy men, a pervading spirit of greed, and crowds of tourists swarming the port amid a maritime folklore scented with beer and fries. There, she had earned her stripes, using her very basic German and a bit of Globish to command her team specialized in medi-cal systems—and more particularly in endoscopes, of which Olympus was the world leader.

After two years of this, wearying of the grind and tired of giving orders, she had decided to interview for positions at various major consulting firms. An old college friend who worked at Ernst & Young had strongly recommended it.

"You'll see, it's really interesting. It changes all the time. Although, if I'm honest, it's not quite what it appears."

"What do you mean?"

And her friend had explained how it worked. While what they claimed to sell was efficiency and performance, consulting firms were actually promising to cut costs. And cost-cutting did not come cheap.

She had interviews at Deloitte, at KPMG, and at a small law firm that was seeking to diversify, but in the end it was WKC who hired her. Each time, the recruitment process was the same: practical scenarios, followed by the personality test. The scenarios were easy, and generally all the same. Some kind of businessman selling windows, waffle irons, or scrub brushes. Depending on the situation for the given territory, the cost of raw materials and manpower, the competition, and other similar considerations, she had to make a rapid mental calculation to help and quantify her market. Hélène knew this routine and the responses by heart. The most important thing was not to say anything too original. At this stage in the process, having thoughts of your own was not considered an asset. For the personality test, the candidate ought to appear lively, lucid, pleasant but rigorous, to have values without coming on too strong, to give the impression that they were dependable, honest, competitive, hardworking, capable of being outspoken without crossing any lines. In broad terms, pragmatism was the key quality they were seeking; there was no place for ideology, unless you counted pragmatism as your ideology, but it was a risk to frame things in that way. Faced with the small committee of examiners, like a reflection of her own future, Hélène put on an assured performance. She was an old hand at this now, and—unlike when she started in the business—could afford to wear Zadig & Voltaire jeans, a Vanessa Bruno top, and Sergio Rossi shoes. A far cry from the Zara suit she wore to her first interviews.

Two weeks later, she moved to Paris and began working with her first client.

———

IT IS DIFFICULT to start with. Her job consists of traveling by train to visit universities that are attempting to improve their organization. In the upper echelons of French government, populated by the same small blue men who proliferate in the big consulting firms of New York, Oslo, or Puteaux, the key words have become "rationalization," "performance," "assessment." Everyone is sick of waste. The country's taxpayers are owed a return on investment; electors deserve consolidated results. That money, granted to local authorities, must now be spent with quantifiable wisdom, in a scientific way, must be assigned to areas where it will produce the largest and most measurable effects. Anglo-Saxon lessons have been learned. They are gradually gaining ground in schools, in the corridors of power, they are flowing through boardrooms, overwhelming departments, informing decisions, reaching every office, soaking into schedules, and at the end of it all they are running through arteries, filling minds, until you can hear your heart beating in time with their efficient, satisfying rhythm: rapid, repetitive, reproducible. You are now part of the process.

It is quite something, when you think about it, to see the path taken by these rules before they establish themselves inside people. Each time, they are met with resistance, because bad habits die hard. But, little by little, they impose themselves, become categorical, unquestionable. And no weapons are required to effect this monumental transformation. All you need are numbers, because nothing is as imperative as a target, nobody can twist your arm quite like a performance indicator. The bottom line is a master that cannot be contradicted, unless you wish to seem like a madman. Or worse: behind the times.

Even so, to lead this revolution and direct efforts in the right way, the organizers of this great enterprise of rationalization require an entire army of consultants and experts who earn their living by bringing down costs, who monetize the science of operational efficiency, who make a fortune from their knowledge of measurement, interpretation, and change. With the aid of certain important-sounding verbs—"identify," "categorize," "prioritize," "evaluate"—they impose this new scientific order, a perfect reign of performance designed to last forever, because it is no longer relative or political or historical, but nothing less than reality itself, transformed into infinitely calculable matter.

Hélène works for the public service business unit at WKC, the function of which is to facilitate—in Bordeaux, Toulouse, or Picardie—the necessary changes taking place at a global level. This is what her dreams of international travel have brought her. She takes regional trains, sleeps at the Ibis hotel near the station, and when she arrives at the office in question is always met by an identical-looking man in a suit and tie. This man looks at her in two different ways simultaneously: on the one hand, she is a woman, which would tend to make him treat her as his inferior; on the other, she comes from Paris and earns more money than he does, which makes her intimidating.

This man, generally a sly old fox in his fifties who enjoys long lunches and wears loafers because that means he doesn't have to bend over to tie his laces, does his best to accommodate these contradictory indicators by being moderately charming and relatively bossy.

"What I want is for us to increase our performance levels while maintaining the same number of employees," he explains, smoothing down his tie.

They all say this. Hélène is used to it. Nobody ever uses the term "wage bill"—it's obscene.

When he introduces her to other, less important men in a pleasant conference room where assistants have set out trays of pastries, and pots of tea and coffee, he will sometimes dare to say: "Gentlemen, I have a pretty young woman for you."

And a union leader will shout out: "How much will that cost us?"

In such circles, women are rarer but just as tough, particularly this one, the head of the applied languages department, with her orange Bakelite necklace and matching clip-on earrings, who announces in a rough smoker's voice: "I have nothing against you personally, but I want you to know that we do not agree at all with this new fashion for private firms."

"I understand," says Hélène.

Sometimes she rents a car and drives halfway across the country to spend three weeks in a town with a river running through it, a town with streets named after Raymond Poincaré, Georges Clemenceau, and Charles de Gaulle. There, she rediscovers the landscape of her childhood: three large high schools and a tax office all built in the same seventies style, cafés called Le Marigny or Le Bar des Sports, flower beds, green benches, a reasonably ugly industrial zone on the outskirts, a boules club, a chamber of commerce, young people sitting on café terraces, old people everywhere.

Here, she does her job.

Confronted by defiant anger everywhere she turns, she responds with smiling calmness, excellent work, and an infallible instinct for sniffing out—amid the mass of information she is given—the weak points in the organizations she inspects: the redundant departments, the places where money is lost, where the mechanism jams. Hélène has never been a grind, but now she gets caught up in the game and becomes one of those people who say things like *I'm going to get to the bottom of this*. Soon, nothing thrills her more than solving a problem connected to a point of law, an administrative rule, or a budget line.

Until that day in Orléans when it all goes wrong.

Two months later, at her assessment interview, she reviews the incident with her manager, Marc Hammoudi.

"Listen, as far as the actual audit is concerned—data gathering and all that stuff—I have no complaints at all. You did a good job. But you failed when it came to the client."

"What? I don't understand. I gave everything for that client."

"You need to learn to manage people. I had to go there twice to whip him into shape. You still think what we're selling is the organization, the process. You need to keep two things in mind. First, time tracking. That's what we're selling: brain hours. If you start giving away your ideas for free, we're screwed. So forget his demands—you only give what we've sold. That's it. Second, the show."

"I don't do that."

"Yes, you do. We all do. Listen, we have a billion-dollar market and no product. What exactly do you think we're selling?"

"What do you mean?"

"The client shells out, but he has nothing tangible to show for it. He doesn't get a new Ferrari in his garage. What we're selling is neurons. That's our business. The problem is that you can't touch gray matter. You're not selling him your pie charts or your graphs, your recommendations or strategies. You're selling him your intelligence. He's paying you because you're smarter than he is. You have to justify your added value. You have to put on a show. At the same time, every client has his own little obsessions. If you don't listen to him, you're screwed."

After this brief interview, which gets her a B and a mediocre bonus, Hélène feels an admiration for her boss that is vaguely reminiscent of someone with Stockholm syndrome.

Yet Marc Hammoudi is no guru; he doesn't even care particularly about being persuasive. His desires lie elsewhere. He is nakedly ambitious. He makes no attempt to conceal his lust for ladder-climbing. He lacks the bourgeois concern for appearances that makes some people transform their greed for money into a taste for art, horses, or haute cuisine. What excites him is power. His desire is raw and always frustrated, but those frustrations only serve to further kindle his ambition.

When she compares him with the other employees at WKC, Hélène realizes he is a completely different beast. She has come to identify three different categories of consultants: the good little soldiers, the zealots, and the tourists. She herself belongs to the first category, those who have always worked hard at school, who wanted a well-paid job with benefits and an aura of prestige, regular promotions, an enviable career, a fulfilling family life. Such employees appreciate high-quality work, like consolidating files, prefer to have a full knowledge of the facts before beginning a conversation, find it interesting to experience different environments, and are proud of their ability to adapt to various contexts, giving the best of themselves each time. They believe that their work is headed in the right direction, that they are part of a general progress: adaptation to a world in perpetual evolution. The zealots, on the other hand, are marked by their categorical conviction, their unrelenting urges. They speak the language of management all day long, impacting and prioritizing even when they are at home with their family, even on Sundays, treating their kids to the same half-baked wisdom that they dispense to their clients: "My job is to help you ask the right questions" and "Information is power." These employees can no longer distinguish between the world of work and the real world. Their vocabularies have been jargonized. Performance is in their souls. You can recognize them from that dreamy look in their eyes, the absolute conviction that gives them the appearance of men who know things must be treated seriously, but without fear. Hélène thought at first that they were just showing off, but they actually believe all this crap. The most surprising thing about the zealots is that they are not defined by their intelligence: they can be half-wits or they can be geniuses, it makes no difference. You see them striding from open-plan offices to meeting rooms, from conference calls to kickoffs, faith shining from their eyes, not a single wrinkle in their suit. They will end up millionaires and on weekends they will wear Ralph Lauren polo shirts, maybe even tasseled loafers. There is nothing to be done with them but to watch them succeed. Lastly, there are the tourists. The beginnings of their careers are usually marked by uncertainty, a moment of hesitation when deciding which direction they want to take, parents who push them the wrong way, a business school chosen out of weakness, conformism, or weariness, an aimless indecisiveness that ends with an improbable and essentially useless PhD. Whatever their background, the tourists seem to have ended up in their current position by chance, and their prevalence largely explains the high turnover in the profession. They never fully grasp the trade vocabulary. They don't really care about client satisfaction; they don't hunger for big bonuses. They do not feel that they have any special authority to give advice to people who have been doing their jobs efficiently for decades. They are like lost souls drifting through the vast transparent offices of WKC, incapable of taking any pleasure from the concierge service or the Japanese garden. They have no aspirations to ascend to the upper floors, where the company's top brass sit at enormous desks and occasionally make fools of themselves after drinking too much at a team-building weekend in the Verdon Gorge.

Marc Hammoudi does not fit into any of these categories. He is, in his own way, a barbarian. He rakes in cash the way others once razed villages. And while he abides by all the rules with his clients, and sometimes even acts quite servile, it is all a strategy, a form of camouflage. Other than that, he has no illusions and a razor-sharp intelligence that makes Hélène question her belief in the company's values.

The president of WKC sends an email every week to all the company's employees, usually on a Thursday. This message is midway between an activity report and a newspaper editorial. Everyone reads it religiously, and while a few may occasionally express reservations about its contents, they do so only in small groups and orally. Anyway, these emails are generally well thought out, featuring not only passages about business news and future prospects, but some thought-provoking ideas and inspirational quotations, with a particular insistence upon values. Because the president is convinced that WKC is an ethical enterprise. The company's values, he believes, are what distinguish it from its rivals, what give it such strength and attractiveness. This philosophy was especially prominent in an email from June 2001 that included four points—"excellence," "courage," "together," "for better" (the latter two in English)—and ended with these lines, which, though written by the president himself, were nonetheless presented in quotation marks: "'Our probity is practiced in our work, our relationships with our colleagues and our clients, internally and externally, but also in the framework of our friendships and our family. The WKC spirit must accompany us wherever we go, in a free and intentional way.'"

Marc, however, does not read this corporate literature.

One day, when Hélène asked him what he thought of the evolutionary model that WKC wished to adopt, with its twin pillars of modification and continuation that defined the path toward transformation, he replied simply:

"I could not give a flying fuck."

Which does not prevent him from producing that kind of bombastic rhetoric himself, nor from backing it up with endless graphs and charts.

Hélène admires his drive, and she tries to follow in his slipstream, to imitate him, to reassure herself by staying close to him. Hammoudi, for his part, does not seem to notice her. He just plows his furrow, blinkers on, carrot dangling, formidable in his power, neckless, huge shoulders, his skin almost gray, his eyes yellow, and his curly hair receding. Hélène knows nothing about his private life. He dresses like everyone else, in blue and gray, plain tie over a plain semi-tailored shirt, soft loafers, no cuff links, an unremarkable Omega on his wrist. He is simple and straightforward. Sometimes he so little resembles a person that he becomes as comforting as a computer.

And one night, Hélène is rehearsing a presentation for some big shots from the Department of Higher Education with Marc and a guy she doesn't really know, Pierre-Antoine, who is noticeable for occasionally wearing a bow tie and being almost surreally kind. The two men fire questions at her in an empty office. She responds without missing a beat, a little dry and academic, but she knows her stuff. The interrogation lasts just under an hour, then her manager looks at his watch.

"All right, that's enough. Very good. On Tuesday, I'll go with you to visit the client."

"In Pau?"

Marc is already packing away his laptop. Pierre-Antoine slips away, shyly wishing them a good evening. The two of them are left together, Hélène sitting and Marc standing.

"Yeah, we'll take the TGV, then rent a car down there. My assistant will send you an email with all the details."

HÉLÈNE SPENDS THE whole weekend worrying about this, wondering what he wants from her, whether it's a favor or a punishment. The following Tuesday, on the high-speed train, Marc does not enlighten her further. He just goes through his emails, slips off his shoes, works on various files, underlining in a two-color red-and-blue ballpoint, and goes onto the platform to make a few phone calls, leaving behind a faint smell of feet and vetiver. They're in first class, naturally—all WKC employees are entitled to this perk—but despite this setting so ideal for nomadic working, Hélène is almost completely incapable of concentrating. The journey lasts practically the whole day, and her boss barely speaks a word to her.

When they arrive at the University of Pau, Marc begins by reassuring the client. At WKC, this is what we do; you're in safe hands; everything will be fine. It's expensive, obviously, but that's the market price. The dean of the university passes them on to an underling who leads them to the office they will occupy—a clean, perfectly suitable room with a window overlooking a river. They are even provided with a Thermos.

"This won't do," Marc says.

"What do you mean?"

"Too small, not enough light. Too far away from the people working here. Find us something else."

"But this is all we have."

"Find something else."

It takes more than two hours, and assistance from a porter, two secretaries, and—curiously—an electrician, before they finally come up with an office that Marc finds acceptable.

There, they are brought the promised documents and they immediately start leafing through them, even though they received almost everything beforehand by email. After three hours of work, Hélène leaves the room for a moment to smoke a cigarette, but her boss stays where he is, his socks on the carpet, his forehead resting on one hand, and his eyes glued to the computer screen.

That night, Marc and Hélène eat dinner together in a small restaurant near their hotel. She orders a steak tartare while he goes for a calzone with a green salad. He stuffs a big leaf of lettuce into each slice of pizza, which he cuts as though he's sawing a piece of wood. They also order a bottle of sparkling water and a carafe of Madiran. Since Marc only ever drinks water when he's working, Hélène takes care of the wine and soon feels the tensions of the past few days easing under the drink's soft caress. She even dares to ask a few questions, to which Marc responds with good grace, reeling off the words rapidly, his voice muffled by food. Then there comes a moment when, fooled by his unusual cheerfulness, she ventures a personal remark:

"I'm glad I get to work with people like you."

Marc turns his yellow eyes toward her, eyelids lowered, and stares at her for a moment, as if to check that she isn't making fun of him.

Hélène feels herself blush.

"I just mean, this is a special company. I'm not one of those corporate people, you know, but WKC is pretty great."

"What the hell are you talking about? We're generally considered the dunces of the profession. Go to Deloitte, or one of those small private firms that deal with high-level mergers. Even at Mercer, they think we're a bunch of idiots."

Hélène sits there open-mouthed for a second or two, before asking:

"Then why?"

"Why what?"

"Why are you here? You could work anywhere."

Just recently, Hélène was told how Marc dazzled everyone during a meeting about the reorganization of a company by skimming through the documents the way a chef might sniff a bisque and putting his finger on the problem in five seconds flat: that's it, that spot in the purchasing department. There's someone in that office who isn't doing their job properly. The client was dumbstruck. It seemed simultaneously absurd and magical. But Marc was proved right.

"The good thing about WKC is that they're not trying to be chic. They don't care about your name or your family. Even your education isn't that important. I mean, you went to ESC Lyon, so you should know that better than anyone."

Hélène sits there, stunned, and Marc, looking pleased with himself, uses his tongue to dislodge a piece of lettuce from between his teeth.

"I'm kidding. All I care about is that they leave me in peace, and they don't turn me down for a partnership just because I've got curly hair."

IN THE DAYS that follow, Hélène has the opportunity to observe his methods up close: the way he manages the client, always listening, satisfying his whims, but mistreating him too, which oddly seems to come as a great relief to the dean of the university.

"You have to understand: a client is always worried, because he has a need, and he doesn't know if it will be met. He's afraid of making the wrong choices. He's afraid of being taken for a ride. A client lives in fear, and he wants a father figure to reassure him."

Hélène could never learn things like this at school or from books. She discovers them in Pau, in their office flooded with beautiful autumn light, in an aura of slight amazement, accompanied by the subliminal aroma of socks and Marc's expensive eau de toilette. What most surprises her is the mixture of insight and cunning, even cynicism. Marc is perfectly capable of saying things like: "Our job basically consists in tidying empty rooms." Or: "A consultant is a guy who borrows your watch to tell you the time and then runs off with your watch." But behind these mercenary haikus, she also observes his sharp-eyed talent for data-crunching, snuffling like a truffle pig, his large and sensitive snout foraging dexterously among the columns and tables, the organizational charts and operating accounts, cutting through the crap like a plowshare, slurping up the swill to expose the underlying numbers, making himself comfortable, his body squelching delightedly in the muck of this sanctuary where dirty laundry is unpacked, where the institution dumps its secrets, where the innermost intimacy of its organs is laid bare.

In this mathematical pigsty, Marc Hammoudi sifts gold from the mud and, with a quiver of pleasure, miraculously unearths unsuspected diamonds. He is not keen on interviews. The men are all smug liars; the women, panicky and vain. In his opinion, this is all just diplomacy, making people believe they've been heard, that their views have been taken on board—delay tactics, in other words. Verbatim records disgust him; surveys leave him cold. As far as he's concerned, all that stuff is just for salving your conscience, and his work, he knows, has nothing to do with morality. He leaves all that crap to others. He's too old to bother with the work of commiseration. His science of mechanisms has no need of actors. Psychology is for bullshitters; he puts his faith in the solidity of facts.

After two days of this, Hélène is forced to admit that he has done a good job, and even if she does not feel even remotely capable of copying his style, she also no longer sees her work in the same light. On Thursday evening, they eat dinner as usual, tête-à-tête in the same little restaurant. He seems satisfied, smiling and expressive in his seat, but he does not say whether it is the prospect of returning to Paris that thrills him, or his disciple's progress.

"Let's order aperitifs. And some wine."

He checks his BlackBerry.

"The train doesn't leave until ten. We can take it easy."

They order Tournedos Rossini and a bottle of Châteauneuf-du-Pape, which he imagines won't be as heavy as the local wines. Their conversation is mostly about work and their colleagues. Marc is paternalistic and petty. He has an acid tongue. Almost nobody is spared. Slackers, ass-lickers, incompetents, rich kids, no-hopers, morons, sociologists ... the insults rain down. Hélène laughs along, adding her own contributions. Out of nowhere, in this interlude of wine and complicity, she finds him very handsome. They have coffee and then, standing up and putting on his raincoat, Marc decides it would be silly to go to bed so early. Hélène is less sure. She instinctively mistrusts this kind of man, the tough guys who sweep you up and impress you, sickeningly sexy, the successful ones who know it all, their bellies swelled with self-importance. The word "executive" pops back into her mind.

"I'd rather get some sleep," she says.

"Don't be a killjoy. One last drink won't hurt."

What reassures her is his detachment: he seems distant, self-absorbed, like a hermit crab with an American Express card. He pays the check and leaves a big tip that immediately wins him the approval of the young waiter. At last, Hélène agrees to go with him, because he's not really giving her a choice anyway, and so they set off through the practically empty Thursday-night streets of that small southwestern town. It's cold and dry, and Hélène follows her boss. He doesn't say a word, but she can tell from his heavy breathing and his wavering gait that he's already three sheets to the wind. Soon they arrive at Le Wilson, a nightclub where entrance is barred by one of those classic heavy wooden doors with a spyhole that slides open. The bouncer points them through a long corridor filled with muffled echoes of the music, then they enter an enormous room with a bar that runs all the way across one wall and a split-level dance floor where a few people are dancing. More than a few, in fact, unless it's just a false impression caused by the mirrors and the strobe lights.

While Marc heads toward the bar, Hélène squints, as if that might help her to bear the earsplitting volume. It's been a long time since she went clubbing. As the bass notes vibrate inside her chest and up to her temples, she finds a guilty pleasure in that feeling of power, of being a girl in this stock market where desires are selling cheap. Not to mention the fact that she's a Parisian in a provincial club, a young woman with money, good references, and an intuitive grasp of the latest fashions that are born by the Seine before spreading slowly through the rest of France. Or at least this is what she tells herself.

But this patronizing perspective is also designed to comfort her, because she already feels unsettled by the sight of those twenty-year-old girls on the dance floor in their bright little tops and the boys with their rugby players' shoulders and their polo shirts. She and Marc exchange a few inaudible words, and she nods, feeling sweat trickle down her back in the heat. As she lights a cigarette, she notices a strange little man, mustache and sweat suit, doing a repulsive dance while watching himself in a mirror. Marc spots him too, and they share a knowing, Jacobin look. Then they sit down on a couch vacated by two couples.

"I can't believe how crowded it is."

"What?"

"I said it's crowded."

"Oh, yeah."

A waitress in a skintight Johnnie Walker T-shirt brings them a bottle of whiskey, a bucket of ice, two glasses, and a bottle of Coke.

"What the hell?" yells Hélène, a little shocked.

"No big deal. It's for me."

She isn't sure if he means that he's paying for it, or if he wants the whole bottle to himself. But he pours her a glass of whiskey and hands it to her.

"Coke?"

Hélène lip-reads this and shakes her head, then uses a pair of metal tongs to drop two ice cubes into her glass. How many times has she found herself in this situation, her head starting to spin, enthusiasm looming like a threat, her body full of urges that are no longer entirely her own. When she was younger, she used to go out all the time; she was a blackout queen, addicted to those moments of pure joy that end in amnesia and suicidal hangovers. She would often wake, early morning, in some strange man's apartment, feeling broken and dirty, and would have to try to reconstruct the story of how she'd gotten there with the aid of a few strobe-like memories. Later, she would send messages to her friends, attempting to fill the gaps in the narrative. *I hope I didn't do anything too embarrassing? What time did we get home?* The replies would come, bringing sighs of relief or gasps of horror followed by the promise not to go through it all again. Hélène had quite a few skeletons of that sort in her closet: boys taking advantage, a line of coke on a toilet seat, dried vomit in her hair, grim Sundays spent under the duvet, ashamed and wanting to die, because she could not believe there was a sponge big enough to wipe all of that away. Because, above all, she did not understand who that other Hélène was, the one who took over her body after she'd had too much to drink. What if that was the real Hélène?

Her boss leans back in his seat, legs crossed, one arm stretched across the top of the couch, blissfully ogling the movement of the nearby bodies. He's taken off his jacket, and the position of his legs allows her to see—between the top of one black sock and the hem of his pants—a wide strip of pale flesh. Hélène shudders. She puts her glass down. Looks at her watch: one in the morning, tomorrow already. The smoke stings her eyes. The bass throbs in her head. Marc leans toward her. She sees his lips, the clamminess of his forehead, the whiteness of his teeth exaggerated by the black light. She points at her ear to make him understand she can't hear. He shuffles closer to her. His arm is behind her back now and despite the cigarette smoke, she can recognize his scent—vetiver and something else behind it, something sweet, almost sugary. He speaks into her ear.

"Want to dance?"

She recoils slightly. And smiles at him.

"No, I think I'm too tired."

Marc's face moves away. She contemplates his impassive expression, the terrible whiteness of his teeth. He stands up and straightens his pants.

"You sure?"

"Yeah, yeah," says Hélène.

So he goes over to the dance floor and starts to dance on his own, the soles of his loafers sliding around within a small radius, his arms raised and his eyes closed. His skin gleams under the colored spotlights. Hélène takes another swig of whiskey and watches her boss moving with perfect serious-ness, taking pleasure in his profound, solitary commitment.

The song ends abruptly and, from the excited whispers that rise from the dance floor, Hélène realizes that the locals are about to have their moment. The youngest ones smile at each other and get ready. A few grab others' shoulders. The singer's voice erupts solemnly and is echoed by the full-throated war-blings of these kids with their tragic faces:

Burned earth in the wind
Of the rocky land.

Hélène knows this song, of course, as does the whole coun-try. In every village, in every town, at weddings and parties, on Radio Nostalgie and at New Year's Eve, "Les Lacs du Connemara" is played, with its stabbing strings, its Gitane-roughened voice, its effortless crescendo, and suddenly that rhythm: *tam tatam tatatatatam*. In front of her, twenty dancers start to jump, reinforcing the drumbeat with their hammer-ing feet, chins raised high, like a parody of soldiers, and Marc disappears, caught up in that crowd of pistons. All that re-main are those unbreakable, twenty-year-old bodies, the same ones Hélène used to see in college at those parties that the student associations would organize every week, and which invariably ended like this, with "Les Lacs du Connemara," because that was how they did it at HEC.

It all floods back. Her studio apartment in Écully, the open-bar evenings and the initiation weekend at a campsite near Montpellier, the new kids being forced to drink and Blanche Goetz in her underwear crying in a tent, no one ever worked out why. A hotel complex grooming its future clients by inviting these students to a skiing weekend in Val-Thorens. Thankfully, having grown up in the Vosges, Hélène did not look too clumsy on a red run.

The song being played again when, just after arriving in Paris, she would see Julien, Léandre, and Clémence almost every night. They were all starting out in life, Léandre and Julien renting an apartment together, Clémence living with her aunt. For a while they lived like overgrown students, going out a lot, and sleeping with one another without any real consequences. Well, they had other fish to fry, didn't they? Because, while they did have fun, the discovery of what could only be called "the world of work" was not without its disillusions. At school they had dreamed of being entrepreneurs, managers, had seen the economy as a land to be conquered. But their real lives consisted of filling out forms, attending meetings, sucking up to bosses and clients, selling hot air, and putting up with their colleagues. When they saw each other, they barely even talked about their jobs, preferring to believe that this rut was just another sort of hazing ceremony, one that would soon be over. At Léandre and Julien's place they would drink cheap, strong Cahors wine that turned their tongues purple. Then they would dance to Jamiroquai and Britney, Daft Punk and Sardou, until the neighbor came around to complain. They would invite him to party with them, and sometimes he would call the police on them. But the cops were generally pretty understanding: they knew there was nothing to fear from young people like these.

Hélène continued to hang out with her college friends, chatting in ad hoc discussion threads on Messenger where they would pass on work opportunities and mess around. They still organized weekends together, barbecues in the countryside or pool parties. The good old days were still going strong. They even went on a cruise together around the Cyclades, saw the sun rise over the Aegean after an all-nighter, stretched out on the deck, suntanned and blissed out, with Sardou's song playing quietly in the background.

In the summer of 2001, Clémence and Léandre got married in the Drôme, at an old, renovated farm that belonged to the bride's parents. Bride and groom rolled up to the church in a Rolls-Royce and some of the men wore morning coats or even military uniform. Hélène's date was a guy from the ESSEC business school who worked with Léandre in the retail sector of the BNP bank. It was at that wedding that she met a cute, well-built man in a pale suit with a silk knit tie, a brazenly British sense of style that appealed to her. His name was Philippe Chevalier and the two of them danced under a pale canvas canopy, to rock songs and to ballads. Late that night, some joker played the famous Sardou song and everyone piled onto the dance floor, jumping around and yelling like they always did. They were still so young, so cut out for success, so in tune with the Zeitgeist. Hélène and Philippe promised to call each other, but neither of them bothered to take that first step. The current of time took them in separate directions then, until bringing them back together much more recently, by chance, at a Japanese restaurant in the seventeenth arrondissement, where he gave her that strange look, at once mocking and eager. Since then, they have gone on a few dates, fucked a few times. To Hélène, that guy is a source both of relief and of anguish. She does not want to let him go.

On the dance floor at the Wilson, the music finally ends. After the usual complaints, the customers reluctantly shuffle off the floor. It is then that Hélène sees Marc, another glass in hand, continuing to shimmy, poignant in his solitude. And in that smoky, cellar-like atmosphere, in the awful, deepening silence after the deafening music has been turned off, she thinks that he looks like a drowning man.

15

GÉRARD MARCHAL WAS not sick.

He might be losing his marbles a little bit, but—whatever the doctors or his son said—he was not sick.

Obviously, at seventy-three, he was no longer able to recite La Fontaine's fables at the drop of a hat. Although he could probably still do a better job of it than most of today's kids. Back in his time, they didn't spend years at university but at least they knew how to read, write, and count correctly. Everything was in decline now, from spelling to morals. And his high school certificate was worth at least as much as the baccalaureates they were handing out these days.

No, Gérard wasn't sick. He was just a bit tired.

That December morning in particular, as he drank his coffee in the kitchen, he felt desperately weary. He had worked so hard, all his life. A certain fatigue was natural. And his father's memory hadn't been great either. He was always losing stuff, could never remember his sons' birthdays. Gérard smiled as he thought about this. That was another age. Men didn't always bother back then. Those memories were still so clear. His father's face, his mustache and pale eyes. And his mother. The word *maman* popped into his head and he was surprised by the emotion he felt. This was happening to him more and more. His day-to-day memory might be failing, but the old memories were more solid than ever. He saw again the playground at the school in Champbeauvert and his friends—Bino, Hubert Lebon, big Monce, and that poor, nervous wreck Robert Spinerni. Once, tidying up the benches in the church, Spinerni managed to get stuck inside, and no one had ever managed to figure out how.

The old man stood up to take his cup to the dishwasher, and the cat surreptitiously rubbed itself between his legs. He stroked the animal's neck before glancing through the window. Outside, the grass was covered with a thin layer of frost. The unchanging trees lined the road just as they always used to. Again, he saw Christophe skating on the frozen pond, and this thought made him smile. His face was bathed in the pale morning sunlight, and the images inside him purred like a wood-burning stove.

He walked upstairs, his old slippers slapping against the steps, and went to the bathroom to shave. He was careful not to leave any hairs at the base of his nose or at the corners of his jaw, as he sometimes did. In the mirror, he no longer really recognized himself. The spreading baldness, the yellowish tinge to his skin, and that thinness, so strange for someone who had always been a little round, even kind of flabby as he approached fifty. Sylvie had put him on a diet then, which pissed him off. He'd been given nothing to eat but beans, not even a potato or a scrap of meat. Nowadays, Christophe worried about his appetite. You must be skipping meals, he said, otherwise this makes no sense. His son had even made him stand on the bathroom scales to check. What a pain in the ass it all was.

In his bedroom, the old man hesitated for a moment in front of his open closet. There were clothes in there that he hardly ever wore anymore, the nicest ones of course: that old habit of putting on your Sunday best for important occasions. But there weren't many occasions anymore, apart from hunting, and when the kid came to visit.

And he didn't come to visit anymore.

He got dressed as he did every day, in jeans, a T-shirt, and his big sweater, pulling the sleeves up to his elbows. Before heading back downstairs, he went into Gabriel's room. It was all still so fresh. His mother had taken him away two days earlier. Gérard hadn't said anything, but since then it had kept churning constantly inside his head. That day, the little boy had hugged him tightly, his head against Grandpa's stomach. He had stroked the boy's hair, so fine and soft, with his old man's hands. He'd been tense as a bowstring ever since.

Back on the first floor, he put on his walking shoes, a jacket, and a red, white, and blue wool hat, which he pulled down to cover his ears. Then he went to the garage, where he spent a moment contemplating the two rifles chained to the gun rack. There was a Browning semiautomatic and his wonderfully balanced and robust Sauer 404, which he'd bought for peanuts at auction. At one point he'd had as many as seven guns in different calibers, for hunting ducks as well as big game. Over the years, though, he'd had to sell them all. His son had found buyers for him on the internet. But he was determined to keep at least one rifle at home.

Because one thing was sure: in this life, you had to stand up for yourself.

He remembered how, as a kid, other boys from the Bellevue neighborhood would constantly pick fights with him. One day, Hubert Lebon caught one of them and beat him with a plank. The boys stopped coming after that.

Back then, Gérard and his friends used to all carry a steel ball that sat in a square leather pouch sewn to the end of a long hemp strap. They would swing this sling over their heads at every opportunity, outside the apartment buildings where their many families lived after the war, pretending to threaten people for a laugh but ready to use those weapons if anyone really messed with them. He had often imagined the damage that sort of homemade weapon might cause. He was sure he could have killed someone with it.

He noticed then that the cat had followed him into the garage, so he picked it up by the scruff of its neck to take it back to the house. The cat wasn't getting any younger either. It was better off staying in the warm. After that he left his rifles where they were and went out. The morning air stung his nose. It was going to be a beautiful winter day, he could tell, clean as a whistle. The temperature had dropped to twenty degrees overnight and the whole landscape was crisp and stiff with cold.

As he approached his van, he noticed a new dent on the sliding door. He stroked it with his fingertips to make sure it was real. The metal was freezing, the damage irrefutable. He had been finding new dents and scratches on a regular basis for some time now, all of them inexplicable. He'd already had to change a bumper and a bent wheel rim. Obviously someone had it in for him—what other explanation was there? He was always careful when he went to Leclerc to park away from the other cars, even if it meant having to walk farther, because those big parking lots were full of idiots and bad drivers, people who didn't care about anyone else. Normally, the discovery of a dent like that would throw him into a rage and he would spend hours fantasizing about retaliations and radical political measures. Because it was undeniable that most of his problems were caused by the general decline in standards: laziness and selfishness were turning the French into dangerous savages. Someone needed to bring some order back to this shithole. For too long, people had been allowed to get away with anything. Civil war seemed possible now. He had sensed it coming long before everyone else, alerted by the early warning signs of his impecunious tenants. But this time, the damaged bodywork inspired only a snotty sniffle and he got behind the wheel without giving it another thought. He had other, more serious things on his mind.

On the brief, narrow stretch of road that led to the center of Cornécourt, he didn't see another living soul. High-voltage lines swung over the road at one point, but other than that it was the same impassive procession of bungalows and traffic circles, a barracks, and the fishing store that was not yet open. A Saturday morning so peaceful it could almost have been declared dead.

Yet when he thought about it, the events had occurred at a dizzying speed. Unless certain facts had been lost in the fog. Gérard would sometimes lose whole days, the way other men might lose their wallet or their keys. Christophe would mention a discussion they'd had, and of course he would nod along, but in reality he had no idea what his son was talking about. Sometimes he would find receipts in his pockets for exorbitant amounts and would have no recollection of spending that money. A hundred fifty euros at Bricorama for paint and light bulbs. What paint? What light bulbs? Or he would receive a pair of flannel pajamas through the mail that he had never ordered. He would open a cupboard upstairs to put away the new pack of toilet paper he'd bought, and the cupboard would already be full. His world was full of gaps, his weeks bristling with surprises and unanswered questions. He had to constantly improvise replies and invent explanations. Because he knew perfectly well that they were just waiting for him to make a mistake so they could send him to the hospital or, worse, to one of those retirement homes that smell of bleach where old people are sent to die. He had to be wary of people he knew and of strangers, had to be constantly on the alert, forever plugging holes in his leaky boat.

Except when it came to the kid.

Gabriel didn't judge him. From time to time, he would say "Poor Grandpa" because someone had explained to him that his grandfather wasn't well, but other than that he continued to regard him in the same way he always had. He did not doubt what the old man told him. When he gave his hand to his grandfather, the trust was palpable, and Gérard would rather have jumped in front of a train than let go of the boy's hand. They went to the woods together for long walks. The grandfather went to fetch him from school and gave him pain au chocolat and sour candy. It wasn't good for his teeth, but it made the kid happy and that was what mattered. They watched a lot of TV together too, those weird cartoons that kids liked these days, with stupid rabbits and superheroes in pajamas. Often, the old man would fall asleep beside the boy, and those were always his best naps.

It had been easy, being a grandfather. With his own kids, it had taken him longer to get used to it. He remembered being at the hospital when Julien was born, that round little red-skinned body, the frog-like face . . . It was obvious the fetus had spent months floating in liquid, and even though it was his kid, his own blood, Gérard had felt a detachment, a disturbance, a sense of duty mixed with something close to repulsion. Of course, the connections had been forged over time, at least until adolescence, when, once again, he had become a spectator, vaguely disgusted by the mutations taking place before his eyes. To put it mildly, he had not liked what his elder son became, the way he spoke and moved, like a little thug, like one of those Arabs from the Vierge neighborhood that he hung out with; he hadn't liked his son's unkempt appearance, his sweatpants and denim jacket, the blasé look in his red-rimmed eyes. Sylvie told him it was just a phase. But the phase had lasted a long time, and they had never fully reconciled. Then one day Julien had packed his bags and rented a studio apartment in town, when he was in technical college, without asking for money or anything. He'll be back, tail between his legs, Gérard had thought. His son had never set foot in the house again.

With Christophe, it was different. That boy had never been as much trouble as his brother. And hockey had given him an outlet. If only he hadn't fallen for that girl, who—twenty years later—would bring them such misery.

When Gabriel was born, Gérard, although healthy, was living an old man's life in his big empty house, with nothing to distract him but hunting, his garden, a subscription to a news magazine, an ever-narrowing field of obsessions, and a sort of vague pain at still being there. Not to mention the feeling that other people were forever in his face, too noisy, always at odds with him, almost like another species. The birth of his grandson had been like a window opening. All he had to do was watch him crawl around or cover his face with mashed potato to realize that everything was worth it, that joy was still possible.

SOON GÉRARD ARRIVED in the center of Cornécourt and, at the traffic circle between the mayor's office and the old vicarage, everything grew blurry again. No longer sure what he was doing there, he drove around it twice before heading toward the new residential zone that they'd built beside the factory, just past the tennis courts.

Some people called this place Turkishland, although it wasn't clear if the nickname was linked to the origin of certain residents or to the nationality of the construction workers. Whatever, the subdivision had spread like an outbreak of hives, starting from nothing and soon covering acres of land. Most of the houses were modest and single-story, but some were enormous, with a tower and antique statues on the lawn, and they all lay in neat rows along streets with incongruous names. In spring, houses beribboned with wisteria and sagging under the weight of rhododendrons would compete in unlikely gardening contests that were always won by the same people. In summer, aboveground pools brought trouble and happiness. In the evenings, the smell of grilling meat would rise in tribute to the nostrils of indifferent gods, and in every garage you could find a lawn mower and a Ping-Pong table.

But the one thing that everyone there shared was a gnawing rage over border disputes.

For, here as elsewhere, freedom was marked out by boundaries. Hence the obligatory portcullises, thuja hedges, metal railings, rows of bamboo, and lovingly stained fences. Each property, in setting its own perimeter, created an outside and an inside, spaces between which the border was never completely sealed but that enabled the idea of dominion: a man's home as his castle. There, at last, you could do what you wished, choosing rusticity or modernity in line with your personal taste, opting for minimalism or ostentation, and nobody could tell you it was wrong. Each house, in other words, was a principality, a domain with its own laws and embassies, because they were not above exchanging a few words with the neighbor, on tiptoes, leaning over the hedge, offering her some vegetables from their kitchen garden, or lending him a power tool that he must not forget to return. Often, they would complain about the noise, about their neighbors who did not know how to behave, about their children who never stopped yelling, about a dog who had somehow made its way into their yard to take a shit, but at least they had their own little territory to defend and the feeling that they could live free from servitude, free from fear of barbarian hordes. Essentially, what was happening in those replicated, individualistic neighborhoods, between the tomato plants and the overflowing pantries, was merely another attempt to find happiness.

That morning, in any case, the area was silent and deserted. Even the canal barely made a sound as its glittering browns and blacks slid under the pale belly of the low sky. On every windshield, the wipers had been glued in place by the night freeze, and the whitened lawns looked like they'd been put under a sleeping spell by some fairy-tale witch. Dreary, asphalt-framed flower beds were the only islands of promise in this desolation. Later, perhaps, a dog would be taken out for a walk, and people would go shopping, but for now nobody dared venture out onto the sidewalks, and the only clues to suggest the place was not completely dead were the lit-up windows and the strings of lights.

Passing a house decorated like a Christmas tree for the second time, Gérard noticed that he had been driving in circles. Not that it really mattered. Nobody was expecting him. He drove slowly, staring at the houses one by one, and sometimes stopping for a second before setting off again. At last he reached the right number, on the correct street. He opened his wallet and checked the Post-it that he'd put in there. Yep, that was it: number 22. He parked on the opposite side of the street, then waited.

His heart beat calmly and steadily.

There was no impatience in his anger.

The kid had gone. Gérard would never be in a rush again.

Just after ten, he got out of his car and crossed the road. He sniffed the air as he walked, breathing in the pleasant smell of woodsmoke and the duller, closer odor of asphalt. He opened the metal gate of 22 Rue Jean-Monnet and it gave a long creak. Instantly, a dog started barking furiously inside the nearby garage, and Gérard hurried up the flight of steps that led to the front door. He rang the doorbell and waited. The dog, meanwhile, was still in a rage, and every time it threw itself against the garage door there was a huge, echoing clatter, almost insulting in that silence, followed immediately by the frenzied scratching of its claws on sheet metal. That racket quickly got on his nerves, and the old man regretted not having brought the rifle with him when he left the house. He imagined firing a couple of large-caliber rounds in there and the thought was so satisfying that he couldn't help chuckling to himself. Still nobody had come to answer the door. He rang the doorbell again. The spaced-out notes chimed cheerfully inside the house while the dog kept barking. Turning around to inspect his surroundings, Gérard thought he saw a curtain twitch on the other side of the street, but perhaps it was just his mind playing tricks. Soon, he heard a man's voice from the garage, authoritative and threatening. There were a few muffled blows, and the dog whined. Then there was silence.

The garage door opened then, revealing the master of the house, in shorts and flip-flops, and a thick yellow sweatshirt. He couldn't be more than five foot three, and he wore rimless glasses. He had sparse ash-blond hair, like the cyclist Laurent Fignon, but there was something less present, almost diaphanous, about his appearance, curiously redolent of unpleasant things like a spider's web or the skin on a cup of milk. After struggling to subdue the fairly large briard sheepdog, this skinny little man took a step forward before rudely demanding:

"What's this about?"

"I want to see the kid," replied Gérard.

"What?"

"Your kid," the old man added. "That little shit."

The man frowned. "Who are you? What do you want?"

Gérard pointed threateningly at him, his mouth deformed by rancor.

"Don't fuck around with me."

The man stood there stunned for a moment, tied to his dog as if to a buoy.

"Are you crazy?" he said. "What the hell are you talking about?"

Gérard shook his head. This was pissing him off now. The guy knew perfectly well why he was there.

"Go on, get out of here," said the man. "Or I'll call the cops."

"It'll be too late," replied Gérard.

"I'll set the dog on you, I'm warning you."

"I don't give a shit about your dog. You have no business being here anyway."

This whole thing was making less and less sense the more it went on, and more than the presence of an intruder, it was this impression of weirdness, of spiraling insanity, that disturbed the blond man. An icy gust of wind blew through the street, and the dog tried to free itself from its master's grip, earning itself a smack on the nose. It whined, ears lowered, then sat down and waited for a better opportunity to disobey. Just then, a boy appeared in the garage. He was barefoot and wearing pajamas. It was Kylian.

"Go back inside," his father said, waving his hand at him.

Pale and wide-eyed, the boy stood still, looking at his friend's grandfather, who stared back at him without a word.

"I said go inside!"

The blond man could feel the situation getting out of hand. He grabbed hold of his son, and the dog immediately flung itself in the other direction and began barking.

"So it's you, you little bastard," said Gérard.

He pronounced these words in a cool, even voice, but beneath it there were hints of sorrow and anger, maybe even of despair. The little boy was half smiling as he tried to get away from his father. He was small with pale blond hair and gentle, slightly lost-looking eyes. One of his pajama legs had gotten hitched up over his knee. Even from a distance, his flesh looked extremely delicate.

"It's your fault," said Gérard.

"For God's sake! What are you talking about?" the man asked.

Gérard did not need to justify himself. He looked for the quickest route to the garage and, his hands stiff and wide open, began to descend the flight of steps. That little shit had hurt Gabriel. And now Gabriel was gone. He clung to this simple logic, which had the merit of pinpointing a cause and naming a culprit for the misfortune that had ruined his life. In his head, this loop had been running endlessly for days. He couldn't stop thinking about it. It explained everything. It blazed brightly at night when he closed his eyes and tried to fall asleep. It drew all his other thoughts into its orbit.

This little boy was all he had left.

A strange noise tore him from these thoughts and he stopped dead, as if waking from a dream. Barefoot on the concrete floor, Kylian was shivering with cold. His teeth were chattering. Gérard heard a deep growl behind him and turned to see a Range Rover stopping in the middle of the street. The mayor of Cornécourt got out.

"What are you up to now, eh? What's gotten into you?"

It took the old man a few seconds to recognize his old friend, but as soon as he did his whole attitude changed and he gave Monsieur Müller a friendly wave. Then, glancing back over his shoulder, he noticed that Kylian, his father, and the dog had all disappeared. All that remained was the empty garage, the metal shelves filled with jars, a pressure washer, a sled, and—lying on the floor—a large, half-eaten buffalo-skin bone.

"Well?" Monsieur Müller asked.

"Well what?"

"One of the neighbors called me. Apparently you're trouble-making again."

"Again?"

Gérard wondered what the mayor meant by that. But he didn't linger on the question. Increasingly these days, the things that were said to him felt like a snare and he preferred to turn a deaf ear. He would rather not hear yet again about how he was losing his marbles.

It had been a long time since he'd seen old Monsieur Müller. Years, maybe. But he remembered it all: the barbecues with the other hockey parents, the tournaments, the raffles, the electoral campaigns, when he worked as an assessor and the same name appeared on almost every envelope: Paul Müller. He had felt flattered by this man's friendship. He had bought the mayor's old BMW, and they had gone out drinking together. And now here he was again, the mayor of Corné-court, in the middle of one last winter. Once again, Gérard had that vague sensation of blurriness. Suddenly, he no longer had the faintest idea what he was doing there. At the far end of the street, a police car appeared. The light on top was not flashing and it came over to them at a crawl.

"I'll sort this out," said Monsieur Müller with a crafty look.

And he put his hands up in a pacifying gesture toward the police car. Gérard, for his part, wasn't worried in the slightest. He was just enjoying this chance meeting, the comforting impression inspired by that familiar face, that thick mountain accent, and that smile, which brought back so many good memories.

16

CHRISTOPHE DOES NOT normally remember his dreams, but when Charlie wakes him that morning he has time to sense images of a swimming pool fading inside his head in an oppressive blue glimmer. When he opens his eyes, though, all that remains is an unpleasant feeling, and his heart racing in his chest.

"It's happening," she says.

She is sitting next to him on the bed, looking very calm. The little night-light in their bedroom illuminates the objects around it with a peaceful, distant sketchiness. Christophe sits up and has a drink of water, his eyelids fluttering as he emerges from sleepiness.

"What time is it?"

"Five," Charlie replies.

They smile at each other in the darkness. Christophe pushes the duvet away and shivers. An instant later, he's on his feet.

"It's okay, we've got time," he says.

But he is already rushing over to the closet where they keep the bag that has been packed for days, containing everything they need: nightshirt, underwear, toiletry bag, a few books to pass the time while they're waiting.

"Don't forget your phone charger."

"I'm going to call my mother."

"Just wait. We can do that later."

Inside their little apartment, they run smoothly through the long-planned actions. From this point on, everything matters. Christophe takes a shower, gets dressed while drinking his coffee, and takes one last look at the checklist magnetized to the fridge door. Charlie, meanwhile, sits in the kitchen, the bag at her feet, and gazes silently at her enormous belly. Sometimes, looking at that swollen bulge, Christophe has the feeling that what he sees is an autonomous object, a perfect egg already leading its own existence. He and Charlie have been drawn into its orbit, and soon the whole world will follow. The young woman seems nervous despite the vast underwater calmness that surrounds her. It is strange being there, so close to the end, just as the sky is starting to lighten. The neighbors are still asleep, the apartment building rests in the early-morning silence, and through the window they can see streetlamps, other buildings, the Moselle flowing quietly below.

"You okay?" Christophe asks.

"Yeah."

As always, he does what's expected of him. He is gentle, he doesn't panic, he checks his pockets, his phone, the car keys, their ID papers, then picks up the bag.

"Okay, let's go."

At a red light, he takes her hand and holds it for a moment. Don't be scared. It'll all be fine. Charlie isn't scared. The town opens like a flower under the lurid pink-orange-blue dawn. The time has come for them to leap into the unknown. Happiness is a strange thing.

At the reception desk, a woman with mauve eyelids takes down their details with robotic indifference, then tells them to sit in the waiting room. Their names will be called. After that,

Charlie's case is processed in a slightly irritating atmosphere of hygiene and slowness. There is something almost incongruous about her contractions amid the sterile white decor of the hospital room. A nurse with braided hair comes to see them at regular intervals, her name badge revealing that she is called Coralie. She chews gum and wears compression stockings and Crocs. Every time they ask her when the epidural will be given, she replies: "Soon." It takes less than ten minutes of this for Charlie to want her dead. Because the pain has already set in, with its peaks and waves that crush her kidneys, break her back. Occasionally Christophe sees her face turn pale and gaunt as she rolls around on the bed, a victim of the battle taking place in her womb.

"Call her!"

Christophe obeys. Coralie reappears, still chewing, and takes the patient's pulse, before offering her a couple of Tylenol. After a few more equally futile visits, she decides to give them one of those prenatal exercise balls.

"Try this, I think it'll help."

Charlie can't believe it. She watches Coralie in her blue scrubs calmly leave the room, the door closing in slow motion.

"She's gaslighting me."

For now, she doesn't dare show the anger she feels to the nurse, so she focuses her resentment on Christophe, who placidly accepts the situation.

"Why don't you try the ball? It might help," he suggests imprudently.

The look his girlfriend gives him leaves no room for doubt about her thoughts on the matter. He needs to find a solution quickly, and something more scientific than that stupid fucking ball.

Ten minutes later, Charlie is writhing in agony, jaw clenched.

"Go and find someone!"

"The anesthesiologist will be here soon."

Charlie kicks one of her sneakers across the room.

"Get a fucking move on! This hurts."

Christophe rushes out and finds Coralie in the staff room, where she is drinking coffee with a few of her colleagues. They do not look too pleased at seeing him barge in on their conversation.

"It's my girlfriend. She's in so much pain . . ."

"The doctor will be there soon."

"Can't you give her something?"

"You just have to be patient."

"But she's in pain!"

With a sigh, Coralie stands up and follows him to the room. Behind him, Christophe hears her Crocs squeaking on the plastic floor. He wants to go faster, but he's too afraid of annoying this nurse, who is the only one that can offer Charlie relief.

"All right, so what's going on?"

Charlie is kneeling on the floor as if praying, butt in the air and arms outstretched in front of her. When she looks up, it is instantly clear that a physical attack on Coralie cannot be ruled out.

"I want the anesthetic," she grunts.

"The anesthesiologist isn't here yet," the nurse replies, unfazed.

Coralie sees women like this every day, the ones who whine all the time and the ones who give birth like they're mailing a letter. She's seen complications too, the bloody bullfight going on for hours on end, sometimes ending with tragedy, a bluish little head, the cord wrapped around the neck. She's seen first-time mothers split open and other women broken in by five pregnancies, the whole industry of birth, no pomp or ceremony, just routine. She no longer gets emotional about it.

Habit is her anesthetic, professionalism her buffer. And then there's the example set by the doctors, who often take pride in their coldness and consider these swollen patients with the godlike gaze of someone boasting seven years of higher education. And seen from those heights, it must be said that there is something a little bestial about these laboring women that does not encourage solicitude.

"Find him," Charlie repeats through gritted teeth.

"I really think you need to go and find him," agrees Christophe, who is starting to feel slightly unwell himself.

"You just have to be patient," repeats the nurse, without departing from her calm indifference.

"Oh fuck..."

A contraction hits Charlie and she writhes again, ending up on her back, arms tensed, fists balled. Then the pain recedes. Her hands open and tears roll over her temples.

"Tell her to go and find that fucking doctor or I really will get angry."

Christophe, smiling weakly, leads the nurse out of the room.

"I think you need to do what she says now."

"You're not the only patients in this hospital, you know."

Christophe has started to sweat. He looks out the window, takes a deep breath.

"Is that the staff parking lot, there?"

Coralie glances outside, with a small frown, and nods.

"If you don't do something, I'm going to have to smash some windshields."

"What?"

"Find someone. Quickly. Or I get my crowbar and I start breaking glass."

The nurse is used to difficult patients, but this is something else.

"Stay here," she says, stalking off.

"Thank you," breathes Christophe.

He wipes his forehead with the back of his hand and slows his breathing down before going back to the room. He knows he will carry out his threat if necessary.

Five minutes later, a tall man with a buzz cut and a signet ring bearing a coat of arms enters the room. He glares reproachfully and says: "What is all this nonsense, eh? Are you the vandal?"

Christophe gives an embarrassed smile.

"This isn't the Wild West, monsieur."

"Are you the anesthesiologist?"

"Are you the father?"

"I thought you hadn't arrived yet."

The man holds out his hand, struggling to conceal his amusement at Christophe's threats of destruction.

From her bed, Charlie has watched the whole scene.

"Hey...remember me?"

After that, things happen with relative smoothness. Charlie is taken to the delivery room, where she is given an epidural injection and falls in love with the neofascist anesthesiologist. And then the real waiting starts. From time to time, a nurse—no longer Coralie—comes in to check the dilation of the cervix. She sticks her gloved fingers into Charlie's vagina while Charlie stares at the ceiling. Each time, the nurse looks disappointed. Charlie is just going to have to bear the pain patiently. Hours pass, filled with a strange fatigue that is both irritating and oppressive. Sitting near his girlfriend, Christophe tries to take her mind off things. He holds her hand, tells her he's there. Not that this is much use to her. At times Charlie wishes she had never gotten herself into this mess. But at other moments she gazes tenderly at Christophe and slowly nods off, while Christophe takes advantage of her sleepiness to play Tetris on his phone or send texts to his friends. When his father finds out what's happening, he replies instantly:

"On my way."

Twenty minutes later, Gérard texts his son to say he is somewhere in the labyrinth of that hospital, killing time by feeding his loose change into a vending machine. Christophe could not do anything to dissuade him from coming, and he's glad of that now. His father's presence, even at a distance, reassures him.

After hesitating for a long time, he also decides to tell Julien what's happening, sending him a brief text and a photograph of himself and Charlie. It has been almost ten years since he heard from his big brother. The last time they saw each other was when Julien came from Montpellier for their mother's funeral.

It was after Christophe's birth that his mother had quit her job at the driving school to take care of her children. Much later, when her younger son had started high school, she wanted to work again, but in the meantime the employment market had changed beyond recognition. In 1975, all you needed was energy and a good work ethic. By 1990, words like "skills" and "flexibility" were all the rage. Beggars could not be choosers.

Sylvie, however, was not the type to kowtow to anyone. She had spent too long living in a bourgeois milieu and was not exactly overflowing with positivity. Thanks to the success of the store, she and Gérard had become recognizable local figures, the kind of people you saw at fundraising parties for the mayor's office, at the Bastille Day celebrations, the kind of people who gave generously for the construction of a new village hall or to help the hockey team. They held small cocktail parties in their home to which they invited other well-off shopkeepers, an educational assistant, a pharmacist couple who lived nearby. Champagne flowed like water and when Sylvie reached out to pick a pistachio from a bowl, her wrist jingled with gold. They weren't exactly rich, but through hard work they had been able to drive a Mercedes, buy a television for practically every room in the house, and have the attic converted. Gérard would periodically think about buying a small chalet so they could spend their weekends in the mountains.

So, really, what was the point in getting some low-paid job that might put them in a higher tax bracket? Following this logic, Sylvie gave up on the idea of a professional career.

"Anyway, I hate being useful," she said, taking a drag on her Winston.

In fact, Christophe had no idea what she did with her time, all those years. A bit of gardening, probably. Some TV soaps in the afternoons. And she spent quite a lot of time looking after her own parents, who weren't getting any younger. No doubt she felt something missing in that indoor life, caught between the veranda, where she watered her plants, and the hairdressing salon, which at least took up an hour of every week. She didn't complain, but perhaps she would have liked to see more of the world, or to learn an instrument. After all, she often talked about that IQ test she'd taken as a teenager, according to which she was in the ninetieth percentile of the French population for intelligence, something that always annoyed the hell out of Gérard. Maybe, too, she would have liked to leave him, but she stayed because she had no income, no savings, only a tiny pension. Sylvie was dependent on her husband, and even if he didn't abuse that power, they were both still aware of it. For a long time, her life had been stuck in a rut.

And then, one day, while she was pushing her cart through the refrigerated aisle of the local Intermarché, Sylvie collapsed. At the hospital, the doctor came to talk to Christophe and his father in the corridor. They had found a sort of blotch, like a little patch of grayish lichen, on the right side of Sylvie's torso, a few centimeters below her armpit. It had probably been there for weeks. She had never told anyone about it and Gérard hadn't noticed it.

"It's a melanoma. We're going to take some X-rays."

"Is it serious?"

"We'll see."

When Gérard asked his wife why she hadn't mentioned it, she just said that it wasn't a big deal. The X-rays begged to differ. There were clearly some pale spots, like bright blisters glimmering in the lung, tiny fingers of whiteness spreading across the rib cage. The oncologist, who knew how to read such images, made an appropriate facial expression. Christophe had overheard him deep in discussion with some interns in a corridor, each of them giving their diagnosis and suggesting the most effective treatments. But Professor Truchy had cut them short. He had seen thousands of cancers, particularly since the Chernobyl disaster, whose effects had supposedly stopped at the Ukrainian border. According to him, there was no point torturing this poor woman. All they could give her were benzodiazepines, antiemetics, and Xanax. Hearing this, Christophe felt a vast emptiness inside him. So it was over, already, without warning. In the space of a few seconds, he became a child again. *Mommy*. It suddenly occurred to him that he barely even knew her. Afterward, he had to put on a brave face, while haunted by the fear that she had done it on purpose, to escape. She had always been a big fan of irony.

Soon, under the effect of the medication, Sylvie sank into a soft and curiously cheerful state, at least when she was conscious. Gérard stayed with her in the mornings, and Christophe came after work. She slept through most of it. She had to be intubated because she couldn't swallow anymore, and she quickly lost a great deal of weight. It was the most amazing thing to witness: what happened to a body in thrall to disease, her skin like taut parchment over the bridge of her nose, at her joints, her belly swollen despite being empty, and those strange bright hues that appeared in various places, a ragged dark blue around her eyes, the rainbows that stretched across her arms even though she never hurt herself, the ultraviolet of her veins, and already that hideous union of yellows and greens that scared away the pretty colors of good health. And, beneath her chin, in the folds of her armpits, the thickly crumped skin reminiscent of a turkey's neck.

The hockey team was wallowing in the middle of the pack that season and, at twenty-five, Christophe no longer had any illusions about his sports career. The highest level of the professional game would remain forever out of reach. But he still loved playing, the sensations of a Saturday night, trips with his friends, and the special status that his position on the team gave him. Now he was the one hazing the younger players, seventeen-year-old kids all wobbly on their skates who went flying when you barged into them.

Once, on a trip to Villard-de-Lans, the players sneaked out of their hotel to go clubbing. They followed the guardrail along the road, twenty of them in single file, in the middle of the night, like Snow White's dwarves. In the end, they found a place called Macumba or something where they could drink and dance, and Christophe even managed to hook up with a waitress, a beautiful brunette with large breasts, a bared midriff, and rings in her nose and ears. Around five in the morning, the two of them went at it in the storeroom where they kept the alcohol, and when Christophe emerged afterward the other freaks were all there waiting for him in the parking lot, applauding. After that, they went back the way they'd come, a bunch of young males numbed by booze and exhaustion, stumbling back to the hotel in a straggly line. When they got there, the coach was waiting for them in the lobby and he gave them the dressing-down of the century. At eight o'clock they all had to put on their uniforms and run around the stadium, which was next to the hotel. Most of them threw up, and the team lost 7–2 to Villard, but Christophe came home happy.

Playing hockey kept him from having to make difficult decisions, sheltered him from the usual age-related losses. And after spending two hours at his mother's bedside, the need to get on the ice became almost unbearable. There, he could empty his head and skate until his body was exhausted. After practice, sitting naked in the locker room, he would look at himself in the mirror, his dick hanging between his thick thighs, his shoulders massive and aching, his hair soaked with sweat, his belly heaving in time with his breaths, his muscles taut under his skin, from neck to hips. And he would see the vitality that was so visible in him, that shone through his skin, reddening his cheeks, making his whole body burn. Every day, he wore himself out for two hours, and when he woke the next day his strength was still there, reborn, apparently endless. He refused to believe in his mother's body, which he no longer dared even touch. Hockey kept him distanced from old age; it denied death. Sometimes he would wake up crying and would not be able to fall back asleep until morning.

After three weeks, her decline steepened. Sylvie was awake for only about two hours a day, and then her eyes and mouth never opened. By the end, she would raise two fingers to show that she could hear, but she no longer had the faintest idea who was talking to her. One night, Christophe kissed her on the forehead for the last time. A chemical odor emanated from her skin, which was almost cold and as moist as a slug. She died a few hours later. By that point, all he felt was relief.

When he went to pick up his brother at the train station, the day before her funeral, Julien immediately made his intentions clear.

"Drop me off at the hotel. I'll be fine."

"Dad's made a baeckeoffe. Your bedroom's all ready."

"I ate on the train."

In the end, Julien agreed to stay the night. In the yard, he stood and looked up at the big house in the darkness, still filled with their mother's fading presence.

"It's like Versailles or something," said Julien, gesturing to the three lit-up windows.

"He's even put the heating on upstairs."

An ironically raised eyebrow. "Wow."

Inside, the two brothers were welcomed by the delicious smell of the baeckeoffe that permeated every corner of the first floor, a smell of patience and prolonged preparation that offered a kind of proof.

Julien dropped his bag in the hallway but kept his jacket on. Then the two boys headed to the kitchen, where their father was waiting for them, sitting in his chair, his half-moon glasses perched on his nose as he pondered a sudoku grid. He was wearing his apron and the table had been carefully set. He had even taken out the Lunéville tableware for the occasion. The fluorescent light above the sink bathed the room in a stark, efficient glare.

Seeing his elder son, Gérard cried: "Ah!," then struggled to his feet. He'd made an effort with his clothes, Christophe noticed. For once, he wasn't wearing the sweatpants that were baggy at the knees and exposed his butt crack whenever he bent over. On the other hand, he had not gone as far as putting on shoes. The old slippers he wore gave him a disarming appearance. The last time Julien saw him, almost eight years earlier, his father had still been a man grappling with the complexities of life and work, worrying endlessly about money and his employees, a man in a state of constant vexation. You could see it in his muscles back then, in the tightness of his shoulders, the lines of his face, in his eyes when you suddenly became one more problem that he had to solve. Now, however, retired and freshly widowed, practically alone and doomed to end that way, Gérard had completely relaxed. He was almost another man entirely, with his slippers and his apron, a man who set the table and didn't mind eating dinner after seven. He and Julien air-kissed, and he asked his son what he'd like to drink. Julien objected that it was already late.

"Come on, we're not in a rush, are we?"

Finally, Julien hung his jacket on the back of his chair and sat down at the table. They raised their beer glasses and made a toast.

"To Mom."

"To us."

The bottles left clear circular imprints on the white table-cloth. The linen was thick and well made, the kind of thing that could be passed on for generations. This tablecloth had seen endless Sundays and Christmases; it had been pressed down by Easter lamb dishes, by the bottles and glasses of many parties and events. It had witnessed men slurping vintage wines and gobbling meat in rich sauces, men with big feet and strong political opinions, laughing like ogres, asses glued to their seats while their anxious, sober wives shuttled between the dining room and the kitchen, the women finally gathering to wash dishes and chat together in secret, their guards down, their tongues sharpened, chuckling as their husbands slouched at the table, belts loosened, pouring themselves a drop of eau de vie and stubbing out a cigarette at the bottom of a coffee cup as they prepared to deliver the final word on whatever subject they had been discussing.

Children's hands had grabbed and smeared this tablecloth, fingers wet with saliva picking up bread crumbs in the pause between a pear and the dessert. The tablecloth had seen an endless parade of simple, hearty family meals—hot pots, sauerkraut, beef stews—and many bottles of red. Around it, bodies had shrunk, husbands had died of old age, women of grief, and vice versa. The stories that tablecloth could have told...In the weft of its fabric were all the secrets of a family, going back years and years. There was even one male cousin who liked boys, and who had once brought home his "friend." It had seen every aspect of ordinary life. Wills that had set siblings at one another's throats, a succession of crises over nothing very much, tears shed and blood spilled, money lost and lives remade. Time had passed, but the tablecloth had remained white. A father and his two sons were eating at it now. They drank a Pinot Noir from Alsace that cheered them up and, in the temporary warmth of a pre-funeral dinner, were reunited.

"You should have come back sooner," said Gérard, after putting the plates in the dishwasher.

Julien, who'd had a bit too much to drink, made a vague gesture, his head moving from side to side. This concession was enough for the father, who made no attempt to drive home his advantage.

Seeing them like that, the hatchet half-buried, Christophe could not remember what had caused the old animosity in the first place. Animosity there had been, though, and plenty of it. They had even come to blows. In fact, they had always fought. Gérard used to give his son a good hiding when he was little—accepted behavior at the time; educational even—but when Julien grew big enough to hit him back, their hostility had immediately swelled to the dimensions of a minor news story. Julien had shoved his father against a wall and said: *Next time, I'll kill you.* Now the mother was no longer around. Even if they'd wanted to fight now, they wouldn't have known how. That relationship had disappeared with her.

The three men sipped a digestif made from raspberries and damson plums and talked about the good old days. Then the father took the old photograph albums out of the cupboard. There were about ten of them, starting with their ancestors and ending in the early nineties. The photos from the seventies had aged badly. Their hues seemed to have lost all life, greens turning diarrhea-colored, whites opalescent, muddying into a sludge of bland brownness. All the same, the two sons were amused by the bold decor of that period: bizarre patterns covering everything from wallpaper to women's dresses. Looking through those photographs, their lives flashed past before their eyes: Julien as a baby, the park, a sandcastle, his face in a balaclava, Christophe in a ski suit standing in front of a snowman. The strangest thing was seeing their parents behind them, and what had been captured on film without their knowledge: their youth, affection, smiles, things forgotten afterward in the tide of gloomy Sundays and family spats. And yet there they were, caught forever, at thirty, at forty, at a campsite, on the beach, with a stroller, holding a child by the hand, so young and fresh-faced.

"Look," their father said, pointing. "Your mother still had long hair back then."

"I don't remember that Chevignon jacket."

"Yeah, I bugged Mom for weeks to get that. I bet you never knew how much she paid for it."

"Oh really?" said their father.

And for a moment, the old hostility was rekindled, the father duped, the mother going behind his back, the little secrets and plots, the undermining of the master's authority.

"Okay, I think that's enough," said Julien.

And he stood up, somber-faced, leaving his glass untouched on the table.

"We prepared your room."

"Thanks. Good night."

"Good night, son."

The next day, a lot of people turned up for the funeral. Sylvie Marchal had lived her whole life in Cornécourt, which naturally forged bonds. Gérard took a quiet delight in his role as widower. He had always enjoyed feeling important, and he didn't deny himself the pleasure even on this sad occasion. It was his vice, this love of pomp and ceremony. The mayor came, and the two men talked for a while. They had also met up for the occasional brioche at Le Narval.

"The prick even trimmed his mustache," Julien observed from the other end of the table, watching his eagerly smiling father, like a campaigning politician.

"Well, you shined your shoes," replied Christophe.

Julien smiled at that, apparently pleased to be there. He asked Christophe about hockey, then fell silent. Christophe had imagined that his brother would want to know more about their mother, her last weeks at the hospice. But those words were never spoken. Julien left that evening, on the train.

"Are you sure you don't want to stay for a while?" his father asked.

"No, I have to go. I've got work tomorrow."

They kissed cheeks outside the café, the son keeping his hands in his pockets, then walking away with his silence and his grievances. That was when Christophe realized he no longer had a mother.

———

CHARLIE, EXHAUSTED, HAS nodded off. When she opens her eyes, she finds Christophe taking a selfie.

"It's for my brother."

"Ah. I doubt he'll reply."

"I don't even know if this is still his number."

"What about your father?"

"He's in the hospital somewhere. I don't want him here—he might start yelling at us for taking too long."

Charlie manages a brief smile. Her head is thrown back, like a swooning saint.

"He really can't wait, can he?"

"I know. Sometimes I wonder if he's more excited about this kid than we are."

The hours pass ever more slowly, but at least Charlie is no longer in pain. Every time the anesthesiologist pokes his head through the door to check on her, she looks at him like a lovestruck teenager and Christophe sighs.

"Look, I can't help having feelings for him."

"It's the painkillers."

The nurse comes by regularly too, to monitor the patient's progress. She smiles at them and speaks in that high-pitched voice that people use when talking to old people or foreigners, but despite her cheerful demeanor they can tell things aren't going the way they're supposed to.

Around noon, the monitor starts to beep.

"What's that?"

The two of them freeze, panic-stricken. The machine that monitors the vital signs of both mother and child continues to emit that stress-inducing beeping noise. Christophe leaves the room and returns ten minutes later with a third nurse, who examines the green sine waves on the screen.

"It's nothing. He's just a bit tired. Let's take a look at your cervix, shall we?"

The nurse puts on a rubber glove and reaches under the sheet. Charlie grimaces.

"Not there yet."

"So what do we do?"

"Nothing, for now. The doctor will be here soon."

The couple are left alone to stare at the trace of the baby's heartbeat. The alarm goes off again, then stops. Charlie breaks down and starts to cry.

"I can't do this. I'm so tired."

"You'll be fine."

"Easy for you to say."

She sheds a few more tears, then wipes them away with the back of her hand, and they smile at each other.

After two weeks of classes with the midwife, after reading all those dumb books on how to be a good mommy and a good daddy to little Mr. Baby, they are now caught in the harsh grip of uncertainty. From time to time, Charlie, having swallowed too much air, lets off a long, odorless fart, but nobody laughs. Christophe, sobered by his helplessness, forces himself not to keep looking at his watch.

A little later, the obstetrician drops by to check on the state of play. Another gloved hand reaching under the sheets. Things are still not really advancing. Four centimeters max, and the machine starts beeping again. In the dark-ringed eyes of the future parents, the same imploring look. The obstetrician, with her impressive chignon, tries to reassure them.

"Everything's fine. There's just a small problem with the contractions. They're starting to tire out the baby's heart. We can't let this go on too long."

"Or what?"

"It'll be okay," the woman in white tells them.

"I want to go home," says Charlie, and again the tears trickle down her gray, exhausted face.

The obstetrician's eyes seem to read her like a scanner, moving one way and then the other.

"Just relax," she says, before disappearing. "There's nothing to worry about."

Another two hours of this—the stress, the uncertainty, the fatigue—and then Charlie tears the sensors off her belly. The beeping stops at last.

"You can't do that..."

But she is already getting out of bed. She puts a foot on the floor, and Christophe catches her just before she collapses.

"Charlie, you can't! Your legs don't work because of the anesthetics."

"I want to go home!"

But by the end of that sentence, her aggression has melted into a sob.

Christophe helps her lie down, then goes off in search of a nurse. This time, there's no one around. The corridor is deserted. Open doors lead to empty rooms. He stands there, panting, all strength gone, his impossible duty weighing him down. He wants to go home too. He sits with his back against the wall and tries to catch his breath. He must get through this. He realizes he has entered a new part of his life, where doing his best is no longer enough.

Another three hours pass in a muffled daze. The room is like a raft adrift on a raging river, the two survivors clinging to it on the verge of killing each other. Thankfully, Charlie slips into a restless sleep and Christophe has time to send some texts to his friends. Greg and Marco reply with brief messages of encouragement, full of short words, clapping-hand emojis, and exclamation points. The obstetrician returns and tells them off for unplugging the monitors. A nurse is called to strap the sensors back in place. Charlie groans. The screen lights up again, bold red numbers, that infernal beeping.

"That's not good," says the obstetrician, leaning close to the screen. "The baby's heartbeat is too slow. How long have you been here?"

"Ten hours."

"Hmm, not that long really."

Christophe sees war declared in Charlie's eyes. In the same unruffled tones, the obstetrician says:

"We're going to have to intervene."

"What do you mean?" asks Christophe.

"C-section."

Although Charlie isn't crazy about the idea of being cut up, she breathes more easily at this news. Finally, a light at the end of the tunnel.

After another injection delivered by the anesthesiologist, she is wheeled to the delivery room. Christophe stays with her while the obstetrician, a nurse, and the midwife get ready at the other side of the surgical area, all of them in blue masks, scrubs, and caps.

"Do you work out?" the obstetrician asks.

"A little. Why?"

"Your abdominal wall is really thick. I can't get him out of there."

"Did you already cut me?" asks Charlie, trying to sit up so she can see.

"Don't move," the obstetrician barks from behind her mask.

Christophe is getting cold sweats. Horrific images flash through his head. He can see his girlfriend's guts, only a few feet from where he stands.

"Wait!" Charlie shouts, feeling a sudden sharp pain in her abdomen.

Too late. Two hands lift up a rounded, bloody shape, the closed features of a face vaguely discernible. This apparition lasts only a second. The tiny body has already vanished. Then they hear wails—distraught, staggering, unimaginably new.

After that, everything happens in a rush. The bundled-up infant is handed to his mother, who barely has time to kiss him, to feel his hot skin against her chest. Seconds later, she is taken away to be sewn up. And the midwife carries the child away, telling Christophe to follow.

"What name have you chosen?"

Christophe, in his surgical gown, trails her into an adjoining room.

"Gabriel," he says.

"Oh, yeah, we get a lot of them these days."

The midwife's tactlessness makes no impression on the stunned father. Then this total stranger, whose face he will forget even while he remembers her gestures, cleans the baby before asking the father to keep an eye on him while she goes off to get some cotton wool. So Christophe finds himself alone with this thing, his son, who is cold and screaming loudly from his small, pink, empty mouth. The father looks around for someone to help him, then leans over the baby, who, lying on the changing mat, is starting to get some color in his face. He puts his forearms either side of the miniature body, tilts his torso down, and kisses the fragile head, the soft belly and arms. He whispers a sweet nothing into the child's ear and the screaming stops.

"Don't be scared. I'm here."

The baby's eyes are still closed, but he clings to that sliver of familiarity, the timbre of that voice. Christophe presses his lips against the infant's forehead, breathing in the sweet smell of hygiene products from the soft fuzz of hair.

"Ah, you're getting to know each other!" the midwife exclaims, coming back into the room with the cotton wool.

She skillfully puts a diaper on the baby, then a onesie, then pajamas, before placing a pale cotton hat on his head and handing this perfectly wrapped parcel to the father, who wonders how on earth he is going to manage not to smash it to pieces.

"No, don't worry, he's a tough little guy."

Now they are in another room, as neutral as all the previous ones, and the nurse is fixing a sensor to the baby's index finger.

"What's that?"

"It's okay, just something to make sure his heart is beating the way it should. I'll leave the two of you in peace now."

"What? Are you kidding?"

Christophe stares in panic at this heavyset woman who actually knows how to look after a baby.

"You'll be fine," she says with casual certainty. "Just wait and see. You'll soon the get the hang of it."

She nods at a chair, and Christophe carefully sits down, as if what he holds in his arms is as delicate as a soap bubble. The midwife makes the facial expression that people make when they are trying to reassure you: duck lips, eyes closed...no problem, you've got this.

And so Christophe is left alone with his son once again. He watches the baby, who is sleeping like a maniac, and listens to his tiny breathing, which is all he has. How can such a creature possibly survive? Then the child wakes up and seems to look for something with his earnest, incapable eyes.

"I'm here," Christophe says quietly.

The baby's eyelids flutter.

"I'm here."

He runs his fingertip along the child's nose and Gabriel's eyes close reflexively.

There's a knock at the door. Christophe's father stands in the doorway, his arms full of gifts, smiling broadly under his graying mustache.

"Everything okay?"

Christophe nods.

"And the mom?"

"They're looking after her. She had a C-section."

"Ouch."

Gérard takes a couple of steps into the room. He's looking for a place to put the flowers, the chocolates, the enormous light brown teddy bear he's holding. After doing so, he tiptoes over to them.

"Can I hold him?"

Christophe hesitates, then stands up to hand him the child.

"What's his name?"

"Gabriel."

"That's a girl's name."

The old man is holding the baby in his arms now.

"He already looks like a Marchal," he says, leaning closer and planting a kiss on the white cotton hat.

Christophe does not have the heart to contradict him.

"Sleep, little one, sleep," the kid's grandfather coos. "You've got all the time in the world."

17

FOR THE CHRISTMAS party, Erwann hired the services of the best caterer in the city. The buffet was a reflection of Elexia's ambition and success. Vegetarian dishes with seasonal ingredients, more than fifteen varieties of cheese, oysters and exotic fruit, and a huge heap of elaborate petit fours that shared a table with piles of empty gift boxes, bottles of Burgundy, and bottled local beers half-submerged in bowls of ice.

But what Hélène and Lison liked best was the Ruinart champagne. Erwann had boasted of ordering twenty cases. Gifts for clients—and therefore tax-deductible.

"How long will this thing go on?" asked Lison.

"A while," said Hélène.

Every Christmas party began the same way. In the open-plan office transformed into a dance floor, earnest discussions about the company's activity would alternate with more light-hearted chatter. Now and then, someone would crack a joke and there'd be a ripple of laughter. Female employees who'd managed to get their kids to bed were already baring their fangs, determined to go a little wild. Later, they would be forced to take a taxi home, and the next day they would regret the excesses of the night; not that this would prevent them doing the same thing again as soon as they possibly could. A handful of men with vertical faces were discussing the future of hybrid cars or the monetary policy of the European Central Bank, incapable as yet of departing from their self-image of dry competence, while the junior consultants swarmed cheerfully, quietly joking like kids taking First Communion, but secretly determined to get smashed and, if possible, laid. Everyone was cheerful, tense, wary.

Because it always went the same way. There was this traditional get-together in the middle of winter, just before the holidays, when alcohol flowed like water and the pressure was momentarily lifted. Indiscreet revelations, shameful couplings, even just an act of clumsiness could ruin years of hard work in the eyes of your superiors. The more reasonable employees could foresee such missteps and promised themselves they would leave early. But the veneer always cracked in the end. After months spent working breathlessly, focused on deadlines, caught between their clients and their managers, they couldn't hope to maintain that stoic detachment for long.

"Where did Erwann go?"

Lison, who that night was wearing an angora cardigan over a Ramones T-shirt, stood up on tiptoes to get a better view, but she could not see him anywhere.

"He's up to something."

"Hmm, that's not a good sign."

"No…"

Just after eight, the intern plugged her phone into a pair of speakers and pressed play on a playlist entitled "Turning Shit into Gold." Within seconds, the atmosphere was transformed. The rising alcohol level in each body also did its work, and soon people were mingling more boldly, talking more loudly, and starting to dance. Out of nowhere, they were wiggling hips, touching arms. Even Parrot seemed to have abandoned his halo for the night. His facial expression was mocking, which made him look juvenile—and rather sexy, if Hélène was honest. She took the opportunity to approach him.

"So...?" she said.

Instantly, she saw wariness transform his features. His big grin shrunk to little more than a faint, ironic curl of the lips.

"So...what?"

"Oh, I don't know," Hélène simpered. "We never talk. I was just wondering if you were happy. How are things going for you?"

Ninon Carpentier and Karim Lebœuf, two junior consultants notorious for following Parrot around like lost sheep in the hope of some kind of reward, exchanged a sideways glance and hid behind their glasses.

"Great, actually. We've done some pretty interesting things so far."

"I heard about your idea. A premium offer for key accounts."

"Yeah."

"Sounds good. What will you give them, gold-plated PowerPoints?"

Parrot forced a smile, but behind this façade Hélène could practically hear the gears grinding.

"I just want us to be ready for the second semester of 2017, that's all."

"The presidential election?" Hélène asked, warily raising an eyebrow.

Parrot confirmed her intuition with a barely perceptible movement of his chin.

"And what are you expecting?"

"A surprise."

"What kind of surprise?"

"We'll see," replied Parrot. "Whatever happens, the State is going to have to tighten its belt and focus on its sovereign powers. The nanny state is a thing of the past. Too heavy, too slow . . ."

"And too expensive, obviously," interrupted Hélène, somewhat irritated by this deluge of truisms.

"Obviously. It's all a question of resources. And finding a new balance. That's where we have the opportunity to do something good."

"Did your friends in the government tell you that?"

A brief frown. Parrot was finding it harder and harder to conceal his annoyance, and his two acolytes decided it was time to retreat to the buffet. To make himself heard over the echoing din inside the office, Parrot put his lips close to Hélène's ear.

"I'm sure there will be some fantastic opportunities out there. Ministers are more and more suspicious of their administrations. The elite of the new generation don't believe the system works anymore. Every time they need to manage a crisis, or implement a reform, or consult experts, they would rather go with small teams."

"The age of the task force," summarized Hélène, gazing into Parrot's eyes in a vaguely flirtatious way.

Then she raised her glass to her lips, ironic yet serious.

"We should work together," said Parrot.

"We'd be so innovative . . ." Then, after considering this for a second, she went on: "But what will we do with all this in the provinces?"

"That's where most of the business will be. Relations between Paris and the regions are at an all-time low. The big regions have to invent everything. Their departments are upset because they get lumbered with the responsibility of reforming themselves, but they aren't given the means to do it. The old regional administrations are on their last legs. Rivalries, shrinking resources, inertia, structural problems . . . it's the biggest shitshow imaginable. There are cracks everywhere.

The guys in the ministries are flying by the seat of their pants. I've seen them do it. They need air traffic control to bring them down safely. They need us to give them the information and do the dirty work for them."

"Yeah, the gray-matter mercenaries. But isn't that what we've been doing for the past twenty years?"

"Of course, but this is the luxury version. Repackaged."

"And more expensive?"

"Naturally."

"Pretty smart."

They clinked glasses.

THREE DRINKS LATER, Hélène noticed the time and thought that, at this rate, her return home might prove complicated. She checked her phone. Philippe had tried calling her several times, and this fact convinced her to have another drink. At eleven, Erwann had still not been tracked down. The dance floor was packed now, and the impertinent intern decided to carry out an experiment. She played "Don't Be So Shy" by Imany, followed by a few other, similarly horny and sensual tracks. Very soon, people hooked up and began to rub their bodies against each other.

"I wonder how many babies will be conceived tonight," Lison said dreamily.

Hélène smiled. She looked at the tall, young intern, like something from a cartoon, and thought how beautiful she was. Her thrift-store elegance, her equine profile, her luxuriant hair, and the space between her eyes: everything about her was enviably unique. Though she wouldn't have admitted it to herself, Hélène was proud to be friends with this girl who seemed to have her finger on the pulse of the age. Drunkenly, she stroked her shoulder and felt a faint urge to kiss her.

"Wanna dance?"

The intern briefly took her boss by the hand, and the two of them moved onto the dance floor. Since Hélène was wearing heels, she stood just as tall as Lison, and they began to undulate, putting on a show for each other, their eyes meeting now and then, evasive but laden with intentions. Hélène felt a desperate need to be desired.

And yet, since starting her affair with Christophe, she had been greatly reassured on that score. Of course she wasn't stupid or alienated, and her existence did not depend on the male gaze. Even so, it made her feel good to see how hard his cock grew at the sight of her ass, to feel how fierce and gentle he became, to sense the weight of his broad shoulders, his sweat-glued stomach, his deep thrusts, when she was naked and her legs were spread for him. Ergo, she was beautiful.

Unfortunately, it made the return to earth—being with her family, the daily routine with Philippe—even more annoying in comparison. What might have been a mild irritation before was now almost unbearable. His late nights at the office and his business trips, the way he always sneaked away as soon as he was supposed to make dinner or give his daughter a bath. Suggestions that had once seemed harmless, like "You should call the Menous so we can have dinner with them," had become triggers for Hélène. Inevitably, she and Philippe were fighting more than ever.

"What is up with you these days?" he would ask her sometimes.

Another question that drove her crazy.

Old loves, she thought, were like those tattered tapestries on the walls of castles. A thread comes loose, you pull at it without thinking, and the whole thing just unravels. In no time at all, you're left with nothing but the bare background: your obsessions and neuroses are exposed; your dreams lie dying on the floor. And no shrink could help you put this mess back together again. There was no solution to the problem, unless you could somehow travel back in time, erase the twenty years of delayed truth that had just exploded in your face.

But the worst part was when they were with the girls.

One night the previous week, when Philippe was absent, Hélène had organized a TV binge. It was an old family habit. When Mom was bored, they could eat toast and drink hot chocolate and watch cartoons. Mouche had jumped for joy at this news, and Clara had unsmilingly declared that it was cool. So the three of them had ended up on the couch, which Hélène had covered with a blanket to avoid any mishaps with Nutella. Mouche had gotten upset over the choice of show, but Clara had refused to compromise. And so, for the hundredth time, they had watched the DVD of *Madagascar*.

"Again?" Hélène had groaned.

"Until death," Clara had replied.

Which had made her mother laugh.

Clara had asked for a smartphone for Christmas. She was increasingly, inevitably being kidnapped by the outside world. When she got home from middle school, Clara was now allowed to hang out with her friends for half an hour, and on weekends her mother let her go on her own to a small park nearby where she would meet up with two or three other girls. Hélène had gone to spy on them once, a handful of prepubescents huddled together on a bench, all laughing, bare-ankled, not a scarf in sight, strangely cuddly and in a bubble of their own. Apart from that, Clara did some ice-skating and was top of her class in school, with an average grade of 18½ out of 20, and she never asked her mother to help her with her homework anymore. She had read all seven *Harry Potter* books at least three times and was now asking to buy her clothes on Vinted. In not much more than two years, she would be in high school. Then the baccalaureate, and it would all be over. Watching her daughters absorbed by the TV screen, Hélène wondered what on earth she was doing. What a terrible mess she was about to make. The days flashed past so fast, the weeks and the years, and in a snap of fingers their whole life together would be gone. Those children who depended on you so totally at the start that it drove you crazy, that their need for you wore you down, all that milk and sweat, and then one day they began to detach themselves, gradually becoming almost like strangers. Clara was twelve now; Mouche, almost eight. And their mother was having a secret affair. The tragedy was right there, within touching distance. Eventually, the whole thing would blow up and their lives would never be the same again. Hélène felt such a pang of anxiety in that moment that she had to take refuge in the kitchen to get her breath back. That was where she was when she received a new message from Christophe.

An emoji showing a pair of lips blowing a heart.

From the couch, Mouche shouted: "Mommy, come quickly!" and, with just a hint of resentment, Hélène put her phone in airplane mode. She rejoined her daughters, and Mouche curled up against her, unthinkingly fiddling with her own feet and bringing a finger to her nostrils now and then to sniff the sweet smell gleaned from the gap between her toes, a habit that disgusted her sister but did not bother Hélène. They passed the whole evening like that, the way they used to, in the cocoon of familiarity, the gentle warmth of hours replayed.

After the bedtime story, Hélène gave in to her younger daughter's latest stratagem to persuade her mother to stay with her a little longer. She got under the covers and Mouche, staring at the ceiling, returned to one of her favorite subjects:

"I don't want you to die, Mommy."

"Me neither."

"Or not for a very, very long time."

"Exactly."

"Like, in two hundred and fifty million billion years."

"Okay, time to turn out the lights..."

Out of nowhere, her daughter asked: "Do you think zombie chickens exist?"

"What makes you ask that?"

The little girl shrugged, and her mother exited the room.

Back in her own bed, Hélène tried to read for a while, but her mind was elsewhere. Five novels on the nightstand, each started and almost certainly doomed to remain unfinished, were sufficient proof that this was not a new problem. So she picked up her phone and forgot everything else while she exchanged messages with Christophe. When she heard Philippe's car in the driveway, she turned out the light and pretended to be asleep. Later in the night, Mouche had a nightmare and she had to get up to calm her down and make her drink some water. Hélène got back into her daughter's bed and did not sleep another wink. She felt that warm, trusting little body pressed against hers. She thought about Christophe. About her daughters. That kind of thing just destroyed her.

"AH, THERE HE is..."

Erwann had just appeared, all smiles, majestic in his pointy shoes, this time wearing a shirt with cuff links under his puffer jacket.

"It's almost one in the morning," said Hélène, checking her phone. "He's not exactly making a big effort, is he?"

In the boss's absence, the employees had let their hair down and the party had taken an alarming turn, with guests smoking in the office in defiance of company rules and bouncing aggressively on the makeshift dance floor, which was now sticky with spilled booze and covered with glitter, since one of their colleagues had facetiously thrown a few handfuls of the stuff during a Britney Spears song. You could see the glitter sparkling from men's hair and women's cleavages, and Lison had even stuck some to her cheekbones.

Erwann's appearance caused a brief stir, but Elexia's employees were too drunk to worry much and soon lapsed back into chaos. The newcomer made his way to the dance floor, where his Merovingian belly hogged the spotlight as he twisted from side to side on his leather soles. Hélène watched him from a distance, wondering what he was up to. At the first opportunity, she collared him:

"So...?"

"So...what?" said Erwann, beaming.

His beard was thicker than usual and gave him a somewhat disturbing hipster-like look.

"Where were you? We've all been waiting for your speech."

"Ah, I'm sick of speeches!" he said, rolling his eyes. "I'm giving up on all that."

Lison hung back, her straw between her lips, ironic by nature. Erwann glanced at her quickly, then returned his attention to Hélène.

"I heard about your exploits at the regional health agency. Bravo, that's great."

"Thank you."

"No, really."

"Thank you, really."

"Well...it's hot in here," he said, and took off his jacket, waving to Parrot, who was standing near the buffet with his entourage.

"Okay, I'll leave you to it. Have fun."

"What a dick!" hissed Lison.

"Take it easy. This isn't high school, you know."

Lison bit the inside of her cheek while continuing to stare at the fat man, who, champagne flute in hand, was ostentatiously dancing the jerk.

"I know why he doesn't want to give a speech," Lison said.

"Why?"

"Parrot's going to become a partner."

"What?"

"In January."

"How do you know that?" asked Hélène, clinging to her glass as her legs turned to jelly beneath her.

"Everyone knows."

It was like gust of cold air flowing between them. Hélène felt the effects of the champagne ebb in an instant, and every part of her that had been soft and available was frozen.

"I didn't know how to tell you," Lison added.

But Hélène wasn't listening anymore. She was staring at those two men, the debonair ginger ogre and his ultra-stylish acolyte, Mr. Perfect with his smooth networking skills and his five-star CV. Her thoughts came in a rush. It had been the same old shit since her student days: the all-boys club, the testicular union, all those men sticking together and finding excuses for their behavior. She finished her drink and immediately grabbed another one. If she'd had a sledgehammer at hand in that moment, she would have smashed their knees to dust.

The next hour was somewhat incoherent. Continuing to drink, Hélène slipped into a happy, vindictive mood. Then she went onto the dance floor to join several colleagues who had taken off their jackets and were swaying like belly dancers, armpits dark and hair dripping with sweat. Finally, she set her sights on little Morel, a cute and remarkably harmless boy with long, curly brown hair, whose girlfriend had recently started work as a freelance naturopath. She flirted with him for a while, until she couldn't stand it anymore and she had to go take a piss.

The women's restrooms were packed, of course, so she went to the men's, locked herself in a stall, sat down without even bothering to wipe off the seat, and pissed like a horse—a long, gushing waterfall of urine—while she stared at her panties between her ankles and gradually regained a little clarity. She sat there for some time, feeling bitter and numb, her head heavy between her hands, incapable of getting up. Afterward, she carefully washed her hands and straightened her chignon. She had to get away from this horrible feeling of futility, of having worked so hard for so little reward. She pursed her lips. And then Erwann came in.

"Oops," he said, instinctively standing on tiptoe.

"Perfect timing," said Hélène waspishly.

Erwann's smile vanished instantly. He looked at her with his hard, hierarchical face.

"When were you planning on telling me?"

"Telling you what?"

"Don't play dumb with me."

After a second's hesitation, her boss retreated into bland neutrality.

"I was waiting for the right moment."

"Don't screw with my head. Everyone knows!"

"What can I say? People talk. I can't control that."

"Explain to me what the hell I'm doing here."

They kept their distance. They both knew that, despite the alcohol and the late hour, this discussion was purely professional. The words they exchanged now could be used against them later, could end up being reported to HR, repeated at a tribunal, even one day in a courtroom.

"I don't understand what you mean," Erwann replied.

"I've been working at Elexia for three years. I'm the most senior executive here, the one who brings in the biggest revenue. I've never fucked up. I'm in the office every day, from morning till evening. So what is the problem, exactly?"

"Jean-Charles can pay the entrance fee, that's all."

"So this is about money?"

"Mostly."

"How much?"

"A hundred thousand."

Hélène had not been expecting such a big amount.

"I could do that."

"That's not what I was led to believe."

There was a flash of pain in Hélène's chest, and she felt her face turn hot.

"What's that supposed to mean?"

"Nothing."

"Did you talk to Philippe about this?"

"No."

But what other explanation was there?

"What did he tell you?"

"Nothing. I didn't talk to him."

She took two quick steps in his direction and had to grab on to the edge of the sink to stop herself falling.

"I want to know."

"I have nothing else to say. Anyway, it's not about the money."

"Then what?"

Rage overwhelmed her suddenly, and tears rose to her eyes. Erwann smiled: her reaction confirmed his feeling.

"We're not going to talk about this in the restroom. You can barely stand straight. I'll see you on Monday."

"Wait."

Eyes closed, she took a deep breath. She refused to let herself yell or weep. All her life, she had battled against that, the logic of the quavering voice. The dam would not burst. In a calm voice, she went on: "I think you owe me an explanation. Parrot's arrival is irrelevant. I can still become a partner."

Embarrassed, Erwann rubbed a hand through his ginger mane, then across his face. He wished someone would come in and free him from this unpleasant tête-à-tête.

"I hate to say this, but I don't think you're in the right state of mind for this now."

Hélène gave up then. She had heard that phrase so many times after her burnout. *You have to take it easy. I don't think you're in the right state of mind. We're going to take the pressure off you.* That whole vocabulary of care and precaution, which was really just a way of sidelining her. If you heard those words, it meant you were no longer the war machine they expected you to be. Which meant you had a choice of the infirmary or a subordinate position. You were now counted among the fragile.

"Everybody wants the best for you," Erwann went on pitilessly. "It's nothing personal. But it's obvious your focus is elsewhere."

Erwann did not want to explain what he meant by that, and she ended up alone in the men's restroom.

LATER, SHE WENT up onto the building's roof with Lison to smoke one last cigarette. The night was drawing to an end, and the silent town below them seemed remarkably peaceful and untidy. It looked as if someone had been playing Lego and had gone to bed, leaving behind a plastic postwar landscape, a city hastily reassembled, where ugliness mixed with legacy, where the concern for beauty was scattered and everywhere dominated by the empire of immediate usefulness.

"What are you going to do?" the intern asked.

Lison had slipped into calling her *tu* again. It was so late now. "I don't know."

"Will you talk to your partner about it?"

"I have to. I need to know what he told that fat fuck. I hate the idea that they were talking about me behind my back."

"Do you think he knows?"

"Knows what?" asked Hélène.

"About Christophe."

"Maybe. Although I'm really careful. I delete all his messages."

"All it takes is something in your search history. Or to forget to close Messenger one time."

"Yeah..."

"No one can hide these days. We leave too many traces behind."

As she uttered these words, Lison made a strange little face, at once frowning and smiling, as if she were explaining to a child that the tooth fairy didn't exist.

"What do you plan to do with that guy?"

"I don't know. My head's all over the place at the moment."

Lison waited a few seconds before asking the question she really wanted to ask, the one that had been eating away at her.

"What about the other two, Erwann and Parrot?"

"What about them?"

"Are you just going to let them get away with it?"

"What else can I do? There's no law against being an asshole."

Lison said nothing, but she had an idea. She flicked her cigarette off the top of the building and the two women watched as the little dot—red, yellow, flickering—was swallowed up by the night.

WHEN SHE GOT home, Hélène woke Philippe, who grumbled about this for a while but did eventually listen to what she had to say. Sitting on the edge of the bed, she asked him three

362

questions. Yes, he knew she was fucking someone else. Yes, he had spoken about it with Erwann—he was his friend, after all. And yes, he knew that Parrot was going to become a partner. Anyway, since her crack-up, he knew that things hadn't been the same for Hélène.

They spoke for almost two hours, quietly so as not to wake the girls, and—for the first time in ages—tried to be sincere, without really succeeding, each sparing the other the gory details, coming to terms with the facts, less to salvage something than to ensure they would have an acceptable role to play in this comedy.

"Do you want to break up?" Philippe asked.

"I didn't say that."

"So what do you want?"

"I want you to stop taking me for granted."

Philippe had to admit that he spent too much time at work, and that he did it because he was bored by their family life. Yes, he struggled with chores and housework. All day long he was in charge of twenty people, managing hundreds of thousands of euros, so when he had to go home and tell Mouche a hundred times to put her shoes away, he felt like he'd been demoted.

"Whereas for me, that's my level anyway, right?" Hélène said, deadpan.

"I didn't say that."

On the other hand, when she asked him if he was cheating on her, he grew as slippery as an eel. He twisted and wriggled so much that in the end she decided to just drop the subject. It wasn't even that she found him irritating. His behavior made her uncomfortable.

For her part, she admitted that she'd been looking for an escape from the drudgery. She also acknowledged that she'd lied to him and came up with some rather pitiful excuses: the passing of time, his neglect of her, the way he looked at her, the feeling that she was just part of the furniture.

"I always supported you," Philippe said. "I listen to you. The sex is still good. We talk about everything. We agree about everything. So what's your problem?" As far as he was concerned, their conversation was becoming ever less comprehensible.

Hélène hesitated. Was it really such a good idea to drag all the skeletons out of the closets in the middle of the night? She weighed the pros and cons. Under her butt, the comforting give of the Simmons mattress pleaded for the status quo.

After that, the conversation turned into a negotiation. Each of them offered efforts in return for concessions, changes in return for promises. Hélène felt hollow, her heart dried out. This man meant nothing to her anymore. She no longer had any desire to touch him or talk to him. All the same, they had sex. A form of reassurance. And then, totally exhausted, they slept side by side. In the morning, Hélène found a Post-it in the kitchen with a little heart scrawled on it, and she hated herself.

LISON, MEANWHILE, WENT back to her apartment, where she found her roommate, Faïza, waiting for her. For some time now, Faïza had been working nights and sleeping during the day. This rhythm had taken over her life after five years spent writing a thesis with the title "Management and Compliance: In Defense of a Legal Approach to the Rules Governing the Distribution of Power Within a Company." She only had two months' work remaining on it, or so she claimed, and she did not want to risk becoming disoriented so close to her goal by resetting her working hours in line with everyone else. Plus, when Lison got home late, the two girls would drink tea together and spend a long time chatting, as if it were five in the afternoon. They talked about their days, the people they met, the books they read or wanted to read. They almost never talked about boys. Lison vaped nonstop. The words came out in a flood. There was talk of Marx, Edith Wharton, Mona Chollet, Emmanuel Guibert, of Asian cuisine and *Ballast*, a magazine to which Faïza had sold two articles, on Jhumpa Lahiri and Beyoncé. If Hélène had seen Lison at such moments, she would not have recognized her intern.

This time, however, despite their closeness, Lison preferred not to tell Faïza anything about the orgiastic office Christmas party, nor about her boss's disappointments. Just after six in the morning, she announced that she was going to bed. After taking a shower, she slipped between the sheets.

There, phone in hand, she sent a WhatsApp message to Erwann, just a brief hello. She sent the same message to Parrot, who would not respond for several hours, but Erwann replied almost right away:

Hi…

You're not asleep.

Nope. You?

I don't really feel like it.

And, after a few seconds of hesitation, Erwann dared to write: *Ah … so what do you feel like doing?*

After that, Erwann began shamelessly chatting her up. Lison teased him playfully for quite a while, dodging his advances and stinging like a bee. This little farce started over again the next day and carried on through the days that followed. The same thing happened with Parrot, although he was a little more reserved, and less candid when it came to using social media. Lison asked both men not to tell anyone. She sent them photographs of herself in her bathroom, paid them compliments, shared secrets and fantasies, and gradually induced them to rise like big cakes full of yeast. By the end of the week, the two executives were in a state of constant arousal.

18

CHRISTOPHE HAD KNOWN from the beginning that this would be a complicated season, and in January the coach summoned him to his tiny office to update him.

"The club president is pressuring me to start you. He thinks it'll be good publicity. His argument is that, given our results so far, it makes no sense to keep you on the bench. So... I'm going to give you a chance. But I need you to start taking this seriously."

Christophe did not play dumb. He knew exactly what Madani was alluding to. Since the beginning of the season, he had missed several practice sessions and had not lost a single pound. He was still paying regular visits to Marco's place for drinking binges, even more so since his son had moved away and his father had been put in a nursing home.

The old man had fought against it, at first. He'd even escaped, and they'd found him in his bathrobe three kilometers from Les Églantiers, on the road to Cornécourt. He'd survived with nothing worse than a heavy cold.

Still, the nursing home was very clean, his bedroom was fine, and he'd even been able to take some of his furniture with him. Christophe had had to fill out a lot of forms and wait a long time on the phone listening to Vivaldi before being accepted by the government welfare programs that would pay toward his father's stay. But he wasn't even sure that they would be enough. He would perhaps have to sell the house and empty his bank accounts, to squander everything on these final few years. It hurt to think of the forty years his father had spent working his ass off, saving all that money, just to trade it in for bed baths, yogurts, and rambling walks through the wooded grounds.

Worse, Les Églantiers had a no-pets policy, which came as a wrench to the old man. Christophe saw him weep when he learned that the cat would have to stay at the house. This man who had once been so tough and uncompromising...it was a cruel discovery to see his strength sapped, his iron will rusted by the ravages of old age. After a certain point, even the ability to control his bladder and bowels, to decide when and where he should fall asleep, to stop his hands trembling, became matters of almost insurmountable difficulty. And Christophe, watching his own hand on the steering wheel as he drove, spotting a new hair growing out of his ear, noticing the changes taking place in his skin—drier, less soft—thought to himself: this is it, I'm on the downward slope. I've barely even lived, and already it's almost over.

The neuropsychologist had warned Christophe: generally, patients like his father went downhill very quickly once they were institutionalized, once they had lost their old markers and habits. They had done all they could to delay this moment, and for a long time Christophe had hoped that some sort of lucky accident would prevent the need to take the fateful step. But after his father had paid that visit to Kylian's parents, he'd been left with no choice. In fact, the police were still planning to charge him with intimidation and threatening behavior, even if it was hard to imagine them arresting the old man in his current state.

To start with, Christophe had gone to visit him almost every day. His father barely reacted. After his escape attempt, he'd been put on tranquilizers, sleeping pills, and all sorts of other drugs that knocked him out. Even so, he fought to stay awake, looking like a baby bird that had fallen from the nest, with the hair around his bald spot growing shaggy and his lips continually murmuring under his mustache. Christophe sat facing him, next to the window. Outside, it was already dark. Agile, energetic women would come into the room now and then to check whether he'd eaten his soup yet. The son combed his father's hair, cut his fingernails, watched him eat, hoping to see a little color appear behind that vast wall of old age. Each time, he left feeling slightly dazed. He'd called his brother so he could let him know what was happening, and ask him to help pay the bills, but that number was no longer in service. He'd searched for him online, all the social networks and so on, but in vain. He would have to deal with this on his own.

Then, in early March, he had found his father in a room belonging to one of the female residents. They were sitting close together, listening to a little radio, the volume turned down low, the two of them looking simultaneously concentrated and miles away.

"Hi, Dad."

His father smiled. He looked better, less passive anyway. He said good night to this somewhat thickset old lady, who smiled back at him, and then his son led him back to his own room.

"Who's that?"

"Who?"

"That woman you were with."

"Oh, no one. She came to find me. I didn't ask her for anything."

It was impossible to get any more out of him.

The next day, he found his father in the same spot, next to this unknown woman with her hands crossed over her belly. This time, the radio was playing a little more loudly, a news debate show about the corruption scandal involving François Fillon and his wife. Christophe asked one of the nurses about the woman.

"That's Madame Didier. She likes to have company."

"And what do they do?"

"Oh, nothing special. They just pass the time."

After that, Christophe would find his father in this woman's company almost every day, so he decided he ought to get to know her. She had worked for the tax office in Paris, then in Le Gard, and finally in Épinal, reaching a senior position, of which she was clearly still proud. Despite her monolithic legs, she was a stylish woman who refused to wear slippers and insisted on having her hair styled every week. Her family smiled from a series of silver-colored frames on her nightstand: fortysomething couples, teenagers, younger kids. On the other hand, there was no trace of a husband.

"But what do you talk about all day?"

"Oh, nothing special," said Gérard. "How's Gabriel?"

"He's living with his mother—you know that, Dad."

"Of course, of course."

In fact, most of the time, Christophe's father and Madame Didier just listened to the radio. They did not get up to anything naughty. Christophe was able to visit a little less often.

THERE HAD BEEN some big changes in his friends' lives too. Greg and Jennifer had decided to keep the baby, which greatly upset poor old Marco.

"You're insane," he lamented, thinking of the life that awaited his friend.

"Yeah, I know," replied Greg, to annoy him.

The baby was due in July, and Jennifer organized their to-do list accordingly. Greg's job was to find them a two-bedroom apartment big enough to house the entire little family, Bilal included, although the teenager was still unwilling to accept the new situation. Jennifer herself would take care of planning their wedding.

"What? He's getting married too?" howled Marco, staggered by this sudden onset of madness.

Indeed, it was crazy to see just how quickly this man—who had, until that point, been totally irresponsible and spent most of his time living with his mother—was growing up. He was taking driving lessons, working nights to earn more money, and looking for a used car on Leboncoin. For the first time in his life, Greg was planning ahead beyond the next weekend, and—having once appeared to be the biggest slacker among the three of them—he was now the only real adult. Not that this was enough to help him find an apartment, given that he had never saved a single euro and he would have to pay a security deposit corresponding to two months' rent.

"I can help out a bit," Marco offered. "Even if I do think you're making a massive fucking mistake."

Greg turned to Christophe.

"Sorry, it's complicated for me."

This was an understatement, with his dad in a retirement home, his kid living in a different department, and a less-than-stellar salary. Greg and Marco made no comment. And then, following a somewhat clumsy chain of thought, Greg asked:

"What about your girlfriend?"

"What about her?" Christophe said.

"No, I just meant, what's going on with you two?"

"It's fine."

"So she's still leaving him?" Greg asked.

"That's the plan."

"But she's not going to...?"

"Not going to what?"

Christophe could not help getting defensive when faced with questions like this. Probably because his relationship with Hélène had taken a strange turn recently.

At first, it had all been so simple. There were those afternoons at the hotel, the constant texting, the newness, fucking like teenagers, exploring each other's bodies, the gradual aligning of wavelengths, finding the best fit, agreeing on the right tempo, switching positions, and the calmness afterward, the tingling of their lips when they kissed, the two of them lying there, stretched out and shattered on the sheets, words passing from mouth to mouth, legs tangled and backs glazed with sweat.

There were the hiding places and the whispers, waiting for each other, choosing a restaurant in a small village or a roadside diner with a good reputation. Later there were seafood platters, a night in a beautiful hotel in the Black Forest, a first argument, morning sex, eyes closed, not daring to kiss because their breath stank, but their bodies didn't care. Learning to use the same words, thinking about her all the time because the world was full of signs that pointed in her direction, knowing her routines and her schedule, listening to her on the phone late at night after she'd had an argument with her partner or because Clara had given up trying at school and it was maybe her fault. Him murmuring *no, no, you mustn't blame yourself*. Feeling the infinite softness within him.

And then, once Hélène's relationship with her partner had started to disintegrate, Christophe no longer felt so sure. Was he going to have to get involved? Were they going to become a couple, live together, share a bedroom, a bathroom, their cars, vacations? The idea was enough to scare him shitless.

But the real problem lay elsewhere.

When he was a teenager, love had been simple. A girl walked past, you thought she was to die for. After that, every time you saw her, you got the same symptoms: you felt sick, your hands were clammy, you couldn't string three words together, and soon that was all you could think about, total obsession. You would hatch crazy plans to talk to her. At night, under the covers, you would listen to music on your headphones and daydream about her. Finally you would ask her out and, if she didn't shoot you down in flames, the two of you would move on to the next stage, finding things in common. Suddenly the world was full of coincidences, shared passions, identical pet peeves. You were amazed that you could have existed without each other when you were obviously such soulmates. You held hands, you looked for each other at the park, and with a bit of luck you ended up sleeping together. And then, in an instant, your bubble burst and all the desire drained out. Love was tragic and temporary. Lust was infinite but bland. After that, you belonged to a world made in your image.

Christophe had experienced all this for a long time— sudden infatuations, lingering obsessions—while Charlie had played an intermittent but clear role in his life, as his soulmate, at least until their separation.

But now he felt less certain. Something had changed. Maybe it was his age, maybe scars that had never properly healed. Whatever the cause, he wasn't as emotional as he used to be. His urges were no longer so lucid. He moved slowly now, his desire like a plowshare. Everything about him had grown bigger—his shoulders, his waist, his need for women. The sharp radiance of the old days had been replaced by something vaguer, murkier, more disturbing. He looked at teenage girls and thought, shit, never again, and that loss stirred up dark feelings within him. He thought about their pert young asses, about the boys who would fuck them, about the beauty of their perfect skin and firm flesh and how he could no longer touch it. Gloomy passions rose through his chest at this thought, a quiver of unease at his throat.

For so long, girls had pursued him. They had chatted him up in bars. They had batted their eyelids at him, shouted his name from the bleachers. He had felt cute, wanted. He'd had his choice of them. He'd even been able to play hard to get.

And then, without warning, that moment was gone. Now their eyes passed over him without even seeing him, and whenever he stared at a woman in a store, or on the street, she would look away, embarrassed, disturbed. So it was that he'd become an old bastard, exiled from the paradise of youth overnight. For young women, he no longer existed. Often he would have to make do with the internet, with the meager relief of his own hand, like a fourteen-year-old. At least there was a lot more choice these days. But at forty, with a kid and an adult life, it was hard not to feel ashamed when you typed "hot redhead" or "mixed-race girls" into a search bar.

These changes left Christophe feeling bitter at times, but he didn't let it get to him too much. That sort of demotion was just one more worry among others; life was full of them. The thing was, he no longer felt capable of saying "I love you." Those words felt alien to him now. Maybe they'd died with his youth. Or maybe Charlie had run off with them. Unless he just felt too disgusting to even try, too sunk in failure, with his body that made cracking and grinding noises when he got up in the morning, an old man, not cute at all anymore. Maybe love was just like all the rest—a moment in life. Or maybe he was just afraid. Whatever, loving wasn't easy anymore.

"Well, she's welcome to come to the wedding," said Greg. "We'd love to meet her."

Marco almost choked: "Are you serious?"

That night, the three old friends were in Marco's living room, with the TV on in the background, although none of them were really watching it.

"Of course," said Greg with a smile. "The crazier you are, the more fun you have."

"She's got a partner, she's got kids. What's wrong with you?"

"But they're separating, right? This could be the moment."

"It's an idea," nodded Christophe, mainly to piss off Marco.

Apparently he succeeded because Marco ran a hand through his thick, curly hair before shuffling into the kitchen, calling back: "You two are unbelievable..."

He came back in with three beers and a new bag of chips.

Christophe looked at his watch. "I should take it easy. I'm playing tomorrow."

"Just drink water, then."

Marco handed out the beers, though, then collapsed into his chair and began flipping through the channels out of habit. That scandal involving Fillon and his wife was still headline news. Hearing the sums of money being mentioned, Greg said: "Wow, fucking hell." Then Marco changed the channel.

MEANWHILE, AT ELEXIA, business was still booming. In January, several employees received five-figure bonuses. Not only that, but Erwann had been contacted by the new party created for the presidential candidate who had appeared out of nowhere, whose demise had been predicted many times but who now seemed to be gaining real momentum.

Emmanuel Macron's rise had, moreover, led to a wave of people all over the country discovering a sudden vocation for politics and many last-minute changes of heart. Everywhere

you looked, the ambitious and the impatient, disoriented socialists and centrists sick of the taste of defeat, human resources managers and minor local figures were ready to jump
on this bandwagon, all of them good, sneaker-wearing people
with modern attitudes, celebrities or regular Joes who had
sensed a disaster looming for the traditional parties and who
unanimously rallied around this refreshing new figure, a
former banker, academically brilliant (and how the French
love academic brilliance), impeccable in his tailored suits, untouched by the failures and ignominies of the past, who was
being compared to Mozart and who contained within him, to
a degree of concentration never seen before, the essence of the
age: an obsession with efficiency.

In his speeches, he threw both the Left and the Right onto
the scrap heap, dinosaurs blocking the onset of the future with
their culture of opposition, their sterile ideologies, the whole
farce that had, since the Revolution, been sapping the country's energy, creating only divisions and stasis. Now was the
time to be pragmatic, to face up to reality, to tackle the chal-
lenges to come, to liberate and innovate, and—of course—to
open ourselves to the world. Though undoubtedly revolution-
ary in many ways, this new movement still seemed wedded to
the old political obsession with infinitive verbs.

Anyway, these slogans won over vast swathes of the public
who were already perfectly at ease with this vocabulary, since
they spent all day at work hearing and spouting it themselves.
At packed political assemblies, the objectives defined were essentially the same as those at strategic meetings, couched in
the same management lexicon, with the same message of team
building and economizing, the nation's president as CEO of
a company, a vision of France created by a sales team, the
corporate spirit finally spreading through the Republic's corridors of power.

Naturally, at Elexia, this world view was highly seductive. At last, they thought, this festering, gangrenous old country of striking workers and vested interests stood a chance of being modernized. Parrot, who constantly boasted about all his friends in high places, was now bragging about all the people he knew in the entourage of the man who appeared, increasingly, the favorite to win the election, particularly given the scandals engulfing Fillon and the traditional right-wing parties. And from everything Parrot had been told, this presidential candidate was very open to advice. They could pass on ideas to him, organize initiatives to help him win. The entire company was abuzz with enthusiasm about the future, each employee wondering how they personally could take advantage of the situation. As for Erwann, he had been approached to run for office in the upcoming legislative elections. In every district, the new party was looking for people like him, self-starters with broad shoulders, extensive networks, strong convictions, and suitable skill sets.

"If he makes it to the runoff, it'll be a huge boost for us," prophesied Parrot, eyes blazing as he stood in front of the Senseo coffee machine in the common room.

"Absolutely. It'll be a massive wave."

"And if he wins..."

Erwann grinned. He had a sixth sense for these things, and he could feel it coming. The growth curves spoke for themselves. A window was about to open for this country, and a whole generation would take the opportunity to rise to positions of power. The primaries had already demonstrated the plausibility of this theory, leading to radical choices, stark divisions that had moderates rushing into the arms of this new candidate. Erwann remained convinced that elections were won by the center. Once the extremists on both sides had stopped shouting, the silent majority would prevail. Except that, for once, this middle way did not pass through the soft underbelly of the provinces, with their banquets and socialism. Nor was there any question now of grand patriotic gestures or any of that Gaullist bullshit. The smart money was on a new kind of governance, like a supreme executive committee of young people, professionals, disciplined teams, with a chic, fun style reminiscent of Silicon Valley. It was an enticing prospect.

But this rosy vision of the future did not take Lison into account.

Ever since the Christmas party, the young intern had continued boldly texting the two horndogs in chief. Each of them believed he alone had the privilege of these seductive messages, and they had been lured into the realms of extreme imprudence. Erotic discussions gave way to widespread badmouthing. Erwann explained why he thought X was a complete dick, while Parrot opined on Y's assholery. They insulted each other, of course, and it hardly needs to be said that they would both periodically send Lison photographs of their anatomy, to which she would reply with appropriate *yum-yum* messages and lip-licking emojis. She and Faïza laughed themselves silly over all of this, sometimes driving home their advantage by taking scary risks, yet somehow landing on their feet every time. The two men, blinded by their libido and incapable of imagining that a mere intern could be smarter than they were, threw themselves into it wholeheartedly.

This went on until March.

Then Lison took a number of screenshots, keeping the photos for herself as a sort of guarantee, and organized leaks using a mailing list that included not only Elexia's employees but the two men's wives, a few clients, and various important local figures, as well as a handful of regional journalists. She took care to delete her own name from all the screenshots, but of course Erwann and Parrot were not so lucky. Soon the two men were the laughingstock of the city, and Erwann's marriage, already struggling, bit the dust. As for his political ambitions, they were well and truly over. He and Parrot hired lawyers and talked about pressing charges, but in the end they decided they'd had all the bad publicity they could take and quietly dropped the matter. As for Lison, she kept working at Elexia as if nothing had happened. Every time she saw them, Erwann and Parrot would glare at her and turn pale, but they wouldn't say a word. They knew that the intern had plenty of other embarrassing evidence against them.

Finally, Lison was summoned to a meeting, and since she had the right to be accompanied by another member of staff, she asked Hélène to go with her. The meeting took place in a conference room on the mezzanine at nine in the evening. That way, there would be no witnesses. Hélène hesitated for a long time before agreeing to accompany her intern, fearing that it would look like she had been Lison's accomplice, and as they climbed the stairs she was probably the more anxious of the two. Lison was wearing a miniskirt, low Docs, sequined socks, her leather jacket, and a silk blouse.

"Good evening, good evening," she said as she entered.

Parrot was accompanied by Maître Bontemps, a fifty-something female lawyer with a passing resemblance to Françoise Giroud: hollow cheeks and high cheekbones, with a spark of mischief in her eyes that clashed slightly with her straight white row of teeth. As for Erwann, he had come on his own, and he had a very specific idea of how the meeting should go.

"I wanted us to meet so we could get things straight." Turning to Lison, he said: "First of all, I just want to say that what you did is one of the dirtiest tricks I have ever seen. Trust me, everyone will know what to expect from you."

Unfazed, Lison placed her phone on the table to record the discussion and said soberly: "I think we should all address each other as *vous*."

Erwann glanced at Parrot, then at the lawyer, who was no longer smiling. He started to breathe heavily and wiped his forehead with a handkerchief. His shirt looked creased and his beard a little scruffier than usual. He gave off the vibes of a man prepared to leap over the table and assault someone.

"I think it would be better if we all remained calm," said Hélène, trying not to show the amusement she felt at this circus.

The meeting proceeded smoothly. There wasn't really anything to debate, in any case. The lawyer reminded everyone of the relevant laws regarding privacy and the secrecy of personal correspondence. Erwann explained that he never wanted to see Lison on the premises again and that he thought she had some nerve continuing to turn up to work as if nothing had happened. As for his partnership with Parrot, there was obviously no reason why it should continue. Then he turned to Hélène, and his words were like nails being hammered into a wall:

"I don't know how involved you were in all this. But you should know that you will never be made a partner in this firm. Or anywhere else, for that matter."

Hélène could have told him that she was not involved at all. She had played no part in their text exchanges, and she had not forced them to make themselves look ridiculous by trying to impress a twenty-year-old girl. But she preferred to remain silent, because she didn't see why she should apologize or justify herself, nor why she should distance herself from an intern who, in her opinion, had done nothing worse than give these men what was coming to them.

After fifteen minutes, Erwann stood up and told everyone to leave. There were no handshakes, and the two men fled the building as if it were on fire. Hélène and Lison went outside to smoke cigarettes together for the last time.

"You know they came to see me too, to ask me to run," said Hélène.

"For the legislative elections?"

"Yep."

"You should have agreed," said Lison, blowing long jets of white smoke through her nostrils.

"I know nothing about politics."

"So?"

The intern was convinced that even a goat would win that election once the new savior had conquered the presidency—an idea that was, by then, widespread and causing mass panic among the deputies up for reelection. But Lison presented her case so adroitly that Hélène could find no objection. The young intern knew people—her stepfather, some cousins, some friends of her mother—who all inhabited that well-informed world of politics, publicity, the press, and she explained the ins and outs of the whole business with an assurance that was simultaneously evasive and irrefutable. Hélène nodded, and in the end she had to admit the truth: that she just didn't feel any desire to get involved in such machinations.

"I don't think I'm really that ambitious, to be honest."

The two women didn't talk for much longer. The babysitter who was looking after Mouche and Clara had to leave at ten, and Lison was meeting some friends at a bar in town.

"What will you do now?" Hélène asked her.

"Not really sure. I might do an internship at a design company."

"In Nancy?"

"No, Paris."

"So you're going home?"

"Well, I'm leaving this place anyway. What about you?"

"No idea."

Hélène knew that Christophe was not her type. And yet... after years spent searching for something so far from where she started, after years spent competing and hauling herself upward, there was something restful about going out with a guy like him. If someone had asked her to explain what she was up to, she would not have known what to say. Obviously it wasn't love. But it wasn't just sex anymore either.

When she got out of bed in the morning and thought about Christophe, her days seemed less oppressive. She was cheerful in a way she thought she had lost for good. She would chat and joke at the breakfast table, to the amazement of her daughters. On the drive to school she listened to music now, instead of the news. Songs by France Gall and Benjamin Biolay played loudly in the car, and sometimes her heart felt so full that she worried it would burst.

"Why are you crying?" Mouche asked from the back seat.

"I'm not crying."

But her eyes were wet, and they were no longer tears of joy.

"Is Dad coming home soon?" asked Clara.

"Tomorrow."

"Good."

Hélène and Philippe had decided to give each other some space until they could come up with a more definitive modus vivendi. In truth, their daily lives had not really been altered by this resolution. Hélène realized that they had been living parallel lives for a long time. Philippe had told her that he didn't care about the other man in her life. And that was probably true. He himself was no doubt screwing around too. They could come to an arrangement.

On the other hand, the next stage would likely be less ami-cable. The house, the mortgage, the cars, the bank accounts, the girls. Sooner or later, they would have to sever those fifteen years of connections, and she knew that Philippe would do all he could to ensure he got the best deal. The gloves would be off. Deep down, he considered himself better and more important than her, and the worst thing was that she had always pretty much agreed with him. He had been born in a bigger city, had gone to better schools. He was an accomplished skier and had spent a year living in the States. His business school was more prestigious than hers, and he was a man. In short, he outclassed her in every sense. None of this was never said aloud, of course. If he'd ever told her: "Shut up, I'm the boss," Hélène would have laughed in his face, then crushed him underfoot. She had, after all, been given the formidable example of her own mother, who had always been so highly strung, so paranoid, the bringer of a storm going back twenty generations, an entire genealogy of good but hypersensitive people who could overturn a table or throw themselves into a canal over a single misplaced word. Then there was her father, the ultimate human time bomb, storing up all his hate and anger until the day when it finally exploded.

It was, no doubt, to these two forebears that she owed the reservoir of brutality on which she could draw whenever faced with an irritation or an obstacle, that sudden rush of rage that had served her so well on her path from Cornécourt to Paris. When people had told her, *This isn't for the likes of you, you'll never succeed*, she had bridled, had redoubled her efforts, hardworking not so much by nature as out of sheer bloody-mindedness. Her parents, each so disciplined in their own way, had filled her veins with this rocket fuel.

But that had not been enough to create a balance between her and Philippe. He already belonged in the world to which she aspired, so he was instantly in a more favorable position.

Plus, obviously, he was a man. She remembered the way they'd looked, those boys coming out of the oral exams when she was a student, the arrogant swagger, the total self-belief, because ever since childhood they'd been venerated, convinced that the world was on their side. This disequilibrium existed in their relationship too. And while Hélène had always acted like an equal, if she was honest she had always felt like the minority shareholder. This had become more evident since she started dating Christophe, because, with him, the balance was inverted: she was the one on top.

Anyway, the net result was that Philippe made the rules. For example, he had told her right at the start of proceedings:

"What you do in bed is your business. But don't try to get custody of the girls. I won't let you get away with any bullshit. Same thing for the house."

"What the hell are you going on about?"

"I'm just warning you, that's all."

Once again, she had blown up. She looked at him and thought how ugly he was, with his macho certainties, in the subdued light of their designer kitchen.

And yet it wasn't exactly all-out war. The two of them still shared a sense of pride, the notion that they were above the fray. So there was no question of their yelling at each other in front of the children. Hélène and Philippe were merely cold, evasive, unnaturally polite at mealtimes: they were, in other words, managers. For example, they'd agreed on this arrangement—temporary, inevitably, but advantageous in many ways—of alternating shifts at home. This solution had the benefit of reassuring the girls, who could keep their familiar surroundings, and of delaying the thorny issue of the division of property. During the week, they cohabited—even if Philippe often slept in the spare bedroom—and on weekends one of them would stay with the girls while the other was free to do as they wished.

It wasn't that bad, really, even if, one Sunday evening, Hélène had found Mouche kneeling on a stool in front of the bathroom mirror, cutting her own hair with a pair of blunt-tip scissors.

"What on earth are you doing?"

She rushed into the room to disarm her daughter, so fast that poor Mouche burst into tears.

"Let me see!"

She made her daughter stand up so she could get a better view of the damage, her lovely thick hair chewed up by the metal blades, her bangs askew, total carnage. And that little face in the middle of it all, streaming with tears.

"How are we going to explain this to your father? Why did you do it?"

It was tempting, of course, to make a connection between this kind of behavior and their separation. But Hélène refused to do it.

"All right, put a hat on or something. You can't let Daddy see you like this."

"Why not?"

"Because. I'll take you to the hairdresser tomorrow."

"I don't want to go to the hairdresser."

"You should have thought of that before."

Naturally, Clara showed up just then and laughed her head off, making fun of her sister for being a "freak."

"I'm not a freak!"

"You're a total freak!"

"No!"

More tears, more yelling.

"Stop!" Hélène barked. "That's enough. No one says another word."

The girls both fell silent, and Hélène offered them a deal.

"We can have a TV dinner tonight, if you stop fighting. I'll defrost some Picard pastries, okay?"

The girls jumped for joy and hugged their mother, telling her she was the best mom ever.

"But you must keep this a secret. You promise?"

"Cross my heart," said one of them.

"And hope to die," said the other.

Mouche spat in her hand to seal the promise, but this time Hélène was too tired to yell at her. She decided just to walk away instead.

HÉLÈNE AND CHRISTOPHE saw each other more often, and in less secrecy. Sometimes at their usual hotel, sometimes elsewhere. Hélène would take charge of finding a nice place on Airbnb, and she would pay for it too. The sex was still good, which translated into sore spots, long sleeps, cystitis. Each was, for the other, a source of joy, an escape from reality. But one day, toward the end of March, Christophe put his foot in it.

"My friends keep pestering me. They want to meet you."

"Oh."

"Greg says you should come with me to his wedding."

Hélène pulled a face at that. Once before, she had agreed to enter his world, and the memory of it was still depressing.

Christophe had invited her to the big house where he lived. He'd given it a spring clean, but somehow failed to rid the place of its ghostly, old-fashioned aura, which lived on in the furniture, the eighties wallpaper, the smell inside the cupboards. They had stayed in his bedroom most of the time, and the first night had been okay. They'd fucked twice, drunk some wine, and eaten croque monsieurs before falling asleep while watching a TV show on the laptop.

In the cold light of day, however, things had appeared less acceptable. Searching for the upstairs bathroom, Hélène had found herself in a little boy's bedroom that had made her feel sick. Then they'd eaten breakfast in the kitchen, and that house had reminded her of others, with its tablecloth, its dresser, and those tiles under her bare feet. She hated the kitchen tiles.

Early in the afternoon, Christophe had convinced her to go for a walk with him. He'd lent her a pair of rubber boots, several sizes too big for her: she'd had to stuff some socks inside to make them fit. The sky was low that day, and the earth waterlogged, as it often was there. The Sundayish, countryside atmosphere weighed heavily on her spirits and made her want to go somewhere warm and noisy where she could eat soup and listen to other people's conversations. Hélène and Philippe had done quite a lot of traveling before the girls were born. During the holidays, they would often spend a few days in Brussels, drinking very strong beers in brown-walled taverns. Those places were always full of laughter and people gorging themselves on medieval-looking meals. She and Philippe would go into all the antiques stores in the Marolles quarter. With full hearts and wallets, they would buy lamps, seventies furniture, and secondhand clothes, before walking to a cobblestoned square to eat waffles. Sometimes they would get too drunk and have an argument. The next day, they would hold hands and visit a museum together. It was an escape, a way of defeating December. But they didn't go there anymore. When had they stopped?

"What's the matter?" Christophe asked.

"Nothing, I'm fine," Hélène lied.

And while they walked through the desolate landscape of Cornécourt, she thought about that previous life, when she and Philippe, still in their twenties, used to live in the twentieth arrondissement. It was their first apartment, between Télégraphe and Porte des Lilas: four hundred square feet at an eye-watering price in one of those old, prewar brick apartment buildings. They both used to work like crazy back then, before meeting up in the evenings, exhausted but happy. In her eyes, Philippe had been peerless, and when they went out at night to a bar she would see all the women looking at him and it would thrill her so much, it was ridiculous. They had everything—youth, money, good taste, a stack of *Les Inrockuptibles* in the bathroom, an expensive espresso machine. They found their clothes in little boutiques in Le Marais and she wore that perfume for men that he adored, Bensimon. On Sunday mornings they would walk to the market in Jourdain and buy a baguette, some cheese, organic fruit and vegetables, saucisson, a bouquet of flowers. She recalled their tartan shopping bag, Philippe wearing Vans, her in ballerina shoes...It was always springtime, at least in her memory.

Before going home, they would sit at a café terrace and watch the passersby. They both loved that neighborhood because it had retained its working-class roots, as they said to their friends late at night when they were drinking at Le Chéri or Le Zorba, those cafés in Belleville that were always packed full of marginally marginal and generally suitable young people. They would enjoy alcohol-drenched feasts together at Le Président, they would eat brunch, force themselves to visit the latest exhibitions, watch movies about which they were expected to have an opinion, go to concerts at La Cigale, Le Divan du Monde, La Boule Noire, to punk gigs at La Miroiterie. To de-stress from work, there was nothing better than those outings in Paris, the kind of thing you could tell your friends and colleagues about: the latest trendy new restaurant, the best bagels in the city, Japanese denim. It was a pleasure and a burden, trying to keep up with the cutting edge of fashion. Philippe excelled at that kind of thing, unearthing addresses and plans, little back alleys where you could find vintage clothing, a cool new bar, a perfect maafe.

Same thing for travel. Zanzibar was better than Senegal; the Shetland Islands beat the Canaries. Barcelona and London were great, but only for a weekend. They would rent a mini-van to explore vineyards in Bourgogne or the Loire Valley, with their best friends, Samir and Julie, who had also gone to business school, even if Julie was already thinking of changing careers.

Hélène had adored that era, when she felt she was exactly where she wanted to be, at an intersection of networks, in the place that produced money, fashion, ideas, the best parties, where the most beautiful people lived. And she was one of them, kind of. Well, she dressed the same way they did, anyway. She experienced the exquisite pleasure of entering a select spot, wearing skintight Acne jeans, a pair of sunglasses from Chloé perched on her nose. So many past slights and snubs were avenged in that way. All those crappy summers as a student when she'd had to work for a pittance to pay her rent, suburban life, and the endless drama of her high school years: that horrible little Versailles with its idols, its hierarchies, and its pitiful falls from grace...all of this had been redeemed in Paris, with Philippe.

All things considered, though, that period when the stress of work was compensated for in lounge bars and chic boutiques had not lasted long. Clara was born in 2004, the year Philippe joined AXA. The Parisian honeymoon had ended in that brief moment between her partner's new job and the start of her maternity leave. As a consolation prize, Philippe had bought her a Goyard purse. Now Christophe was inviting her to a wedding. So much had changed between those two events that you might have believed a war had taken place. And, now that she thought about it, Hélène had absolutely no idea where she had left that two-thousand-euro purse.

19

EVERY TIME HÉLÈNE went to see a hockey game, she left the girls at her parents' house because it was on the way. At least the death throes of her relationship with Philippe had brought this benefit: Clara and Mouche got to see their grandparents more often. And Hélène's parents, thrilled by this turn of events, almost forgot to criticize her.

This time, as usual, the two girls jumped out of the car as soon as it came to a halt and rushed through the yard. Their grandfather had just installed a playground set there, and Clara and Mouche fought over who would get to sit on the swing first. Mouche lost, which was a shame because she was too small to reach the monkey bars.

"Good trip?" Mireille asked, kissing her daughter on the cheeks.

Hélène shrugged. "It's not far..."

"That's not what you used to say."

Hélène did not rise to the bait. Mireille was shading her eyes with one hand, even though she was wearing dark glasses. She found exposure to sunlight increasingly painful.

Hélène kissed her father, who was wearing his usual old loafers—perfect for the yard as well as for trips to town—and his favorite old blue T-shirt. She instantly recognized the scent of his cheek, the smoothed leather of the skin, the aftershave he wore. Then she took a moment to look at him. He hadn't changed: he still had the same slim body he'd had in the army. Old age did not seem to have attacked his inner core, as it did with so many people. Jeannot was simply crumbling around the edges, growing ever thinner, his hair turning to a sort of down, his skin growing diaphanous at the temples and under his eyes, poignantly revealing the meandering river of a mauve or blue vein, and his body—not a single inch shorter or a single pound heavier—taking on a volatile, almost cloud-like appearance.

"Well," said her mother.

Her father announced that he would go look after the girls, and Hélène watched him walk serenely away.

"How are you for time?" her mother asked.

"I'm not in a rush," said Hélène, emerging from her reverie.

They went into the house. The curtains were partially drawn to spare Mireille's eyes. Hélène sat in her usual spot at the kitchen table and touched the plastic tablecloth with its design of cherries.

"I was about to make some tea," her mother said.

"Perfect."

Through the French door, she could see the girls playing outside. Mouche had finally been allowed on the swing, and Clara was hanging upside down on the monkey bars. Their grandfather stood, hands in pockets, watching them have fun. Since he had quit smoking, it was as if a part of his physiognomy was missing. Wherever he was, he always looked now as if he was waiting for something that was never going to happen again.

The water began to gurgle inside the kettle and Mireille put two cups on the table, then poured the boiling water into them before adding the Lipton tea bags. While the tea was brewing, she told Hélène about a conversation she'd had with the new neighbors, a young couple who had just moved in. The woman worked at the hospital and the man sold cars at one of those lots that lined the road between Cornécourt and Chavelot.

"It's strange how all the car lots are in the same place."

Anyway, the couple wanted to have children, but they were "struggling." Three attempts at IVF had already ended in failure, but they weren't giving up.

"They should just enjoy being young," her mother observed. "They've got plenty of time to have kids later."

This was an old refrain. Before starting a family, Mireille had insisted on "having a life." No doubt her own mother's example had influenced Mireille's determination to remain free. The poor woman had given birth to five children before her husband was killed in a cycling accident at a railroad crossing. Throughout her childhood, Mireille had watched her mother wear herself out washing dishes, doing laundry, ironing clothes, a stew constantly simmering on the stove, looking ever more ravaged and pilfering whatever cash she could to stay afloat.

"Not for me," Mireille would say whenever she thought about this or saw such sacrifices in a movie or a TV documentary.

She'd had Hélène quite late in life, and that was the end of her childbearing. In the family mythology, it was often said that Mireille was not one of those "perfect women" who gave everything to their family, and nothing annoyed her more than having to listen to someone drone on about self-sacrifice when she happened to meet some old acquaintance at the supermarket or the newsstand where she went to buy her lottery tickets.

"I saw that Christiane Lamboley. There's one who never talks about anything but her kids and all her aches and pains."

Jean might well have wanted another child, but it was never a possibility. Instead, he'd had his vegetable garden, which had grown considerably smaller over recent years, and then—after their daughter had left home—the two of them had discovered the pleasures of package tours. When it came down to it, a postcard was just as good as a family photograph.

Hélène drank her tea and listened as her mother told her the latest news. There were stories of cousins she never saw, neighbors she had never met, and—with sour little asides—an assessment of Hélène's own situation and how it affected the lives of her parents. After this little tirade, though, her mother still asked her how she was doing.

"Yeah, I'm okay..."

Mireille observed her daughter from behind the photochromic glasses that had become transparent again now that they were in the dim interior.

"The kids see everything, you know," she said in a serious voice.

"Have they said anything?"

"A few things," her mother replied. "Clara's worried she'll have to leave her room."

"Yeah, I know. I'm explaining stuff to her gradually."

"The important thing is to keep hold of your job."

"I've never had any problems with that, have I?"

"Do you have some savings at least?"

"Yeah, yeah, don't worry."

Her mother gave a satisfied nod.

"I always worked. That's what matters."

Hélène agreed. Her cup was empty, but she was not yet thinking about leaving. It was the strangest part of all this, how comfortable she felt at her parents' house these days.

Of course, if she stayed here much longer, the situation would soon deteriorate. Her mother would want to start bossing her around, asking her why she did this and not that, she'd have to start taking her shoes off inside the house and all her parents' old habits would once again feel like an unbearable straitjacket. All the same, she had to admit that Cornécourt and its surrounding area no longer filled her with disgust the way they used to. Several times, visiting Christophe here, she had felt curiously relaxed walking around the streets of her adolescence. Now that she was no longer imprisoned in these walls, behind these façades, now that she felt sure she had escaped the fate of becoming one of those women who settle for a little dog and dyed hair, she no longer lived in dread of this town. On the contrary, there was a kind of sweetness in seeing again the same light, at dusk in a back alley, that she had seen at fifteen, at passing the same storefronts on the high street. Every bridge brought back a memory, and the basilica with its remnants of a maze reminded her vividly of sneaking out there with Charlotte on freezing nights to smoke cigarettes in the ruins. Above all, the smell of earth from the gardens and on the banks of the Moselle, in the evenings, after rain, was exactly the same. In fact, she felt so comforted by this homecoming that it was starting to worry her.

"They're not like you at all," her mother said, watching the girls play outside. "Neither of them."

Mouche had given up on the swing and was now digging a hole in a corner bordered by big stones that her grandfather had created for her. As for Clara, she was following the old man, who, incapable of doing nothing for more than a few minutes, was now busy watering the flower beds.

"What was I like, at their age?"

"Don't you remember?"

Hélène tried to excavate a memory, but nothing came.

"I don't remember anything at all until I was eight or ten."

"Well, that's nice," said her mother sarcastically.

"So what was I like?"

Her mother stared at her, trying to work out if her daughter was making fun of her, then said: "You laughed all the time."

THE WOLVES WERE a strange team that season, with no fewer than four players aged over forty and three under eighteen. They'd had to deal with this motley crew, an ever-lengthening injury list, and their Canadian goalkeeper, Jimmy Poulain, leaving in January because his brother was in a car accident back home. In the end, ironically, the club had to take the number-two goalie from Strasbourg, their biggest rival, on loan for the rest of the season. The only major investment the club had approved was for the transfer of a Slovakian international named Tomas Jagr, who, despite his eagerness and hard work, did not make much of an impact, barely reaching double figures for goals scored.

Even so, the Wolves had done reasonably well, beating the weaker teams and defending stoutly against the better sides such as Dijon and Reims. Overall it had been a tough season so far. They'd enjoyed a few moments of glory, and suffered a minor crisis in January. As things stood, they still had a vague hope of being promoted to D1. Now they were getting ready for a home game against the Colmar Titans, having already won the away leg.

Christophe had not had much game time and had scored only two goals. He'd had some big fights with the coach, Madani, who had finally lost patience over the player's failure to lose weight. "I don't need a calzone on ice," Madani had declared two weeks earlier. Christophe was now a benchwarmer again.

That night, in the locker room, Christophe looked at his teammates as though they were already fading into the realms of memory. The same routine was going on around him, the same familiar sounds—sticky tape being unrolled, the thud of blades on ice, men sniffing and clearing their throats as they stared with concentration, and the voice of Gilles, the gear guy, as he thundered out his usual mantra: "Come on, boys." Christophe felt outside all of this, impatient, frustrated, a spectator.

After a while, unable to bear it any longer, he decided to go and see the coach in the little hut that served as his office. Madani was on the phone while inspecting the tactical diagrams spread out across his desk. The game would not start for another half hour, but already the hubbub from the bleachers was audible.

"I wanted to talk to you," said Christophe.

The coach looked up and asked him to wait a minute while gesturing for him to take a seat. The two men had known each other for more than twenty-five years. They had never been friends. Christophe sat down on the chair in front of the desk. He had a bad stomachache and thought he might throw up.

"Yeah?" said the coach, after hanging up.

"I know I've had a shitty season."

Madani laughed. He was wearing a baseball cap in the club's colors and a fleece jacket, and was aggressively chewing gum. The softness of his caramel eyes seemed to clash with his edgy, almost vindictive attitude.

"I'm not just talking about hockey," Christophe went on. He was struggling to get the words out. Thankfully the coach was not interested in hearing the details. After a sigh, Christophe continued: "I know I'm not going to play anymore."

"What's your point?"

"This is my last season. It's over."

Madani was tempted to tell him that it had been over long before this, that he spent too much time drinking and not enough training. But he just nodded.

His thighs spread, his forearms resting on his knees, his head lowered, Christophe cleared his throat before adding:

"My son's in the crowd tonight."

The coach's face twitched. He didn't like it when people played on his feelings. Christophe sniffed again, then looked up. His lips had practically vanished, leaving just a horizontal slit. It took him a massive effort to get the next few words out.

"He's never seen me play."

"Go on."

"I'm not asking for a lot."

"Hmm," said the coach. "We'll see."

Christophe waited. He would have liked some kind of promise. Since his son had been living in Troyes, he had seen him only during holidays and on the occasional weekend. People had asked him why he didn't move there too. Others had wanted to know why he wasn't fighting it. They said he should get a lawyer and take the case to court. As for Marco and Greg, they just bitched about Charlie even more than they had before. Only Hélène abstained from giving a firm opinion. She knew what it was like to have a life at the mercy of opposing forces, and she knew that in such situations no one was entirely to blame, nor entirely innocent.

At first, Christophe had thought it wouldn't be a big deal. He would see Gabriel less often than before, but they would be able to spend quality time together, as people said these days. He would spoil the boy. Gabriel's time with his father would be like a permanent vacation. But he had not considered the speed at which children changed. Every time he saw his son, he was almost a different person. Away from Christophe, he had grown thinner, less naive, more handsome. He spoke new words, knowing words, and could curse fluently in Arabic after a few months in the mini-Bronx of the school playground. He had also adopted some new tics, like sticking his fingers up his nose or grunting like a piglet. At least Christophe could blame Charlie for all of this, which was compensation of a kind.

Some Sunday evenings, when Christophe dropped him outside his mother's house and watched him cross the street with his backpack, he could almost feel the sands of time slipping through his fingers. In no time at all Gabriel would be ten, twelve, sixteen; he would become an annoying little prick, a rebellious teenager who never listened to advice and cared only about his friends; he would fall in love; he would struggle with school, his grades, the stress of exams; he would pester his dad to buy him an Eastpak backpack, an expensive puffer jacket, a scooter so he could get hit by a car; he would smoke weed, make out with girls, learn to like the taste of cigarettes, beer, and whiskey, get bullied by rugby players, find other people who would listen to him and hold his hand; he'd want to have sleepovers, vacations without his parents; he would want them to give him more and more money while he gave them less and less of his time. Christophe would have to go to the police station to pay his son's fines, would have to read teachers' reports describing a total stranger, a creature capable of groping girls or insulting a truant officer...unless he just sank beneath the surface, became the school whipping boy, faded into the background. Christophe didn't know which possible fate he feared more.

And then one day, with a bit of luck, while they were driving in the car or eating supper in the kitchen late one night, that child would tell his father something about his life. Christophe would then discover that he no longer knew him at all. That this boy had found his way and was now stronger than his own father, with a better understanding of objects and their uses, and the son would gently mock his old man for being out of touch. Christophe would discover that the kid was outflanking him in every way possible, and that would be the best news he could ever hope to hear. But he would not be there to witness most of this. Gabriel would do his growing up out of sight. That time would be lost forever.

THE ÉPINAL PLAYERS came onto the ice amid a deafening roar that mingled shouts, bravos, and the sound of foghorns. Two thousand people were gathered inside that rink, Freddie Mercury was singing "We Will Rock You," and in the whirl of green and white spotlights it looked like the entire town had come together, their hearts beating as one. Soon, under the vaulted roof of this strange cathedral, the announcer's fairground bark would list the players' names. Christophe's would not cause much of a stir, but there would be a brief roar when Théo Claudel's name was spoken. This kid had scored three of the four goals that secured victory a week before, and he had already become a kind of star. Christophe's teammates looped gracefully around the ice a few more times, then stood in line while Colmar's players emerged to the habitual boos.

Standing inside the arena, Christophe felt the hammering of his heart inside his chest once again. It was not the kind of thing you could get used to. The cauldron of noise, the will of a people. That joy, boundless, and yet bound to end. He started looking for his son's face among all those that filled the bleachers, but the din was too loud and there were too many people standing up, blocking his view. Marco, on the other hand, was easy to spot in the middle of the hard-core support-ers, with his bass drum, his enormous stature, and the scary faces he kept pulling. Finally, the music stopped, the lights came back on, and Christophe saw his little boy sitting next to Hélène, along with Greg and Jenn. He immediately noticed that Gabriel was not wearing a hat, and felt irritated. But he had to go back to the bench.

Épinal started the game at full speed, the three lines of players taking turns to move forward in waves. Théo Claudel scored in the second minute, then twice more during the first period, sending a frisson of excitement through the supporters, who felt they were witnessing the birth of a legend. High on confidence, he even tried a slap shot from ten meters out. It was stopped by the goalkeeper, but its power, audacity, and sheer artistry were thrilling. Even the opposition goalie saluted the attempt.

It soon became apparent that this was one of those exceptional nights when the atmosphere reaches fever pitch, when the rink starts to vibrate like a locomotive, the jubilation in the bleachers transforming into speed on the ice, the screams and shouts coming from two thousand mouths translating into a single, unending dull roar. Everyone seemed caught helplessly in the rotation of the game, as if inside the drum of a monstrous machine where destinies and actions, desires and fears all tumbled at dizzying speeds. And inside that drum, Marco banged his own drum, grimacing as he made it boom, like a semaphore amid the infinite movement of flags.

Christophe, meanwhile, sat still on the bench.

To him, minutes had never felt so brief. He watched the game, then the spectators, glaring, sniffing, spitting, his legs twitching, his whole body bathed in sweat despite his inaction. One way or another, something was happening for the last time, and he felt this in every pore of his body. He was like a beached fish, dying. He had to get out on the ice.

Standing behind the barrier, the coach was organizing the game as always, sending mysterious signals to his players and ordering the rotations. From time to time, he would squat down to scrawl tactical ideas on his whiteboard, which he generally kept to himself. This was his way of thinking, of channeling his anxiety. The first period came to an end. Christophe had still not touched the ice. He returned to the locker room without a word.

AT FIRST, HÉLÈNE had had to be persuaded to come and see the games. It all brought back too many memories. But ultimately, the rink proved to be more like a tranquilizer than a time machine. As soon as she was sitting in the bleachers, her head was emptied of thoughts, all her worries dissolved. All she had to do was shout along with everyone else, clap at the same tempo, follow the movements of the puck on the ice, and the outside world just vanished. This time, it was slightly different because the atmosphere was more febrile and Christophe had asked her to look after his son. The kid had followed the game enthusiastically at first, yelling and making lots of comments. But tiredness had overcome him, and now he was resting against her, looking very pale, his eyelids growing heavy behind his glasses. After a while, he turned to Greg and asked: "Uncle, is it almost over?"

"Almost," Greg lied.

At the intermission, Greg went to fetch three cups of Picon and one of Coke, which revived the boy's spirits a little. Then he asked Jenn to switch seats so he could sit next to Hélène. They made a toast.

"So, I've given it some thought..."

"Given what some thought?"

"The wedding."

"Well, I should hope so."

The game had started again, as had the deafening roar in the bleachers, so they had to press close and speak into each other's ear. Greg smelled strongly of cigarettes and deodorant, which Hélène didn't mind.

"No, I mean...I want you to come."

"I don't know if I'll be free that day."

"You don't even know the date yet."

Hélène smiled.

"When is it?" she asked.

"May sixth."

"Really?"

"Yeah, why?"

"That's the day of the second round of the election."

Greg was speechless for a moment, unsure what her point was.

"So?"

"No, nothing."

"Who cares about elections?"

He took a swig of Picon, and Hélène did the same. He was a really nice guy, she thought.

THE GAME WENT on in the same supercharged atmosphere. By the end of the second period, Épinal was leading 9–1, but Christophe still hadn't played. In the locker room, the coach congratulated his players and urged them to take care of themselves. From that point on, what mattered was avoiding injuries. There were other games on the horizon, the season wasn't over, and as far as Colmar was concerned, it didn't really matter how many handfuls of dirt they threw on their coffin.

The players listened in silence. Steam rose from their bodies, like racehorses, and they just sat there sniffling, breathing hard, hawking, and spitting on the floor. Some nibbled cereal bars; others bit into bananas. They drank water straight from the bottle, their Adam's apples rippling quickly up and down their throats. They were tired, but they knew they had to keep going. The whole room was filled with a mixture of exhaustion and electricity. The goalkeeper, who was having a problem getting his pads to stay on, asked for help, and Desmarais knelt down to tape them in place.

Christophe watched all this as if from afar. He wanted to say something, but what?

"Come on, boys..."

The game restarted. The opposing team seemed drained of confidence and barely dared to attack anymore. As the seconds ticked past during this final period, Christophe's throat tightened. He felt increasingly unwell. In the ninth minute, he stood up and walked over to the coach.

"I need to play."

Madani continued watching his players move around the ice, whiteboard in hand.

"Please," Christophe said.

This time, the coach looked up at him and, after a few seconds of thought, gave a firm nod.

"You can replace Kevin," he said.

"Okay. Thanks."

Christophe skated onto the ice as part of the next line. There were only eight minutes left. The lines were usually swapped every forty-five seconds. There were four lines in the squad, three of which played regularly. Christophe probably had only one or two minutes of play before the game ended. Thankfully, Colmar's players seemed incapable of maintaining possession of the puck.

During his first stint on the ice, Christophe had two chances and fired both at the goal, but didn't score. There was a strange feel to this final period: the tempo had slowed, and the exhausted players seemed to be moving around in a daze. In the bleachers, the hard-core fans were still yelling loudly, and Marco was the loudest of all, banging his drum and screaming so hard that the veins in his neck swelled and throbbed.

On his way back to the sidelines, Christophe received a pat on the back from his coach before collapsing onto the bench. Forty-five seconds of play and he was shattered, drenched in sweat from head to foot. While he watched the game, drops of perspiration rolled down his face, falling from his fast-blinking eyelashes. Licking his lips, he recognized the pleasant salty taste.

This was it. He had started playing hockey thirty years before and he had only forty-five seconds left before the end. Inside his chest, his lungs were filling and emptying as fast as they could. He closed his eyes, trying to compose himself, and gripped his stick with both hands. Desmarais turned toward him and saw his lips twitching in a silent whisper. He elbowed the guy next to him and all the other players on the bench turned to watch Christophe, his handsome face streaming with sweat, his brows knitted, his voice inaudibly begging some higher power: *Please, just give me one more chance.*

Back on the ice, Christophe could feel that his legs had gone. Thankfully, the Titans were even more drained. They tried desperately to hold off Épinal's attacks, defending aggressively, almost angrily. Christophe tried to make up for his physical shortcomings with smart positional play. Soon, the puck slid toward him along the boards; he tried to dribble it for a few meters before making the pass, but he didn't have time. A Colmar defender came hurtling toward him out of nowhere and smashed him into the Plexiglas barrier. It was such a brutal, flagrant foul that the crowd let out a collective gasp.

For a moment, Christophe knelt on the ice, unmoving, struggling to catch his breath. Then, hanging on to his stick, he clambered to his feet. There was not much more than twenty seconds left. He skated forward as Kamel Krim was aiming a shot at goal. But Colmar's goalie blocked the puck and one of the defenders sent it speeding up the other end of the ice. Desmarais intercepted it and skimmed it back into the box. Christophe emerged from behind the goal. Using his last reserves of strength, he curved his trajectory to meet the straight line of the puck. And, with a mixture of gracefulness and skill, gave a glancing touch that altered its direction. The net bulged.

A roar rose from the bleachers, punctuated by the blaring of foghorns, while the announcer spoke the words "Number twenty, Christophe Marchal" for the very last time. He went on a lap of honor to thank the supporters, his stick raised above his head. When he reached the stand where his son was sitting, he noticed the weird expression on his face. Greg had woken him just then so he could witness his father's triumph. Gabriel looked as if he was crying.

BY THE TIME Christophe walked out into the parking lot, his heavy bag slung over his shoulder, it was practically deserted. The Titans had cleared out long before, and only a few of the players' friends remained, a handful of fanatics hoping for an autograph or a selfie with their latest idol. Hélène was waiting with the others inside Jenn's Duster. In order not to wake the little boy who was sleeping with his head against her chest, she and the others were all talking in murmurs, although they had drunk so much that they kept bursting into hysterical laughter. Hélène had made them laugh especially hard when she had marveled at the passion-fruit scent of the little orange fir tree hanging from the rearview mirror. Intoxicated by the combined effects of victory and Picon mixed with beer, she had declared with absolute sincerity:

"Mmm, I have to get one—it smells amazing!"

After a while, unable to hold it in any longer, she had gotten out of the Duster to relieve herself between two other cars, an action of which the others had heartily approved. She wasn't as stuck-up as they'd thought, this girl—even Marco had to admit that. After pulling up her jeans, she stayed outside a little longer to smoke a cigarette, and they all watched her without a word, tall and ponytailed, in skintight jeans, smoking like a cowboy.

"Okay, that settles it," said Jennifer. "She's coming to the wedding."

Back in the car, Hélène was not given a choice. They made her promise, and she thought, yes, it was good to be with these people, in this place, to be surrounded by their thick accents and their simple kindness. It was a little like putting on a comfortable old sweatshirt discovered at the bottom of a drawer. She kissed Gabriel's forehead.

"LOOK, THERE HE is," said Marco, spotting Christophe.

Hélène got out of the 4x4 and ran toward him, then threw herself into his arms. He caught her midflight and they kissed, all their worries forgotten, two kids in the easy night. Christophe's hair was wet and gave off the clean, fresh smell of shower gel. Hélène held him at arm's length so she could look at him.

"Hi," she simpered.

"Hi."

He dropped his bag on the ground and held her around the waist. In her eyes, the lights of the rink traced angles of luminosity, and her smile, for once, was free of irony, suggestiveness, any subtext at all. He asked her what she thought of the game.

"It was great," she said, with total sincerity.

In the darkness, he thought she was truly beautiful. She kissed him again. She smelled of alcohol, but what did that matter?

"I want to go home," he said.

"What about your car?"

"You can drop me off here tomorrow."

"Are you sure?"

The Dacia's engine roared behind Hélène and the headlights shone full beam through the night. They moved apart from each other, and Jenn honked the horn a few times. Now they had to explain to their friends that they were going back to the house instead of out to a restaurant as they'd planned.

"What's wrong with you?" said Marco, disappointed.

"The kid's shattered."

"Next time," said Hélène.

The others argued about it a little longer, then left them there, honking the horn several times as they departed. Christophe was carrying his son in his arms, and Gabriel's sleeping face gave the whole scene a sort of sweetness.

"They're really nice," said Hélène, slinging the strap of the sports bag over her shoulder.

They headed toward Christophe's station wagon. She felt at peace with the whole world.

WHEN THEY'D PUT the little boy to bed, Hélène took a shower and Christophe went to the kitchen to make them a bite to eat. He'd turned the heating up and the house seemed to purr around them. When Hélène came downstairs, in panties and a T-shirt, a pair of old slippers on her feet, she found the table set and her boyfriend in an apron. He'd cooked an omelet and toasted some bread.

"Have a seat. Do you want some salad?"

No, just the omelet was perfect. They drank wine and Hélène, feeling merry again, scraped salted butter over the toast and dipped it in the runny egg mix. It was rich, fatty, delicious.

"Cheers," said Christophe.

They clinked glasses and talked about the game, the team, the season, Christophe's friends.

"I think I basically promised them I would go to the wedding."

"Well, good."

"Yeah, I don't know…"

Christophe ate hungrily, using his fork to cut into the viscous egg mixture, stuffing his mouth with big hunks of bread, and doing it all so eagerly that he ended up with egg-stained fingers. He licked the yellow liquid from his fingertips and caught Hélène staring at him.

"What's up?"

"Nothing. Just eat. I like watching you."

She gestured encouragingly with her chin, then poured herself a third glass of wine. But Christophe put his fork down and wiped his mouth with his napkin. They both felt good, relaxed and pleasantly full. They had world enough and time. And the child's presence upstairs contributed in a strange way to this simple, almost routine pleasure. Hélène hoped they weren't going to stay too long at the table. And yet she was the one who spoke next:

"Have you always lived here?"

"In this house, you mean?"

The cat came over then, begging to be petted, and Christophe's hand disappeared under the table to scratch its head.

"No, I mean in Cornécourt," said Hélène. "Have you always lived in this area?"

"Yeah."

"It's not a criticism, you know..."

"I know."

He used the tip of his tongue to prize a piece of bread from between his teeth, and she watched him chew it, his lips pursed.

"I'm not friends with anyone from that part of my life," she said.

"What do you mean?"

She could sense his suspicion but couldn't help articulating what was in her heart.

"I don't know. Didn't you ever want something else?"

"It's no worse here than anywhere else."

"I was so desperate to get away."

"But you came back."

"Not really."

The cat jumped onto Christophe's lap. With his enormous hand, he caressed its spine, and it began to purr loudly.

"So you've never been anywhere else?" Hélène asked.

She saw him tense.

"What for?" replied Christophe, his face suddenly as hard as wood. "It's the same everywhere."

Hélène raised an eyebrow and Christophe stood up, forcing the cat to jump to the floor. It ran out of the room with an indignant yowl while its master began clearing the table. Hélène felt guilty, but she couldn't help herself. She liked him so much that night that she felt compelled to pull him closer to her.

"I didn't mean to upset you," she said.

"I'm not upset."

She stood up too and joined him near the sink. She needed to reduce the distance between them. She wanted to be happy, then and there.

"Come on, leave that. Who cares?"

She kissed him on the mouth and immediately began rubbing her hands over his chest, under his T-shirt, as if she were trying to warm him up. This touch was enough to empty both of their heads. Christophe held her tight. He felt her breath on his skin, her teeth biting his neck. She breathed in his smell, then licked him with the tip of her tongue, just to taste him, pressing herself harder against him, against his huge hockey-player thighs that made him seem almost superhuman, like a slightly gross but beloved centaur. When he held the back of her neck to kiss her deeply, she moaned with pleasure and felt herself melt inside. Her fingers reached for the fly of his jeans, popping the buttons one by one, then she reached her hand inside his pants and felt his erection straining the soft fabric of his underwear. Hélène began to pant. She bit him again, and their foreheads bumped together. He grabbed hold of her ass, feeling the smoothness of her skin, the softness of her flesh, through the fabric of her panties. Hélène was a centimeter or two taller than him, and it felt good to be taken like that, enveloped, her eyes deep in his, her big ass just for him, her fingers around his dick. Her other hand gripped the back of his neck. They kissed each other on the lips a few times, and Hélène began to undulate, breathing hard through her nose. He picked her up and shoved her against the sink and she gave a little cry of surprise when she felt the cold enamel against her butt. Christophe had already pulled her panties halfway down her thighs. She twisted her body to help him and, when she felt them around her ankles, kicked them across the kitchen.

Christophe was very hard now, and she plunged her hand deeper inside his boxers to squeeze him, her fingers brushing the bristly disorder of his pubes. The need burned inside her. They kissed each other a few more times, their mouths fused occasionally, their tongues heavy, their pupils magnified, their breathing out of sync. When he pulled her hair, Hélène moaned louder, a sound that rose from her chest, and she rotated her hand around his dick, leaving a deliciously viscous film on the back of her wrist. When those drops of semen, beading at the tip of his glans, touched her skin, it felt like fire flowing through her veins.

She grabbed Christophe's hand and guided it between her thighs, standing on tiptoe so she could support herself against the sink and open her legs wider. He slid two fingers into the fold, then inside the slit, the shimmering frills where the skin grew so fine and so sensitive. Hélène felt a shiver run up her body to the tips of her hair and sighed with pleasure, as he moved his fingers inside her, lightly, almost subliminally, probing the hot interior before touching her clitoris, rolling it between his index and middle finger, pressing allusively on the hidden, unmysterious little bulge. He kept moving his fingertips until Hélène felt herself grow deep and wet, then she buried her face in the hollow of his neck, her hand continuing to jerk him off, pulling away the fabric of his boxers to get a better grip.

"Come on," she said after a while because she wanted to feel him inside her.

Instead of which, he kept going, stubbornly, subtly, his fingers sliding over her lips and inside her pussy, deep within the burning flesh, then back to the clitoris, which sent its inevitable waves radiating through Hélène's body. He wanted to make her come, but she held herself back: for fun, to make it last, out of pure spite.

"You won't beat me that easily," she panted, her lips curled in a smile.

Instead of speeding up his movements, Christophe continued with the same inexorable delicacy, grazing the crenellations of the mucous membrane, pressing the blood-swelled organs, pulling at her pubic hair. Hélène's fingers, meanwhile, were making a slow, flutelike movement and she could feel how stiff he was, veins bulging, shaft quivering, on the verge of orgasm.

When she spat into her hand, he couldn't help cursing. It had become a game, a contest of wills. He accelerated his movements in the hope of making her surrender first.

"In your dreams," she said, and they both laughed.

She grabbed his arm, tensed against the edge of the sink, so she could arch her back more. It was coming. They were soldered together, interlaced like snakes, their hair tangled, their eyes closed, their gestures narrowed to the smallest of movements, and she felt his cock throbbing against her palm. He couldn't hold it in much longer. Christophe turned his face away to catch his breath. She was right at the edge too, her feet balanced on the end of the diving board. She whispered a few words into Christophe's ears, and there was nothing he could do.

He came, standing there in the kitchen, all over her, and Hélène removed her hand to let him finish what he'd started. Only a few seconds later, she came too. She had won.

20

HÉLÈNE HAD HESITATED until the last moment, but when Philippe told her that he was seeing someone, a woman at his office (how original!), she thought oh and then fuck it, before texting Christophe to give him the good news: *Okay, I'm coming to the wedding.*

Even so, it was heartbreaking, a life built together over fifteen years ending like that. Now and then, Hélène found herself wishing she could rewind time. She and Mouche still played the "magic slate" game, so if her daughter did something really naughty like gluing her plastic animals to the carpet, Hélène was willing to wipe the slate clean as long as Mouche said sorry and truly meant it. But at Hélène's age, sincere apologies were no longer enough. Every act was like a scar, a tattoo, and while your choices could take you far, your cowardice and your inaction were no less fearsome. On the practically vertical slope of adulthood, everything mattered.

In any case, this much-anticipated wedding was bound to mark a turning point. Which was why she had hesitated for so long. Now that Philippe had a girlfriend, Christophe inevitably became more than a fling. And it was dumb, but suddenly she was afraid of losing him.

The first thing she did was to rush out and buy a new dress. The second thing was to worry about her date's suit.

"It's okay, I already have a Hugo Boss suit," Christophe explained. "It's perfect."

"What color is it?"

"Blue."

"When did you buy it?"

"I bought it in Troyes, at a factory outlet. Fifty percent off."

Hmm...

"I said when, not where."

"I dunno, four or five years ago."

"Send me a photo."

"Now?"

"Well, yeah, the wedding's on Saturday. Send it to me."

"Okay, I'll call you back afterward."

Five minutes later, she received a photograph of Christophe wearing his suit. It was exactly as she'd feared. It was too big, the jacket came down too low, the shoulders were square, and the fabric was pinstriped, making it better suited to winter. Worst of all, Christophe had tried it on without bothering to wear dress shoes, and the effect of the outfit with tennis socks was absolutely appalling.

She called him back.

"We need to get you another suit ASAP."

"Huh?"

"Come to Nancy. We can go shopping at Printemps."

"I'm not going to splash a thousand euros on a suit I'll only wear once."

"My treat."

"You're joking, right?"

And when the time came to pay for the fitted blue De Fursac suit, which made him look wonderfully elegant, they had their first serious fight. In the end, Christophe paid, but

413

Hélène made him promise he would let her buy him a pair of shoes. After that, they went all around town in search of an appropriate pair of oxfords. Eventually Christophe started enjoying himself and was soon walking with a spring in his step beside Hélène, for whom money was no object and who was determined to spoil him. There was an undeniable pleasure in wandering around a city with the feeling that everything you saw might belong to you, that all the store windows were like open bars. By the end of the afternoon, he had a completely new look: Paul Smith shoes, Smalto belt, silk tie, and agnès b. shirt. It would have cost him a month's salary to buy all that. Then they went to a tailor to have his new pants taken in. They rewarded themselves for all this effort with a coffee on Place Stan. Looking down at the shopping bags at their feet, Christophe shook his head and sighed.

"It was my pleasure," said Hélène.

"I don't really like the idea of being a kept man, though."

"Don't be misogynistic."

"What?"

"You heard me. Anyway, you can pay for the coffee."

For now, this discussion settled the balance of power between them.

ON THE BIG day, Hélène set off for Cornécourt with the altered suit and they each got dressed in separate rooms before meeting in Christophe's bedroom to check out their reflections in the full-length closet mirror. Standing there side by side, her in heels, him in his new suit and impeccably white shirt, they were forced to admit that they looked like a million dollars.

"Not bad," said Hélène.

"Yeah..."

Outside, it was the first weekend of May, and the air was alive with that fresh scent of greenness that makes hearts swell with hope.

There was a knock at the bedroom door, and Gérard poked his head inside. Christophe had picked him up the day before and he had slept in his old room. He was already dressed in a gray suit, his shirt buttoned all the way to the top.

"Ah . . ." he said, seeing this tall, unknown woman in a flower-pattern dress. "Excuse me. I was looking for my tie."

Christophe hurried over, embarrassed.

"Your teeth, Dad."

The old man's gummy mouth fell shut with a wet snap and his eyes rolled comically up in their sockets.

"Come on," said Christophe.

They left the room, followed by the cat, which had not let Gérard out of its sight since his return. Hélène was left alone in her beautiful dress, with her reflection, and the immensity of spring glimpsed through the half-open window.

IN THE BATHROOM, Christophe helped his father tie his tie then, taking him by the shoulders, checked that he had everything he needed: teeth in mouth, glasses in pocket, cash in wallet. He had shaved, combed his hair, trimmed his nails. His suit hung very loose on his shrunken frame, but overall he looked fine, thought Christophe. Pretty good, in fact. Although Christophe did notice two hairs growing out of his nose and removed them with tweezers.

"What about Gabriel?" his father asked.

He had already asked this question dozens of times since the previous day. Christophe had even found him in the little boy's old room, just standing there in silence.

"I told you, he's at his mother's house."

"Oh, yeah."

A delicate smile appeared on Gérard's face.

"I'm losing my marbles a little bit."

Christophe touched his arm and smiled back. Everything was fine.

"We should get going."

"Already?"

"We're going to the mayor's office, remember?"

"Oh, yeah," said the old man.

But Christophe knew perfectly well that his father was lying: he had no idea what they were supposed to be doing next. He reminded him that Greg was getting married, and that Monsieur Müller was officiating. At the mention of that name, the old man's eyes lit up.

"That guy's such an idiot!"

Christophe also reminded him that they were going to the mayor's office with a friend of his called Hélène.

"Yeah, your girlfriend."

"Right."

Christophe hesitated for a second, then asked:

"What do you think of her?"

His father just shrugged. "Oh, you know me. I've never understood women..."

GREG AND JENN arrived outside the mayor's office just before four, in a convertible Citroën 2CV, honking the horn and executing a wild, screeching curve in the square that scared the hell out of some of their guests before being met with a round of applause. Clinging on in the passenger seat, Jenn was in her seventh month of pregnancy and did not seem entirely appreciative of the groom's acrobatics. As soon as the car had come to a standstill, she gave him a sharp talking-to.

Greg nodded enthusiastically before jumping out of the car, all smiles, arms raised, a bolo tie decorated with a turquoise stone around his neck. After giving victory signs with both hands, he walked around the 2CV to help Jenn out of her seat. The bride was wearing a long white dress that made her swollen belly look like an egg. She was smiling too, but with a detectable tension, and there was a hardness in her gaze that betrayed the anxieties caused by the organization of this event. She made a few impatient gestures in the direction of her son, Bilal, who was staring vacantly among the guests, indifferent and apparently deaf. She had to shout out his name before he snapped out of his trance and trotted over to carry out his role as groomsman, holding his mother's train along with a candy-pink cousin who could not have been more than ten.

Christophe and Hélène stood toward the back with Gérard, who seemed fine, his mustache quivering in the wind, happy as a lark in the cool spring sunshine.

"Hey, losers!"

Marco had just appeared behind them, looking chic in a pale summer suit and a red tie.

"You look strangely handsome," said Hélène.

Marco laughed, then raised his finger toward the sky and pretended to start dancing.

Then, after greeting Christophe's father, he opened his jacket and showed them the metal flask that he'd slipped into the inside pocket.

"Are you worried they'll run out?"

"These ceremonies can drag on, you know."

"It's not a church wedding—it'll be over before you know it."

After that, there was a discussion regarding the thorny question of the best man that had beset them for weeks. There was no problem on Jenn's side: she had picked her best friend, Florence, but Greg had delayed his decision for as long as possible, unable to choose between Marco and Christophe. Two days earlier, he had delivered his verdict: the job was to be given to one of his great uncles, an old farmer called Jacques who lived somewhere in Haute-Saône and was on the wrong side of eighty.

"He's supposed to be driving here on his own."

"Maybe he'll turn up in an ambulance?"

Hélène, intrigued, asked for more details. According to what Greg had told them, this Jacques was a widower who lived alone in an enormous farmhouse. To make things easier, he had moved everything necessary to his daily life into the largest room on the first floor. This room functioned not only as his living room and kitchen but as his bedroom too, since his bed was positioned next to the fireplace, and even his bathroom, since he washed himself at the sink. He had a small vineyard, enough to sustain his personal consumption at least, which amounted to a bottle of astringent purple liquid with every meal. Consequently, his teeth looked oddly porous, as if the acidity of the grape juice had eroded all the enamel. Everyone imagined him to be rich, even if he lived quite frugally. In short, he was one of those countryside legends, a stubborn and indefatigable man, a Gaullist regional councillor, tough on crime and eager for profit, who would, when he died, leave behind photographs of mustachioed ancestors in golden frames, a pile of money in his savings account, and a houseful of rustic furniture that his heirs would give to charity.

Marco was really excited at the prospect of meeting this man, a fact that made Christophe laugh but Hélène found slightly disturbing. But the hand of the church clock was turning and soon Monsieur Müller appeared on the front steps of the mayor's office. At his command, the guests stood in line and began filing up to the wedding hall on the second floor. Monsieur Müller and Gérard Marchal exchanged a few words in passing, with the mayor looking at his old friend attentively, as if seeking out the precise marks of his illness in his expression. After this brief inspection, he told Christophe's father that he was looking well.

"Why wouldn't I?" replied the old man, with total candor.

Monsieur Müller smiled politely, and Gérard was swept up the broad stone staircase by the procession of other guests.

In the wedding hall, everyone took their seats. At first sight, Greg's uncle did not seem particularly exotic. He was just a reasonably attractive old man with a slightly red face, bearing little resemblance to the portrait his nephew had drawn of him. Hélène, though, noticed his hands and pointed them out to Christophe. They were enormous and stone-hard from years of manual labor, so thick that they remained permanently half-open, like the hands of a Playmobil figure. To look at them, you would have guessed they were capable of cracking walnuts or breaking spines, but not typing on a Mac keyboard. They were hands from another age, when men worked the earth, and they seemed incongruous in the civilized world of screens and sensitive skin. They also appeared at odds with the rather shy man to whose arms they were attached. They took up a lot of space.

Monsieur Müller loudly cleared his throat and the murmur of conversations died down. The names of the bride, groom, bridesmaid, and best man were read out. Promises were made to respect, help, and remain faithful to each other. Both parties were obligated to live together as man and wife. Hélène, who was not married, found all this embarrassingly old-fashioned, maybe even inappropriate. What business was it of the mayor of Cornécourt or the French government whether two people were monogamous? Sitting in the second row, she turned around to judge the effect that these words had had on the other guests. In that row of faces, she found nothing to reassure her. These people were society incarnate, unanimous in their placid anonymity, their tacit consent. Looking at all those faces, strangely similar despite their infinite variety, she felt a sort of disgust. Outside, the leaves of a large chestnut tree in the school playground were rustling in the wind. She felt Christophe's hand on her thigh. Jenn and Greg signed the register, then their witnesses did the same. It was over already. A life sentence had been pronounced.

IT TOOK THEM quite a while to drive to Moudonville, the small village thirty kilometers from Cornécourt in whose hall the wedding would be celebrated. Greg had waited too long before trying to book somewhere, and in May—when weddings were all the rage—he had not been able to find anywhere closer. To get there, they had to follow a narrow, winding road that passed through some woodland, several villages, and vast swathes of rural nothingness. The guests drove in procession, their cars bedecked with ribbons, horns honking whenever they passed any kind of habitation. It was like the Tour de France minus the bicycles.

"It'll be carnage on the way back," observed Christophe's father, who was sitting in the passenger seat, to the right of his son.

"Yeah, totally," agreed Marco. "Drunken roadkill everywhere."

"Who's the designated driver?" Hélène asked.

The three men were silent.

"Well, I'm warning you now," she said. "I plan to drink."

"I don't mind driving," said Christophe's father.

Christophe shook his head. "It's okay, I'll go easy on the booze."

Hearing this, Marco took the hip flask from his pocket and offered it to Hélène. She swallowed a mouthful of whiskey and immediately felt her face flush with heat, her hair start to curl. Well, at least she had won brownie points with Marco, who winked at her as he took a swig himself.

THE VILLAGE HALL was an ugly, cube-shaped building located at the top of a small hill surrounded by featureless countryside. Only one road led there. It was hard to imagine how it could possibly function as a business. In a nearby field, tents had been put up in advance by the more farsighted guests. As they approached the building, Gérard pointed out a small white dot moving near the entrance.

"What the hell is that?"

Marco laughed. "It's a goat!"

"Huh?"

"It's for Greg's big brother. Since he's the only one who isn't married, they got him a goat."

It took Hélène a few seconds to get her head around this. "Seriously?"

"Yeah, yeah, it's the legionnaire's gift. You know, there were no women in the desert so they'd..."

Marco made an obscene gesture, and Christophe glanced in the rearview mirror to check his girlfriend's reaction to this. He was feeling pretty tense and preoccupied himself. The idea of having to keep an eye on his father was bad enough, but if he had to watch how much he drank as well...But what bothered him most was sensing the distance that Hélène was keeping with all those around her, without even realizing it. He didn't know what he could do to make her feel more at ease. All day long, he'd been asking her how she was, and

421

in the end she'd snapped at him to cut her some slack. On top of all that, she was determined to go home that night so she could vote in Nancy the next day. It was not going to be simple, that was for sure.

Meanwhile, a group of guests had already gathered around the goat, and the poor animal, tied to a stake, was frantically shaking its head, making the bell around its neck ring, and bleating pathetically. The children were crowding around it, like flies around a carcass, elbowing each other out of the way so they could pat its head or offer it a handful of grass, their parents standing back and immortalizing this bestial harassment on their cell phones. The climax of this ritual came when Didier, the unmarried brother, agreed to pose with the animal in his arms, holding the goat close as if it were his bride.

"Not exactly subtle, is it?" Hélène said.

Christophe shrugged. "What do you want me to say?"

They observed this sad sideshow from a distance, champagne flutes in hand. The waitstaff consisted of kids from the local hotel and catering school, who walked clumsily among the guests, their trays loaded with glasses and canapés, blushing as they mumbled "Monsieur" or "Madame," the gravel crunching loudly beneath their feet. As the sun slowly set, the guests chatted in small groups, enjoying the champagne, which loosened tongues and made faces look more familiar. Around them, the geometry of fields and meadows rolled all the way to the horizon. A few cherry trees in blossom caught the eye, and, near the setting sun, several black-and-white cows were chewing the cud with a slowness that seemed to contaminate the whole landscape. To counteract this impression of sluggishness, there was only a thin, almost invisible stream, its dark water cutting a line through the fold of the valley.

But Christophe did not have time for such bucolic musings. He had to keep watch over his father, check on the mood of his girlfriend (who was at that moment chatting with one of the bride's female cousins), and tirelessly greet a series of acquaintances who came over to him one after another, an aunt dressed up like the queen of England, an old friend he hadn't seen since that famous barbecue at the Lac du Perdu, you remember, it was the summer of the vuvuzelas, oh yeah, of course, good times. Meanwhile Greg, beaming and panoptic, went around handing out drinks and slaps on the back. It was bizarre to think that he and Jenn were going to have a family.

"You want a little *schluck*?"

Marco had resurfaced, hip flask in hand, and Christophe noticed that his tie had already disappeared.

"Dude, there's champagne. Why would I want to get drunk on Label 5?"

Marco did not have time to take offense. The groom had just climbed onto a chair and was banging a teaspoon against the rim of his glass.

"Your attention please..."

The hubbub of conversations died down.

"So... I wanted to say something now, because who knows what kind of state you'll all be in an hour from now. I wanted to say that Jenn and I are happy you all came today. And we got nice weather too! So... yeah. I'm not really a speech guy, I just wanted to say that this is a great day and I'm really happy. I mean, we're happy."

He raised his glass toward Jenn, who was sitting in a corner surrounded by women of various ages, including her mother, her sister, and her best friend, all of them magnetized by her enormous belly.

Next, Greg launched into a series of thank-yous to everyone from his close family to his colleagues at the factory. The last word was reserved for his father, who was no longer with them, but they were all thinking of him. And for the Cetelem bank too, without whom none of this would have been possible. Talking of which, there was an urn near the DJ booth for anyone who wished to contribute.

"And don't forget to vote!" shouted Didier, the unmarried brother, who was already half-smashed.

Some people thought this was funny, others less so.

Ever since Marine Le Pen had reached the second round, that phrase had become the national mantra. In newspapers, on social media, on TV, an endless parade of celebrities and influencers had turned up to analyze the causes of the disaster and rebuke the voters who had put them in that situation. The mayor of Cornécourt himself, who was an independent and was "not into politics," had still given his opinion on the matter after the wedding. We had to come together, for the Republic and for our children; we couldn't play with fire like that, particularly with the eyes of the world upon us, even if we should of course listen to people's anger, understand their difficulties, etc. The guests had listened politely to this before shuffling out of the mayor's office, whispering darkly. The old people seemed especially alarmed by the situation, even though theoretically they were the ones least affected by the future. Among the younger people, however, and particularly the men, this commotion caused a sort of grim jubilation. There was a satisfaction, after all, in seeing the country's great and good thrown into a panic, hearing the fear behind their sanctimonious twaddle. It was about time the rich felt the ground give way beneath their feet. For two weeks, the natural order of things had seemed suspended, the balance of power wavering.

At the wedding, as elsewhere, it was impossible to avoid this subject for long. Everyone's heads were so stuffed full of poll results, of analyses and figures. That interminable campaign had set the entire population on edge. But there were almost as many views as there were French people. Some had watched the debates between the two rounds, while others had not. There were those who never missed a single edition of the news and others who didn't want to hear another word about it. Macron had his fans, Le Pen her sympathizers. The hard-core supporters on both sides were obsessed. The niches, the variants, the focus groups, the singularities were examined under the microscope by analysts who pretended they knew what was going on. Well-intentioned people pleaded for more education, resources, time, responsiveness. Others, more severe, saw only decline, deterioration, regression, and spoke in favor of tightened belts. The blasé no longer believed in any of it. The compulsive optimists dreamed for the thousandth time of hypothetical reorganizations. On either side of these lines that were considered moral but that were more often related to origin, geography, educational level, or income bracket, the fiercest spewed their hate at the enemy, symmetrical in their opposition, equally convinced, all of them miserable and filled with certainty. The country had become this dreadful pressure cooker, about to blow, inside which simmered a decades-old stew of denials and deafness, of bitterness and suffering, of nostalgia and fear of the future. Every day, it was the same old list of Muslims, Europe, the climate occasionally, money always, of the national debt, which was becoming a personal wound, disturbing the sleep of people who had not for a single second in their lives been in the red. But, deep down, the only subject was the world that each person wanted to make with his own hands, according to his power, protected from the storms of the outside, this raft on which he would finally be with his own kind. And the disciples of openness, although they gave themselves an aura of universality and positivity, were ultimately doing the same thing: circumscribing their ideal atoll, welcoming in theory, shareable in dreams. As for the apostles of isolation, they were generally content to oscillate between the need for a haven and the fantasy of revenge.

Christophe was just waiting for it to be over. He and Hélène never talked about it. Politics just led to arguments, he thought, and things never changed that much anyway. The next Monday, he would still have to go back to work, would have to sell pet food at the same rate, would watch as the prices of electricity and health insurance kept rising, would feel as if every benefit he possessed was being stolen from him one by one, would try to stand firm against this gradual erosion of his happiness, and would think about the kid's next visit, whether he should drive or take the TGV, and where could he take him on vacation?

"What are you thinking about?"

Hélène towered over him in her heels. She draped an arm around his shoulder, smiling mischievously, and kissed him on the forehead. She smelled of alcohol and perfume.

"Nothing," said Christophe.

"I saw the seating arrangements."

"And?"

"We're with your father. And Didier, the unmarried brother."

"Maybe he'll let the goat sit in his lap."

"What a pile of crap that whole thing was. The poor little animal. You guys are morons."

"That's our charm."

Christophe put his arms around her waist and the two of them stood close together, feeling young again, cheerful in the caress of evening, comfortable as kittens.

Just then, Greg told everyone to come inside. It was time to eat.

Inside the village hall, tables had been laid with paper table-cloths, and every place setting was marked with a pack of

426

sugared almonds. Christophe examined the menu. Beet chips with a turnip mousse, rack of lamb, cheese plate, and vacherin for dessert. At their table, there was also an unremarkable-looking couple who were there because the man, Michael, liked to go fishing with the groom. His wife, Giovanna, had dyed hair and blue eyelids and worked in childcare. Everyone smiled a lot, trying to be friendly and laughing too hard at Didier's jokes. Christophe's father seemed happy. There was a gleam in his eyes and he kept nodding, like those little toy dogs that people used to keep in their cars.

After the first course, Hélène excused herself and went outside for a smoke. Christophe went with her. The effects of the champagne were starting to fade, and she was drinking water. She was still fixated on the idea that she couldn't spend the night with him.

"You okay?" Christophe asked.

"Yeah. Maybe we shouldn't stay too late, though."

"We just had the starter."

"I know, I'm just a bit tired."

Christophe took a hard drag on his vape. Alongside the patio doors that had enabled the guests to enjoy the sunset and were now looking out onto nighttime stood an ever-changing cast of a dozen or so smokers. A squeal of feedback from inside the building made them all turn around, as surprised as if they'd heard a gunshot.

"Ladies and gentlemen..."

A small man, almost bald, with a goatee and wraparound glasses, had just appeared in the DJ booth. He spoke in a nasal voice peculiar to cheap amplifiers and asked everyone if they were having a good time. When no one responded, he asked them again and they responded with a unanimously apathetic "Yeah."

"Wow, what an atmosphere!" he joked.

There were then a few hackneyed jibes about the perils of marriage and the virtues of a good wife, after which he picked out from the assembled guests a cousin in a Mao collar, who joined him onstage.

"All right, now for the serious stuff!"

And the DJ rubbed his hands, smiling demonically and revealing a row of black-and-white teeth.

Christophe turned to Hélène, who was staring at this scene as if it were causing her physical pain.

"Shall we head back inside?"

She nodded, smiling ruefully, and Christophe held her hand as they went back through the doorway. But just as they entered the room, all eyes converged on them. Hélène froze, wondering what she could have done wrong, thinking about her hair, her dress. In the DJ booth, the cousin in the Mao collar was pointing at her.

"Her!" he said.

And the guests murmured unambiguously.

"Come up here, please, madame," said the DJ.

Hélène was blushing fiercely.

"What's going on?"

Christophe didn't know; he was looking for a way to get her out of this awkward situation. But the DJ had read her lips and he explained:

"We're going to play a little game. We need you. Come on, come on."

"All-ez! All-ez!" shouted the teenagers, who were all sitting at the same table, banging it with their fists and their silverware.

Hélène went past her seat and downed her glass of white wine, to a smattering of applause and a few approving remarks. Then, like an ocean liner, she moved through the crowded room, her cheeks bright red, her chin raised high, swaying majestically on her high heels.

A few minutes later, there were five women sitting on the stage, all in dresses or skirts, their knees pressed tight together.

"All right, now we need two volunteers."

The groom immediately called out Marco's name, and the teenagers chorused: "Mar-co! Mar-co!" The atmosphere was changing, the veneer of polite aloofness starting to melt. The real party had begun, the pagan moment of burning ships and laughing like the devil.

Marco stood up and, not without a certain flair, waved his napkin above his head. Once again, the guests applauded. One of the bride's uncles was chosen next, and he rushed comically toward the row of women.

The DJ introduced the two men to the candidates, who gave their names one after another, from left to right and then from right to left. This was repeated until Marco and the uncle had memorized everyone's names—Cathy, Hélène, Rolande, Samia, and Christelle—which took quite a while, provoking some laughter and a few remarks. Then the two men were blindfolded and the DJ, microphone in hand, helped them to their knees. Christophe had guessed where this was heading soon after it began, but it was only when Marco was kneeling in front of her that Hélène understood what was about to happen.

"And nowwwwww..." bellowed the DJ, like a drumroll.

And he explained the rules of the game. Marco and the uncle would have to fondle the calves of the five women sitting in front of them and try to guess which legs belonged to whom. But to make things a little more difficult, the five participants were asked to switch places. This game of musical chairs went on for a while, the DJ giving a series of orders: stand up, sit down, stand up, sit down. From his spot in the audience, Christophe did not take his eyes off Hélène.

Thankfully she looked to be enjoying the festivities. At last the contest began, and Marco was told to go first.

When the first woman felt a hand on her tibia, she gave a little cry, which sent the guests into hysterics. Marco soon gave up groping her leg, presuming that this must be Cathy, and the audience gave a sigh of disappointment.

"Shhh!" said the DJ. "Don't give him any clues."

Marco shuffled across to the next woman and began stroking Rolande's calf. It was uncomfortable, kneeling on the stage, and the blindfold had been tied too tightly. Not only that, but the interior of the village hall was stiflingly warm. But he had to keep going until the end. When it was Hélène's turn, he guessed right away and removed his hands as if her skin was white-hot. Hélène's eyes found Christophe's, ten meters away in the audience, and they exchanged one of those wounded smiles that are beyond reproach. The game carried on cheerfully. At one point, a man with hairy legs replaced Samia and the uncle guessed that it was Rolande, who looked deeply hurt. While this went on, Christophe drank three glasses of wine. Finally, the uncle won the contest 4–2 and the women returned to their places amid cheers from the audience.

"Let's give them a big round of applause!" the DJ shouted.

The young waitstaff had begun serving the rack of lamb, scurrying around in their black-and-white uniforms, putting plates of steaming meat in front of the seated guests before rushing back to the kitchen. Hélène, having returned to her place, asked Christophe to fill her glass. Her hand was trembling, but she smiled stoutly.

"Are you sure you're okay?"

"Oh, please stop," she said.

Thankfully, the lamb was succulent and was accompanied by a gratin dauphinois and a ballotine of green beans, and the conversations around the table grew loud and enthusiastic once again.

The children had left their table. They had stuffed themselves with cakes and peanuts during the aperitifs anyway. Now, having found a box of streamers, they were pelting them at one another in the corridor that led to the exit, and every time a smoker went out there he would emerge outside enveloped in brightly colored paper. At one point, the goat burst into the dining room and Greg's brother made it sit in his lap, continuing to eat his meal while gripping the animal firmly with one hand. Outside, the landscape had vanished behind darkness, and the only things visible were the vague silhouettes of the smokers, the brief red glow of a cigarette end whenever someone took a drag. There were more games, lots of wine, and then it was time for the cheese course. Christophe's father stood up and his son pulled him back by his shirtsleeve.

"Where are you going?"

"I'm allowed to take a piss, aren't I?"

The groom, meanwhile, had begun a tour of all the tables, handing out kind words and thank-yous to everyone present, moving from an uncle who had traveled from Reims to a friend who'd had to take time off work, expressing his gratitude to the branch of the family that had bought them the Thermomix, which was of course the highlight of the wedding registry, then kissing his mother, who was starting to wonder what she was doing there. He asked everyone if they were enjoying their meal, had a laugh on the sly with his friends, and proposed an endless series of toasts. The guests all obligingly congratulated him and asked how Jenn was feeling, while the bride herself sat looking majestic and weary, presiding over the festivities like some goddess of fertility.

Greg seemed happy, in the way that a saint or a simpleton is happy. It was a pleasure to witness. Hélène said to

Christophe: "He seems like a really nice guy, your friend." Christophe agreed, and with this shared observation of another's happiness, they half forgot the painful episode of the calf-fondling game.

Inevitably, they played the garter game too, but—taking into account the bride's current predicament—it was a fairly tame version. Then it was time to dance. The DJ lowered the lights, and red-green-blue spotlights began sweeping the dance floor while a disco ball sent countless bright glimmers scattering over the walls. To open the dance, the newlyweds waltzed for a few minutes, alone and centrifugal, then the DJ played "Spacer," an old disco hit by Sheila, and Christophe was struck by the poignancy of its old-fashioned sophistication. Couples started slow-dancing while the synthetic, French-accented voice delivered the bland English lyrics.

It was strange seeing them all there, tapping their feet, hands raised, following the naive rhythm of the singer in the crisscrossing ballet of beams of light. Serious faces, fleeting smiles, they all got really into it, sinking into the amnesia of Saturday nights, the naked desire of nightclub dance floors. But the DJ did not seem satisfied with this trancelike state, so he pressed a button on the dry-ice machine. Instantly a thick cloud of smoke spread across the room, causing a few old men sitting at their table to start coughing. It was almost midnight. The cheese course was served. Green lasers shot from the ceiling, drawing modernistic lines and fanlike shapes through the mist, while the groom's mother returned to her nursing home in a Renault Modus.

Christophe got to his feet and invited Hélène to dance. Together, they entered that space marked out by the realm of music and smoke, then abandoned themselves to the rhythm of the song, among all those other faceless bodies, in the repetitive pulsing of bass notes, the clean crack of the snare drum, the patches of dry ice floating parallel to the floor. Hélène spun on her heels, and Christophe caught her by the waist, breathing in the smell of her hair, her neck. She let him kiss her. Sadly, the song ended just then, and Christophe noticed that his father still hadn't come back to their table.

He quickly scanned the room, then muttered a few words to Hélène, whose shoulders slumped as she watched him walk away. Oh well. She felt like having fun. She saw an unclaimed glass of champagne on the nearest table and drank it. The DJ played a Daft Punk song and Hélène returned to the dance floor. Eyes closed, she surrendered to the music.

"Have you seen my old man?"

Looking up from his cell phone, Marco shook his head. Christophe wanted to ask him if everything was okay, but it was clear that Marco was not having the time of his life, so instead he just said: "You should drink some water."

Then he set off in search of his father, beginning with the restrooms, before asking the smokers outside if they'd seen an old gentleman with a mustache, about this tall, putting his hand up at eye level. Of course, no one had seen him. Christophe searched the parking lot. It was starting to get cold outside, and the combination of his anxiety and the dampness of the night made him shiver. He used the flashlight on his phone to check inside each car, but the battery was close to dying and he still hadn't found his father. He kept searching, calling out "Dad! Dad!" His voice rang out in the void, sounding almost ridiculous. He even went out into the fields, but the earth was so wet and spongy that he felt like he was getting sucked into the ground. He stood there for a moment, completely still, aware of the countryside's dark indifference, stretching out into the distance in every direction. His father might be anywhere in that landscape, perhaps dying of hypothermia, lost in the darkness like a child.

"Da-ad!"

The word fell to his feet, sounding meager and hopeless, producing no echo. He went back toward the light and, inside the village hall, moved from table to table asking the same question as briefly as he could. His muddy shoes were making a mess on the floor, but he didn't care about that. When Greg asked if he needed help, Christophe shook his head, probably because he didn't want to ruin everyone's night. Anyway, the old man couldn't have gone very far.

He looked in the kitchen and behind the stage. He checked the restrooms again. He was feeling more and more anxious, calling imploringly into the emptiness, his words following the old paths that lead up to the sky, the path of frightened prayers. Marco joined him and they started questioning the staff in the kitchen.

"We should make an announcement."

"Let's take another look around first."

On the dance floor, people were still moving to the beat. Some of the old people had complained that the music was too loud, but the DJ ignored them. His job was to get people dancing, and you could tell from his bulging eyes and his megalomaniacal attitude that this idiot thought he was playing Madison Square Garden. Even so, when Marco tapped him on the shoulder, he did lift up one of his headphones.

"If I make an announcement now, no one will dance to 'The Chicken Dance.' You know that, right? It'll kill the atmosphere."

Marco did not argue the point. He went over to Christophe, who was talking to one of the waiters.

"Have you looked in the cloakroom?"

"What cloakroom?"

The waiter explained that if you went past the restrooms and into the recess to the right, there was a door that was normally unlocked and, behind it, a large room where people could leave their winter coats. Marco and Christophe hurried that way. The waiter had been right—the door was unlocked. Christophe groped for the light switch with one hand and, when he found it, the room filled with light.

His father was there.

He was asleep, his fists balled, curled up inside some thick brown curtains where he had made a sort of nest, his lips vibrating delicately beneath his white mustache. Christophe swore under his breath. He was so relieved, he could have wept. He crouched down near the old man and listened to him breathe for a moment. His respiration was deep and regular. He smoothed down a strand of hair that was sticking up from his temple.

"What should we do?" Marco asked.

Christophe answered him without turning around: "Nothing. He's fine here. Let's just let him sleep."

Christophe stood up, looking preoccupied.

"Aren't you thirsty?" Marco said.

"Fuck, yeah. Like you wouldn't believe."

Marco grinned. He was in the mood to party too.

WHEN THEY GOT back to the tables, a slice of vacherin was melting on their plates and the room was less packed than before. Some of the families with children had left, as had some of the more elderly guests. On the dance floor, aunts, couples, and teenagers were still shimmying, among them Bilal, who had found himself a rather cute dance partner. She was tall and skinny with short hair, wearing thick-lensed, round glasses and a white T-shirt with a red heart, tucked into a pair of dark blue pants, a very plain outfit somehow rendered stunning by the high heels she was wearing. Marco and Christophe, in a daze of alcohol and fatigue, watched the dancers for a while, then went back to the table for a rest. There, elbows on the tablecloth, they drank wine. They were soon joined by Greg, who—armed with two bottles of eau de vie—was doing another tour of the tables.

"So, you happy?" Marco asked.

"Ha ha, it's digestif time, guys!"

He handed out some heavy little glasses and filled them to the brim.

"Cheers!"

"To love!"

"Your good health!"

They downed two shots each, exchanging some solemn words about friendship and the passing of time. It was the manly hour of self-satisfaction, of deep drunkenness, when ties are loosened and it's okay to hug.

"Hey, I have a surprise for you two," said Marco.

"Oh?"

"But we need to hit the john."

Greg and Christophe smiled. You didn't have to be a genius to guess what would happen next. They followed him to the restroom, where Marco poured three nice, thick lines of coke on the edge of the sink. Christophe stood in front of the door while this was going on, to make sure no unwelcome visitors interrupted their fun. Eventually, someone rattled the door handle.

"It's occupied," yelled Greg.

"Who's that?" said a voice.

"Your mother!" Marco replied.

They laughed like hyenas. The other person went away.

They took turns snorting, then Marco poured out another three lines. All three of them were sniffing, giggling, hopping about excitedly. Greg even started windmilling his long arms around. Another three lines, to finish off the bag, and then they looked in the mirror.

"Oh, wow," said Greg.

"We look fucking wasted."

"No shit, Sherlock."

The image reflected back at them by the mirror was not exactly a high school class photograph. It showed three men in their early forties, hair receding, bellies expanding, wallets empty. Tomorrow, even the day after, they would pay a high price for this sleepless night. It might even be the last time they went crazy like this. None of these thoughts were spoken aloud. They had to stay dumb and have fun. They were happy and they loved each other very much.

"Come on, boys," said Marco. "Let's do this!"

They went back onto the dance floor, and it was only then that Christophe realized he had no idea where Hélène was. He'd forgotten all about her. He felt a fleeting ripple of guilt, but the music (Donna Summer) was even louder than before, the air thick with dry ice, the other faces damp with sweat under the colored spotlights, and Christophe himself was in a state of mind that left no room for mixed feelings. He let himself be swept away by the wave of sound, eyes closed, body following the rhythm, fists beating the air, his heart ready to explode, and fucking hell he was thirsty. He kept going back to the tables between songs, grabbing the closest glass or bottle he could find, whether water or champagne, and pouring its contents down his throat before going back to dance, doggedly, as if the dance floor were his job. He was no longer aware of anything but the sweltering heat and the endlessly spinning lights and faces.

Hélène, meanwhile, had gone to fetch her toiletry bag from the car so she could freshen up a little before leaving. Back inside the hall, she was surprised by how loud the music was and by the chaotic scenes on the dance floor. Not that she was unhappy. Despite those idiotic games and the inevitable "Chicken Dance" (which that bastard Christophe somehow managed to escape), it had not gone too badly, she thought. Of course, she couldn't help finding the whole thing a little corny, but she'd had her fun and she'd done her duty. And now, since the dessert had already been served, they could leave without upsetting anyone. She also wanted to have sex, and she thought that if they didn't hang around too long the night might still have a very happy ending. She imagined herself kneeling in front of Christophe, looking hot in his new suit, and the idea really turned her on.

She started searching for him amid the magma of colors and bodies on the dance floor. The music was so loud now that it seemed to be coming up from the floor and rattling her ribs, almost like a drug in itself. The DJ had taken off his T-shirt and, in the strobe lights, his white body shone like a manatee. Every time he raised an arm to wave it in time with the bass, she saw the little tuft of hair in his armpit. At last she spotted Christophe, who was jumping up and down, out of time with the beat, in his socks. She had never seen him like that before, and she was slightly disturbed by how different he seemed. His drenched hair kept rising and falling in slow motion as he jumped, his transparent shirt was glued to his chest, and his eyes were shut so tightly that they looked like little mouths. Hélène gaped. He was obviously in no state to drive her home.

Then suddenly, the sound began to fade, the spotlights converged on the floor, the song ended.

There was a silence then, and everyone stayed where they were, panting like dogs. Some voices rose in protest. They wanted to keep having fun, to lose themselves in the music. Christophe was swaying, in a total daze. He turned and saw Hélène, and smiled at her. His eyes were dark and watery, with an oil-like sheen that gave her the creeps. Hélène wanted to go and talk to him, but the first bars of the song were playing now, and everyone knew what it was. The ominous opening chords, the whistling of the wind...

And then Michel Sardou's voice, and those lyrics that pretended to talk about another land, although everyone here knew what the song was actually about. Because the earth, the lakes, the rivers...they were just images, folklore. This song was not about the lakes of Connemara. It had nothing to do with Ireland. It was about something else, an ordinary epic, the story of their lives, which did not arise from the moors or any crap like that, but was situated here, in the countryside and the suburban streets, in the slow pain of unchanging days, at the factory, in the office, in the warehouses and supply chains, in the hospitals where nurses wiped the asses of old people, this life with its depressing inequalities, its endless Mondays and occasionally the beach, keeping your head down, a small raise now and again, forty years of work and more, all to end up hoeing your tiny patch of garden, gazing at the blossoms on a cherry tree in springtime, feeling at home, and then your eldest daughter coming around on Sundays in her Renault Megane, baby seat in the back, a child to reassure everyone: it was worth it, after all. All of this they knew instinctively, from the first notes, because they had heard the song a thousand times, on a transistor radio, in the car, on TV, bombastic, unmistakable, a melody that wrenched your guts and swelled your heart with pride.

Hélène saw the dancers sling arms around shoulders and open up their throats to sing along, husbands and wives in chorus, the left-wingers who hated the singer but knew every word, right-wingers the same, even the kids, she'd seen it at her business school, the cream of French youth, blind drunk and drenched with sweat and spit, the men in a scrum, the girls with their eyes closed, under the deluge of colors, defying the dawn. Then the wedding guests began to jump in a circle, united in vulgarity, scarily archaic, stamping the floor in an alternating explosion of white light, feet drumming in time with the beat of the song. Even the ones who'd stayed seated at their tables stood up now and clapped along. Hélène didn't move. She felt almost afraid.

Just then, a woman took her partner by the hand and led him away from the dance floor. Hélène saw the woman climb onto a chair, then onto the first table. Everyone watched, breath held, before clapping even louder. The DJ, showing himself more skilled than he'd first seemed, kept the song going while this impossible couple tiptoed from table to table, careful yet quick, to the rhythm of the music and its carnival scansion. *Tam tatam tatatatatam!* Others followed suit, fat men, drunk men, Christophe and Marco among them. Under their weight, the tabletops bent alarmingly, the folding legs creaked, but no one was sober enough to prevent the disaster. The music seemed to rise from the depths, fierce as pure alcohol, and in that thunderous night, a screw came loose. Christophe happened to be standing above it. Hélène saw the table give way beneath him and he disappeared in a crash of dishes and white paper, head first, feet in the air. His fall sobered everyone in seconds. Suddenly, it was clear that this was no laughing matter. The music stopped, leaving each of them alone with the violence of the reality and the silence. Hélène had witnessed it all, the barbaric joy, the debacle, and that strange dive to earth, like something from a viral video. She also saw Marco rushing over and pushing people away.

"Call someone!" he yelled.

The lights were turned on and the guests found themselves at the mercy of the fluorescent ceiling lamps, feeling almost naked in that stark hospital glare. They exchanged embarrassed glances. Some were finding it hard to stand straight, while others looked disheveled, almost dirty. Bilal's dance partner ran out of the room, and he disappeared in her wake, following the precise clicking of her heels along the tile floor. Everyone was in shock. It was almost cold now.

Hélène walked over, followed by a handful of distraught revelers, and behind the overturned tables she found Marco kneeling on the floor, holding Christophe to his chest, his friend's wet nape cradled in his heavy hand. There was a circle around this curious scene, vaguely reminiscent of pious images, ancient tragedies, stories of miners, factories, the unfortunate accidents that populated family trees in that region. Marco looked up.

"Call someone," he said again.

But his voice was just a croak now, barely audible, and there was a glassy look in his eyes.

"Is he dead?" asked a kid standing nearby, thrilled by the horror of that possibility.

"No, of course not," his father replied coldly.

Hélène didn't dare move any closer. She felt like an outsider, in a way that was hard to articulate. But there, in the chaos of that village hall, among these people whom she barely knew and yet recognized so easily, she was sure of one thing: she was mad at Christophe. He moved just then, first his head, then his arms. Everyone distinctly heard a sort of relaxed sigh and Hélène felt the relief of all those around her. Then his body shuddered, and they saw his face come to life again. After a few hesitant blinks, he smiled. On his forehead, there was already an egg-sized lump in all the colors of the rainbow.

21

THE EARLY RISERS emerged from their tents around nine in the morning, like survivors of a nuclear war venturing out of bomb shelters. At first, they began wandering through the fields, their hair sticking up, often wearing the same shirt they'd been wearing the night before, but now with sweatpants and flip-flops, cigarettes dangling from some of their mouths, many of them in sunglasses. Soon there was a line outside the portable toilets. Some of the men even shaved. The sun was already hot.

The bride's parents, who had been the last ones to bed after clearing up the hall, woke early and returned to the campsite, in tank tops and crop pants, the father a giant, the woman short and round, the two of them wearing the same Puma sneakers. They made sure that the guests had everything they needed. The wife was maybe more like an army officer, but they were both cheerful and accommodating. In the kitchen, they toasted the previous night's leftover bread and brewed coffee to fill the pump pots, and the delicious smell of Sunday morning soon pervaded the village hall and spread out through the fields, tickling the nostrils of the last sleepers. There was still some wine and beer and several bottles of

Picon, and the refrigerator was packed full of pork chops and sausages. Aldo, Jenn's father, poured charcoal into a grill and watched, arms crossed, with Neanderthal satisfaction, as the embers glowed red. Finally, some other guests went inside to help set the table, to distribute bread and pats of butter, jars of jam and mustard, to take enormous salad bowls filled with vegetable macédoine or potato salad out of the fridge.

Little by little, people found something to do. Some gave a hand; others stretched out to enjoy the sun or dropped an aspirin into a glass of water. Most were content just to chat, their voices quiet with the residue of embarrassment, that pale reserve of the morning after. When Gérard emerged from the cloakroom, his back was aching but he looked happy. For some time now, he explained, he had been sleeping more and more, maybe because of the pills they gave him at the nursing home. Anyway, he seemed in an excellent mood and he joked around with various people before sitting down to eat breakfast. It was only then that he realized he'd forgotten to put his teeth back in.

At eleven o'clock sharp, Uncle Jacques left his tent. He didn't bother brushing his teeth, but he did smooth down the remnants of his hair with a drop of Pento hair cream. He, too, was in top form despite his advanced age and a night roughing it in the fields. Greg had taken his new wife home early that morning and, thanks to the distance from the village hall, they had been spared the traditional wedding-night visit from their more boisterous guests. So, when he returned on his own to Moudonville, since Jenn preferred to get some rest, he was given a special surprise. No sooner had he gotten out of his car than he was kidnapped and covered in shaving foam and confetti. Then Marco took a handful of toilet paper smeared with Nutella and rubbed it on the top of his friend's head. Greg took it all in stride. He barely struggled, and even posed for photographs afterward. He'd been expecting something like that and had brought a change of clothing.

"So where's the stuntman?" he asked as he was cleaning himself up in the restroom.

Marco, who was drinking a Mexican beer, shrugged.

"Sleeping it off, I imagine."

"I didn't see his car."

"His chick went home on her own."

"Oh?"

"Yeah, she took his keys. It was *imperative* that she went back last night."

"Ah…"

Around noon, Christophe finally crawled out of the tent where he'd taken refuge the night before. He felt like he hadn't slept a wink, and when he looked in the restroom mirror and saw the massive bump on his forehead, he whistled. It had doubled in size and its rainbow colors had faded to an ugly yellow-blue-black. He checked his phone. Hélène had not replied to any of his messages. He was not in the best of moods.

All the same, he ate breakfast with his father and drank a beer, which perked him up a little, enough at least so that he could smile when someone spoke to him. But he knew. This was going to be one of those lost days when even the beautiful weather feels like a form of torture and your friends look like murderers.

They decided to move the tables outside. Lunch went on for hours. The air was fragrant with the smell of barbecued meat and the guests shuttled between the grill and their tables, helping themselves to more food, while Aldo kept an eye on the browning chops, voice booming loudly. There was plenty of cheese left, and the guests drank red wine to their hearts' content without exhausting the stock, giving rise to more songs and laughter. At one point, Uncle Jacques stood up and sang a legionnaire's song, which everyone found very moving. They sat there, looking thoughtful, listening to the patriotic lyrics, the sluggish rhythm designed to keep soldiers marching in time, the deep voice of this ancient uncle who stood there with his hand on his heart. It was quite something, after all, to love one's country.

"Maybe we should go vote," said someone.

This idea was met with onomatopoeia and a few objections. What was the point? Why the fuck should they care?

They thought about the whole circus again then, the fascists and the startup merchants... What kind of world were they living in? Thankfully, conversations soon gravitated to their usual topics. Politics was not a suitable talking point for the day after a wedding. Christophe stared down at his cardboard plate, smeared orange and brown by the merguez sausage he'd just eaten. The bride's mother and two of her sisters were busy wrapping the remains of the food in aluminum foil. The party was drifting toward its end, for good this time. Christophe got to his feet and whispered to Greg. He still hadn't heard from Hélène. He needed to get back to Cornécourt.

"Already?" said Greg, looking at his watch. "It's still early."

In the end, Christophe told him he was planning to vote. He also wanted to make sure that Hélène had gotten home safely.

"Can't you call her?"

"I already did," Christophe replied.

Greg regretted asking the question.

"All right," he said, struggling to his feet. Then, to the assembled guests, he called out: "Anyone want to go back to town?"

"You're leaving already?"

"I'm just gonna make a quick return trip. I'll take anyone who wants to go."

It was just after four. The day had flown by and most people felt a little discomfited by the idea that this beautiful weekend was coming to an end. They'd had fun, laughed a lot, eaten well, and drunk too much. Their cell phones were full of photographs they would look at later. No doubt the parents-in-law would make an album and from time to time someone would take it out of the closet and bathe in the happiness that was frozen there forever, the face of a grandmother or an uncle who had since died, the impossibly small bodies of those children, the slow hemorrhage of time held back by the dam of a rectangle of glossy paper. They would smile, seeing the fashions of that bygone era, the haircuts, the shape of people's pants. With hindsight, Christophe's fall would take on a legendary, burlesque dimension. *And that tall girl, who was that?* someone would ask. Hélène's name would have been forgotten. All that would remain was the imprecise outline of her face in the background, to the right, her back glimpsed during aperitifs, a blurry profile of her seated at the table. She would have pursued her life elsewhere, leaving behind a scattering of light between the album's pages to become…what? No one would know.

In the meantime, Greg's question had made several people think: maybe it is time we got ready to leave. The tents were dismantled and Marie, the bride's mother, insisted that everyone take some food back with them. Then the first cars began to file out, horns honking cheerfully, before driving back to Cornécourt, side mirrors still trailing lace ribbons.

Around them, the countryside was round, the fields downy, and the water in streams and puddles glittered under the gentle May sun. In the flat blue sky above, a few shreds of cloud kept stretching and dissolving. On the way back, the four men did not say a single word. They just blinked slowly as they watched the landscape move past. Marco was the first to be dropped off.

"Well, see ya, guys."

"See ya soon, big man."

Then it was Christophe's turn. He asked Greg to drop him and his father outside the mayor's office.

"How will you get home?"

"Hélène was supposed to leave my car behind Le Narval."

Greg did not probe any further. He just said: "Well, it was fun..."

"Yeah. It really was."

They smiled at each other. Christophe's father, who had climbed out of the car, asked where they were, and his son reminded him.

"Oh, yeah," said the old man, as if remembering.

As they walked away, Greg jokingly called out: "Don't forget to vote!"

Christophe smiled, but his smile instantly curdled into a grimace. His head was aching again. He gingerly felt at the bump on his forehead. It was still there, a solid reminder of the night's events.

"That must have been quite a fall," his father said.

"It was. You remember you're sleeping at my place tonight?"

"Will Gabriel be there?"

"He's at his mother's house, Dad, you know that."

"Oh, yeah, that's right."

On the terrace of Le Narval, none of the regulars paid them any attention. It was a warm evening, and the customers were having a drink or playing a game of Morpion, enjoying the peacefulness of the moment, the almost nonexistent traffic, the cloudless sky. And yet there was a hint of vexation behind this tranquility, the feeling that even these sweetest hours were numbered. It was a new impression, and no one could work out when it had begun or why. Every pleasure seemed now to contain within itself that end-of-vacation mood, the idea that each moment of happiness might be the last. As if spring were not guaranteed to follow winter, after all.

Around that nondescript little square, with its bar, its bakery, its real estate agent, not far from the always empty church, a country was making the most of its reprieve. And on that lovely spring Sunday, now drawing toward its final hours, the weather was so beautiful, life so patient, that it was almost impossible to imagine the vast accumulation of gas hissing in the basements of a world anxious that its end was nigh.

EPILOGUE

CHRISTOPHE NORMALLY PREFERS to park near the entrance, but the Castorama parking lot is packed that Saturday afternoon and, after driving around for a while, he settles for a spot at the other end.

"We'll have to walk, sweetie."

In the backseat, Gabriel is reading a Donald Duck comic book. Christophe has dressed him in too many layers as usual—sweatshirt, puffer jacket, scarf—and the kid's cheeks are bright red.

"You're not too hot, are you?"

"Yeah."

"Well, take your scarf off, unzip your coat."

Gabriel puts his book down and obeys.

He's eight years old now. His hair is darker these days, and it falls over his eyes, behind his glasses. He doesn't want to get his hair cut. Anyway, his mother likes it that way.

Every time Christophe picks his son up, he can't help noticing the changes. Gabriel is no longer that little blond kid with a disproportionately large head and a body made from bits of wood, looking up at him with those innocent, faun-like eyes. Sometimes, late at night in bed, Christophe will scroll through old photos on his cell phone. He stares at the little boy sitting at a miniature table with his friends from day care, all of them in smocks, working hard on their paintings, and he has to admit to himself that he has no memory of that period. He was too busy dealing with all the shit in his life: work, the separation from Charlie, hangovers after partying with his friends. Sometimes he thinks that he missed all the good stuff. Depressed, he gets up and goes out to smoke on the doorstep. That time is lost to him forever, he thinks. Maybe he should delete the photos, condemn himself to the present for good. But he doesn't have the guts to go through with it.

Gabriel shuts the car door and takes his father's hand, and the two of them walk toward the store. In the parking lot, people push carts filled with bags of compost, curtain rods, and rolls of wallpaper. They all look in a rush. They wear jeans and sneakers and down vests and talk with strong accents that make him smile. At the entrance, a woman wearing lots of makeup and a paper chef's hat is selling waffles, and the sugary smell makes their mouths water.

"Can I have one?" asks the boy.

"Maybe on the way out."

Christophe picks up a shopping basket and, after checking his list, sets off in search of a smoke detector. He forces himself to walk slowly so his son can keep up.

"I wish I had a toolbox."

"Really? What would you do with it?"

"Home improvement, of course."

"Well, you could ask Santa for one."

A roll of the eyes. "Santa doesn't exist."

"Oh?"

"Come on, you know he doesn't."

"I wish you'd warned me, I could have saved some money to buy presents."

"Ha ha, very funny," says the kid.

In the electrical supplies aisle, Christophe picks out two power strips and grabs a two-meter stick because it's always handy to have around; then he heads toward the gardening section at the back of the store.

"I need to check out the Weed Eaters, see how much they cost."

"Okay."

On the way there, his eye is caught by a figure in the bathroom aisle. A tall woman in skintight jeans, a checkered shirt, and Converse sneakers, with a ponytail tied high up on her head. He stops, heart pounding.

"Dad...what is it?"

"Nothing, sweetie, it's okay."

Hélène is there, chatting with a salesman. Beside her are a preteen girl and her younger sister, about the same age as Gabriel. He can't see the woman's face and he doesn't need to. The way she stands with her hand on her hip, the way she tilts her neck, the curve at the base of her spine, the straight shoulders, and that prominent, denim-clad butt...he recognizes her in a second, instinctively. A whole world rushes back into his memory, full of light and details.

"Are we going?"

"Just a second, honey."

Christophe shakes his head and squeezes his son's hand more tightly.

"Let's just go home," he says reluctantly.

"We're not going to look at Weed Eaters?"

"Another time."

"What about the waffles?"

"We don't have time."

"Why not?"

Christophe gets dragged into a series of annoying negotiations. He tries to usher his son toward the exit, but Gabriel digs his heels in.

"You're going too fast!" he complains. "And what about my waffle?"

"Come on, we're in a rush."

Christophe glances over his shoulder. Hélène is standing in the middle of the central aisle, watching him flee. He stops then and she smiles politely. They take a few steps toward each other.

"It's strange, bumping into you here..."

"Yeah. What are you doing in the area? Don't you live in Nancy anymore?"

"I do, I do."

Christophe can tell that she's affected by their meeting too. Her cheeks have flushed pink, as they always do when she's excited, and the hair on her head is curling slightly. He recognizes the signs. She used to look the same way after they'd made love. He also recognizes her scent—a blend of detergent, perfume, and her skin—which hasn't changed at all. The children stare stonily at each other. Hélène's started telling him about her life, mostly out of a fear of awkward silence. She tries to be cheerful, to seem perfectly at ease. She comes off like a TV host.

The house she and Philippe used to own has sold (and sold well, she adds, with a satisfied raise of the eyebrows), so she's managed to buy a really nice two-bedroom place in a modern apartment building, and best of all she's found an old farm in the Vosges, near Saint-Michel-sur-Meurthe: a beautiful spot, surrounded by fields, hardly any neighbors, and a great view.

"I'd forgotten how nice it is to live in a place where no one can see you," she says.

Christophe nods. He's let go of Gabriel's hand, and Hélène gives her daughters a ten-euro bill so they can go and buy waffles with their new friend.

"It's a lot of work, though. I spend most of my weekends fixing it up."

"How's your job?"

"I'm not so invested in it anymore. When my little one's a bit older, I'm planning to start my own firm. I've got so many ideas."

"That's great," says Christophe. "So how are you coping with the home improvement?"

"Not too bad." Then, for good measure, she adds: "You and Gabriel should come visit sometime."

"Sure," says Christophe with a smile. "I'd like that."

He looks at her. She's beautiful. Beautiful like memories of past vacations, like those familiar faces that flash through your mind at the smell of cut grass, or are resurrected when the afternoon sun filters through the blinds, stirring the memory of a nap in a house where you were once happy. Hélène contains all that shared time. Six months of life in a single breath.

"So what about you?" she asks.

"I'm fine."

"Are you still working at the same place?"

"Yeah. And I'm kind of the hockey club's general manager too."

"Whoa, that's great!" says Hélène.

He can tell she is relieved that his life has moved on too.

"We're aiming to reach the top division in three or four years. It won't be easy, but we're building from a solid foundation."

"Absolutely. You have to believe!"

Christophe gives a little snort of amusement. She hasn't changed. Nor has he. And yet nothing is the same anymore. He feels his shoulders tense, and he smiles.

"It's great seeing you again."

"Yeah. For me too."

Just then, the children reappear, overexcited and sticky with sugar.

"Oh, fantastic. No, no, no, don't touch me with your disgusting hands!"

Hélène is standing on tiptoe, eyes wide like someone in a horror movie, which makes the kids laugh. Christophe notices that Clara is giving him a strange look as she bites into her waffle.

"Well..." says Hélène after a short silence.

"Yep."

They move as if to kiss each other's cheeks, then back out.

"I've got a couple more errands to run," says Hélène.

"Okay. Well, enjoy the rest of your weekend."

"Thanks. You too. Bye, Gabriel."

The little boy gives a thumbs-up before taking another bite out of his waffle. His chin is covered with powdered sugar and there's a sort of white halo on his chest. Christophe feels his son's sticky, trusting fingers insert themselves into his hand. They head to the checkout, then out to the car. Before leaving the parking lot, Christophe slows down in front of the store's entrance.

"Who was that?" asks Gabriel.

"A friend."

"I remember her."

"You do?"

"Sure."

"Are they nice memories?"

"They're fine."

Christophe turns to the backseat and sees his son forcing a smile, just as he does for photographs. He is already lost in Donald Duck again. Christophe's cell phone buzzes. It's Nadia. He picks up.

"Yes, honey?"

The station wagon sets off on the road to Cornécourt. Christophe looks up at the sky, where a few gray clouds are massing. But he says, yeah, absolutely, a barbecue is a great idea. The first of the year. They exchange a few more words, blow kisses, the call ends, and he steps hard on the gas, his heart in pieces. Behind him, the little boy, surprised by the sudden acceleration, calls out excitedly:

"Come on, boys, let's do this!"

Acknowledgments

Sabine Barthélemy, Édith Bernez, Gaëlle Bona, Guillaume Chassard, Thierry Corvoisier, Cindy Couval-Mathieu, Sabine Desilles, Pierre-Henry Gomont, Elsa Grimberg, Thaël Huard, Jean-Nicolas Lecomte, Éloïse and Philippe Martin, Hélène Martin, David Mathieu, Nicolas Matyjasik, Anthony Maurice for his precious help, Lucie Mikaélian (for her wonderful adolescent journal "Mes 14 ans"), Cécile Moizard-Matyjasik, Brigitte and Patrick Nouyrigat, Cécile Rich, Anne Rosencher, Romain Sarmejean, Manuel Tricoteaux, Faïza Zerouala.

Lastly, I would like to thank Nicolas Martin and the players and staff of the Épinal ice hockey team.